darkest light

A Ravaged Skies Novel

fire in the sky
book one

A.M. Geever

For Aunt Eleanor, *who told me I should write about something besides zombies.*

I'm pretty sure this isn't what she had in mind.

prologue

SATURDAY, MAY 24
10:37 AM

On a Sunday morning, New Life Baptist Church should be humming. Families should be pouring out of their cars and SUVs, kids chasing each other across the parking lot and through the doors, the swell of organ music and songs of praise filling the air.

Through his open window, all Cody heard was silence.

His car rolled to a halt a hundred feet from the impromptu command post. He checked the live stream on his phone one last time. Better cell reception let him see a smooth video feed for the first time. The young white male in tactical gear paced back and forth at the front of the church, holding an AR-15 rifle. He twisted his wrist to check his watch, then grinned like he'd just won the lottery.

Cody caught stutter-stop fragments of the live stream on the drive here. At one point, the gunman punctuated his point with a muffled burst of gunfire. Cody had flinched at the terrified screams that followed.

"Asshole," Cody said under his breath. He shoved his phone in the back pocket of his jeans as he climbed out of his government-issue sedan. The trunk popped open with a *squeak*. He reached inside, picked up his ballistic vest, and put it on. Despite the warm temperature, a windbreaker with US MARSHAL emblazoned across the back was next.

He trotted over the cracked asphalt to the line of state police cruisers and sheriff's department SUVs ringing the parking lot. The first 911 call came in nineteen minutes ago. At the last update Cody had heard the FBI's Crisis Response Team was twenty-four minutes out. Cody had monitored their ETA on the drive here, but it had been several minutes since he'd heard an update.

"US Deputy Marshal Cody Greer," he said.

A stocky, middle-aged man, his blond hair a haystack and uniform sweat-stained, took Cody's extended hand. "Sheriff John Semanski, Loudoun County."

"Good to meet you, sir."

Beside him, a tall, pale man in tactical gear lifted his chin in greeting. "Trooper Warner, Virginia State Police Tactical Team. I'm coordinating our side of the entry plan."

Cody nodded. "Where do things stand?"

"We've got an active shooter in the main sanctuary and approximately one hundred fifty people trapped inside. At least ten confirmed deaths. The asshole is live streaming this," Semanski said, anger making his voice rough as sandpaper. "Now that you're here, the Marshal Service has perimeter control."

Cody nodded. That wouldn't happen in practical terms until more of his colleagues arrived. "You've got a positive ID? This is the guy from Indiana with the warrant for interstate transport of stolen firearms?"

The sheriff nodded.

"Is anyone from FBI on-site yet?"

The sheriff shook his head. "Crisis Response Team is about..."

He checked his watch. "Eighteen minutes out, but the Hostage Rescue Team is closer to twenty-five."

Cody raised his eyes, surprised. Given the distances involved, both ETAs were fast. If the FBI was sending both Crisis Response and Hostage Rescue—its elite hostage rescue unit—this situation was more complicated than he'd realized. A lot could happen before they arrived. He made it to the scene quickly, because he was in the area after a prisoner transfer.

Semanski handed Cody an earpiece and radio. "Channel one-alpha for the inner cordon, and radio silence until Hostage Rescue arrives."

They had to wait for FBI Hostage Rescue. Federal response protocols were clear. The Marshal Service established the outer perimeter, local SWAT—or in this case the state police—secured entry points, and Hostage Rescue would execute the breach.

"Still no direct contact with the gunman?" Cody asked. He looked across the parking lot at the white clapboard church. The green fields behind it made it look like a postcard.

Sheriff Semanski shook his head. "Nothing."

"Sir!" A sheriff's deputy sprinted toward them along the line of police vehicles. "We've got a hostage! She climbed out a bathroom window."

Cody, Semanski, and Warner followed the deputy to the ambulance where EMTs were evaluating a slender, middle-aged woman. She was missing a shoe. Her stockings were torn and dress rumpled. Cody could see the slight sheen of bur marigold seeds sticking to her gray-blond hair. Mascara streaked her cheeks, and tremors racked her body.

"He planted bombs," she gasped. "I heard him talking to someone on his phone before he started live streaming. He said it was the grand finale."

Cody's stomach plummeted like a condemned man falling through the gallows trapdoor. "Did he say where?"

She nodded, her head bobbing up and down. "The choir loft, right behind the pulpit. I think he said fifteen minutes, but that was five minutes ago. There's some sort of timer on his wrist. He kept checking it and he'd laugh this..." The woman shuddered. "He sounded like a lunatic."

An icy shiver made Cody's neck and shoulders twitch.

"Do we have any confirmation on that?" Warner asked.

"I saw it when I got out of my car two minutes ago. I thought he was checking his watch," Cody said.

This new information escalated the situation from a 'regular' hostage situation to domestic terrorism. He looked at Semanski and Warner. "Is there any ordnance disposal on-scene?"

Semanski's face went white. Warner spoke into his radio. After a pause, he said, "The state team is fifteen minutes out."

Cody keyed his radio. "Greer to FBI command. What's the ETA on HRT?"

A crackle of static. "Sixteen minutes."

"Command, we have intelligence the gunman has planted explosives on a ten-minute timer. We may need to breach. Is there anyone closer?"

Time crawled before they got the answer. "Negative. EOD specialists are en route with the Crisis Response Team, updated ETA thirteen minutes. Maintain perimeter positions. Do not breach. Repeat: do not breach."

Cody's mouth felt stuffed with crumbled autumn leaves. The FBI's order to wait and follow protocol wasn't arbitrary. Usually, protocol kept law enforcement officers alive and civilians safe, but not always. Cody always followed protocol. He had never been one to flout the rules or go in guns blazing. That cowboy crap got people killed—except when it didn't.

A burst of gunfire rattled the stained glass windows. Screams, then the staccato *pop, pop, pop* of a gunfire burst. The escaped woman cowered like an abused dog. A current of barely contained forward momentum—the need to act—crackled down the line of assembled officers like static electricity. Over a hundred people were inside that church and law enforcement was stuck out here, running out of time.

"My tactical team is staged and ready, Sheriff," Trooper Warner said. "I have a go to breach the north entrance on your authorization."

The sheriff swallowed hard. "The FBI doesn't want us going in. This is beyond anything my department has trained for." To Cody, he said, "You're a fed. What do you think?"

The bright morning sun spattered jewel-colored reflections from the stained glass windows. Bomb or no, the gunman in that church was intent on mass murder. They had about eight minutes on the clock. Someone had to make the call.

"Warner, how many tactical officers do you have staged?" Cody asked.

Warner blinked. "Enough."

Cody's mind raced. He knew what he should do; he should respect the chain of command and follow orders. He didn't have to like them or agree with them, only follow them. And over a hundred people would die on his watch. "EOD won't be here in time if there are bombs inside. It might be a bluff, but if it's not and we wait, everyone in that building dies."

It was a reckless gamble based on secondhand intel. Cody didn't know what the right call was, only what his gut was telling him: they needed to act.

Sheriff Semanski said, "You're saying we should breach?"

"I'm saying it might be more dangerous to wait."

Warner nodded. "If this is a go, VSP Tact will neutralize the shooter. The rest of you can evacuate the hostages on our signal."

Semanski stood frozen, staring at the church. "All right," he said. He spoke into his radio. "All units, this is Sheriff Semanski. We have credible intelligence of explosive devices with an active countdown timer. Federal response is plus ten minutes and the threat is imminent. VSP Tactical will breach on the north entrance. We will evacuate the hostages on their signal. We have minutes to do this, people." To Warner, he said, "Let's do it."

The sheriff caught Cody's gaze. Calm washed over Cody as he nodded his agreement. This wasn't about protocol anymore, nor the insubordination he had just committed. This was about the oath he had sworn to protect against all enemies, foreign and domestic.

Warner's cool voice buzzed through Cody's earpiece. "North entry teams, stack up. We breach in sixty seconds."

chapter
one

CALEB

FRIDAY, JULY 11
7:30 PM

The tires squeaked as the pickup slowed to a halt. The red glow of the restaurant's neon sign sparkled through the drops of rain on the windshield, then the wipers swept them away. Caleb switched off the wipers and stared out the windshield. He rubbed his eyes, then scrubbed his face. The long drive tugged at every muscle. He sat for a moment, indecisive, then picked up the burner phone. He punched in Ruth's number and pressed the dial button.

The ringing of her phone buzzed in his ear twice before she picked up. "Hello?"

"Hey, Ruth," he said.

"Hey," his sister said, relief in her voice. "It's been a while. I was worried. Is everything okay?" She didn't ask where he was. It was safer that way.

"I'm okay. Tired. Been driving most of the day."

Ruth said, "It's been raining in Coeur d'Alene, maybe the last this year."

He almost said, 'Here, too,' but that might imply he was near. He wasn't, but that wasn't the point; discipline was. It kept them both safe. Caleb thought of what to say that wasn't inane chitchat. Were they really reduced to discussing the weather? "How's work?"

"Good," she said. "I just changed hospitals. Northcrest Regional just got certified as a Level 1 trauma center."

"Really?"

"Yeah. I finished up the Trauma Nursing Core six months ago. The timing was perfect."

Pride swelled in Caleb's heart. His sister was capable of anything she set her mind to. "I'm so proud of you."

"It's not the Nobel Prize or anything," she said, laughing.

"It's not nothing, either."

"I know, I know. The hours have been a bear with the kids, but my neighbors help me out with babysitting."

"That's good," he said. He hesitated, then said, "If you need any help, Ruth, you—"

She interrupted him. "I appreciate it, Caleb, but you know I can't."

Silence stretched across the connection before he answered. A familiar sense of frustration bubbled inside his chest. "You can, if you ever need to."

There was a trust in Costa Rica. Because of Costa Rica's exceptionally protective legislation, it wasn't possible to trace it back to him. The authorities could never seize it. He would never say more on the phone, however. They'd tapped her line before. In all his time on the run, the only thing Ruth had ever let him give her were the burner phones.

When she didn't answer, he said, "How are the kids?"

"Oh, they're good," she said, her voice warming. "Jodi's starting fourth grade in the fall, and she's in the play for her summer camp. She got a scholarship, so it's next to nothing. Peter will be starting second grade." She sighed, her voice getting wistful. "He looks just like you at that age, Cay."

Caleb wanted to smile at the use of his childhood nickname but the twist in his gut made it impossible. He hadn't seen his nephew since Peter was an infant. Peter's sunny smile from pictures on Ruth's social media filled his mind's eye. Caleb thanked God for social media, even if it was today's whipping boy for society's ills. Ruth's social accounts let him watch the kids grow and feel like he had a connection to them.

That feeble connection was the only thing that kept him going sometimes—especially when loneliness hit so hard he couldn't breathe. Lately, that feeling came more and more often.

"I saw Mr. Jacobs yesterday," Ruth continued. "He's getting close to retirement. Still doing JROTC at the high school."

The heavy knot in Caleb's stomach tightened. He hadn't seen Mr. Jacobs since before his last deployment. No, he realized, that wasn't right. He hadn't seen him since after the fiasco of the court martial. "Tell him I say hello next time you see him."

Ruth sighed, a sound Caleb was so well acquainted with he knew what was coming next. "Caleb, what are you doing? This is no way to live. I miss you. Mister Jacobs does, too. The kids don't even know you."

Caleb ran his hand through his hair. "Can we please not do this right now?"

"You never want to have this conversation," she said, the frustration in her voice scraping over his eardrum like a knuckle on a cheese grater.

"What do you want me to do?" he said, his own frustration making him snap at her. "I can't turn myself in, and I'm not spending the rest of my life in prison. Is that what you want, for me to die in prison?"

Ruth sighed over the line. "Of course not, but I'm worried about you. You sound depressed all the time. Detached."

The rain hit the truck with an insistent drumbeat. "Look," he said. "It's getting late and I need to eat. I'll call you later?"

"Sure," she said, letting it go. "I love you, big brother."

She had infused her words with so much emotion—love, longing, missing—that his eyes flooded with tears. "I love you, Ruthie," he said, trying to mask the tightness in his throat. "Talk to you soon."

Caleb hung up, his spirits lower than before he'd called. His little sister sounded resigned and frustrated, which was how their calls ended more and more of late. Caleb hated that he was the reason. Even more, he hated that she wouldn't take his help, even if he understood. Her ex-husband was uninvolved and not very consistent with his child support obligations. If anything happened to her, he wouldn't step in and care for his children. With no extended family on their side, if Ruth ran afoul of the law because of him... She'd never risk it. Never. And if she did, the circumstances would be so desperate that he'd hate himself forever for not being there. He might as well take the money in that trust and burn it in a parking lot.

Caleb pinched the bridge of his nose. Ruth's question echoed in his head because she was right. What the hell was he doing? What was this accomplishing? He was a stranger to his niece and nephew. He couldn't settle down and have a life, not a real one, especially if he stayed in the States. He couldn't help his sister in any way that mattered, because they both knew what happened to kids who had no one.

Bitterness filled his mouth with the taste of dirty pennies. All the time—the years—he had felt like he'd never get out from under the cloud of what his father had done, only to conjure up a cloud of his own.

Caleb shook himself, shoving the melancholy aside. He pushed the door of the truck open, his booted feet light on the wet pavement. He locked the truck with the keys. It was the only way to do it with this old beater, though calling it that wasn't fair. The truck's beat-up appearance had no bearing on how well it ran.

Caleb hunched his shoulders against the rain. He didn't

mind, though, for the rain had cooled things down enough that he wore a windbreaker. He walked close to the buildings of the quaint main drag to the diner he'd stopped in once before, a few years back. It was a little place, the sort of mom-and-pop establishment common in small mountain towns, especially the ones that weren't tourist destinations. He wanted to duck his head as he walked inside, even though he knew his head wouldn't hit the jamb. It always felt like it, though.

He waited to be seated, asking for a booth along the back wall of the narrow dining room near the window that wrapped around the corner of the building. He wanted a sightline of the side parking lot, just in case. The booths jutted out from the back wall perpendicular to the rest of the dining room. The one he'd chosen backed up to the next booth on just the one side, with the window on the other. After folding the wet exterior of the jacket in on itself, he set it on the seat by the window and slid into the other. Outside, the inky dark of twilight descended all the more quickly because of the rain.

The waitress approached his table, a tired-looking woman, her waist thickened by middle age. The lines on her face hinted at a life of struggle, but the laugh lines around her eyes showed joy, too. "Here's the menu, hon," she said, her brown eyes regarding him warmly. "Would you like something to drink?"

"Some coffee, please. How's your night going?"

"It's going," she said. "I'll be right back."

Caleb studied the menu, settling on a bacon cheeseburger and fries. He looked up when the bell over the door jingled. A police officer walked in, shaking rain from his cowboy hat. The waitress greeted him with a smile. "Hey, John... Wet enough for you?"

"Rain in July, now I've seen everything. I'd complain but it's the last we'll see till next April," he said, smiling. "I'll be at my booth."

Caleb looked down at his menu again so as not to bring attention to himself. His large frame commanded attention. He'd been told by more than one person he reminded them of Jack Reacher

—from the television series, not the movies. Caleb didn't like being memorable these days, but the comparison pleased him. Most people meant his physique, which didn't matter to him. His job—past and present—demanded it. What he liked was what Jack Reacher represented: a modern-day knight errant, a force for good in the world. He'd had that once. Then they made a joke of it.

He felt a thump through the back of his seat as someone settled into the booth behind him. He looked up at the window, catching its reflection, and cursed. It was the police officer. He'd been so busy trying to avoid notice that he hadn't seen the lawman's approach.

He checked his watch—7:41 p.m.—and decided to leave. The lodge was only fifty more miles. If he wasn't paying enough attention to notice the police officer heading for the booth behind him, he shouldn't be here.

He reached in his jacket for his wallet, put a twenty on the table, and eased out of the booth, ducking his head to avoid notice. The waitress rounded the corner of the coffee counter and stopped. "The bathrooms are the other way," she said.

"Turns out I can't stay. Sorry to waste your time."

"Don't worry about it."

Caleb offered her a smile and continued toward the exit when the TV over the coffee counter caught his eye. He almost looked away, then stopped, shock rooting him in place.

"We're joined tonight by former US Army Ranger Avery Scott," the program host, Jack Winters, said. "You may have seen or read his book, *Honor Restored*, where he tells his incredible story." Winters turned to his guest with a warm smile. "It's good to have you here, Avery. Thank you for joining us."

The familiar smile and twinkling blue eyes of Caleb's former C.O., his former friend, glowed on the television screen. "Thanks so much for having me on the show, Jack."

Caleb stared at the television, stunned. He wrote a book?

Jack Winters said, "Avery, why don't you tell the audience who you are and a little bit of your story."

Caleb's former C.O. nodded. "I wrote *Honor Restored* to tell my side of the story. You can't prepare for this kind of experience. I wanted to show the human cost of false allegations."

Caleb's teeth clenched with a sharp scrape. Every allegation made against Avery Scott was true.

"Fifteen years as an Army Ranger. Eight deployments in Africa and the Middle East. Then the men you called brothers turned on you."

Avery nodded. "Yeah," he said, sounding as if he had trouble articulating even that one word. "There's no—" He stopped, blinking hard, and swallowed. "These were guys who had saved my life on more than one occasion, and I'd saved theirs. And that's okay. That's the job. But they accused me of stealing and selling the weapons we need to defend this country to the highest bidder. They even accused me of being the ringleader and I gotta tell you... Special operators are trained to withstand a lot. Nothing prepares you when it's your name and reputation on the line in that kind of situation, but that's what happened to me and my family."

"Not to mention your liberty was on the line," Jack Winters said, his expression grave.

The cook came out from behind the stainless steel counter that separated the kitchen from the coffee counter. He wiped his hands on his apron as he looked up at the television. "Have you read his book?"

It took a moment for Caleb to realize the man was talking to him. He ripped his eyes from the screen, which had gone to a commercial. "No."

"It's a crazy story. It's hard to believe his own unit would do that to him."

Jack Winters' serious face returned to the screen. "Tonight's guest is Avery Scott, decorated Army Ranger. Scott was accused of running a criminal enterprise that stole and sold millions in

American weapons. A court martial convicted him—supporters called it a kangaroo court—before the president pardoned him.

The camera zoomed out to show both men on screen. Winters said, "Avery, what do you think was behind the allegations that led to the charges and court martial?"

"I still don't understand what the guys who concocted this fairy tale thought they were doing." The face of Caleb's former C.O. looked as guileless as a child's. "I served alongside them for years. I went to their kids' birthday parties, their weddings." He shook his head. "I still can't make sense of it."

Winters said, "Do you think any of them were involved in the theft ring and trying to cover their tracks?"

A jolt that scorched like lightning ripping across the sky raced through Caleb's body. A photograph from his last deployment filled the screen, the shot zoomed in tight. He and Avery squinted into the bright sunlight in front of the ruins of an Afghan village obliterated by Islamic State fighters. A superimposed circle, several shades lighter than the rest of the picture, highlighted Caleb's face.

"It's not a stretch, is it?" Winters continued. "Caleb Frost, the man who initiated the allegations against you—he's highlighted there in the picture—went on to commit several armed bank robberies, stealing millions of dollars. In fact, he's still at large."

A static roar filled Caleb's ears. The television's colors sharpened, the smell of food and sizzle of the unattended grill increased tenfold. The police officer's silhouette in the booth along the wall seemed to pull the light in the room toward him, making him glow like a beacon. Caleb didn't catch what the cook said as the man's eyes narrowed.

He had to get out of here right fucking now.

He turned away and headed for the door, not hurrying, his eyes darting everywhere. Was anyone following? Had the cook recognized him? Of all the damn things to show up on television when he was standing right there.

The evening air, warmer than when he'd entered the restaurant, caressed Caleb's face as he opened the diner door. The rain hadn't stopped but had lightened. He pulled the keys from his jacket pocket and walked down the sidewalk, heedless of the rain. Caleb unlocked the truck door and got inside, buckled his seat belt, and turned the key in the ignition.

He looked down the main drag, scanning for trouble, but all he could see was red. That son of a bitch was making even more money from what he'd done? Spreading more lies about what had happened? It wasn't enough that he'd escaped punishment for his crimes. Now he was playing the victim and rewriting history? Turning Caleb and the other members of his unit—who had agonized over what to do—into villains?

Caleb's hands gripped the steering wheel so tight it seemed it should snap in his hands. His body felt too small for the emotions roiling inside him, humming and buzzing under his skin like a tempest.

Get hold of yourself.

He took a few breaths and shook out his shoulders. Then he turned on the turn signal and checked his mirror before pulling away from the curb onto the quiet main street. He didn't dare stay the night at his place after this. If he'd been recognized, this location was burned.

He stopped at the light, even though it still glowed yellow. Being pulled over for a ticket was something he couldn't afford. A few blocks down the road, a police cruiser turned onto the main drag and headed his direction. His pulse sped up like an excitable puppy wagging its tail. Not a big deal, he thought. When the light changed—any second now—he and the cruiser would pass each other. Caleb would go on his way like he always did.

The police cruiser's lights bloomed red and blue. The rotating lights washing over his face burned like fire. Caleb assessed the situation with combat-honed reflexes. He put the truck in reverse and twisted around, his arm along the top of the seat. More police vehicles raced toward him along the main street of the sleepy little town.

If it was just the one car, a lone officer doing his job on a crappy, rainy night, he'd brazen it out. Say 'Yes, sir,' and apologize for inconveniencing the officer with whatever dumb thing he hadn't realized he'd done. Show the man the respect he deserved before going on his way. But this was different. The cook must have recognized him.

Caleb had the training to get out of this. He knew he could do it—he was certain of that—but he might need to hurt someone. He hadn't served to keep Americans safe only to kill some poor schmuck trying to do the same thing—a guy just doing his job, who wanted to get home safe to his wife and kids.

Inevitability swirled around him like water circling a drain. Ruth's voice echoed: *Caleb, what are you doing?*

The police cruiser pulled through the light and cut across the intersection, blocking his path. Behind him, two officers climbed out of their vehicles and approached the truck. Their movements were stiff, more rigid than a warrior's would be.

Caleb switched off the ignition. He rolled down the window, put his hands on the steering wheel, and waited. He wasn't— would never be—a killer of innocents. Reality stared him in the face. His time had run out.

chapter
two

CODY

FRIDAY, JULY 11
8:00 PM

Cody's hands rested on the crib rail as he watched Grace sleep. She lay on her back, both hands flung up beside her head like she was playing cops and robbers. Her straw-colored hair curled around her ears. He marveled again at how much of it she had, right from the beginning. He stroked her silk-soft cheek with the back of a finger. Cody couldn't stop smiling whenever he looked at his daughter. Whenever he thought of her. It still amazed him that someone so small could fill up his entire world.

After a parting glance, he got up and left the nursery to eat dinner with Emma. Brown moving boxes of all shapes and sizes were stacked in every room, some open, some sealed shut. A small but growing number were now broken down and leaning against the wall, flat as pancakes. After three weeks in their new house, it still looked like a bomb had gone off. The last time they moved, he and Emma had unpacked and set up in ten days, but they'd been childless and had a lot less stuff. Tomorrow he'd be home all day. Emma could catch up on her sleep, and he would scale these cardboard mountains if it killed him.

A sharp scrape raked his bare ankle. "Ow!" he cried out, yanking his foot up and hopping on the other. On the floor, something with a sharp corner stuck out between two boxes along the wall. Cody bent and picked up a picture frame. He flipped it over to see teenaged Cody sitting beside his mother, his sandy-colored hair not quite in his eyes. In the picture, he looked like he wanted to be anywhere but there, which had been true. His father stood beside his mother, and Cody's little sisters clung to their father like starfish. Cody studied the picture for a moment—his eyes drawn, as always, to his father.

I wish you were here to see your granddaughter, dad.

Kind eyes. Quiet strength. Cody still remembered how safe he'd felt just being near him. In the photo, his father was ten years older than Cody was now. What would it feel like, he wondered, to outlive his dad?

"Cody! Dinner's almost ready!"

Cody blinked, then lay the picture on top of a box labeled FAMILY PICTURES. He slid the picture over the gap between the box it had been in and the one beside it. That way, it wouldn't slip between the boxes.

Emma stood at the kitchen sink, steam rising around her from the pasta she dumped in a colander. He walked up behind her, sliding his arms around her waist and pulling her close. She smelled faintly of the lavender soap she liked and strongly of baby spit-up, but most of all, she smelled like Emma. He couldn't describe it but knew it all the same. He kissed the back of her neck, his lips skimming her skin. "Dinner smells good."

"Thank you for saying so," she said. She turned her head and twisted halfway in his arms, still holding the hot pot off to the side, and kissed him. "Let's eat. I'm starving and so tired. I don't want to fall asleep over my plate."

Cody released her and stepped back. "I'll set the table."

A few minutes later, they sat at the kitchen table, Emma's legendary spaghetti and meatballs filling the kitchen with the scent of heaven. Cody finished a bite and dabbed the corners of his mouth with a napkin. "Thank you so much, Em. You know I'd have made dinner if you'd waited, right?"

Emma nodded. "You were up with Grace almost as much as me. Besides, I don't have a commute."

Cody smiled. Emma was in a good mood. The last few months had been stressful. He hadn't been sure they would make it, if he was honest. Things still weren't right between them, but they were both trying.

He tried to hide the wince when he thought about how they'd ended up in a small Idaho town with a ten-week-old baby. Apart from the baby, none of it had been the plan. Emma had been furious about the move at first; silent seething followed. She'd lightened up a lot since Grace was born. He understood her reaction, even if he had trouble admitting it. Throw in the stress of being a new mother, a two-hour breastfeeding schedule that kept her perpetually sleep-deprived, and a cross-country move, and he was lucky she even spoke to him.

"Grace took an almost four-hour-long nap," Emma said. "It feels like I haven't had that much uninterrupted sleep since she was born."

Emma had the bags under her eyes to prove how tired she was, but she also glowed when she held Grace in her arms or fussed over her as first-time mothers do. Still, he worried. She'd had to leave her OB/GYN who had gotten her through the high-risk pregnancy, and they'd both loved the pediatrician who had taken care of Grace those first few weeks. Too many changes in too short a time, but it would get better. It had to.

"I've got the whole weekend plus Monday off," Cody said. "Maybe by Tuesday it won't feel like we're living in a packing store."

Emma grinned. Her sense of humor was the second thing he'd noticed when he'd met her. He would be lying if he'd said it was the first. Emma had long blond hair, blue eyes, and legs that went on for days. And just a couple freckles on the pale skin of her face. He'd always been a sucker for girls with pale skin and freckles. If he told anyone he'd noticed her sense of humor before her beauty, they would rightly call him a liar.

"You know," she said, "I think I've figured out that neighbor's name."

"Which one?" Cody asked.

"The lady in that first house past the bend. I think it's Samantha. Unless it's not... It might be Sophia?"

Shit, Cody thought, not hearing anything more of what Emma was saying. Samantha Young still hadn't returned his call. The chaos of moving and starting at a new office had left him scattered. He'd fought long and hard to stop that transfer. In the end, it had counted for nothing.

"Honey," Cody said, interrupting Emma. "I just realized I need to make a WITSEC call. I'll be right back."

Emma raised her eyebrows and said, deadpan, "Off all weekend, huh?"

"After I make this call, yes. I promise."

Leaving the table, Cody got his phone and went into the living room. He'd just punched in the last digit of Samantha's number when the phone rang.

Shit, he thought, his heart sinking. It was Abner, his boss. Cody almost crossed his fingers as he swiped the screen to answer.

"Cody," Abner said. "Sorry to interrupt. Have you ever heard of Caleb Frost?"

Cody's new boss' lack of small talk took some getting used to. Abner wasn't unpleasant, but his lack of social niceties was jarring.

Cody frowned. The name rang a distant bell but he couldn't recall details. "I've heard the name."

"He's a bank robber, a good one, too. Nine counts of armed bank robbery in seven states over six years. He and his crew have stolen close to sixteen million dollars and never fired a shot. Never got so much as a parking ticket. He was just picked up in Montana by local law enforcement. You're low man on the totem pole, so you're going to get him and bring him here to Coeur D'Alene."

"Montana? Shouldn't the field office in Missoula or Billings bring him in?"

"They should." Cody could hear the shrug in Abner's voice. "Frost is from Idaho, Bonner's Ferry. Someone called in a favor to bring him here, probably political. I don't know who and I don't care. That crap is above my pay grade. Either way, he's coming home."

Cody cast a glance at Emma, who looked at him through narrowed eyes. She knew something was up. That was another thing he'd been attracted to, her intelligence.

"You still there, Cody?"

Cody walked farther into the living room. "Yeah, I'm here. When do I go?" he asked with a marked lack of enthusiasm.

"Is there a problem, Cody? Is the baby sick?"

"No, no, nothing like that," he said hastily. He dropped his voice lower. "It's not gonna go over well with Emma, but that's not your problem, sir. When do I go?"

"First thing in the morning. Darlene will send over the details. You're flying into Kalispell, Montana."

"Flying?" Cody said. When he heard Emma huff, he knew he'd blurted that out too loud. Voice lower, he asked, "Is Frost that big of a deal?"

Abner chuckled. "He is around here. Let's just say if terrorism and drug trafficking hadn't bumped bank robbery from the FBI's Most Wanted list, Frost would be on it."

"Okay, sir. I'll get it done."

"That's what I like to hear. Look, Cody," Abner said, an avuncular note creeping into his voice. "You got a raw deal, I know that. Never pull that sort of crap on me, mind you. If that bomb had gone off, you'd be a hero. You still saved a lot of lives.

"I know how hard it is with the first baby, never mind moving across the country when they're as young as your Grace. Do a good job, put in your time, kiss a little ass if it's still required, and you'll be back where you want to be in three years, tops."

Cody barely held back a groan. He knew it would take that long to fix the mess he'd created. Hearing it out loud hadn't gotten any easier.

"Bringing Frost in is a big deal, especially around here. It might shave a few months off that," Abner continued. "By then, you and Emma might love it here. You might decide to stay."

"Maybe we will."

As if. Idaho was too small. Coeur d'Alene ranked in Idaho's top ten cities—with under 55,000 people. It was beautiful and the people welcoming, but it wasn't Virginia—wasn't the center of anything. Back East meant family, connections, real opportunities. Cody might adapt, depending on how things went, but Emma never would.

"Talk to you soon, boss," he said. "Have a good weekend."

"I'll see you when you get back. Just don't lose him."

Cody chuckled at Abner's joke, not because it was funny but because it was expected. Emma's good mood would soon be missing in action and he couldn't blame her. He hung up and stuck the phone in his pocket, then rejoined Emma at the table. She had resumed eating, but he could see the annoyance in her eyes.

"I'm sorry, Emma," he said. "I have to go retrieve a fugitive—"

"It's fine, Cody," she said, sounding too resigned to get angry. "Don't worry about it."

"I'll make it up to you. I promise. It's just my job, you know?" The moment Emma looked up, he knew he'd said the wrong thing.

"If you'd taken my advice about how to deal with the situation at your job, we wouldn't be here. I don't want to hear that it's just your job, Cody. I'm sick to death of your job."

"I'm sorry, Em."

"I'm tired, Cody. I never get enough sleep. I love Grace so

much, but I'm stuck here all day, in a place I don't know. I have no support except you, and that's hard. If we were in Virginia, I'd have my parents and sisters." Tears flooded her eyes. She sat back and threw her napkin on her half-finished pasta. "All you had to do was swallow your pride a little, but you wouldn't. Don't sit there and tell me 'it's just my job.' This entire mess is about you and your pride, Cody."

"Emma," he said, feeling helpless but also defensive. "It's not as simple as you make it sound."

She pushed away from the table and carried her dish to the sink. An unhappy cry started up in the nursery. Emma sighed and turned around, pushing her golden hair behind an ear. "I'll get her," Cody said.

Emma shook her head. "She's hungry. Just... eat your dinner."

Cody's attention stayed at the end of the hall, where Emma had disappeared from view. When he finally looked down at his dinner, his appetite was gone. Worry gnawed at his gut, fear whispering in his ear that Emma would never forgive him for uprooting them, for letting his pride drag her away from a life she loved at a time when she needed her support system more than ever.

All of this—and his part in making it happen—had blindsided Emma. He hadn't understood what that might stir up. "Three," he said, sighing. "Two and a half if I'm lucky."

He got up to clear his plate and put away the leftovers. He would go to flipping Montana tomorrow, then come home and unpack like his marriage depended on it, because it might. Making this up to Emma—that was his real job now.

day one

chapter
three

EMMA

SATURDAY, JULY 12
  11:00 AM

The July heat pressed against Emma like the creep at the office Christmas party brushes by just a little too near. It didn't matter where you worked. He worked there, too.

Sweat trickled down her spine, pooling at the small of her back. Ten weeks since having the baby, and her body still felt like it belonged to someone else—someone softer, exhausted, and leaky.

The baby monitor crackled. Emma froze, her hand hovering over a stack of case law books. Was this just the soft snuffle of a sleeping baby, or would the rustling from the monitor soon escalate to full-blown wails? Grace had fallen asleep after a nighttime cluster of feedings that had Emma's eyelids drooping. *Please don't wake up, sweetie.* After a few seconds, it seemed Grace had granted her wish. She continued sorting the contents of the moving box labeled EMMA'S OFFICE.

A picture of her and Cody on their wedding day stared up at her. She'd been radiant with optimism despite the train wreck of her first marriage. Emma ran a thumb over Cody's face, remembering how his eyes had barely left hers during the ceremony. He'd spent the entire day grinning like a man who couldn't believe his good luck. She had felt the same.

"And now, we're here," she said. Here was Specter Lake, Idaho, a small town an hour from Cody's office in Coeur d'Alene. Specter Lake had a population of who-the-hell-knew, and Emma knew precisely two people: her husband (currently absent) and her infant daughter (currently unconscious).

The garage creaked around her. She didn't know the sounds of this house yet, which only heightened the sense of dislocation she felt. Their ranch-style home sat on the edge of town among a cluster of self-contained streets, surrounded by ponderosa pines and neighbors she barely knew. Normally she'd make more of an effort, but a cross-country move with a new baby had wrung Emma out.

She did know their next-door neighbor Martha a little. The silver-haired woman had introduced herself the day they moved in, presenting Emma and Cody with a casserole to welcome them to the neighborhood. Emma had thought that kind of thing only happened in movies and found it charming. The woman her age who lived across the street had also tried to be friendly—Emma couldn't remember her name. Whatever it was, she seemed to understand that Emma was too overwhelmed to make the first move. The ugly truth was she barely managed waves and brief pleasantries at the grocery store.

They probably think I'm an East Coast snob.

Emma huffed out a breath that caught her bottom lip, sending a few strands of hair lifting from her forehead before they settled back against her damp skin. Maybe she was being a snob about living in such a small community. Then again, she had a baby hell-bent on never sleeping through the night and a husband she wasn't used to being on the outs with. When it came right down to it, Emma didn't have the energy to care.

A wave of dizziness made her head swim. She braced herself against a stack of boxes, waiting for it to pass. It was the heat, most likely. It had been a while since she'd had anything to drink.

"You should be helping me with this," she said aloud, as if Cody might materialize from behind the Christmas decorations. He was halfway to Montana by now, transporting a bank robber apprehended along the Idaho-Montana border. It wasn't the first weekend Cody had been called away, and it wouldn't be the last. But this time, the space where her understanding should be was filled with simmering resentment that lingered sharp as iron filings on her tongue.

She carried the items destined for the extra bedroom inside and put the box in the living room. A frame slipped off the top and hit the hardwood floor. Emma picked it up, taking the time to look at the certificate. Emma White, Anne Arundel County District Attorney's Office Distinguished Service Commendation. She smiled, remembering how surprised she'd been to receive the commendation. She'd only been with the district attorney's office for a year, but it had been a good one. It felt like a lifetime ago.

She dropped the commendation back into the box. She'd sort through this mess later. First, she needed to clear enough garage space to justify a nap.

The air-conditioning felt glorious after the heat of the garage. She closed her eyes a moment. A mistake, since a different conversation in a different living room started looping through her brain like soft rock on repeat. She had paced back and forth across their old living room, seven months pregnant, her belly leading the way like an autonomous entity. "Just bend your knee and apologize, Cody. Your boss can't protect you if you don't take some responsibility."

Cody shook his head with that stubborn set to his jaw that attracted or infuriated her, depending on the situation. "I'm not apologizing for doing my job. Thank God the bomb was a dud, but what if it hadn't been? Everyone in that church would have died if I'd followed procedure."

"I know that, Cody. You had a choice between following the rules and doing what's right, but this is politics. Right and wrong don't matter when they're looking for a scapegoat." She took his hand in hers and gave it a squeeze. "Sometimes you have to play the game."

Cody's frown twisted his mouth into a crooked line. "I don't play games with the truth, Em," he had said. "That's not who I am."

Not who I am. Cody had acted as if compromising would irreparably corrupt his essential Cody-ness. As if his moral stance was worth uprooting their lives when they had a newborn. She'd spent three years building a reputation at her firm, but what did that matter when Cody's principles were on the line?

Gritting her teeth, Emma returned to the garage, the temperature hotter by a good fifteen degrees. They'd been experiencing a heat wave that her weather app characterized as having 'abnormally high temperatures.' She couldn't wait till it broke. Her phone buzzed in the back pocket of her shorts. She pulled it out to find a text from Cody.

Just landed. Reception spotty. Will call when I can. Love you both.

Emma stared at the screen. She should reply, even if it was only 'Okay.' Instead, she tucked her phone back in her pocket. The problem wasn't that Cody had principles. She loved that about him. Cody's moral compass never wavered. It always pointed true north. The problem was he'd chosen those principles over what she and Grace needed, just like—

She cut off the thought, clamping down hard when it tried to slither through anyway.

Wind chimes tinkled outside at the exact moment the baby monitor erupted with Grace's hungry cries. Emma's breasts responded immediately, her milk letting down with a tingle that radiated through her chest. She couldn't let go of how all of this had unfolded, and it was making her miserable. Maybe if she wasn't so tired all the time—but she was. Some days, it felt like that was all she would ever be.

Grace's cries had worked up to a squall by the time she reached the nursery. It was the only room they'd completely unpacked. Emma lifted her daughter, the baby's face screwed up tight and bright pink, and inhaled the powdery scent of her head. The angry knot in her chest loosened as Grace's tiny fingers clutched the edge of her tank top. "I know, sweetie," she murmured, settling into the rocking chair to nurse. "Everything's different and weird for both of us, isn't it?"

Grace latched on to Emma's nipple with the determination of a tiny velociraptor. Emma stroked the downy hair on her daughter's head, loving how it curled around the pink shell of Grace's ear. Grace's brilliant blue eyes glazed over while she suckled, grunting like a little piglet. Emma barely knew this little creature, yet she loved her completely. She still hadn't wrapped her head around how it could be so true. It just was.

After Grace fell back asleep, Emma returned to the garage. She yawned so wide her eyes screwed shut.

"You look like you need a break."

Emma blinked, trying to hurry the yawn along. Her neighbor Martha stood in the open garage doorway holding two sweating glasses of iced tea. Her silver hair was pulled back in a short ponytail stub, and she wore a white polo shirt, tan shorts, and white canvas Keds. Light-pink lipstick completed the look, making Martha appear like the sort of woman who played tennis with ladies from 'her club.'

"I saw you before. You looked hot, so I made iced tea."

Emma smiled. "That's so sweet of you. Thank you."

Martha waved the thank you away and pressed an icy glass into Emma's hand. "What do you have Cody doing? I haven't seen him all day."

Emma shrugged. "He had to work." The cold glass against her lips was followed by the bitter bite of the unsweetened iced tea filling her mouth. Emma winced when a flash of pain from the icy drink lit up her front teeth like bursting lightbulbs.

"I know what that's like. My Jack used to work every weekend. Well, you're an attorney. You know how that is."

Emma's throat tightened. She didn't miss the seventy-hour weeks, and she wouldn't trade Grace for the world, but she didn't really know who she was without her job. When she'd become a mother, it felt like everything else she had been was suddenly irrelevant, whether she liked it or not. Then they had moved and everything else about her life changed.

Martha gave her arm a squeeze. "Why don't you come over for supper? You're new in town with a new baby and your husband's away—that's three strikes right there. You shouldn't have to cook, too."

Martha didn't look anything like Emma's mother, but the longing her simple acknowledgment triggered made her eyes fill with tears. Emma felt her face crumple, the tears spilling over before she could stop them. "I'm sorry," she said as she swiped at her cheeks. "I'm just tired."

Martha set her glass on a box and wrapped her thin arms around Emma's shoulders. "You're not just tired. You're everything, aren't you?"

Emma nodded against the older woman's shoulder, inhaling the earthy scent of garden soil. Martha's garden was something to see. "It's all so different," Emma said before pulling back and wiping her eyes. "Moving here wasn't part of the plan. Cody's work got—" She sighed. "It got complicated, so here we are."

Martha's dark, shrewd eyes studied Emma's face. It made her feel like a kid caught stealing candy at the corner store. "And now you're stuck with the consequences of his choices."

Emma shrugged. "Something like that."

Cody had offered to go to Idaho on his own so she could stay in Virginia near her parents and sisters. Emma had rejected it almost out of hand. She couldn't imagine parenting without Cody, nor could she deprive him this time with their child when it was all so new. She just hadn't counted on it being so hard, nor how much the fallout of him putting his pride above her hurt.

Martha's soft smile was filled with a knowing sympathy. "My Jack was stubborn as a mule when he thought he was right, and even more when he knew he was wrong."

"Yeah?" Emma said. "What did you do?"

"I talked to him when I didn't want to and cussed him out when he needed it." Then, speaking with exaggerated care, she added, "And when I had a new baby, I slept when the baby did."

Emma felt her body sag. "I want to get something done today. Grace kept me up most of the night."

"Then go sleep." Martha held out her hand for Emma's empty glass. "Supper's at six, if that works. Come over earlier if you want. I'll be home. Bring whatever you need for the baby."

"Are you sure? I don't want to be..."

Emma's voice trailed off under Martha's don't-make-me-come-over-there stare. "If she wakes you up to eat and you're still tired when she's done, go back to sleep."

A half smile tugged at the corner of Emma's mouth. "I will. I promise."

"Maybe I'll tidy up a little while you sleep," Martha said.

"I can't ask you to do that," Emma said. She was simply having a bad day. She wasn't a total basket case. At least, she hoped not.

"Just a few dishes," Martha said, brushing aside her protest with a wave of her hand.

"Thank you. I—" Emma hesitated, then settled on repeating her thanks.

She stopped at the nursery door before continuing down the hall to hers and Cody's bedroom. Grace lay on her back, her head turned to the side. One arm was flung up over her head, a mirror image of Cody when he slept.

"Talk to him when I don't want to and cuss him out when he needs it," Emma whispered to herself. She bit her lip, considering Martha's advice. It couldn't hurt to try.

chapter
four

CODY

SATURDAY, JULY 12
 2:30 PM

Cody stretched his arms overhead, groaning. He checked his watch: 2:30 p.m. *When are we getting out of here?*

His prisoner, Caleb Frost, barely spoke. Cody arrived in Kalispell, Montana, at eight, figuring it would take two hours at most to pick up Frost and get back on the plane. Another three hours for the flight, handing Frost off to the transportation detail, and driving home. Best-case scenario, he'd be home by one, maybe two.

If only.

The prisoner transfer from local authorities had taken far too long. The sheriff struck Cody as competent and no-nonsense, but they were giddy about having caught Caleb Frost—decorated US Army Ranger turned bank robber—in their small mountain town. Cody wasn't used to being treated like a minor celebrity for taking custody of a fugitive, but that was the position he'd found himself in.

Retrieving Frost's belongings had also dragged on. Cody always made sure prisoners checked their items, just in case. When he saw the Rolex Submariner among Frost's possessions, he was glad he had. He didn't need the headache if it went missing. Abner had said the man stole millions. Something about seeing such an expensive watch had made it seem a whole lot less like Monopoly money.

Upon returning to Kalispell City Airport, Cody was informed the plane he'd flown here in had mechanical problems. *You have got to be fucking kidding me,* he had thought, his irritation rising. That killed any hope of salvaging his day with Emma, because a plane appropriate for prisoner transport was required. They'd been waiting for a replacement ever since.

Cody looked around the passenger lounge. It was small, on the nicer side of the many municipal airports he'd frequented over the years. Caleb Frost commanded attention in the bright-orange jumpsuit he wore. The handcuffs, belly chain, and ankle shackles didn't help his anonymity, nor did the two local deputies flanking him. Against the muted tones and clean but worn gray upholstery of the airport lounge, the orange jumpsuit burned bright as a flame.

Cody knew from reading his file that Frost had been a decorated Army Ranger in the 75th Ranger Regiment, with several deployments under his belt. Once he dug into the news stories online, he remembered the court martial of Avery Scott, Frost's commanding officer, and the subsequent pardon. At the time, Cody hadn't followed the story closely but it had been all over the news.

What Cody hadn't known was that Frost, along with every other member of his unit who had accused Scott, had left the service within the year. Cody found that odd. Honorable discharges all the way around, but these were enlisted soldiers, not officers who could resign their commissions. Nearly an entire unit cycling out in the same year? They'd been pushed out, if Cody had to guess, but quietly, without official punishment.

Cody stole a glance at Frost. *Why does a guy like that become a bank robber?*

Cody didn't know what Frost's commanding officer had or hadn't done. The man had maintained his innocence throughout the court martial and several members of the unit had defended him. That Frost's commanding officer had been convicted and subsequently pardoned by the president mattered to Cody not at all. Such things were beyond his newly reduced pay grade.

And still... Cody couldn't stop puzzling over how being pushed out of the Army led to a run as a bank robber. His brain kept turning the scenario over like a dryer that wouldn't stop running. If the guy had been guilty and got away with it, Cody could see being angry. Getting forced out of the service under those circumstances might leave a man feeling betrayed, even. But going from serving his country to stealing millions of dollars? Because Frost and his crew, which many people thought included at least one of his former unit members—on Reddit, anyway—were that good. They had pulled off their heists with the precision of the special operator Frost had once been, to the tune of millions.

The door to the passenger lounge opened. The pilot's head poked through. "We're ready to go. I'm sorry about the delay."

Cody nodded. "I'd rather be late than dead." He straightened his sports coat as he stood, then said to Frost, "Time to go."

Watching Frost stand up was like watching a mountain rise into the air, especially contrasted with the two deputies, neither of whom were ninety-eight-pound weaklings. *Thank God he's coop-erative,* Cody thought to himself. If Frost somehow slipped his handcuffs and ankle shackles, there was no way Cody could take him. Saying the man was big and tall was like saying Mount Everest was a hill. Frost was so muscular the jumpsuit strained at the seams.

Cody wasn't a gym rat, but he stayed in shape. He wanted

Emma to find him attractive enough to keep having sex. Having made a promise to be monogamous, Cody didn't think it would be fair to let himself go. One of Frost's biceps, his tan skin bulging along the edge of the short sleeves, was larger by a third than both of Cody's put together. The man's torso was so broad that Cody was pretty sure he could stand behind him and disappear entirely. But it was the shrewd intelligence in Frost's eyes—a piercing, icy blue that matched his name—that gave Cody the most pause. Caleb Frost might be cooperative, but Cody wasn't fooled. The man was dangerous.

Cody held the door as Frost and the deputies followed the pilot. Sweat popped out on his forehead almost as soon as he stepped into the bright sunshine and warm, moist air from the previous day's rain. It had been warm this morning but now the paved runway broiled, throwing off the kind of sweltering heat that forced shadows to seek shade.

The small group walked toward the high-winged Cessna 206 Stationair, a plane Cody was familiar with. As soon as he saw the suicide-style doors, he smiled. When the pilot opened them, Cody got confirmation that the passenger seats were configured the way he preferred. Two passenger seats were flush against the back of the pilot and copilot seats, facing the plane's tail. The other two passenger seats faced the plane's nose, with a space between them for people's feet. "Last row," Cody said to Frost, indicating the seat he wanted him to take.

"Yes, sir," Frost said. His tone was slightly mocking, which undercut the polite reply. A smart-ass, just Cody's luck. But Frost complied and Cody let it slide. For someone wearing cuffs, a chain, and shackles, he moved with surprising grace. He must have been something on the battlefield.

Once Frost was situated to Cody's satisfaction—seat belt fastened, wrist cuff locked to the seat frame and his right ankle shackle attached to an anchor point on the floor, plus a headset to cover his ears—Cody thanked the deputies for their help. He removed his sports coat with a sigh and tossed it on one of the empty seats. Sweat trickled down his back, despite the garment being made of lightweight cotton seersucker. Cody wore a sports coat to conceal his weapon and shoulder holster, though for work he'd have worn it whether armed or not.

The pilot walked around the plane, conducting the exterior safety check. Cody stepped away from the open door to catch the breeze. He pulled out his phone and tapped out a quick text to let his boss, Abner, know they were about to leave. The pilot came around the plane's nose just as Cody tapped the green dial icon to call Emma. "We're already hours behind schedule," the pilot said. "Your call needs to wait."

"Two more minutes won't make a difference," Cody said as the call connected, followed by a ring.

"The plane has a satphone. You can call when we're in the air. I'd like to be home in time for dinner. I'm Bill, by the way."

The second ring of Emma's phone buzzed in Cody's ear. She usually picked up immediately. 'Before the first ring finishes' was what he liked to say when he teased her. By the third ring, he was sure her phone wasn't nearby or she was sleeping. If it didn't mean waking Emma up, he'd ignore Bill's instructions, but it probably did. With a sigh, Cody ended the call.

Emma had rallied and put on a good face, enough that they'd salvaged the rest of their evening. He'd left her to sleep this morning, leaving a note with his departure and when he hoped to be home. He knew she was annoyed about the trip—so was he. Grace hadn't slept well again. A bad night for the baby meant Emma didn't sleep, either. Emma hadn't been able to reach her mother, whom she talked to every Friday night. Plus, there was the small fact of him not being at home with her, taking care of the things he was supposed to be taking care of.

And there was the move. A few months ago, he would have said his marriage was rock solid. But that was before he failed to take into account what Emma might need when everything blew up at work. The buzzing twang of his conscience demanded he be honest. He really didn't see how he could have handled it differently, because he wasn't sorry for what he'd done. There had been a bomb in that church. It hadn't detonated because the guy wasn't a good bomb maker, but that was beside the point.

For all his rebellious impulses, Cody followed the rules. He needed a damn good reason to break them, and he'd had one. But he'd dug in his heels immediately, even before telling Emma he'd been called up on the carpet. And then he hadn't listened to her. He'd gone through the motions of listening, but he'd already made up his mind.

Christ, I'm an idiot.

He had offered to move to Idaho on his own and fly home every month. Emma had refused. He'd known she would, which made the offer feel hollow even though he'd meant it. Deep down, he believed they'd get through this, given time and a lot of heartfelt groveling on his part. But dragging her across the country as a first-time mother when the whole thing could have been avoided? There was no polite way to say it. He had screwed the pooch.

Cody shoved his phone into his pocket and boarded the plane, Bill following him. He pulled a magazine from the pocket against the plane's far wall, then sat down in the second row, facing Frost. "Do you need anything, water or something to read?"

"No, sir," Frost said.

Bill reappeared and handed Cody what looked like a walkie-talkie: the satellite phone. "Wait till I tell you it's okay to call."

"Sure thing. And thanks."

Cody slipped his headset over his ears and plugged it into the jack. He could hear switches being flipped as the plane powered up. He twisted in his seat to look out the windshield. The propeller was a gray blur as they taxied down the runway.

The dark blue-green of the mountain's forested slopes gave way to granite just below the jagged-toothed peaks. Kalispell was a beautiful town, with Glacier National Park less than five hours north. He and Emma had talked about camping in Glacier. A soft smile played over Cody's mouth when he thought about bringing his blond-haired girls here sometime.

Bill spoke to the tower, and the tower answered with a largely incomprehensible string of words. The plane turned and picked up speed. With a whining scream of engines, they lifted into the air. A few minutes later, Bill's voice buzzed through the headset. "Is this your first trip to Montana, Marshal?"

Frost's head lifted, and he looked at Cody. They were on a common channel. "It's not," Cody said. "But it's been a while. Ten years at least. I was in Jackson to ski."

Bill laughed. "Saw lots of celebrities, I'm sure. I'll never say Jackson isn't Montana, but it's not the Montana it used to be."

Cody smiled. His own hometown was a few hours outside Memphis, Tennessee. Memphis had experienced the same phenomenon. Change wasn't always a bad thing, but he knew what Bill meant.

"I guess you do this sort of thing all the time," Bill said. "Prisoner transports and such."

"It's part of the job. You have to go when and where they tell you. I'm in the doghouse with my wife this weekend. I was supposed to be at home."

"Any kids?"

Cody smiled. "A daughter, Grace. She's ten weeks old."

"Your first?"

"Yeah," Cody said. "She's such a pretty little thing."

As Cody finished speaking, the plane's radio crackled to life. "Salt Lake City ARTCC advises all aircraft: Solar event in progress. Possible intermittent communication and navigation system interference. No significant disruptions expected. VFR flight conditions are otherwise normal. Maintain standard communication procedures."

"What's going on?" Cody asked.

"Just a weather advisory because of solar activity. We might have some minor radio static. The satphone might get a little twitchy, but it's nothing to be concerned about. They happen all the time."

Cody's grip on the satphone tightened. "Can I still make my phone call?"

"Yeah. If your call doesn't connect, just give it a couple minutes, but I've never had problems."

Cody sighed, relief loosening his grip on the phone. That would just be his luck, to be unable to make his call. He pushed one of the headphones aside and started to dial the area code when he remembered. He still hadn't called Samantha Young! Grace and Emma weren't the only ones who didn't get enough sleep.

He cleared the call he'd started and punched in Samantha's number, which he knew by heart. Cody had only encountered Steven Silva once when they passed in the courthouse hallway. It had been enough. One glance at those empty eyes told Cody everything: Silva would have killed Samantha slowly, savoring every second.

Two years into his career as a US Marshal, still so green he had moss growing behind his ears, Cody had been assigned to Samantha's protection detail after her escape from Silva's captivity. She was Silva's only known victim—emphasis on known. Something about the man's methodical nature suggested practice, though he'd never been connected to other disappearances.

Throughout the trial and her subsequent relocation into witness protection, Samantha had shown remarkable resilience. Years later, when she requested Cody as her WITSEC inspector despite living outside his district, he'd been honored and uneasy for the same reason: Samantha trusted him. His transfer meant she had a new WITSEC inspector now, but that didn't mean Cody had stopped trying to keep Silva where he belonged.

Steel bands seemed to cinch around Cody's chest as he waited for the call to connect. The judge's ruling to transfer Silva to MacDougall-Walker Correctional Institution made no sense.

Level 4 and 5 security or not, Silva belonged exactly where he'd been the last twelve years.

Just as he thought the call wouldn't connect, the phone began to ring. One ring, two, then the line picked up. "I'm sorry you've missed me. Please leave a message and I'll return your call when I can." A high-pitched beep followed the message.

Goddammit, Cody thought. He hated leaving messages, especially when all he could do was apologize for things he didn't control that shouldn't be happening.

"Hey there, it's Cody," he said, raising his voice to be heard over the noise. "Just checking in again to see how you're doing and how I can help. I can only imagine how anxious you are, but I'm not giving—"

The line went dead. The hiss from the headphone cushion hugging his other ear quieted. Cody pulled the satphone from his ear. The display had gone dark.

The Cessna's engine sputtered. Frost ripped off his headset and leaned forward in his seat. "Something's wrong."

The Cessna lurched as the engine died. They hung in the air for a breath, suspended. The nose began to drop. "What's happening?" Cody said, twisting in his seat to talk to the pilot.

"Mayday, mayday! This is Charter Flight 227, departed from Ravalli County Airport..."

Cody's heart thudded, stuttered, then hammered like hot tongs on an anvil. He squinted through the gap between the seats, searching the readouts on the instrument panel. Everything that had glowed among the dials and switches was dark. Only one— the altimeter—had a functioning display. Its two needles spun counterclockwise, one fast, one slower.

"Charter Flight 227 out of Ravalli County declaring an emergency. Complete power failure, instruments dead, requesting immediate assistance from any towers receiving."

A vibration hummed under the soles of Cody's feet until the plane shook. Frigid dread contracted his stomach and snatched air from his lungs. He wasn't a pilot, but he knew what those needles meant. They were losing altitude—fast.

"Calling any receiving stations! Cannot maintain altitude!"

The plane plummeted, the low slant of the afternoon sun setting the mountain on fire. The restraints constricted around Cody's body like a python. A sharp crack drowned out the pilot's frantic maydays when one of the spear-like treetops snagged a wingtip. Then they were spinning, around and around and around, like a child's whirligig. Branches clawed the fuselage. The plane tipped, dipped, cartwheeled through the forest.

Cody had left Emma and Grace at home. His golden girls, he'd left them behind. He'd never see them again.

Cody's arm was wrenched up, the pain blinding bright. His vision hopped and jumped, head cracking against his seat. A roar of sound—crashing, splintering—assaulted his senses. The windshield atomized in a mist of glass and pine needles. Then they slammed to a halt like an overripe tomato thrown hard against a wall.

The *tick-tick-tick* of cooling metal and his own ragged breath filled Cody's ears. Aviation fuel mixed with the astringent scent of pine. The shadows were deeper below the trees. The Cessna's frame groaned as it settled. Cody hung suspended, tilted at an angle. The ground below him felt miles away. The singe of bile mixed with the coppery taste of blood filled his mouth before his sick splatted on the metal of the suicide doors.

"We are so screwed."

Frost's voice rasped over Cody's ears like a saw's sharp bite. His chilly blue eyes snagged Cody's like razor-sharp hooks. Cody opened and closed his mouth, like a fish suffocating on a creek bank. He reached out a hand to the only person he could see: Caleb Frost.

chapter
five

SATURDAY, JULY 12
3:10 PM

Emma jerked awake, heart thundering. She couldn't remember where she was. The angle of the light through the curtains was wrong, the shadows on the ceiling unfamiliar. Then she remembered: Idaho, their new house, Cody gone to catch a criminal.

She checked her phone. It was eighty-seven degrees at three in the afternoon. She'd slept longer than she'd meant to, but Grace hadn't made a peep on the baby monitor. The silence felt like a gift wrapped in delicate paper. She didn't want to tear it.

Cody might be home by now, or soon, she hoped. There was no way to know how long the fugitive retrieval would take. He'd left the house at seven this morning, landed in Montana around eleven; now it was three. He wouldn't wake her if she were sleeping, and it was probably a little early to expect him. Home yet or not, she hoped he'd bring dinner.

Emma swung her legs over the side of the bed, her body as

heavy as waterlogged wood. The sheets had left creases on her forearm that she traced with her fingertip. Her mouth tasted stale, like day-old coffee. "Cody?" she called as she walked down the hall. "Cody, are you home?"

No answer. She checked the house and the yard, front and back. She checked the kitchen for a note, in case he'd come home but needed to go out again. No note. Disappointment stole over her like a heavy cloak. But he'd be home soon. She yawned as she stretched her arms over her head.

I'll text him to bring takeout.

In the bathroom, she flicked on the light and splashed cold water on her face. The air-conditioning hummed, raising goosebumps along her arms as she brushed her teeth. The radio played in another room, the volume just low enough that she could hear the melody but not the words. Maybe Martha had left it on after she'd gone home. It was nice to wake up to a human voice, especially when it wasn't a crying baby.

Dinner with Martha, she thought, remembering. At least she hadn't texted Cody to pick up food. Emma studied herself in the mirror. The dark smudges under her eyes looked like faded violets, and her golden-colored hair hung limp around her face. She gathered it up into a messy bun. Not great, but better. She padded down the hallway, pausing at the nursery door. Grace lay on her back, the rhythm of her breathing even and deep. One tiny fist was curled beside her ear, the other splayed open on the mattress. Emma's chest squeezed with a swell of love so deep her breastbone ached.

I'll take a quick shower while she's still asleep.

The bathroom light flickered once, twice, then went dark. The hum of the air-conditioning ceased and the song from the radio vanished. Silence settled over the still house. Emma flicked the light switch off and on. Nothing.

"Well, shit," Emma muttered, hoping the power would come back on soon. It was broiling outside. For now, the house was cool. She'd close the curtains to help it stay that way.

She went to her bedroom to get her phone, then to the living room. The hardwood floors were cool under her feet, like a chilly stone patio. Their place in Virginia had carpet. They'd planned to rip it out but hadn't gotten around to it. She was unhappy about moving, but she had to admit having hardwood floors again was nice. They lived in a much nicer house than they could afford in Virginia. She reminded herself of this every day. In the living room, she pulled the curtains closed, then checked her phone for a power outage alert.

The screen's black reflection shined up at her, even in the dim light. She pressed the power button but it didn't flicker to life. She kept on holding it, expecting the phone to reboot. Nothing. That's odd, she thought, her lips pursing in a frown. When she'd checked the time after waking, she'd noticed the battery was at sixty percent. It couldn't have died that quickly.

She walked to the kitchen, her gaze falling on the refrigerator. Two bottles of breast milk she'd pumped yesterday were in there, along with what was left of last week's groceries. She and Cody were supposed to go shopping today, but she thought they still had some orange juice. She reached for the fridge handle, then stopped. With the power out, she really shouldn't open it unless she had to, so she decided on water instead. She'd filled a pitcher earlier and left it by the sink. She didn't like cold water; it always hurt her teeth. On the way to the sink, she plugged in her phone at the kitchen island. The built-in charging ports were nice—not that she'd admit that to Cody. Not yet.

Now that she wasn't running on fumes, she regretted not answering Cody's text. If he'd texted her again while she was sleeping, she wouldn't know till her phone recharged. Except she hadn't heard the soft, ascending *ba-doop* when she plugged it in. She checked her phone again to find it wasn't charging. *Because the power's out, idiot.*

Anxiety crawled up Emma's throat like marching ants. Being alone with the power out and Cody away unsettled her. Since having Grace, she worried about things that never used to faze her. She loved being a mother, but it was turning her into a worrywart.

She couldn't let go of the oddness of her dead phone. Even if there was no service, the phone shouldn't lack power.

Maybe Martha will know what's going on.

Emma slipped her feet into sandals and grabbed the baby monitor. The green power light indicator on the monitor didn't glow, either.

"What is going on?" Emma muttered, feeling confused. She checked the base in Grace's room and found it and the other monitor also inoperable. Even if the base, which was plugged into the wall, wasn't drawing power anymore, the two charged monitors should be working.

Emma checked on Grace again. She still slept soundly. It wouldn't hurt to leave her in her crib for a few minutes to run next door. She had complained to Cody many times that kids today grew up in a surveillance state, their every activity monitored and parents always in attendance. She still thought this was so. Now that she had a baby of her own, however, she understood the impulse to want to keep her child safe in a very different way.

After the cool interior of the house, the late afternoon heat swirled around her like a warm towel. Martha answered after two knocks on the kitchen door. Her silver hair looked mussed, like she'd been holding it back from her forehead. "Emma? Is Grace all right?"

"Yes, she's fine. I'm just wondering if you have power?"

Martha frowned. "I don't know. I've been reading in the sunroom." She reached for the light switch beside the door, flicking it up and down. Nothing happened. "I guess I didn't notice."

"What about your cell phone?" Emma asked.

Martha's eyebrows knitted together. "My cell phone?"

Emma nodded. "Mine's totally dead. I looked at it a few minutes before the power went out. It was at sixty percent. I'm not sure how that can happen."

Frowning, Martha stepped away from the door, waving for Emma to follow. Emma stepped into Martha's kitchen. Martha walked through to another room, returning a minute later with her phone. One look at her face gave Emma her answer. "Mine's not working either."

"That's kind of weird, don't you think, for the power to go out and our phones die at the same time?"

"It is strange." Martha's eyes narrowed. "Let's see if there's anyone outside we can ask."

"I don't know," Emma said. "It's kind of far."

"And the baby monitor isn't working, I guess," Martha said, looking like she was sorry she'd brought it up.

Emma nodded. "I don't think it has that range anyway."

"I understand, Emma, but she'll be fine." Emma must have made a face because Martha added, "It's just a few hundred feet. For most of human history, we didn't have baby monitors."

Emma knew Martha was right, but she still felt squirrelly about it. She remembered her older cousins sharing how they'd left the house all day in the summertime as kids, barely seeing their parents apart from mealtimes. To a one they felt sorry for kids who no longer had that freedom. Besides, Grace was sleeping. "You're right. Let's go."

She followed Martha through the house and out the front door. The neighbor from across the street stood outside. Relief flooded through Emma now that it appeared they wouldn't be going far.

Their house, Martha's, and the house across the street sat on a bend in the road. Their lot was almost an acre—easily two to three times larger than others in the neighborhood. Small woods backed both their house and Martha's. Most of their lot was wooded, but it extended to where the road straightened, about an eighth of a mile. Martha's lot was similar, with a significant distance between hers and other houses on that side.

A bluff rose abruptly across the street, though it dropped off on either side after a short distance. The only section deep enough for a decent lot was directly opposite Emma's house. The three houses felt more secluded than the others. Dog walkers provided steady activity mornings and evenings, so it didn't feel isolated. Still, more people usually meant more information. Emma had assumed they'd need to walk to one end of the bend or the other for news, but now they had their neighbor just across the street.

A few hundred feet beyond Martha's house, a man stood beside a car stopped in the middle of the street with its hood up. Beyond him, three more vehicles sat in place in the street. None seemed to have been in an accident; they just weren't moving.

Emma and Martha walked down the driveway and crossed the street. The woman who lived there stood on the sidewalk, her copper-colored hair pulled into a braid. Emma racked her brain but still, the name wouldn't come.

"Hi, Martha," the mystery neighbor said when they reached her. "I'm Diane," she added, as if reading Emma's thoughts.

"Emma," Emma said.

"Are your cell phones dead?" Diane asked them.

"Yes," Martha said. "The power, too."

Diane frowned. "My Apple Watch died, and I just charged it this morning."

"What's going on with the cars?" Emma asked.

Diane shrugged. "I was just going to see."

Emma hesitated, looking back at her house, then down the street. She wanted to know what was happening. *Grace is fine*, she thought, forcing her feet to move her along.

Every driver reported that their car had simply died and wouldn't restart. No one had a working cell phone, which made it hard to call for a tow truck. Who had a landline anymore? A balding man with a round face, whom Martha greeted and said was named Pete, arrived. He organized people to push the stalled cars out of the way. Emma cast an anxious glance toward her home, thinking of Grace. Surely she had enough time to help. She had always heard small communities pulled together in emergencies. A power outage hardly constituted an emergency, but the pulling together part seemed true enough. She'd worried earlier about seeming like a snob. Helping out would show she wasn't. Besides, it was the neighborly thing to do.

After the cars were moved, Emma heard someone say, "Martha! There you are."

A tall woman with the kind of short hair middle-aged women often favored strode toward them. She wore an expensive-looking pink athleisure track suit with a skirt that Emma was ninety-nine percent certain was in fact a skort. Despite the heat, her makeup had no smudges. Emma couldn't find a drop of sweat anywhere on the woman's tanned skin.

"Hello, Janice," Martha said, her tone cool.

"This is exactly why I've been pushing the HOA to invest in a generator for the community clubhouse," Janice said, not bothering with pleasantries. "We'll need to convene an emergency meeting without power now."

"An emergency meeting?" Emma said. "For a power failure?"

Janice seemed to notice of Emma for the first time. She looked down her nose at her. "You're new, aren't you? The Grays, right, in the house next to Martha?"

Before Emma could reply, Janice thrust out a hand adorned with a diamond ring so large Emma wondered how she could lift her hand. Her grip was painfully firm, like she used handshakes to establish dominance. "Janice Westfield. I'm the HOA president."

"It's Greer," Emma replied. "Emma Greer." The woman's imperious attitude rubbed Emma the wrong way. "My husband is Cody but he's—"

Not bothering to let Emma finish, Janice said, "You'll need to secure your property, Emma. Any loose items need to be stored." Janice's gaze flicked over Emma's slightly disheveled appearance. Her narrowed eyes gave the impression she found Emma lacking. "I hope you have emergency stores. You know," Janice said, her tone of voice becoming that of a parent addressing a particularly inattentive child. "Water and non-perishables. And make sure your garbage cans are properly stowed. The last thing we need is trash everywhere."

Emma's jaw tightened. An unpleasant tingle, like biting aluminum foil, sent a shiver down her spine. "I'll get right on that," she said, not bothering to hide the sarcasm.

Either Janice didn't notice Emma's tone or chose to ignore it. Then her lips pressed into a thin line. She'd noticed. "Well, excuse me. I need to go speak with Ted about organizing a neighborhood watch for tonight."

Janice turned on her heel and marched away. Did the woman watch too much true crime on television? Once she was out of earshot, Emma said, "Organize a neighborhood watch for a power outage? Emergency water stores? The real estate agent said the water here is gravity fed."

Martha sighed, like she'd heard all of this before and still found it irritating. "That was Janice being friendly. The water here is gravity fed once it's pumped into the towers. Don't worry about her. She treats the HOA like it's her personal war effort."

Great, Emma thought. An HOA president with a power complex.

"Are you still coming over for dinner?" Martha asked. "I haven't seen your car, so I know Cody's not back yet."

Emma and Cody only had one car since moving. They'd sold the other; it wasn't worth shipping. They'd get another eventually, probably before winter. Their house was within walking distance of downtown, but Emma didn't want to trek there in cold weather.

She wondered if cooking for another person might be too much just now. "Are you sure? I don't want to put you out."

"I've got ground beef and a propane grill. If Cody comes home in time, we can feed him, too."

"Okay then," Emma said. "I'll see you in a bit."

Back at the house, Emma found Grace still asleep. The nursery felt stuffy without the air-conditioning. Emma opened the window to catch the breeze. Grace didn't stay down very long, her hungry cries demanding sustenance. After changing and nursing her, Emma gathered what she needed—diapers, wipes, and a change of clothes for Grace.

The sun hung low in the sky as she carried Grace across the front lawn to Martha's front porch. The day's heat lingered, but its oppressive bite had lessened. Neighbors still clustered in small groups on the sidewalk, their conversations an anxious hum. Emma caught fragments as some walked by. "...do you think all the way to..." And "...nobody's phones are working. I heard..."

They all sounded on edge. The cell phones not working really freaked people out, Emma included. I hope Cody's phone is working, she thought. *He's all the way in Montana... His phone is probably working just fine.*

She'd feel better if she heard Cody's voice, but she was a grown-ass woman. She could take care of herself and Grace.

Martha sent Emma to the back patio, joining her a few minutes later. Potted flowers gave the outdoor space bright pops of color. Martha had already set the patio table and silvery beads of condensation slipped down the glasses of water even though they didn't have ice. A ceramic bowl held a simple but appealing salad. The propane grill hissed softly as Martha flipped the burgers with a turner, then rolled the corn on the cob to cook it evenly. "Dinner's almost ready."

Emma settled Grace in the portable bassinet she'd brought. Grace's eyes began to droop. The heat, most likely. "For a baby who keeps you up all night, she's a good day sleeper," Martha said, then smiled at Emma. "But it looks like it's caught up with her."

"Thanks again for getting me to take a nap," Emma said. "I needed it. Have you heard any news?"

Martha shook her head. "Nothing more than what you already know. Cars aren't working and cell phones are dead. Other electronics, too. Someone said it might be connected to the solar flare."

"What solar flare?" Emma asked.

"You must have missed the alert. There was a text about a

solar flare that said electronics might be disrupted for a few minutes. Chuy said it may have been stronger than predicted."

"Who's Chuy?"

"A neighbor. He's a mechanic and specializes in classic cars. He knows so many constellations. I think it's kind of a hobby for him."

"Did he have any idea how long this will this last?" Emma said. She always found newspaper stories and magazine articles about the natural world—and universe—interesting, but she was hardly an astronomer.

"No," Martha said, transferring the burgers onto buns on a platter. "We've got food, water, and each other. I see no reason to get riled up."

Emma smiled. Martha's no-nonsense manner reminded Emma of her mom. She sat at Martha's urging, looking up at the sky's faint rosy glow. Emma loved when the light did this. She didn't know why it happened, something about the angle of the light and which colors of the sun's rays were more visible. Whatever the reason, it felt magical, like fairy lights might appear suspended in the air.

They ate as twilight crept closer, the food simple but satisfying. Emma realized she was hungry despite her unease about not being able to get in touch with Cody. Then Martha said, "Emma, look at the sky."

Emma looked up. The darkening twilight sky shimmered with glimmering filaments of light, vivid shades of red, pink, and green, bleeding into one another like watercolors.

"Is that the Northern Lights?" Emma whispered.

Martha stood. "We don't get them here very often, but I think so. They're not usually so much..." She paused, then said, "More."

The lights pulsed and swirled, casting an otherworldly glow over the neighborhood. Emma stood, transfixed, but also unsettled. No power, dead phones, cars that wouldn't run, and now the Northern Lights, all in one day. She couldn't deny how beautiful they were. Was Cody seeing the same sky in Montana? Then she shivered despite the warmth of the summer evening, a sharp stab of fear piercing her heart. Had Cody been in the air when the flare happened? Would the same thing happen to his plane as the cars stalled out in the street?

Oh, for crying out loud, she thought. The nap had helped, but she was still overtired. She wasn't going to let her imagination run away with her. Even so, the faint sense of unease lingered.

Grace stirred in her bassinet, oblivious to the silent spectacle above. Emma reached down to touch her daughter's cheek, her skin as soft as dandelion fluff. "What's happening, Martha?" she asked, wanting reassurance despite herself. She looked back up at the sky. "It's kind of odd, all these things happening at once, isn't it?"

Martha's hand lighted on her shoulder. "Maybe, but isn't it beautiful?"

chapter
six

CALEB

SATURDAY, JULY 12
  3:40 PM

Caleb took a gasping breath. The *ba-ta-ta-dum, ta-ta-dum, ta-ta-dum* of his thundering heart began to slow. The marshal hung suspended above him, held in place by his seat belt and shoulder strap. Caleb thought the marshal had been awake throughout the crash. He'd seen his unfocused stare as the plane came to rest. Now he was out.

Carefully, Caleb moved his limbs. Everything hurt, especially his neck, but he seemed to have escaped serious injury. He'd have a better idea once he got out of the plane and moved around.

He flexed his right hand, then sucked in a breath. The wrist cuff the marshal had locked to his seat frame had twisted. It cut into the soft flesh of his inner arm. Nothing serious, but it hurt. A smear of blood welled around the bright metal.

"Son of a bitch," he said, huffing out a shallow breath. Then he noticed the links between the cuffs had also broken. "Guess I'll take it, though."

The plane had come to rest on its side. Its doors were against ground. A massive tree branch had speared and knocked out the windshield before stabbing through the seat beside him. He'd just been in a plane crash, but today was still Caleb's lucky day. He'd have to climb around the tree to get out. Once he was free of the rest of the restraints, that wouldn't be a problem.

The cut on his inner forearm didn't look deep. He pulled the broken metal out. Blood welled and flowed over the curve of his arm, steady but not heavy. He pressed the seat belt button and tugged the buckle free. The seat belt released with a pop. He turned onto his side to slide off the seat, ending up with one foot on the doors. His other foot, still shackled to the floor, was raised up a little in front of him, but not so much he couldn't move around.

First, he needed to get the manacles and shackles off. With some difficulty, he climbed onto the seat next to the marshal, taking his time so he didn't lose his balance. His legs still felt shaky, which made sense. He checked the closest front pocket of the marshal's jeans for the keys but didn't find them. He had better luck with the other. Easing back down, he used the small silver keys to unlock his wrists, the belly chain, and then the shackles that slowed his gait to a shuffle. He circled his wrists in both directions once both cuffs were off. It felt good, even with the cut on his arm.

Caleb climbed back up on the seat, ignoring his neck. The flare of pain at impact was settling down to an achy throb. He felt for a pulse in the marshal's neck. It thumped under Caleb's fingers, strong and steady. Passing out had likely helped his body calm.

His second order of business was to relieve the marshal of his weapon. Caleb gripped the gun and pulled it from the marshal's shoulder holster; a Glock 23, nice and reliable. After he stepped down, he released the magazine and removed a bullet. FC 40

S&W was stamped on the metal jacket. Good, he thought, reloading the bullet and reseating the magazine. He preferred Smith & Wesson .40 caliber to 9 mm for its superior stopping power. And he liked how the Glock handled using the .40 caliber.

His third order of business was to find his stuff and the first aid kit. It took a few minutes with the disarray in the cabin, but he found both. He unzipped the jumpsuit, stuffed the bag with his belongings inside, then zipped it back up. He had to hold the hard-cased first aid kit in one hand; he needed the other free. He crawled under the branch and squirmed between the front seats. One glance told him the pilot was dead. Definitely not getting home in time for supper.

Caleb crawled through the windshield and slid down the plane's nose to the ground. His right ankle flared with a dull pain when he landed. He'd walk it off. Behind the plane mangled trees, some knocked over, some with tops snapped off, showed the path of the plane's fatal fall from the sky.

As soon as he'd been apprehended in that small mountain town, he had regretted his decision not to flee, or at least not to try. If he hadn't just spoken to Ruth, hadn't seen that bastard on television, he wouldn't have been so rattled. He could have gotten away without hurting anyone, he saw that almost immediately. By then, it had been too late.

Now, the situation was different.

Cleaning the cut on his arm confirmed the wound was superficial. He disinfected it, then applied antibiotic ointment and a bandage. Then he ripped the belongings bag open and reached inside. He pulled out his clothes: jeans, tee shirt, belt, boxer briefs, and socks. He reached into the bag again and found the Rolex, which he slipped on his wrist. He frowned as the second hand glided over the clockface. It was going on four o'clock; still a good four to five hours of daylight. More would be better, but that wasn't the hand he was playing. When his fingers brushed against his phone, he could tell it was a lost cause before he saw it. Sure enough, not only was the screen smashed but the casing had cracked open. No cell service out here, but he'd find some eventually. He'd have to buy a burner.

He kept searching in the bag until his hand closed around the shield-shaped piece of metal. He smiled as he looked at the bottle opener that bore the insignia of the 75th Ranger Battalion, which he also had tattooed on his right upper arm. Mister Jacobs, his high school teacher and JROTC sponsor, had given it to him when Caleb passed Ranger School. Even with how things had gone, he felt a swell of pride seeing the red lightning bolt slashed across the shield's center, the sun and stars over its blue corners. The arched yellow and black ribbon with RANGER across it above the shield left the space for the opener tooth and fulcrum. In a survival situation his clothes were more important, but this reminder of his service was the only possession he cared about. The watch was important. It could be sold or traded should the situation demand it, but the bottle opener... Caleb didn't like to think of himself as sentimental, but he'd be sorry to lose it.

Whatever, he thought, shutting down the train of thought. Get moving, Frost.

He dropped the opener back into the bag and changed his clothes. He couldn't find his boots and had to crawl back into the plane before finding them under the marshal's seat. He could hardly hike through the wilderness in the crappy slip-on prison shoes he'd been given.

There's got to be an emergency kit here, he thought, scanning the debris littering the cabin. It was finding it that would be a bitch. Eventually, he found a duffel bag marked Emergency Supplies in the cockpit. He hoisted it over his shoulder. The bag wasn't large and probably lacked what he truly needed, but it beat nothing.

Caleb glanced back when the marshal groaned. The man blinked his eyes. He looked at Caleb with an unfocused gaze. "Help me," he croaked through a raspy throat.

Caleb didn't answer. He'd have preferred an escape that didn't strand the man in the wilderness, but this was his chance. He had to take it.

Once outside the plane again, he squatted down and unzipped the emergency kit to inspect the contents. He found a second, more comprehensive first aid kit—bandages, gauze, antiseptic wipes, and the like—four flares, a whistle, some water purification tablets, bear spray, foil emergency blankets, a knife, paracord, a flashlight with spare batteries, a small folding camping shovel, and a small packet of waterproof matches. There were also three one-liter bottles of water and a selection of energy bars. He removed one of the bottles of water, half the energy bars, and a few other supplies. Then he climbed the nose of the plane and dropped what was left inside. Might as well minimize the chance of attracting bears if he was leaving food for the marshal. He was a thief, not a murderer. If the marshal knew anything about the outdoors, it should be enough. Search and rescue would arrive in a day or two.

A prickle of unease crawled across Caleb's shoulders and down his back, causing a shiver. He wasn't a pilot but he knew a little about planes. He knew the emergency locator would be triggered by the impact of the crash. What he didn't know was how quickly they would respond. Depending on where they were, rescuers had a lot of ground to cover.

"Not my problem," he said aloud.

He needed to figure out where the hell he was. Probably still Montana given how long they'd been in the air before the plane lost power. This far north, most likely the Salish Mountains or the Cabinets. Thank God the Finleys had loved to backcountry camp when he and Ruth had lived with them. No familiarity with the area would make this a lot harder.

Caleb squinted up at the sun. He needed somewhere to go to ground. His place outside Bonner's Ferry was probably closest; it was practically at the Canadian border. He'd have to be careful, but with a little luck he could do it. West first, then north.

He felt every ache and pain as he left the plane behind. The grade of the incline was steep, about thirty degrees, but the peaks above weren't too far. After that, he'd be going downhill a while. He sipped water sparingly as the sun beat down. A hat or sunscreen would've been nice, but given how his day started, he was doing okay.

A daughter, Grace... She's such a pretty little thing.

Caleb stopped mid-stride when the marshal's words echoed in his head. How old had he said his daughter was? He couldn't remember. And it wasn't his problem. He continued up the slope.

A daughter, Grace... She's such a pretty little thing.

"Not your problem, Caleb," he said aloud. "Keep your ass moving."

For another ten minutes, he did.

A daughter, Grace... She's such a pretty little thing.

"Fuck," he almost growled, stopping again.

Caleb scrubbed his face with his hands. This was his chance. He had to take it. He'd taken measure of the marshal in a minute flat and knew the type: a Boy Scout. The guy wore a seersucker sport coat in July! Seersucker was as lightweight as it got, but still, who did that? Caleb knew who. The guy who follows the rules. He needed the sport coat to keep his weapon out of view, but the guy's vibe was a hundred percent Clark Kent taking off his glasses on his way to the phone booth. It wouldn't matter if he was a marshal or an insurance salesman. If this guy was on the clock, he'd be wearing the damn sports coat.

He hadn't even been too much of a prick. When one of the deputies who'd collared him mentioned the marshal being the man to put Caleb behind bars, his response was unexpected. "All I do is bring them in. The rest is up to other people." Then he'd added, "I think he's going to spend a very long time as a guest of the federal government, but you never can tell, especially if he's got a good lawyer."

Caleb had an exceptional lawyer.

It had almost seemed like the guy had no stake in the outcome, which of course wasn't true. Clark Kent was all about truth, justice, and the American Way. Caleb's first CO, the guy before Avery Scott, had loved that saying about sheepdogs and wolves and which one they, as Rangers, needed to be. The metaphor was corny as hell but Caleb had enjoyed how much his CO liked it. The question burned bright, as if it were scrolling text from a news program: What was he, a sheepdog or a wolf?

A daughter, Grace... She's such a pretty little thing.

"I am such a fucking idiot," he muttered, turning around. He was going to regret this. Caleb knew he'd regret this decision till the day he died, but he was damned if he'd be the reason that little girl went from having a father to being an orphan.

The marshal had crawled out by the time he got back and sat in the shade of the nearest tree. He looked up as Caleb approached, his brow furrowing. His eyebrows knitted together, and his mouth actually fell open.

"What are you doing here?"

"Something I already regret," Caleb said. "Are you hurt?"

"My lower leg and foot," he said. "I'd like my gun back."

Caleb squatted beside him. "I'm sure you would. Let me see."

The marshal complied, sucking in a breath as Caleb pushed up his pant leg. He could see swelling over the top of the marshal's shoe. He felt along the swelling shin, stopping at the sharp intake of breath halfway up.

"I've got to press on this. We need to know if it's broken."

The marshal nodded, and Caleb pressed. Sweat popped out above the marshal's upper lip and his mouth was pressed tight like a vise. Caleb pressed harder, trying to determine the extent of his injury. The bones didn't seem out of place, judging by the way the marshal huffed, trying to manage the pain. "I don't think it's broken. Fractured maybe, or a bruised bone. Let me check your foot."

One look at his foot told Caleb there were broken bones. The top of his foot was already a dark purple, like an overripe eggplant. By the time he finished palpating the metatarsal bones, the marshal had turned a shade of pasty that had overtones of green. "Some of these are broken."

"My foot's broken?"

"Two of the metatarsal bones, I think." Caleb's finger hovered in the air an inch away from the marshal's foot before he swiped it toward his toes like he was swiping a phone screen to unlock it. "The ones along the top here. What's your shoe size?"

The marshal stared at Caleb. His incomprehension at the change of subject made him look like a confused pug. "My shoe size? Why?"

Caleb just stared at him.

"Ten," the marshal said.

Caleb sat and began unlacing his work boot. "Your ankle and foot are swelling, so I need to know if you can wear mine. A boot will keep it from getting worse, but you have to get it on now before it swells more. If we walk out of here, you need something on your feet."

"Walk out on broken bones?"

Caleb nodded. "It'll hurt, but it won't kill you."

"But we won't have to walk out. Search and Rescue will come."

Caleb didn't reply and they traded footwear. The laces were loosened enough to pull out of the top two eyelets. Even so, the marshal winced as he eased his foot into the boot. "Tie it as tight as you can to the top of the boot. I'll find something to splint your leg, just in case."

The marshal nodded. Caleb took the marshal's athletic shoes and put them on. It felt strange to wear another man's shoes, like stepping into someone else's life. Each of the four men he pretended to be had a house and a quiet life in remote corners of the country. After all this time, he'd never gotten used to it.

"The pilot's dead," the marshal said when he'd finished lacing up Caleb's boots.

"Yeah, I know."

"Thanks for leaving the water and the food. Do you have any idea where we are?"

"Salish Mountains, I think, or maybe the Cabinet range. The middle of nowhere."

The marshal looked around. Pain carved grooves at the corners of his eyes. Caleb got the medicine kit and gave him ibuprofen. "The plane must have some kind of beacon. They'll know we crashed. We should stay put and let them find us rather than become more lost."

Caleb waited before answering. He should be trekking away on his own, not babysitting an injured US Marshal who wanted to haul him off to jail. "I know bigger planes have them and I think these do, too, but..." He shrugged. "If we have to activate it, it won't work without power."

The marshal ran his hand through his hair and let his head rest against the tree trunk. Almost under his breath, he muttered, "Emma's gonna kill me."

"Emma your wife?"

"Yeah. God, what a mess. So, we're stuck with each other for a while."

"Looks like."

Caleb scowled. This guy had a wife and kid who'd want him home alive. He didn't strike Caleb as an outdoorsman. He lacked the skills Caleb had learned as a Ranger. Skills that would get him out of here, especially were he alone.

Not leaving the man to die was the right thing to do, and Caleb already regretted it. It wouldn't matter if he saved this guy's life. If he wound up in custody—real custody, not this farce—he was going to prison. This marshal's wife and kid weren't his responsibility, and yet...

I'm getting soft, he thought. *I'm getting tired and soft and sentimental, for Christ's sake, and I damn well can't afford to be.*

"I'll get some wood and make a fire," Caleb said. "It'll get cold when the sun goes down."

He got to his feet and dusted off his jeans. He was here for now. Didn't mean it had to stay this way.

chapter
seven

CODY

SATURDAY, JULY 12
10:16 PM

Cody rubbed at his eyes and blinked, trying to remember where he was. A vicious headache thumped from temple to temple, like a bouncy ball smacking back and forth against the inside of his skull. His neck hurt, too, especially at the base of his skull. The tight muscles clamped onto his spine like barnacles on the hide of a whale.

He pushed himself up to sitting from where he lay on the ground. An emergency blanket slipped away, light as paper sliding from a table and fluttering to the floor, the foil crinkling. His right foot and ankle tingled, squeezed inside a too tight boot that felt like a boa constrictor. Cody looked up to the sky and squinted, confused. A symphony of shimmering lights danced across the heavens, like incandescent streamers of orange and red, green and purple, stretched from one mountain horizon to the other. An owl hooted softly, as if it were admiring the night sky.

Everything rushed back. The plane, the crash, the gunshot cracks and snaps as they careened through the forest canopy like a cannonball. The bouncing and spinning from one obstacle to the next—like being a pinball in a machine designed by the devil.

A small fire crackled nearby, white and yellow flames dancing over red coals. The light it cast was nothing compared to the sky. The night sky brightened everything—brighter than moonlight. The darkness that should cloak such a remote location was beaten back, still night but glowing. Cody searched the sparse campsite. He was alone. After coming back earlier, Frost had abandoned him again.

A coyote yipped. Cody looked up to the stars, trying to identify constellations he might use as a navigational aid.

Who the hell am I kidding?

He had missed the sunset, which would have helped with orienting himself. The dippers and Orion's Belt were the extent of his knowledge of the constellations. Besides, there were more stars here than he'd ever seen before. Even the few constellations he knew were hidden among them. He had no chance of navigating by the stars.

A sticky anxiety wormed between Cody's organs, coiling around them like unclean antennae. Frost was gone. He scrambled to his feet as well as he could, anxiety on an express train to frenzied panic.

I'm an idiot.

How could he have been so foolish and fallen asleep? He hadn't planned to. He hadn't even been lying down when he last remembered doing anything. That didn't change the fact that he had woken on the ground and Frost, opportunist that he was, had seen his chance to escape. He was a criminal and a fugitive. He'd already said he regretted coming back. Perhaps he'd needed to salve his conscience, if he had one. Assure himself that he wasn't so cold that he'd left Cody for dead without a backward glance. Obviously, the man's pragmatism had caused him to reconsider.

The fire popped, sending a puff of sparks skyward. Having

lost the warmth from the emergency blanket, Cody felt the cold. It couldn't be more than fifty-five degrees. He limped along the fuselage of the plane, searching for signs of his prisoner. He reached the tail, squinting into the strangely illuminated darkness. His body began to tingle, aware before he was that something was different. A moment later, barely discernible movement sharpened into a shape coming toward him. For a terrifying moment, he thought it was a bear before the shape became a man.

"How's the foot?"

Frost stepped into the light of the fire. He carried a small, folding camping shovel in his right hand. A jacket, jeans, and shirt were draped over his left arm. He held a pair of hiking boots by tied laces in his left hand.

Cody stared at the items Frost held for an uncomprehending moment. Then, aghast, he asked, "Are those the pilot's clothes?"

Frost nodded. "I buried him. He doesn't need his clothes anymore. We might."

Cody blinked at Frost, shocked. "You buried him?"

Frost brushed past him, his large frame intimidating. No wonder he'd mistaken him for a bear. Frost dropped the shovel and boots near the plane. He folded the clothes and set them on top of the boots, then continued to the fire where he warmed his hands. Without turning around, he said, "We can't have scavengers coming over here for his body."

Scavengers. Body. Cody's head spun as he limped after Frost to the fire. Pain flared in his foot with every step. He felt small under the strange glowing sky, inside the circle of the fire's comforting illusion of safety. Apprehension that felt like the snap of static electricity burrowed into the base of Cody's skull. Scavengers coming for the body. He was no longer at the top of the food chain. *Maybe Frost is, since he has my gun, but I'm sure as hell not.*

Cody's indignation bubbled up. "You shouldn't have buried his body. The search and rescue teams will be here tomorrow or the day after."

Frost turned to look at him, his frame a dark silhouette in the firelight. Barely controlled anger rolled from Frost's body. Cody took a step back.

"I just spent three hours digging a hole big enough for that man's body with a kid-sized camping shovel. After I filled it back in, I looked for enough rocks to stack over his grave in the dark. If anyone comes for us, they'll dig him back up." Frost's voice roughened to a predatory growl. "Save your middle-class morality for someone who cares."

Frost turned back to the fire. Cody stared at him. This man was supposed to be in his custody, but there was no doubt about who was in charge. Frost had Cody's gun and fewer injuries, but it was more than that. Frost wore his authority like a weapon, dangerous even when holstered. He could leave whenever he wanted and Cody couldn't stop him. He might technically be Cody's prisoner, but right now that meant nothing.

Cody's heart began to pound, his lack of control of the situation tightening his chest and constricting his throat. He backed off to the plane and sat down heavily, the absurdity of his situation hitting him. He was stranded in the wilderness with a ruthless, efficient criminal. The man had been an Army Ranger, had done several tours in Afghanistan and other, more remote, hot spots. Frost had the skills to survive and could leave if he wanted.

Cody shook his head, disbelief at his situation and worry for his family mingling to form a toxic stew. His wife and new baby were at home alone. He knew help would arrive eventually, but what if he died out here? There were bears for sure, black bears and grizzlies. Mountain lions. A wolf howled in the distance, long and mournful. Another answered, then a few more. And wolves, he thought, surprised he'd forgotten them.

Wolves don't attack people, you moron.

He knew this because he'd just read a book about the history of wolves in North America and their reintroduction to Yellowstone. There were only two confirmed instances of a wolf attacking a human since 1900. Like most wild animals, wolves didn't want humans anywhere near them. Had wolves made their way to Idaho from Yellowstone or been reintroduced separately? He didn't know.

"Wolf attacks," he muttered to himself. "Might as well start chanting about lions and tigers and bears."

Cody raked his hair with both hands. Emma must be sick with worry. She would have gone from anger at his being late to concern, then fear when she learned the plane hadn't arrived. He knew how he'd feel were the situation reversed: sick with worry and fear. None of this would be happening if he'd done things differently, if he'd thought of Emma instead of how he'd been wronged. He had dragged Emma and Grace across the country because he'd been too proud to kiss some ass and what had it accomplished? Tension in his marriage, a demotion at work, and now this. Would Emma become so unhappy she'd leave?

The nighttime rainbow of colors rippled above him. Stars studded the sky among the colors, like pieces of glitter that stuck in the carpet months after being spilled. A bat swooped by with a flutter of leathery wings. Cody ducked, instinct kicking in despite knowing the bat had been far too high to buzz him.

Frost said, "How tight is the boot?"

With his attention directed back to it, the discomfort in Cody's foot kicked up a notch. "Like a boa constrictor is wrapped around it. It won't kill me."

Frost joined him at the plane, sitting a good six feet away. "The pilot's boots are a size bigger than mine. If you're still that uncomfortable tomorrow, you can wear one of his." Then he fell silent and studied the sky.

Cody said, "They're the Northern Lights, right? I've never seen them before."

Frost took a deep breath, then sighed. "I saw them a fair bit growing up, especially near the Canadian border. Not this time of year, usually, and not like this."

Cody stopped swatting at an insect buzzing near his ear mid-motion. Something in Frost's voice sounded tentative. Cody looked at him. In profile, Frost's face looked carved of alabaster, his furrowed brow and slight frown pensive.

"These colors are more..." Frost paused. "Vivid. And bright." Then he added, more gruffly, like he realized he'd revealed something he hadn't meant to, "Take more of the anti-inflammatory from the med kit. Eat an energy bar and drink some water. It's easy to get dehydrated at higher elevations."

Who the hell is he to order me around? Cody thought. His stomach growled, not giving a damn about his identity crisis. Frost was helping him, yes, but he was still a criminal. A criminal who had gained control. Some professional I am, Cody thought. "You were a Ranger before you started robbing banks. That's quite a career change."

Frost didn't answer. It hadn't been a question. He looked at Cody and blinked once. "What's it to you?"

Cody smiled. "Not a thing. Guys like you keep me employed. I read your file. I guess it's not really a surprise."

"What's that supposed to mean?" Frost said, his voice sharp.

"Your old man's in prison, right?"

"If you read my file, you already know that."

"Apple didn't fall far from the tree in the end."

Frost pinned him with a cold glare. "What did your dad do?"

Cody didn't want Frost to know anything about him. "What my dad did for a living doesn't matter."

Frost snickered. "You're one of those guys. You can dish it out, but you can't take it."

Cody bristled. "He was a police officer. The police chief, actually."

"So, you went into the family business. Must have made your daddy proud becoming a fed."

Frost made it sound like an insult. Without thinking, Cody said, "He died in the line of duty. He didn't live to see me become a marshal."

Frost stared at Cody like he could see right through him. He didn't seem embarrassed, like an acquaintance might if this happened at a dinner party. Then he shrugged. "You can say your dad died a hero. Mine's just another third-generation drunk who killed someone at a bar."

Cody hadn't known that. The alcoholism wasn't in the file—why would it be? It was irrelevant to Frost's crimes. Frost said it matter-of-factly, not asking for pity or offering any. It caught Cody off guard. He no longer felt like he had to establish authority. He felt like a jerk. He looked back at the sky and said, meaning the lights, "How long do they usually last?"

Frost took so long to answer, Cody thought he wouldn't. "I don't know about these."

They lapsed into silence, both of them watching the sky. Cody had always thought he'd see the Northern Lights with Emma. His spirits sunk lower, recalling the resigned disappointment that had dimmed Emma's face last night when she learned he had to leave to collect Frost. He had a lot to make right between them. As soon as he got home, he'd do just that.

chapter
eight

CALEB

SATURDAY, JULY 12
11:00 PM

"I need to take a piss," Greer announced, struggling to his feet like someone three times his age.

Caleb watched the marshal's labored movements, cataloging his injuries. The foot was the worst, obviously, but Greer had taken hits all over. The man's limitations gave Caleb options. Melting away into the wilderness was never far from his mind. Funny, how he couldn't seem to do it.

"Me too," Caleb said, rising to join him. Every muscle in his body ached as he pushed himself upright, a souvenir from when the plane had dropped like a stone. The headache was the worst, but he hadn't experienced blurred vision or been nauseous. The crash had thrown him against his restraints hard enough to leave what would soon be impressive bruises. Still, he'd had worse.

They walked away from the camp, the distance between them carefully maintained. Caleb guided them deeper into the woods, his steps quiet from years of training—old habits. The light in the sky illuminated their path in shades of red and violet, casting everything in an otherworldly glow. The aurora painted the wilderness in colors that reminded Caleb of Afghanistan when a dust storm was rolling in—terrible and ominous, but also beautiful in its way. He listened to the normal forest sounds—the rush of wind through pine needles, the distant call of an owl. Something normal below the abnormal sky.

When they stopped to relieve themselves, Caleb kept his senses alert, scanning their surroundings. Standing still made him feel vulnerable. He didn't like feeling vulnerable—not in war zones, not during jobs, not as a kid in new homes, and not now. As they headed back toward camp, Caleb watched Greer's face soften at the sight of the fire's glow through the trees. The man was scared, trying not to show it, but his relief at returning to their makeshift camp was plain. A trained observer could spot tells like that. Caleb had gotten good at reading people early as a matter of survival.

Greer stopped, gazing up at the aurora. His posture shifted, shoulders dropping as tension left his frame. Caleb understood. The sky was alive with colored lightning. It made you feel small but connected to something eternal. The difference between them was the marshal thought this was temporary. That rescue was coming and his life would continue as planned. Caleb was beginning to think none of that would happen.

"Did your phone make it through the crash?" he asked, careful to keep his tone conversational. "Mine got smashed all to hell."

"Yeah," Greer replied, sounding annoyed at being pulled from his moment of wonder. "But there's no service out here." He pulled a phone from his pocket and gave it to Caleb. "It doesn't even turn on."

Caleb pushed one of the side buttons. As expected, nothing happened. "Was it charged when we got on the plane?"

The marshal's posture stiffened. He'd noticed something in

Caleb's voice. "I had it plugged in at the airport, but if it's searching for wireless that isn't available, the battery runs down pretty quick." His voice turned wry. "I didn't think to change the settings after we crashed."

Caleb nodded. He'd been hoping he was wrong but everything fit. The plane's sudden power loss. The aurora. The dead electronics. He'd read about it, trained for similar scenarios. The suspicion that had been growing all day settled in his gut like a stone.

"I don't think there's a rescue coming."

Caleb felt the marshal's eyes on him. He kept his gaze on the rippling colors above but his pulse quickened. He didn't want to face what this meant—for himself and the marshal, for his sister, for everyone—any more than the next guy, but facing reality was what Caleb Frost did. Caleb dealt with facts and evidence, not speculation and conspiracy theories.

"The solar flare, the aurora, the plane losing power, and now your phone not powering up." He turned to meet the marshal's gaze. "I've been trying to talk myself out of it."

"Out of what?" Greer asked, alarm creeping into his voice.

"I think there was a CME, in addition to the solar flare. That means the lights aren't coming back on."

"The lights? A CME? What are you talking about?"

"A coronal mass ejection," Caleb clarified, realizing he had to back up. "Solar flares and CMEs almost always happen together, but they're different. Both are caused when the sun's magnetic fields get twisted and snap back into place. The flare is just the flash of light from that explosion, like the muzzle flash from a rifle. A CME is what happens when that same explosion throws billions of tons of magnetized solar particles into space. That's the bullet. If that bullet's aimed at Earth, and the magnetic field of those particles lines up just right with Earth's magnetic field, that's when you get the really bad stuff: a geomagnetic storm that can knock out everything electronic. That's what I think happened to our plane and your phone, and why there's no rescue coming."

"So there was an EMP?" The marshal's question was hesitant, like he was having trouble connecting the dots.

Caleb shook his head. "EMPs are different; they're man-made. They pretty much happen when a nuclear device explodes in the—"

"Are you saying someone set off a nuclear bomb?" the marshal interrupted, eyes going wide.

"No. I am not saying that," Caleb said. Panic wouldn't help either of them. "Remember that alert the pilot got about a solar flare? That he said might mess up your call? I think there was a CME, too, because the plane lost power. If it was strong enough to knock us out of the sky, it was strong enough to knock out everything else."

He watched Greer process this information, his face reflecting the aurora's glow, like he was trying to fit a piece into a puzzle. "Are you saying most things, like cars and power plants, have quit working?"

Caleb nodded. "Anything with electronics. Older cars will work, and electronics that have been hardened against EMP attacks. Batteries if they weren't in an electronic device or if they were shielded. If it's mechanical, it's fine." He held up his wrist. "My watch is mechanical, so it works, but your phone, the plane, the emergency transponder that's supposed to call for help..." He let the implication hang between them.

The marshal didn't want to believe him—denial in the face of catastrophe. He'd seen it overseas when civilians couldn't comprehend the new reality war had thrust upon them. He'd seen it on his own face when he realized the Army was screwing him over. He said, "Whatever the cause, if I'm right, there's no rescue coming for us. We move out at first light."

"Move out? Are you crazy?" Greer's voice rose. "If they find the plane and we're not there— You're supposed to stay in one place if you're lost in the wilderness." His expression hardened.

"You want to stay out of prison so bad you think I'll just buy some story about an EMP or CME or whatever the hell it is you're selling? Do you think I'm that stupid?"

The accusation stung more than Caleb expected. Not because he cared what the marshal thought, but because he wasn't lying. He wasn't manipulating anything. He was trying to help this idiot who'd rather see him behind bars than accept his offer.

The marshal turned away. Something moved in Caleb's peripheral vision. His hand shot out, gripping the marshal's arm before his brain caught up. Thirty feet away, a black bear investigated their wrecked plane. Its fur absorbed the firelight—a void against the dark landscape. Then two smaller shapes emerged. Cubs. Caleb's stomach dropped.

A sow with cubs... For Christ's sake. I really need a beer.

Their plane had crashed because of a CME and he'd been fool enough to come back. Now a bear with cubs. The kind more likely to attack. Were he a churchgoing man, Caleb might think someone was trying to get his attention.

"Don't flip out," he whispered to the marshal, who had gone rigid beside him. "No sudden—"

One cub spotted them, startled, and ducked under its mother. The sow's head rose, nose twitching as she caught their scent. She huffed a warning.

The marshal vibrated with fear. Caleb forced his breath to slow, drawing on his training. Fear was natural, but panic was optional. He'd faced down insurgents and armed security. He could handle a bear.

He straightened, projecting confident authority. "Hey bear!" he called out, his voice firm. "Move along now!" He raised his arms slowly, making himself larger. From the corner of his eye, he saw the marshal follow his lead.

The cubs retreated toward the plane, bleating like sheep. The sow advanced, huffing again. Louder this time, more threatening.

"Stay still," Caleb murmured. "She's not charging, just worried about her cubs." He kept his voice steady. Confident.

He'd talked men down from violence before—this wasn't so different. He clapped sharply. "Hey bear!" he said, raising his voice just a little more. "Time to go!"

The bear rose to her full height. Even at this distance, she towered over them. Caleb clapped again. She dropped down, shaking her head.

"Go on!" he said, channeling the authority he'd used to help his unit get through firefights. "That's right... Nothing here for you. Take those babies with you."

With a final warning huff, the bear turned away. Her cubs scampered after her. They melted into the darkness, leaving only paw prints behind.

The marshal slumped. Caleb realized he'd taken a step closer, positioning himself between the man and the bear. What the hell was wrong with him? Jump in front of a bear for the marshal? What was it about this guy who was—frankly—a bit of an asshole?

A daughter, Grace... She's such a pretty little thing.

Fuck him and his pretty little thing of a daughter, Caleb thought, annoyed with himself. He knew better than to get involved in this shit, or he ought to.

"So," Greer said with surprising steadiness. "We're leaving at first light."

Caleb snorted a laugh, a half smile tugging at his mouth. Maybe the guy wasn't a total lost cause. He could still make a run for it once they reached civilization and he off-loaded the marshal somewhere safe. For now, he was stuck with the guy. Caleb didn't need a US Marshal dying within ten miles of him. Something bad might still happen, something he couldn't control. If it did, and despite the fact that he'd helped this man, they'd throw the book at him.

Caleb gave himself a mental shake. That wasn't going to happen. He looked up at the aurora, a celestial tapestry woven with threads of crimson, so bright that he cast a faint shadow. The stars were smeared like butter across the sky, thick and heavy and shining. He'd never see the stars if he ended up in prison. He'd never see the Milky Way, or taste the air after rain.

He'd rather die than let that happen. If he was right, the world had changed. Into what, he didn't know, but his sister was out there alone. He needed to survive and stay free, for her sake as much as his own.

day two

chapter
nine

EMMA

SUNDAY, JULY 13
  9:00 AM

The sheet under Emma's back felt damp when she woke the next morning. It hadn't really cooled down last night, despite Martha's claim summer nights here were usually cooler. She rubbed at her itchy eyes and blinked them open. Sunlight streamed through a gap in the curtains, its intensity blunted by the pines sheltering the house. A soft breeze, more akin to a half-hearted puff, caressed her cheek.

She rolled over and reached for her phone on the bedside table, the fullness of her breasts uncomfortable. She needed to nurse or pump soon. Just before she turned the phone's dark surface her way, she remembered there was no power. She pressed the button anyway. Nothing.

She and Martha had stayed up past midnight watching the aurora, its undulating ribbons of ruby red and emerald filling the sky with an ethereal glow. Emma stood up and stretched, tired but still feeling better rested than she had in weeks. The house was so quiet. No whirr of air-conditioning nor the roar of a neighbor's lawnmower. Even Grace hadn't woken her.

Her heart missed a beat, fear squeezing her chest like a tightening noose. Grace never slept through the night. Emma ran from the bedroom, her stomach trying to force itself up her throat. She lurched to a halt over the crib, barely able to breathe. Grace lay on her back. Her tiny arms waved like kelp in a gentle current. Her blue eyes widened, and her face lit up when she spotted Emma.

Emma blew out a shaky breath. Relief made her feel light as thistledown. "Good morning, sweet girl," she said, lifting Grace from the crib. Her pounding heart slowed. She kissed Grace's head, the slight dip of the soft spot of her skull warm against her lips. "You're in a good mood."

Grace's diaper was soaked. Emma changed her, grateful for the stockpile of disposables in the closet. She'd considered cloth diapers before Grace was born—environmentally conscious, more cost-effective over time—but ease won out, especially once it was clear they were moving across the country. Now she wondered how long their supply would last. If the power was still out, would stores be open? No power meant no registers, no monitoring of stock, no debit and credit card transactions. It meant most stores would be shadowy, if not outright caverns.

Hardly anyone shopped with cash anymore, herself included, but Cody did. He insisted they keep a thousand dollars in cash in the gun safe. She'd always thought this idiosyncrasy antiquated. Now, she was grateful.

Where was Cody? Emma bit her lower lip, worry stirring in her stomach. Had his plane landed yet? Was he stranded at the airport in Coeur d'Alene without a car? Maybe he was still in Montana. He'd mentioned the town, but she'd been so angry with him she hadn't really listened. All she could remember was somewhere near the Montana/Idaho border. She couldn't even call his office. Even if he'd gone as far east as the Montana/North Dakota border, he should be home by now. He wouldn't leave her and

Grace to fend for themselves if this was an emergency. The power's out, Emma, she told herself. Since when is that an emergency?

She gave herself a mental shake. The power was out—that was all. Some food might go bad and the A/C didn't work; it wasn't the end of the world. If he'd been forced to drive for some reason, there were mountains between there and here. Whichever road he took, she shouldn't expect him for at least another twelve hours. If he got home earlier, that would be gravy.

She settled into the rocking chair to nurse, the familiar weight of Grace centering her in a way nothing else could. Grace latched on eagerly, her small hand splayed against Emma's breast. Through the window, Emma saw neighbors congregating on the sidewalk farther down the street. Maybe someone had news. If nothing else, they were adults she could talk to. She couldn't spend all day talking to herself.

After Grace finished, Emma changed into shorts and a tank top. She finger-combed her hair and twisted it into a knot at the nape of her neck. Her reflection in the bathroom mirror looked tired, but better than yesterday.

"Ready to be social?" she asked Grace. Grace wriggled, burped, and looked at Emma with wide eyes, as if to say, 'Did I do that?' Emma laughed. Motherhood might be turning her into her own mother—an unnerving idea—but she wouldn't trade Grace for the world.

She slipped into the Baby Bjorn harness, got Grace snuggled in, and then put the tiny sun hat on her head. Emma opened the door and warm air spilled through the outer screen. Should she close the door to keep what cool air remained inside or opt for a breeze? It would get hot anyway, she reasoned, so the breeze won out. She'd open more windows when she came back inside.

Breeze or no, stepping out from under the pine trees, the sun beat down with a ferocity she still wasn't used to. The elevation here was ten times that of home and the weather stayed dry.

Clouds didn't play much of a role in Idaho summers. She needed to find a sun hat, or she'd be sunburned by day's end.

Emma squinted against the brightness, letting Grace grab her finger as she walked to the end of the bend where some neighbors had gathered. Martha spotted her first, raising a hand in greeting. "Morning, Emma. Sleep okay?"

"Better than I expected. Any news about when we'll get power?"

Diane, whose name Emma remembered this time, said, "No."

Diane wore a uniform type top with a name tag, which made Emma feel less impressed with herself for remembering her name. It had probably registered subconsciously. Specter Lake Market, Manager was etched across the top of the name tag.

"I hear they're working on it," said an older man Emma hadn't met. He stepped forward, extending his hand to her. "Tom Wilson, pleased to meet you."

His short silver-white hair almost sparkled in the sunlight. He had the relaxed air of a man enjoying his retirement. Emma took in his canvas pants and button-up shirt with the sleeves buttoned at his wrists. How was he not melting? Tom looked her in the eye as she introduced herself, his eyes a light brown. Emma liked him immediately. "I'm Emma. It's nice to meet you."

Tom leaned down to look at Grace. "And who is this pretty little thing?"

"This is Grace."

Grace batted her hand at Tom. He smiled and let her clutch his forefinger in her hand. "Goodness, she's a charmer." His eyes flicked up to Emma. "I have to get Carrie over here to meet her. She's caught the grandma bug, but so far the kids aren't obliging her."

"I'd like that," Emma said.

A woman in her forties whom Emma hadn't met yet had approached from the direction of Emma's and Martha's houses, joining them but waiting for a break in the conversation. "I hope they fix this soon. My freezer's going to be a mess."

"Bring your food over to our house, Karen," Tom said. "The gennie for our freezer is running and we've got room."

Karen blinked at him, obviously surprised. "Thank you, Tom. That's very generous of you."

"The rest of you, too," Tom said. Then he added, "But not too much. Eat up first."

The newcomer held her hand out to Emma. "I'm Karen White. I live three doors down from the first house after the bend."

Karen was so thin the pointy bones of her elbows threatened to erupt through her skin. She pushed her blond hair, cut in a practical bob, back from her face.

You really need to get out more, Emma thought to herself. Grace squirmed, giving an unhappy whimper. Usually, she was placid while awake. It had to be the heat. Emma bounced her a little, hoping it would help.

"What's strange is that the cell phones aren't working," Emma said. "Are any of yours?"

The group exchanged glances and shook their heads. "Nothing," Diane said. "And no cars are running except old ones. It's weird."

"What I've been wondering about," Tom started, then stopped, when a midnight-blue Dodge Charger rolled slowly down the street, its engine purring like a contented beast. The driver, a broad-shouldered man with close-cropped black hair and bronze skin, stopped alongside them. He leaned out the window, his expression friendly beneath the shadow of his baseball cap.

"Morning," he said, nodding to the group. "I was just in town. The power's still out there, too." It seemed to Emma that all of them wilted at that news, herself included. Then the man added, "Diane, I saw Randy at the grocery store. He asked me to see if you might come in."

Diane stepped closer to the car. "I'm going there now." She started to check her wrist, then stopped. The watch she must usually wear, for her wrist was bare, must not be working. Still, the habit remained. "Hardly anyone uses cash anymore. It's going to be tricky. Randy will want to open if we can. Sunday is shopping day for a lot of people."

"Do you want a ride?" he asked her.

Diane nodded. "That would be great, Chuy. You're a lifesaver."

While Diane rounded the car, Martha placed a hand on Emma's shoulder. "Jesús, this is Emma and her daughter Grace. They moved in next door to me, along with Emma's husband, Cody. Emma, this is Jesús Rodriguez."

"Chuy," he corrected with a small smile. "Only my mother and Martha call me Jesús. Nice to meet you, Emma. Wish it was under better circumstances."

"Me, too," Emma said, her next words slipping out before she could frame it as a question. "Your car works."

"Yeah. Old cars are still running. Anything new is dead in the water." He frowned, his face clouding over as if he wanted to say something else. Instead, he patted the dashboard. "This old girl never lets me down."

Emma frowned. No power, no electronics. Her brain began to tick. This fit a pattern but she couldn't quite catch it. Maybe something Cody had mentioned? "Anyway, it's nice to meet you, Chuy."

"Nobody's heard any news?" Chuy asked the group. By now Diane had gotten into the car and had her seat belt buckled.

Tom shook his head. "Not that I've heard."

Chuy said, "Randy said they have ice at the store. I'll get some for all of you when I drop Diane off."

A round of thankful exclamations followed. These people are great, Emma thought. If she had to be here alone, she couldn't have asked for better. Maybe Idaho wasn't as bad as she'd thought. Maybe, as her father was fond of saying, she needed an attitude adjustment.

Chuy waved, then guided the car in a U-turn. Emma watched the car recede. What was it she couldn't remember? She needed coffee to puzzle out anything more complicated than feeding Grace this morning. Grace began to fuss in earnest, her tiny face reddening with the effort. "I should head back," Emma said. "I haven't eaten yet and I need to check the refrigerator."

"Keep it closed as much as you can," Martha advised.

"I need to go to the store," Tom said. He added, for Emma's benefit, "I own the hardware store in town."

"Oh," Emma said. "Wilson's Hardware, of course. I've been to get lightbulbs but must have missed you."

"Everyone comes by eventually," Tom said.

Emma nodded. "I'll see you all later."

She was almost at her door when the pieces clicked—an electromagnetic pulse. She'd read up on it for the HardNetworks patent application. HardNetworks, her client at the firm, developed hardened electronics for military use. EMPs could fry electronic circuits in modern devices. The nonfunctioning cars, dead phones, no electricity—but older cars still working. Her heart thudded against her ribs like a trapped bird. Could a solar flare do something similar?

The power might not turn back on for days, maybe weeks. Specter Lake wasn't so small it wouldn't have a disaster preparedness plan. Did that plan include an EMP? They were popular in some genres of books and movies, but Emma wasn't sure how much the general populace knew about them. She hadn't before she'd been assigned to the team handling the HardNetworks patent application. Then a second realization hit her, but this one sent a cold wave of dread through her stomach. Specter Lake's water system. The real estate agent had explained it as a selling point. It was gravity-fed from elevated water towers, which meant they had water during power outages, but Martha had said those towers were filled by electric pumps. How long before the water towers emptied? How long before the backup generators running them ran out of fuel?

Did anyone else realize what was happening? Emma looked back down the street, to where Martha, Tom, and Karen still chatted on the sidewalk. They'd all seemed concerned but not worried, the same for Diane and Chuy. Just like her until ten seconds ago. No one was talking about the water supply, but if this went on for a while, it would be an issue.

I need to fill everything I can with water right now. And get more food.

She thought about going back to tell the others when Grace whimpered again, sounding unhappier than before. Her daughter couldn't fend for herself. Grace depended on her and Cody for everything. They'd brought her into the world; it was their job to protect her. Emma knew she was a smart, competent person. She could take care of Grace just fine. She still wished Cody was here.

A wave of dizziness hit Emma. She had to grip the doorframe to steady herself. What if Cody had been on the plane and it had been affected too? Was he even alive? In an instant she felt alone and inadequate, even though she had no proof of her fears. But if she was right, they were facing something much bigger than a power outage.

Not knowing where Cody was, if he was safe, hollowed out her stomach and singed her throat with acid. The familiar precursor to morning sickness triggered a wave of nausea. When would the water give out if the worst happened? If everyone rushed to fill containers at once, the pressure might drop before she could get enough for her and Grace.

Ten minutes, she told herself. *Ten minutes to fill containers, then I'll tell them.*

She hurried inside, heart racing. The quiet house felt alien now, its contours transformed by what she feared might be happening. She buckled Grace in her bouncy seat on the floor by the couch. Immediately, Grace began to cry, loud, angry squalls that normally would have Emma running to soothe her.

She didn't have time to soothe Grace.

Emma moved through the house with quick efficiency, first to the hall bathroom, where she plugged the tub and turned on the faucets. Water gushed out, the pressure normal. It felt like mercy.

She hurried down the hall and did the same in the master bath. Despite the normal pressure, both tubs filled with agonizing slowness.

Next, she collected every container she could find—pitchers, pots and pans, empty gallon milk jugs she'd been meaning to recycle. She pulled glasses, cups, and bowls from the cupboards and filled everything. Anything without a lid she covered with plastic wrap. Grace howled but Emma stayed on task. She scrubbed the double washtub in the garage by the washer and dryer, wincing at the rinse water running down the drain. She found several five-gallon buckets left by the previous owners and washed them out on her back patio with the hose. Then she started on every sealed moving box, looking for anything that could hold water.

Emma kept looking for the time on the kitchen clock and appliances, even though nothing was working. Sweat trickled down her back and dampened her bra. How long had it been? Ten minutes? Twenty? She should go back outside and tell the others, but there were more containers she could fill if she kept unpacking. If she kept looking a little longer and gathered just a little more.

The quiet in the house felt oppressive, like the tension after she and Cody had argued but before they'd made up. Grace had stopped crying. Emma hurried to the front room. For the first time, she'd left Grace to cry herself out. She slept in her bouncy seat, her face tear streaked and pink. Emma knelt in front of her daughter, running her hand over her head, but lightly so she didn't wake her.

"This is for you," she whispered. "Grace, this is all for you. You need clean water."

As the minutes stretched, her rationalizing felt less justifiable. The Emma who had graduated law school with honors, who had built her reputation on hard work and ethics, would have alerted everyone immediately. That Emma would have organized the neighborhood response.

That Emma hadn't had a baby who depended on her for everything.

This Emma filled pot after bucket after tub with water. She counted the gallons, trying to remember how much an adult should drink every day. *I can't Google it,* she thought, and a borderline hysterical laugh bubbled up. She'd never had to remember such a thing. You turned the tap and water came out. That was how it worked. That's how it always worked. In her naivety, in the abundance of the First World, she had assumed it always would.

She walked to the living room to check on Grace again—still sleeping. She peered through the window. Martha stood in her front yard. She stared up the street, a pensive expression in the pinch of her eyes. Emma returned to the kitchen and her containers, but with every minute that passed, with every shot glass she filled, the weight of her silence grew heavier.

What was she doing? She had always disdained people who only cared about what affected them without bothering to think of others, especially those less fortunate. Now she was acting just like them. She turned off the kitchen sink and stepped back. "I'm better than that," she whispered. If not for herself, she'd do it for Grace. If she couldn't live her values when it was hard, what was the point of having them at all? Why bother teaching Grace to do the right thing when she wasn't?

She would share what she suspected, beginning with Martha, who had been so kind to her. She would help her community get organized for however long might be necessary. What she had now —water in containers littering every flat surface of her house— would have to be enough. Hopefully, the only emergency was in her head. When he got home, she would tell Cody, and they'd laugh about how the scariest thing in the house had been her imagination.

Grace still slept in her bouncy seat, oblivious to her mother's decision. A swell of love so deep it hurt held Emma in its viselike grip. "I'm going to talk to Martha," she said aloud. "I'm going to do what I can."

chapter
ten

EMMA

SUNDAY, JULY 13
  10:04 AM

Martha's eyebrows pulled tight as she pulled her silver hair back into its usual ponytail. "How much do you think we need?"

"I don't know exactly. A gallon a day for an adult? With this heat, it's probably more." Emma rocked Grace in her arms. "If the power is back on in a day or two, I think we'll be fine, but if goes on longer..." She shrugged.

"If it goes on longer, the National Guard will be deployed. They'll bring those— I don't know what they call them, but they have water trucks. I've seen them on TV after hurricanes."

"If those trucks work," Emma said. "None of our vehicles are working. Why would theirs?" Martha frowned. She—and everyone else—were still thinking in terms of what they were used to. Emma was struggling with that herself. She added, "What if this drags on?"

"But it's not everywhere," Martha said. This time, her denial was not as strong as before.

When she'd gone back to talk to her neighbors about the water, Emma would never have guessed the toughest nut to crack would be Martha. Martha, like most people, hadn't considered how widespread this might be. "I don't know how much area an EMP can knock out, Martha. But I think it's better safe than sorry. I'll feel better if you fill some containers for yourself, just in case."

She needed a printed copy of the HardNetworks case file. Had she brought it with her when they moved or sent it back to the office? Her work situation hadn't been settled when she left. On her mentor's advice, Emma had left it that way. She was only on six-month maternity leave because her pregnancy had been high risk, so she was still an employee. She just didn't live there. They had pared down their belongings before the move and Cody had been in charge. He had left her work stuff alone, but she'd been even more sleep-deprived then than now. She may have sent the case file back. She couldn't remember.

Martha's eyes darted around her kitchen. "I have some large containers in the garage. Jack kept them for camping."

"Fill everything you can," Emma said. Had they kept their camping cooler? That would hold gallons of water.

"Don't apologize for being cautious, especially with a baby to take care of." Martha placed a hand on Emma's arm. "I'll get started right away."

Emma nodded, feeling more relieved than she expected. "I need to go grocery shopping. Cody and I were supposed to go yesterday. Do you want to come?"

Martha nodded. "Give me fifteen minutes."

Back at her house, Emma placed Grace in her bouncy seat. She set it on the kitchen table to catch the breeze coming in the window. She secured it in place with a clamp Cody had made. His paranoia that Grace might bounce herself off the table had made Emma feel better about her own. They'd laughed about how silly they were being, since Grace could only wriggle in place.

Tiny beads of sweat dotted Grace's forehead. Her fine hair was damp. Emma pulled the plastic wrap off the edge of a jar of water, carefully wetting a corner of a washcloth. Gently, she dabbed her daughter's forehead and neck. "We're going to be okay," she whispered.

Emma surveyed her water vessels covering almost every level surface in the room. She opened the cupboards, where she'd stashed the filled glasses and cups, bowls and pots and pans. There were more in every room of the house. Would it be enough? It has to be, she thought.

Cody would know exactly how much they needed. He always knew random things like that. Her throat tightened and tears filled her eyes. Where was he? Every time she thought about him being on a plane when this happened, she wanted to throw up. She realized her hands were shaking and pushed the thought away. She couldn't afford to think this way. Cody would be home as soon as he could. He had to be. The alternative was unacceptable. She had to stop feeding her fear for him. She had to concentrate on keeping Grace safe. She didn't have time for anything that interfered with that.

A knock at the back door helped her shake off the mental downward spiral. A woman stood waiting, her chestnut hair pulled back in a bun at the base of her neck, loose strands framing her heart-shaped face. She looked to be around Emma's age but had a fragility about her. Then again, looks could be deceiving. It might just be her petite build that gave Emma this impression.

"Hi," Emma said, opening the screen door.

"Hi, I'm Kate," she said. "I live farther down the road on your side, where the houses start again."

"Hi," Emma said. "I'm Emma."

Kate smiled but seemed nervous. "I was just at Martha's. She said you're going to the store?" When Emma nodded, Kate said, "Do you mind if I join you?"

"Of course not," Emma said. "We're leaving in about fifteen minutes."

"Great," Kate said.

Kate stood there, not leaving. Maybe she wanted to wait here? "Do you want to come in?"

"Um, sure."

Emma ushered Kate into the kitchen. Kate looked around at Emma's array of water-filled containers. "Thanks," Kate said. "Martha mentioned you were collecting water."

"Better safe than sorry," Emma said, but her cheeks warmed with embarrassment. Based on her kitchen, she must look like a lunatic.

"No, it's smart. I did the same thing this morning." She reached up to toy with her necklace, skimming it over her breastbone. "Martha thinks we're overreacting. She says we'll all be laughing about this tomorrow, when the power's back on."

"I hope she's right," Emma said, forcing a lightness she didn't feel into her voice, even though she didn't believe it.

"Me, too," Kate said. "Meet you at Martha's, then." She smiled, but it didn't reach her eyes. As she turned away, Emma saw Kate frown, her cheerful mask slipping away. Well crap, Emma thought. Kate was just as concerned as she was. Rather than making Emma feel better, it made her feel worse.

chapter
eleven

EMMA

SUNDAY, JULY 13
   11:00 AM

The late morning sun beat down as Martha, Kate, and Emma, pushing Grace's stroller, walked into town. Emma had dressed Grace in the lightest cotton dress she could find and draped a light percale sheet over the stroller's sunshade. With extra water, diapers, and a change of clothes for the baby inside, the diaper bag strained at its seams. She'd stuffed the bottom tray of the stroller with a small backpack and cloth shopping bags.

Emma eyed Martha's folding granny cart with envy, sure the feeling had colored her face green. *I can't believe I'm eyeing her granny cart... What am I, eighty?* Still, she made a mental note to find one. They were close enough to town to walk, so she might as well, even if it made her lamer than lame. *I'll get a cane while I'm at it to shake at teenagers.*

Martha walked with purpose and energy. Kate moved at a

more measured pace. "Are you all right, Kate?" Emma asked when Martha walked ahead to greet a neighbor.

Kate nodded. "I'm fine. It's just the heat."

They stopped in some shade while Martha chatted. Two police officers on bicycles passed by. One of them waved, and Emma waved back. For a crisis—if that's what this was—the police presence seemed minimal. Martha and the man she was speaking with finished their conversation and the three women continued walking.

Emma heard the hum of running machinery before she saw the grocery store—the generator for the store's freezers. Since the large windows at the front of the store were dark, the market appeared closed. The line of people waiting at the entrance belied appearances. As they neared, Emma saw people enter as others left. It reminded her of waiting in line to shop at Trader Joe's during the COVID-19 pandemic. As had been the case then, everyone waited patiently. Unlike then, people stood close together. The sight made Emma relax, though what had she expected—a food riot?

"Five people at a time, store policy until the power's back on," a young man in a store smock announced as they approached. "If you don't have cash, talk to Randy on your way in."

"Do you both have cash?" Martha asked. "I do if you're short."

"I'm okay," Emma said, and Kate said she was okay for funds, too. The line moved in fits and starts, all of them slow. Grace began to fuss in her stroller, her tiny face reddening with frustration. Emma pushed the stroller back and forth, trying to lull her. She didn't want to pick Grace up. It would only make her hotter.

"Martha!"

Diane waved from the store entrance, her copper braid gleaming in the sunlight. She looked hot and harried. Martha went to the door to see what Diane wanted. When she returned, she said, "Diane said to meet her at the back door. If we can give her cash and lists, she'll get everything together for us."

"I wish I'd known that earlier," Kate said.

"Me, too," Martha said to Kate. Her eyes darkened with what looked like worry, as if she didn't like what she saw. Kate didn't seem to tolerate the heat well.

They walked through the parking lot to the alley behind the building. Emma hadn't known the lot was accessible that way. The few times she and Cody had shopped since arriving in town, they entered and exited the lot from the road. The alley lay in deep shade. *Why did we roast walking down the street? We should have come this way.*

Diane stood in the open back door by the time they reached it. "Come in," she said. "I don't have time to do your shopping for you, but I couldn't say I'd let you jump the line. You'll have to leave this way and cut through the alley."

"It's not fair to everyone waiting their turn," Kate said.

"I've got boob sweat and a hot baby," Emma said. "I'm going."

The storeroom was cooler than outside, and when the door closed behind them, it was almost completely dark. Diane turned on a flashlight and scooted around them. "This way. Randy's being cautious with limiting the number of people in the store. I can't blame him, with the lighting being so bad and the security cameras not working. We're only using the generator for the freezers and meat cooler." Diane stopped just short of the wide, swinging doors to the sales floor. "Leave the stroller here, Emma. I brought carts back for all of you. They're just out there. And there are flashlights in the baskets."

"This is so nice of you, Diane," Emma said as she felt for the latches to detach Grace's seat from the stroller so she could set it in her cart. "I was waiting for Grace to cry. You know, like the shrieking child from hell on a plane."

"Don't mention it," Diane said. "Like, *really* don't mention it."

The light was better here than in the storeroom, and brighter still at the front windows. Emma could see the dark silhouette of a shopper searching the shelves with a flashlight.

"I'm going to catch my breath," Kate said. "I'll catch up."

"Are you sure?" Emma asked.

"I'm sure," Kate said.

Martha held out her hand. "Give me your list, Kate. I'll get you started."

"Martha, I'm—"

Martha cut Kate off. "Just give me your list."

"Okay." Kate held out her list but her voice had an edge.

When they were halfway up the aisle, Martha said to Diane, "I tried to get her to wait or give me her list, but you know Kate."

Diane nodded. "It could just be the heat."

The gossipy side of Emma was dying to know what they were talking about. So was the practical side, because if Kate was unwell and needed help, she'd like to know. "Is everything okay?"

Martha shrugged. "I'm probably being overprotective. Kate has a heart condition. Her mom and aunt did, too. She got a pacemaker last year, and she's fine, but I worry."

"She's young to have a pacemaker," Emma said, shocked.

"Which is why I worry," Martha said. "And why Diane let us in."

"Is it serious?" Emma asked. "I know it's none of my business... She doesn't seem to tolerate the heat very well."

"Kate has never tolerated the heat well, even as a girl. The heart condition isn't that serious, really," Martha said. "It's more about making sure her blood pressure doesn't drop when she stands up because of how her blood circulates. Her heart won't stop beating, but she could get light-headed, pass out, and hit her head."

They had reached the end of the first aisle when a stocky man with thinning brown hair approached. Emma thought he might be Randy, Diane's boss, from the way Diane straightened and trained her attention on him. "Heath's here," he said.

Even in the poor light, Emma saw the color drain from Diane's face.

"Are you sure it's him, Randy?" Martha asked, putting a hand on Diane's shoulder. "Where is he?"

"In the parking lot. I told him to leave. He says his car isn't working so he can't go into Athol."

"What use is having a restraining order when he uses anything as an excuse to ignore it?" Diane said. She sounded angry but also apprehensive.

"Don't worry, I'll handle it," Randy said, placing a hand on Diane's shoulder. "I just wanted you to know. Go to the office and lock the door. I'll come get you when he's gone."

Diane looked uncertain for a moment. Then she nodded and left. Randy sighed. "Like today isn't complicated enough. Excuse me," he said, then left Emma and Martha alone in the aisle.

Emma caught Martha's eye. "I take it things didn't end well."

Martha snorted. "They didn't begin well. Let's finish our shopping and get out of here."

Emma moved through the shadowed aisles, selecting canned goods, rice and dried beans, anything with a long shelf life, as well as candles, bleach, and other home supplies that might be useful. Even though she was still breastfeeding, Emma added dry baby formula to her cart, too. By the time they checked out, Diane's ex had come and gone without incident.

Grace slept, oblivious to the tension swirling around her mother like fog. Her tiny chest rose and fell, like perfectly timed clockwork. As she and Martha pushed their carts to the back of the store, a fierce protectiveness surged through Emma's body. She would keep Grace safe, whatever it took.

chapter
twelve

CODY

SUNDAY, JULY 13
   12 NOON

Despite never being more than a light social drinker, with every painful step, Cody wished he had drugs. The kind that would make him hallucinate animated woodland creatures. After his father died, his mother needed him. That had crowded out the more unwholesome but typical teenage pastimes. Being out of control had never appealed to him anyway. But that was then. Now he hobbled through the Montana wilderness with broken bones in his foot, a screwed ankle, and an Army Ranger turned criminal for a guide.

Frost stopped. "Take a breather while I scout ahead."

Cody nodded and sank to the ground at the base of the nearest tree. Now that his foot wasn't bearing weight, a faint numbness crept through it like gangrene. If the boot he wore got any tighter, that might come to pass. Frost disappeared through the trees, his pace more than doubled without Cody trailing behind him.

"Show-off," Cody muttered, but without conviction. He was frustrated, that was all. Frost was, too.

After last night's bear incident, Cody had quit questioning Frost's judgment. His distrust was based on the man being a criminal, but if the former Army Ranger with survival training thought they should hike out, Cody would hike out. He wanted to go west? They'd go west. Midmorning, they'd adopted a southerly route. West, south, whatever Frost decided, that was the direction Cody would go. They were in a survival situation and Frost was the expert.

Cody wasn't sure he believed Frost's suspicion that the plane had crashed because of a CME. He'd heard of EMPs, solar flares, even coronal mass ejections, but knew little about them. After the bear incident—even though it amounted to nothing—Cody felt his vulnerability more keenly. But more importantly, if there was the slightest chance Frost was right, he needed to get home to Emma and Grace. If Frost was wrong, every step closer to civilization was a step closer to putting the man behind bars.

Cody tugged at the bandana tied around his neck. It had been the pilot's. He pressed the thin fabric against his sweaty face. Every inch of his body felt wilted from the heat. It had to be close to ninety and it wasn't even noon. The cover of the forest helped but his dampened clothes stuck to his skin like a rash.

The crack of a stick caught Cody's attention. Frost walked toward him through the trees. "There's a hiking trail ahead," he said as he neared. "It follows the ridgeline. Looks like we didn't crash as far out as I feared."

Buoyancy, like a hot-air balloon breaking free of the ground, lifted Cody's spirits. "That's good news." Frost gave him a hand up. Cody said, "If I've done all this walking on a broken foot for nothing..." He shifted his weight and a flash of pain almost took his breath away. "Ow!"

Frost said, "You better hope that's the case. The alternative is a lot worse."

His comment hit like a punch. Apprehension bloomed in Cody's gut. He was right, of course. Cody wanted this trek to be for nothing. Then Emma and Grace would be at home with working lights and air-conditioning and cold food in the fridge. They'd be safe.

Frost shoved one of his massive hands into the backpack and pulled out a water bottle. He took a few swigs and then handed it to Cody. "Finish it and we'll go."

They set out a minute later, Frost slowing his pace for Cody's benefit. Frustration leaked through Frost's all-business veneer. He never said as much, but his constant scanning and anxious looks ahead betrayed his agitation. If he hadn't returned after leaving Cody behind, he'd be miles away by now. More importantly, he'd be free. Cody had no illusions about his situation. He needed Frost. That didn't mean he wouldn't do his duty when they reached a town. The first thing he'd do was get help and reassert control. He had to get Frost back into custody for real.

Cody bent over, hands on knees, when they reached the trail. His legs trembled like he'd run a marathon. The forest thinned, and the sun beat down like an anvil. Frost had gotten ahead of him. Cody pushed himself upright and followed, not wanting to fall any farther behind. The astringent smell of sap and heat flooded his senses. Two steps later, his foot snagged on a rock. He tumbled down.

He hit the hard, earthen path with an *oof*. Dust filled his nostrils and coated the inside of his mouth, the coppery tang of blood tickling his tongue. Shards of pain streaked upward from his broken foot through his ankle and into his calf, causing the muscles to spasm. He groaned, then climbed to hands and knees. When he spat, the parched earth absorbed the red-streaked spittle in an instant. He wanted to stay where he was, on his knees in the dusty path, just for a little while. He closed his eyes and thought of Grace's chubby face, the pink roses of her cheeks and her blue bird bright eyes.

Cody groaned as he pushed off the ground. He swayed a moment until he got his balance. Foot half-numb, he took a step, then another, dust puffing around his ankles as he continued along the trail in Caleb Frost's wake.

EMMA

SUNDAY, JULY 13
12:15 PM

They collected Kate, who had more color in her cheeks after resting in the relative cool of the storeroom, and exited through the store's back door with their purchases. None of them had purchased so much they couldn't manage. Cody had chosen the stroller and Emma thought it was too big. Now she was thankful for its size. It meant one less bag on her shoulders.

Diane had given them each a bottle of water. Emma had started to refuse when Diane jutted her chin toward Kate. Seeing how Martha and Diane looked after Kate sparked hope inside Emma. Friends from small towns had often said one thing they valued about living there was that people looked out for one another. Among these women, at least, that seemed true. Emma hoped they were indicative of the townsfolk in general, but she shivered all the same.

The shady alley stayed the sharp lash of the sun's rays. Emma's steps slowed as they approached the end of the alley where they'd have to step out from the shade. When they reached the main street, she blinked, raising her hand against the glare. Her shadow shrank to nothing, as if it sought escape from the merciless glare, too. She adjusted the drape over Grace's stroller, making sure none of the sun's sharp rays slipped inside.

They rounded the corner toward the town square. A small crowd, maybe thirty people, had gathered on the far side in front of Town Hall. Some fanned themselves with pieces of paper. Almost everyone was talking—in pairs or huddled in larger groups.

"Is there something going on?" Emma asked. "A meeting we don't know about?"

Martha said, "Let's go see."

Emma adjusted the cloth shopping bag on her right shoulder. Even though she'd put heavier items in the bag on the stroller, she could tell her shoulder would hurt by the time she got home. How was that possible when she carried Grace all the time?

She pushed the stroller through the small crowd, steering around elbows, though most folks stepped out of her way. Town Hall's wide double doors were closed. A hastily handwritten note was tacked on them. People crowded around to read it.

"What does it say?" Kate asked, standing on tiptoe.

A bearded man in overalls stepped back from the sign. "There's a meeting tomorrow at ten a.m.," he said, raising his voice. "It says the mayor and emergency services will update us on the situation then."

"Is anyone there?" Martha asked.

The man shrugged. "Must be, since the note is there, but the door's locked. It's usually closed on Sunday."

"They might not have much information yet," said a woman standing nearby. She wore rumpled scrubs and a name tag that read Amanda Benning, RN. Strands of hair escaped her ponytail and stuck to her neck. She looked dead on her feet. "We're having trouble getting information at the hospital."

"You came all the way from the hospital?" Martha said, her surprise plain. "How did you get here?"

The surprise that widened Martha's eyes and parted her lips ramped up the disquiet percolating at the back of Emma's mind. The hospital was twenty miles away. Emma hadn't been happy about it when they looked at Specter Lake. She was used to having several hospitals nearby, but there was an urgent care in town. Right now, twenty miles seemed like the other end of the country.

"I borrowed my friend's bike," the woman said, shrugging. "I had to get home to take care of my dogs."

"Are things okay over there?" Kate asked.

The nurse nodded. "The hospital's running on generators until power is restored. The real problem is most of the equipment isn't working. When I wasn't looking after patients, I was digging through storerooms for anything that worked."

"Any idea what's behind this?" Emma asked. She felt Grace wriggling through the frame of the stroller and started pushing it back and forth.

The nurse shook her head. "Nothing official. Some people think it's the solar flare. One guy at work thinks there's been a terrorist attack on the electrical grid." Her voice became dismissive. "Why he thinks there'd be an attack in small-town Idaho is beyond me. Whatever it is, anything with electronics—which is almost every piece of equipment—isn't working."

"The water's still running at least," a man in a short-sleeved button-down shirt said. "My cousin's son rode his bike over from Coleman. Their water pressure is half what it usually is."

Martha's quick intake of breath confirmed it; Emma had been right about the water. Conversations bubbled around them, snippets floating past like a mirage winking in and out of focus.

"...can't reach my daughter in Seattle..."

"...pharmacy's giving out medications, but they're limiting how much..."

"...Does Ed still have a HAM radio?"

"...if this lasts more than a few days..."

The door of Town Hall opened. As if pulled by a magnet, everyone turned toward it. A middle-aged man with a sheriff's department cap looked over the crowd. "Hey there, folks. We've set up a communication station at the firehouse. Anyone with working radios, CB equipment, anything that might help us establish better communication, please bring it by."

"What about Gerry's Salvage?" Martha called out. "He might have something useful."

The officer nodded. "We've already sent someone. We're trying to cobble together what we can."

Emma's stomach contracted like a fist. *Cobble together what we can? They don't know what's going on any more than we do.* She searched the faces in the crowd, looking for signs: hunched shoulders, tightened jaws, brows beetled tight with confusion or concern, but didn't see them. Had anyone else heard what she had? Had the implications of what the officer just said registered with anyone?

Emma's mouth felt tacky, like it was coated with half-dried paint. The sun still beat down, but a chill settled over her perspiring skin. The surrounding voices became a low murmur, like rushing water from a distant creek. Their faces were concerned or flushed with heat or frustrated, but everyone's composure seemed intact. Emma didn't see any sign that others were freaking out like she was. It felt like she was standing at the center of a collectively held breath of willful self-deception that this was a temporary inconvenience—like a blown clutch or clogged kitchen sink—when the appropriate response should be more along the lines of what the actual fuck? "I need to get back," she heard herself say. "I need to get Grace out of this sun."

"We'll come back tomorrow for the meeting," Kate said. "By then, they'll know something concrete."

As they walked away, Martha said, "You were right about the water."

Emma nodded. "I wish I wasn't. What will we do if the water stops running?"

Martha said, "We live on a lake, Emma. I'm sure we can figure it out, not that I think we'll have to. When we get back, I'll finish walking the neighborhood and suggest everyone fill some containers."

"Without freaking people out," Kate added.

Martha smiled. "Of course not. Just being neighborly and practical."

Kate grinned. "Both of which happen to be true of you."

Emma followed Kate and Martha, as unaware of her surroundings as Grace was in the cocoon of her stroller. The two women discussed who in the neighborhood might need help while Emma's mind spun like a broken compass needle.

Maybe I'm wrong. Maybe the mayor and...

Emma paused for half a step as she realized she didn't know if there was a town council or board of supervisors. Law enforcement was involved, of course, and other emergency services would be. Perhaps someone in that mix would know more by tomorrow. They might even have answers and plans for what to do next.

Perhaps.

Might.

Maybe.

Emma didn't like those odds. None was a bet she wanted to make.

chapter
fourteen

CALEB

SUNDAY, JULY 13
   4:14 PM

The journey was far from over, but Caleb breathed easier when the sign came into view: Troy, Montana, Population 889. He'd guessed right—they had crashed in the Cabinet Mountains, just not as remote as he had feared. Their entire journey as the crow flies ended up being a little upward of fifteen miles. Unfortunately for them, they hadn't been flying, and the trek had been much longer because of the marshal. The late afternoon sun hung low in the sky, but the heat of the day showed no signs of abating.

The marshal slumped against him, having given up refusing the help Caleb offered a couple hours ago. It had taken the entire hot, miserable day to get here. Sweat beaded on the lawman's face, which he blotted with the damp bandana he clutched in his other hand. The *scritch* of his dragging foot grated against Caleb's ear. The marshal's sunburned face winced with every step, his eyes narrowed by a permanent squint of pain that pinched his lips tight.

Caleb knew they had been lucky to survive the crash. Being so much closer to civilization than he'd thought was nothing short of miraculous. Even so, he couldn't shake the growing frustration bubbling in his chest. If he hadn't been such an idiot and gone back for the marshal, he'd be long gone by now.

A daughter, Grace... She's such a pretty little thing.

Would he have made the same choice last year? Caleb couldn't decide, and that bothered him. He had always been a protector. He protected Ruth when they were on their own. Maybe that was what Mister Jacobs, his history teacher, had seen in the sullen teenager he encouraged to join JROTC, and later the Army.

As a Ranger, he'd protected others. Those he'd fought endangered regular people just trying to live. Caleb took pride in protecting them—Americans or foreigners, it didn't matter. His brothers fought the bad guys over there so they wouldn't have to fight them at home. For Caleb, it was simpler: just stop the bad guys. The moral clarity of his mission was never in doubt, and his determination to execute it never wavered.

He lost his way after the army. Lost the sense of belonging he'd fought so hard to find. Lost the purpose, the mission. The worst part of it was he did it to himself.

Being pushed from the army when his truth-telling became an embarrassment was beyond his control. But what followed? That was on him. He'd given in to the anger and bitterness, the sickening feeling of being used. He had repurposed his expertise to serve his own ends. He would stick it to the man who had stuck it to him. After a while, he did it for the rush. Then, it was just what he did. He couldn't recall when it started to feel pointless, but it had without him knowing until he knew it all at once. Was that what Ruth had been trying to tell him? Was an unconscious recognition of the fiction of his righteous cause the reason he'd hesitated and been captured?

"What's the plan?"

The marshal's question pulled Caleb from the thoughts swirling inside his head. "Find out what's going on."

They passed several small businesses as they entered the town outskirts. Some cars on the street were neatly parked; others were a jumble. It looked like they had stopped when the CME hit and were later pushed to the side of the road. Farther down the street, people walked and gathered in small groups. A woman pushed a shopping cart overflowing with canned and boxed goods and bottled water. Two men hauled boxes of supplies from a storefront, glancing around like they feared being watched. There was no threat, no imminent danger, but nervous tension hummed in the air.

At the gas station on the corner, Caleb took a second look. Ten dollars a gallon.

"That's not good," the marshal said.

At first Caleb thought he meant the prices but realized he referred to a man holding a shotgun beside the service station door. Caleb's lips flattened, forming a line. "No, it's not."

As they continued down the road, Caleb caught sight of an older man standing in the open door of a mechanic shop. A mix of cars and trucks filled the small parking lot beside the building. An old Buick caught Caleb's eye—early eighties based on the sedan's boxy lines. That Buick would run if he was right about what had happened.

"Let's check that garage," Caleb said, nodding toward the shop. "See what we can find out."

The man at the shop stepped onto the sidewalk. He looked them up and down, his eyes as sharp as an eagle surfing thermals and looking for prey. His gaze settled on the marshal. "Looks like you've had better days."

The marshal straightened, bracing himself against the building and releasing Caleb's arm. "You could say that."

Caleb stepped forward, extending his hand and looking the man in the eye. "I'm Caleb. This is Cody. Do you have a chair he can sit in for a minute to get off his foot?"

"Roy Jenkins," the man said, shaking Caleb's hand with a firm grip. Caleb thought he was in his late sixties, maybe early seventies, but he'd lost little, if any, vitality. He stood erect, shoulders back, eyes alert; Caleb was pretty sure Roy had been in the service. Roy's eyes settled for a moment on Caleb's bicep, where his Ranger tattoo peeked out from under his tee shirt. "This is my shop," Roy added. "Come on in."

As they entered the shadowy auto shop, Caleb scanned their surroundings. He stopped just inside the open roll-up door. The smell of grease, oil, and mineral spirits filled his nostrils, the walls and floors a drab, stained gray. The grit under his boots, like every shop he'd ever been inside, made him feel like he'd been here before. Roy, the owner, had walked ahead of them and disappeared through a door. He returned with a folding chair. The marshal collapsed into it with a groan.

"Want something to drink?"

"That would be amazing. I can't remember the last time I was this thirsty," the marshal said. He extended his hand. "Cody Greer."

They traded handshakes before Roy disappeared again. He returned with two cans of Coca Cola. "I'm afraid they're warm. No refrigeration since the power went out."

"Thank you," Caleb said, accepting a can. When the sugary, fizzing liquid hit his tongue, he groaned with pleasure.

"Army?" Roy asked, his chin jutting toward Caleb's tattoo.

Caleb nodded. "Yes, sir. And you?"

Roy gave Caleb the tiniest of approving nods. "Marines. You boys look like something the cat dragged in."

Before Caleb could answer, the marshal said, "Our plane crashed yesterday."

Caleb's headache, which had settled down to a steady dull throb, suddenly felt like a spike through his brain. It wasn't that the plane crash needed to be a secret. He didn't know what the marshal would say next. His military service had sparked a tiny rapport with Roy. If the marshal told him why they were together, that rapport would disappear.

Roy's eyebrows climbed his forehead. "A plane crash?"

"Yep. It was a small plane. I'm a US Deputy Marshal. I was on official business."

Caleb shifted his weight and moved his hand around his hip, ready to pull out the marshal's gun. Meanwhile, the marshal showed his credentials.

Roy looked at the marshal, then at Caleb, and grinned. "He's not your prisoner, I hope."

The marshal shook his head, returning Roy's grin. "If he was my prisoner, he'd be wearing an orange jumpsuit and slippers."

The adrenaline spike puddled around Caleb's feet. A slithery nervousness replaced it. What was the marshal's end game here?

"Do you have any idea what's going on?" Caleb asked. "Our plane lost power and dropped out of the sky." He tipped his head toward the road. "It looks like the same happened to those cars pushed to the side of the road."

"The price of gas has gotten high," the marshal added.

Roy shook his head, his mouth twisting down like he'd tasted something rotten. "They didn't miss a beat, the fools. I'm sure it's cash only with nothing working."

"Nothing at all?" Caleb said.

"Not a damn thing," Roy answered. "I think it was a CME, myself."

The marshal said, "Why is that?"

"Like your friend here said. Your plane dropped out of the sky. We've been without power two days now. Nothing works, apart from older cars and trucks, older generators, batteries. Electronics are fried, not a peep from the power company. And the sky..." He shrugged. "I've seen the Northern Lights plenty, but I've seen nothing like this. Depending on the light, you can almost see it during the day."

Silence stretched, supple as warmed wax, before Caleb said, "I think so, too. It's why we hiked out. I worried the emergency transponder on the plane wouldn't work, and the—" He caught himself before he said 'the marshal.' Roy might think it odd. "Cody's foot wasn't going to get better sitting out there."

"Didn't get any better on the hike," Cody said dryly.

Roy's smile was small but mischievous. "I don't imagine it did."

"Has anyone come in an official capacity with any news about what's happened?" Caleb asked.

The older man shook his head. "Not yet. I don't expect anyone anytime soon, either. Folks here are pretty self-sufficient. Not all, but most. Up here you have to be. Most people have generators and pretty good stores of food, but..." He shrugged. "You know how it is today. Everyone orders everything online and it comes two days later. People think they won't be cut off from anything anymore."

"What about local government and law enforcement?" Cody asked.

"They've been keeping a close eye on things," Roy said, leaning against the workbench behind him. "Checking in on folks, especially old coots like me. I've known the mayor and most of the city council my whole life. A few of them go to my church. They're doing what they can to reassure people. So far, it's working." He cast a dark glance in the direction of the gas station. "Mostly.

"People in small towns like Troy have more of a preparedness mentality than people in the city. We're used to winter storms cutting us off and power outages that last a day or two, but not everything stopping at once. The grocery store looks like old news clips from Soviet Russia."

He frowned, then said, "If this keeps up much longer, things could change fast. The vultures at the gas station aren't helping when they hike prices and stand outside with shotguns."

"The veneer of civilization is thin," Caleb murmured, thinking of the time he'd spent in war-torn countries. Cultures were different. Values, too. Caleb had difficulty trusting people, but in his experience, most people just wanted to get on with their lives. When the world around them functioned as it should, that was easy. You found out just how fragile the social contract was when it broke down.

Roy huffed out a breath. "Where are you headed?"

"Specter Lake," the marshal answered. "My wife and baby are there. I need to get back to them."

Caleb said, "My sister and her kids are in Coeur d'Alene." The marshal shot him a sideways glance but said nothing. Just try to stop me, Caleb thought. He didn't plan on being taken back into custody. If this was a CME, which seemed more likely every second he spoke to Roy, then all bets were off.

Roy whistled. "That'll be one hell of a journey with so few cars running. You saw the Buick in the lot."

Caleb nodded. There was no point denying the obvious.

"You won't be getting anywhere tonight, and someone should look at you," Roy said, jutting his chin at Cody. He plunged his hands deep in his pockets, squinting out the door as if weighing something. The shadows had lengthened outside, casting the shop in deeper gloom. The sky hadn't darkened as much as the poor light inside suggested.

Roy pursed his lips and nodded, as if he'd decided. "I can't promise you transportation, but why don't you come have a meal with me and my Sylvie? We have a gennie, and we're on a well. You look like you could use a shower."

Caleb's chest caught mid-breath. It was quite an offer from someone they'd just met, even if he and Roy had their service in common. His suspicion flared, trying to find the right question to expose an ulterior motive. He'd stayed off the radar this long that way. As he looked at Roy, however, he couldn't find one.

"That's very kind of you," the marshal said. "A pail and some soap are more than enough."

Caleb sighed, the decision taken out of his hands. "It's much appreciated."

"The truck's out back," Roy said. "Let me lock up."

"What about the Buick?" Caleb asked. "Don't you want to move it inside?"

If he and Roy thought this was a CME, other people did too. There had been enough books and disaster movies with EMPs and solar flares. Caleb couldn't be the only person to have eyed it up.

Roy grinned. Even in the dim shop, Caleb saw a sparkle of amusement in his eyes. "It's here because it's not running. And I removed the distributor cap, just to be sure."

Hope that Ruth was with people as generous as Roy snagged Caleb like a rabbit in a snare. The civilization they all took for granted was fragile; he had seen that fragility firsthand. He had put his life on the line—willingly—to hold it together, to spare others needing to see what he had seen. As he stood in Roy's shop, watching the canny smile of the man who had made them such a generous offer, he thought maybe that fragile veneer hadn't cracked just yet.

chapter
fifteen

CODY

SUNDAY, JULY 13
   6:00 PM

Ninety minutes later, sitting on the back patio of Roy and his wife Sylvie's tidy ranch style home, Cody felt a thousand percent better. When they built the house, the area was probably more remote. Over the years, people built more houses, but not in a planned development, more the mark of a growing community. Cody wasn't sure that was the case anymore. The town's welcome sign had said the population was less than a thousand.

Roy had stopped on the way to his home to call on a friend. It turned out that the friend was a retired doctor. He diagnosed Cody with two broken metatarsal bones and had a severe ankle sprain. His advice—icing, analgesics, crutches, a medical walking boot, and two weeks of rest—was not something Cody intended to follow. He did take the ibuprofen, a bandage for his ankle, a crutch, and instructions for rewrapping and reinforcing his boot.

Now Cody's foot was in a pail of ice-cold water. Roy's wife

Sylvie had wanted him to take some ice from their deep freezer, but Cody had refused. The well water was cold enough that he didn't need ice. Roy and Sylvie had already insisted both men take showers, explaining that they'd been running their generator an hour or two to keep the food in the deep freezer from defrosting. Cody wasn't sure he believed they weren't turning the generator on just for him and Frost, but Sylvie had insisted. He couldn't deny his spirits felt revived now that he was clean.

The kitchen door opened and Frost stepped out. "Dinner's ready."

Cody leaned forward and motioned to the pail. "I'll be in as soon as I take care of this."

Frost nodded, then disappeared back into the house. Cody dried his foot and put on his sock, which was really Roy's, then wrapped the stretchy bandage around his foot and ankle in the figure-eight pattern the doctor had showed him. He eased his foot into his boot, wincing. It still hurt—a lot. He stood, grabbed the crutch from the wall, and limped inside.

Sylvie stood in front of the open oven, pulling a baking dish out and setting it on the stovetop. Cody had, based on nothing, expected Sylvie to be a small roly-poly sort of woman. Instead, she proved tall and whipcord thin, with a ready smile and dark-brown eyes. Cody had seen the liquid propane tank alongside the house when they arrived, so cooking as usual made sense. Cody breathed deep, the smell of cooked meat almost making him dizzy. His stomach growled.

Sylvie closed the oven door. "Go on to the dining room. I'll bring this right out. It's a good thing we've got LP or we'd be eating sandwiches."

"I'm sure they'd be wonderful," Cody said, then he allowed himself to be shooed from the kitchen.

He joined Roy and Frost, who sat opposite one another. Cody took the seat next to Frost and Sylvie followed, carrying a plate of pork chops. The chops, mashed potatoes, and green beans made Cody's mouth water. After saying grace, he and Frost fell on their dinners like wild animals.

"I'm sorry for wolfing down my food down," Frost said a few minutes later. "Twenty-mile hikes on energy bars doesn't cut it."

Roy smiled. "I have no such excuse. I always wolf down whatever Sylvie fixes for dinner."

Sylvie swatted him, amusement sparkling in her eyes. "You're still doing the dishes."

Roy grinned at her and winked. "Can't blame a fella for trying."

Longing squeezed Cody's chest. Roy and Sylvie were what he hoped he and Emma would be fifty years on. He should be with them, not hundreds of miles away.

"Roy tells me you're headed for Coeur d'Alene," Sylvie said.

"Yes, my sister and her kids are there," Frost said. "The marshal isn't going as far." He said to Cody, "Specter Lake, right?"

"Yeah, Specter Lake," Cody said, trying to keep his annoyance from his voice.

Frost spoke to their hosts like he was a regular guy just trying to reach his loved ones, not a fugitive. Cody wasn't advertising the reality of their situation. He should have alerted local law enforcement and had Frost jailed, but Frost could get him home—if the man didn't ditch him. Cody couldn't bring himself to give that up.

The conversation had continued without him. Cody refocused his attention. "...a long trip, especially if things don't get back to normal soon," Sylvie said, frowning. Her brow furrowed, then she said to Roy, "Are you thinking that old Indian?"

Roy nodded. "I have a '52 Indian Chief motorcycle, if either of you knows how to ride. She's a little temperamental, but right now she's purring like a kitten. It should get you home."

Cody's heart leaped in his chest. He hadn't let himself hope Roy might help them with a vehicle because he didn't think he could handle the disappointment. "I know how, but my foot..."

"I do, too," Frost said. "Though it's been a while. Don't you want to keep it for yourself? You might need it."

Cody looked at Frost, trying to keep his mouth from catching flies. In his experience, criminals were opportunistic. Frost had used his military training to commit bank robberies for years. No criminal stayed successful that long without reading situations and exploiting every advantage. What was he playing at here?

"We've got two trucks and a car that are older, so they're running. It's not like I don't have the skills to keep them that way. I like the oldies stuff. Easier to work on and more reliable."

"That truck of yours was in your shop more in the last six months than Tracy's Toyota was the last six years," Sylvie said.

"Bet that Honda's not so reliable now," Roy said, a sly grin quirking up the corners of his mouth.

"Well, there is that," Sylvie allowed. "But there's no need to gloat."

"Besides," Roy said, his voice sobering. "If this goes on a while, I expect I'll be giving it to someone to use or someone will steal it. I'd rather choose who gets it."

"That's... I don't know what to say, except thank you," Cody said, his throat getting tight.

"You have your sidearm?" Sylvie asked Cody. "You can't go out there without a way to protect yourselves."

From the corner of his eye, Cody saw Frost stiffen. Cody realized he might have a card he could play, and that Frost knew it. He hadn't even bothered to try getting his gun from Frost. He was injured; Frost was not. Frost was a former Army Ranger and could be the Incredible Hulk's little brother. But now, if Cody revealed they'd been on that plane because he'd been retrieving Caleb Frost, wanted in seven states for armed bank robbery, Roy and Sylvie might sing a different tune. All of Frost's attentive guest and grateful thanks might go out the window and they'd help him regain the upper hand. Being right wouldn't help him get home, however. He said to Sylvie, "I've got my sidearm. We're good."

Frost's posture softened. He glanced at Cody sidelong, the knowledge that Cody could have changed the terms of their uneasy truce in his favor reflected in his eyes.

"Well, that's settled," Sylvie said. "Let's have dessert. I'm worried it's a little stale since I made it a couple days ago, but it's still dessert."

Frost practically leaped from his chair to help clear the table. Cody knew the man wasn't a sociopath—he'd come back for him when he didn't have to. But he couldn't shake the feeling that this attentive guest act was just that: an act.

Sylvie and Frost returned with slices of bundt cake and coffee. Sylvie said, "I'll be right back. I forgot to take my pill."

She went back to the kitchen. Roy's face sobered. "Sylvie's got high blood pressure. We just got the three-month refill. Mail order because of the insurance. It's three times the price if we fill it at the local pharmacy." His voice dropped lower. "I'm worried about what'll happen if we can't get more when we run out. We're just as dependent on online shopping as anyone, I guess."

Sylvie returned, and Roy's face brightened. Now that he knew of Roy's worries, Cody could tell Roy's smile was a little forced. He and Emma didn't have much food in the house after their recent move. No odd cans of beans and forgotten boxes of noodles that accumulate at the back of the cupboard, forgotten until it's cleaned out. He hoped Emma had gone to the store before this happened or played it safe and went shortly after. She was still nursing Grace, so at least they didn't have to worry about formula, as long as Emma was getting enough food herself.

The rosy buzz of Roy and Sylvie's generous offer of the motorcycle leached from Cody's body like air from a tire with a slow leak. He had to get home.

Frost said something he didn't catch and Cody refocused to pay attention—again. Cody's first duty was to his family. He was supposed to have Frost in his custody and deliver him to Coeur d'Alene to face justice. That he might not fulfill the duties of his job scraped at his conscience like a carpenter's rasp on a piece of wood. But when push came to shove, he'd choose Emma and Grace every time. There might be a way to fulfill both obligations. He just didn't know how.

After mapping the next leg of their route, Frost made his excuses and went to bed. Cody followed soon after. The curtains of the guest bedroom they shared were open. Frost sat on his bed, back to the wall, his face red-washed through the window. The bright reds and greens filling the sky glowed as brightly as the first time Cody had seen them. Cody stood by the nightstand separating the two twin beds.

"It's hard to believe something so beautiful is so destructive," Frost said.

Cody glanced down, catching the glint of Frost's teeth. He looked back out the window. "It is."

"Thank you."

Cody looked down, his brow furrowing. "For what?"

"For not telling them who I am and that I had your gun."

Cody shrugged. "You still have my gun."

Frost shook his head. "It's on your bed."

Cody turned to look. Dark against the lighter bedspread, his gun lay on the bed. He reached for it, the familiar heft in his hand comforting, the gnawing anxiety of Frost having such a lop-sided advantage over him receding. Frost still had the upper hand. He was injured, while Frost was not. Frost was also close to being a professional body builder. If he didn't have a wife and daughter at home, and a fugitive to apprehend, Cody might ask to stay with the Jenkins a while longer to allow his ankle to heal. His injury, not to mention his personal and, ironically, his professional obligations, kept him dependent on Frost.

Cody sat on his bed, the gun resting alongside his thigh on the bedspread. "I had my own reasons for not saying anything."

Frost shrugged. "I'm still grateful."

Frost lay down, eschewing the light bedspread in favor of lying on top of it. Cody wondered what had Frost—

Don't be ridiculous, he told himself, cutting off the idea

forming in his mind. He set his service weapon on the bed beside him as he lay down. Frost had given it back unprompted, changing the terms of their unspoken temporary alliance, but that didn't mean he might regret doing so and want the gun back. One decent act didn't mean Cody could let his guard down.

The ibuprofen he'd taken earlier had softened the sharp edges so that now his aches and pains thudded like a distant drum. He closed his eyes, felt his mind drifting. "I'll make sure you get to Specter Lake if you don't interfere when I leave to find my sister and her kids."

There it was, the catch. Cody said, "That's what returning my gun is about—a show of good faith."

A long beat, then Frost answered. "Something like that."

Cody's mouth twisted in a frown. For getting home, Frost was an asset he was loath to lose. For his job, bringing Frost in was a duty he was sworn to fulfill. There was no telling how bad things might get. Maybe the world had fundamentally changed, but this could be localized. The rest of the world might be mobilizing to help. Right now, there was no way to know.

"Whatever is happening out there, I'm still a lawman, and you're still a fugitive. It's still my job to bring you in."

Frost's low laugh filled the space between them. "You're not telling me anything I don't already know. I pegged you as Clark Kent the minute I saw you. It's good to know I'm not losing my touch."

Cody felt a flush warm his neck and creep to his face. He would not rise to the bait Frost had thrown. He also would not admit that Frost might have sized him up accurately. "This thing may only affect a small area. We might get closer to Coeur d'Alene and find everything is okay."

"If that's the case, my sister and her kids are fine."

No way he's saying what that sounds like, Cody thought. "So, you'll come in without a fight?"

Again, another just too long silence before Frost spoke. "I'll get you home, Marshal. We can cross other bridges when we get there."

Cody knew what his answer should be. He should tell Frost to quit deluding himself—this was a bribe, nothing more. Normally, he wouldn't trust a criminal's word about anything, but Roy thought it was a CME, too. Their host struck Cody as honorable. More than that, Roy's worry about his wife's medicine hit too close to home. He was genuinely scared for Sylvie's life. Just like Cody was for Emma and Grace.

It rubbed against everything Cody believed about himself, like sandpaper over an open wound, when he said, "Okay. You've got a deal."

day three

chapter
sixteen

CALEB

MONDAY, JULY 14
5:55 AM

The floorboards creaked under Caleb's boots as he slipped from the bedroom. The marshal snored, but not loud nor often enough to drive Caleb from his bed. He paused before closing the door and watched the lawman's chest rise and fall. The marshal's face, slack with sleep, looked younger, unburdened by the pain that had creased his features throughout yesterday's trek. Caleb shut the door and crept downstairs.

Dawn painted the horizon in muted purples. The aurora was still there, fainter but unmistakable in the brightening light of dawn. Caleb's skin prickled with unease at the sight.

The smell of coffee filled his nose as he neared the kitchen. Roy stood at the counter, his back to Caleb, pouring steaming liquid into two chipped mugs. "Thought I heard someone moving around," Roy said without turning. "Coffee's ready."

Caleb's mouth twitched, a smile tugging at one corner. The old man's hearing was as sharp as a bat's. "Thanks."

Roy pushed one mug toward him as Caleb approached. "I thought you might be an early riser."

"Old habits," Caleb said, wrapping his hands around the warm ceramic. The heat seeped into his palms, as warm as a shared secret. An old-fashioned alarm clock, twin bells atop, showed the time on the stove.

Roy nodded toward the back door. "Let's take these outside."

The morning air bit at Caleb's face as they stepped onto the patio. The temperature had dropped overnight, like a whisper of autumn in mid-July. An early winter. That's all we need, Caleb thought. They settled into the wooden chairs, neither speaking for several minutes. The silence was uncomfortable, but the quiet of men used to early mornings and time to themselves.

"I might have something for you," Roy said after a few minutes. He went to his garage and returned with a wrapped bundle, which he set on the table. He pulled back the wrapping to reveal a revolver, well used but well maintained. "Smith & Wesson .38. Not fancy, but reliable."

Caleb's pulse quickened. He studied the weapon, then Roy's face. The old man's expression remained unreadable, his eyes steady beneath his bushy eyebrows.

"I appreciate it," Caleb said, making no move to take it. "But maybe you don't mention it to the marshal."

"You two have an interesting dynamic. Almost as if you're both play-acting."

Caleb's jaw tightened. He stared into his coffee, watching the surface ripple with his breath. Then he looked back at Roy. He could maintain the fiction they'd established yesterday, but something in Roy's steady gaze made it impossible. "I'm his prisoner." The admission scraped Caleb's throat. "He was hurt when the plane crashed and I couldn't leave him there."

Roy's eyebrows rose, but he showed no other reaction. "I thought something was off. I didn't figure you'd cop to it."

Caleb's fingers tapped against his mug. It was that or squirm. "You've been generous. More than generous. It feels wrong to keep lying to you."

Roy nodded. "So, why are you still here? He's safe. You could be long gone by now."

Caleb snorted a laugh, Roy's question a mocking echo of his own. "I've been wondering that myself."

"If I give you this," Roy said, and Caleb knew they were back to the gun, "will you use it on the marshal?"

Caleb opened his mouth, but the words wouldn't come. Everything he'd done since the crash had been stupid, against his interests. Yet all of it had been the right thing to do. He tried again. "No, I won't."

"The hesitation doesn't inspire confidence, son."

Caleb set his coffee down, leaning forward with his elbows on his knees. His shoulders bunched tight under his shirt. "It's not about the marshal. I'd never—" He shook his head. "I was thinking about how stupid I've been, because I did leave. He was unconscious and the pilot died in the crash. He couldn't even have asked me to stay. I got my stuff, took his gun, and split. If I had even an ounce of self-preservation, I'd have kept going."

"But you didn't."

"No, I didn't," Caleb almost whispered. "Before we took off, I heard him talking to the pilot. He's got a little one at home, a baby. Her name is Grace."

The name hung in the air between them. It felt like the grace people said you should grant yourself and others when getting your act together was out of reach. It filled the air, curling around Caleb like a warm hand over his own that offered solace. Acceptance. Maybe even forgiveness.

"I know what it's like when no one's looking out for you," Caleb said, his voice rough with emotion that took him by surprise. "My sister and me, our dad went to prison." Caleb's eyes slid away from Roy's. He had carried the burden of his father's actions, even though they weren't his own. "He shot and killed a man when he was drunk. We bounced around the system after. Some homes were okay. Others... weren't."

Caleb shrugged, his throat closing around memories he rarely examined. He looked up at Roy, wanting him to see he meant it. "If that little girl becomes an orphan, it won't be because of me."

The first real rays of sunlight broke over the horizon, striking Roy's face. His features had softened, but he looked much older than a moment ago. "My son Robby died in Afghanistan," he said. "2010."

Caleb recognized the pain in Roy's voice. He had heard it too many times. "I'm sorry."

Roy nodded. "He was a good kid. He always looked out for others, even when it cost him. You remind me of him."

Heat flooded Caleb's face. He wanted to protest, to explain that he was nothing like Roy's son. That he'd spent years taking what he wanted because "the system" had taken everything from him first.

"You know what gets me?" Roy continued, sounding more confused than anything else. "Not a day goes by that I don't think about my boy joining up to help people. Didn't matter if he knew them. He got over there and it wasn't as black and white as they'd told him, but he still tried. He died trying to help, and people here at home won't even help their neighbors."

Caleb thought of the gas station with its inflated prices, the man with the shotgun, the way this small community was already fraying at the edges. He thought of Ruth, alone with her kids in Coeur d'Alene, and the marshal's wife and baby, waiting for him in Specter Lake. "People look out for themselves, especially when they're scared. That's just how it is."

"Is it?" Roy fixed him with a piercing stare. "You've been looking out for Cody."

Caleb shook his head. "That was different."

"How?"

A daughter, Grace... She's such a pretty little thing.

Roy's question hovered between them, simple but so very hard. Caleb had no answer that didn't undermine the walls he'd built around himself. Walls that somewhere along the line had become a prison, fixed in place and too high to scale.

"Sometimes we're better than we think we are," Roy said. He held the revolver out to Caleb. "We just need reminding."

Caleb stared at the weapon before taking it, feeling the weight of more than just metal in his hand. The faith Roy placed in him was there too, fragile as a spider's web heavy with dew. He wasn't sure what to say, didn't have the words to explain just how precious that faith, this moment, was to him, so he said something true. "Thank you."

Roy nodded once, satisfied, and picked up his coffee again. He took a sip. "Your marshal friend seems like a decent sort. Stubborn, though."

The sound Caleb made was somewhere between a laugh and a groan. "You have no idea."

"The kind who still does his job even when the world's falling apart?"

"Exactly that kind." Caleb's smile faded. "It makes things complicated."

"The worthwhile things usually are." Roy drained the last of his coffee. "Sylvie's going to be up soon. She'll be making breakfast. Bacon and eggs, the works, and she won't hear of you two leaving without eating."

Caleb nodded, grateful for the shift—the return to lightness in their conversation. "I wouldn't dream of arguing with her."

Roy stood, his knees cracking. "That's fifty years of kneeling on concrete for you."

Roy headed inside, but Caleb stayed where he sat, watching the sunrise creep across the yard. The gun on the cushion felt like a reminder of the choices he'd made and those still to come. He thought of his sister and her kids, of the lawman sleeping in Roy's guest room, and his wife and baby.

The cool morning air filled his lungs as Caleb took a deep breath. For the first time in years, the path ahead didn't seem as dark.

chapter
seventeen

EMMA

MONDAY, JULY 14
  11:08 AM

An air of resigned hopelessness pervaded the stifling town council meeting room of Specter Lake's town hall, not unlike the waiting room at the DMV. The windows were thrown open to catch the breeze outside, to little effect. About three hundred residents had crammed into a space designed for half that number, radiating heat and anxiety.

Emma stood against the back wall. Grace had been fussy all morning and only settled down when Emma stood and rocked her. Holding her too warm baby against her own too warm body had Emma's crankiness veering toward full-blown crabby. Two earlier attempts to use the Baby Bjorn harness had resulted in a very unhappy baby, and Emma raised the white flag. It was going to be a barnacle baby day.

Emma looked down, twisting her wrist before remembering

she wasn't wearing her nonfunctioning watch. The man next to her said, "It's just past eleven."

Emma smiled her thanks. "Your watch still works?"

He nodded. "Never did like digital readouts." He dabbed at his forehead with a handkerchief. "I've never come to a town council meeting, but they're over an hour late starting. I expected this to be better organized."

Emma had, too; or rather, she had hoped. Everything she could think to bring—two water bottles, three bananas and a few granola bars, baby wipes, diapers, baby powder, a nursing drape, her breast pump, and even some dry formula—filled the diaper bag at her feet. She'd thought it overpacked before she left the house, but now she was glad of it.

As five people took their seats behind the curved table at the front of the room, the crowd grew restive. In front of the man at the center, a sign identified him as Ken Dawson, Mayor. The police chief joined them, taking one of the end seats. Emma had met him the second week after they'd arrived in town and thought his first name was Brian. Maybe. It might be Bill. Cody had stopped by the police station on their way home one afternoon to introduce himself. "Professional courtesy," he'd said.

Another police officer, who looked like he was sixteen years old, stood near the door. The rest of the town's small police force was elsewhere, patrolling or maybe finding a place for the spillover attendees to gather.

A glimpse of silver caught Emma's eye. Tom Wilson had slipped just inside the door from the hall, then stopped, apparently unable or unwilling to push through the crowd any farther. Emma held up her hand to catch his attention. "Tom!"

He turned at the sound of his name and sidled over. After greeting the man who'd told Emma the time, Tom joined them. He ran a hand through his hair. "I thought I'd missed it, but then someone stopped by the store to say things still hadn't started," he said. "It's an oven in here. How's the little one doing?"

Emma shrugged. "She's hot, but when I try to put her in the Baby Bjorn, she cries, so I guess we're being hot together."

"Poor little thing," Tom said, pursing his lips. "I know how she feels. At least she's sleeping now."

Emma smiled. "Ten bucks she wakes up when it's least convenient." She paused, then asked, "Were things okay at your store?"

Tom nodded. "Yeah, though folks are antsy."

A palpable tension hung in the air, heavier than the Selkirk Mountains looming over the town. "I closed up to come over rather than leave Carrie on her own."

"Where is she?" Emma asked. She still hadn't met Tom's wife.

"She doesn't like crowds, so she stayed outside."

The mayor stood, and the room quieted. He tapped the hand-held megaphone before raising it. "Hello, everyone. Thank you for coming. If you're up front, I'm sorry if this is loud, but we want everyone in the hall and outside to hear. I know everyone's got questions about what happened and what we're going to do."

"Understatement of the century," the man on Tom's other side said.

Mayor Dawson continued. Despite the projection of the megaphone, his voice sounded strained. "What know a massive power surge took down the electrical grid. Not just in Specter Lake, but everywhere we've been in contact with."

"Which isn't far," a woman on the town council added. She had leaned forward in her seat and cast an exasperated glance at the mayor. Emma squinted, making out her name: Councilwoman Kendra Owens. Her comment suggested they hadn't done much, or as much as she would have liked.

"We're working on establishing communication with larger population centers," Dawson said, not acknowledging the woman's interjection. "In the meantime, we need to focus on community needs right here. Are there any questions?" Hands shot up across the room, including Emma's. The mayor pointed to an older man in the front. "Mike, what's on your mind?"

"What about the water treatment plant? My tap was running low this morning. At this rate, there won't be any water soon."

"That's an issue we're working on," the mayor said. "Perhaps Chief Walters can speak to that."

The police chief? Emma thought. Why was he passing off an infrastructure question to law enforcement?

The police chief stood and stepped out from around the table. "We've stationed an officer at the plant just to keep the works secure. Obviously, the main pumps are down, but they're working on getting the backup generator online."

"Why isn't it working?" someone asked.

The police chief looked at the mayor. The mayor hesitated. "Come on, now" and "What's the problem?" volleyed at him from the crowd.

"The problem is the bond issue that was voted down last year." It wasn't the mayor who had answered, but Councilwoman Owens. "If you don't remember, some of us on the town council backed the county bond issue on the ballot last year while others"—she cast a pointed glare at the mayor—"opposed it. That money would have allowed us to upgrade the water treatment backup systems. Because it didn't pass, we're working with the antiquated system we've been limping along with for years. Except now it's not working."

A rumble of discontent filtered through the assembly. Tom leaned into Emma and said, "Because Lord knows nobody wants to pay more taxes."

Emma sighed. That sentiment was everywhere. Emma's hand remained raised. The mayor passed over her. Grace squirmed against her shoulder, making small, fussy sounds that threatened to grow louder.

"What about medical supplies?" a woman in the back said. "My mother needs insulin."

The mayor cleared his throat. "Dr. Meyers has opened his clinic as a triage center. Anyone with immediate medical needs should go there. The county hospital is running on generator power. We're asking only those who truly need that level of care to go—"

"The county hospital is twenty miles away," someone shouted. "How are we supposed to get there?"

Emma thought of the nurse she'd talked to yesterday, who had looked so bedraggled. The mayor continued speaking as if no one had interrupted him. "Dr. Meyers' clinic and the urgent care are working together to get people the care they need."

The room grew louder with overlapping voices and questions. Emma bounced Grace, trying to keep her calm while still maintaining her raised hand. The mayor continued calling on others—mostly men, and from the way he greeted them by name, mostly longtime residents.

Beside her, Tom raised his hand. Mayor Dawson called on him almost immediately. "Tom Harper, good to see you here. What's your question?"

Tom tipped his head at Emma. "My neighbor's been trying to ask something for a while now."

The mayor's gaze lit on Emma, his smile leached of the warmth that had been there for Tom. "Of course. Miss...?"

"Greer," Emma supplied. "Emma Greer. I have two questions. First, is anyone from the water treatment facility here to share specifics about what the plan is for providing drinking water if the backup system stays out of service? Second, what's the plan for communicating with state and federal emergency services if this continues and standard channels remain down?"

Mayor Dawson's chilly smile didn't waver. "Well, Miss Greer, as I mentioned, we're working on communication. As for the water situation, we have people handling that."

Which didn't answer her question. Emma decided to press him for an answer. "Is someone from the water department here or not?"

Councilwoman Owens jumped into the conversation. "No," she said, annoyance plain in her voice. "It wasn't deemed necessary."

The mayor's posture stiffened, like his joints were half-frozen. Emma didn't know the history between the mayor and Councilwoman Owens, but it was clear they didn't see eye to eye. "Dave has more pressing concerns than attending a meeting," the mayor said, giving the councilwoman a death glare, his words clipped short like he wanted to bite. "He's working on the problem right now."

"Do you have an emergency communication plan in place?" Emma persisted.

"Miss Greer," the mayor said, his tone shifting to one you might use with a confused child. "In small communities like ours, we handle things differently than you might be used to in—where did you say you were from?"

"It's Ms., and I didn't." Flashbacks of trying to reason with Cody about the mess at work, how dismissive he'd been, sparked against the dry tinder of her repressed anger about the whole fiasco. "Where I used to live is not relevant to my question, which you still haven't answered."

Grace chose that moment to wake up, whimper, and then bawl as if someone had set her diaper on fire. Emma shifted her from one arm to the other. The mayor gave her an indulgent smile. "Maybe you have more immediate concerns right now, like tending to your little one?"

Heat flushed Emma's body, her grip on her temper snapping like an overwound guitar string. "I can't attend to my daughter if there's no water. You don't seem to have any plan beyond platitudes."

The mayor's eyes widened, then narrowed. Shit, Emma thought. She'd get nothing from the man now, not that she expected to. He was an idiot. Tom said, his voice raised, "I'm also concerned about coordinating with other government agencies."

"The sheriff's department has a backup radio system that they're working on," the mayor said, his tone different from the one he'd used with Emma, like he was talking to an adult. "And we've sent several of our officers to nearby towns and the county seat on bicycle. We're confident we'll establish communication with larger emergency agencies by tomorrow."

"After the buzz saw they've taken to everything in Washington, DC?" someone called out. "Good luck with that."

The room erupted into overlapping questions and concerns: Where was the National Guard? What about people with chronic health conditions? Who in town had a working vehicle? The council members exchanged tense looks. The police chief whispered something to the mayor, who frowned and shook his head.

"Everyone, please!" The mayor raised the megaphone. "One at a time!"

Emma leaned in to Tom. "They don't have a plan."

Tom nodded, his lips pursed and frowning. "Not one that works without electricity."

Grace's crying got worse. "I have to get her outside and feed her," Emma said.

She started to pick up the diaper bag, but Tom got there first. Emma squeezed through the crowd and slipped out the door, with Tom following. The crowd in the hallway and foyer was almost as large as the crowd in the council meeting room. Emma breathed a sigh of relief when they left the building, even though the hot sunshine offered no respite from the heat.

"Thank you, Tom," she said. "What a waste of time."

Tom pursed his lips. "Ken Dawson's a good man, but he's in over his head. He never could admit a mistake, but I'm surprised by how bad that was."

Emma rocked Grace gently, wondering where she could go to nurse. The grocery store, maybe, if Diane would let her in the back. It had been cooler there the other day. Grace continued to squall, her face red as a beet.

"I need to go," Emma said. "But we should meet later and at least get our neighborhood organized. I'm happy to host it."

Tom nodded. "Good idea. I'll get the word out."

"Thanks, Tom."

From the foyer of Town Hall, Emma could hear angry voices

—a lot of them. The meeting was doing nothing to allay anyone's concerns. Emma hoisted the diaper bag on her free shoulder and crossed the square, glad to be free of the tension in the council meeting room. It had inched up like the mercury of the thermometer outside of Tom's store. If the town council didn't get a handle on this soon, it was going to boil over.

"It's okay, Grace," she whispered, wishing for the millionth time that Cody was here.

chapter
eighteen

MONDAY, JULY 14
   12:09 PM

Mountains often came to mind when people thought of Idaho. Caleb could attest to the veracity of this, but it wasn't the case everywhere. Where he now stood on Idaho State Highway 200, a few miles north of Ponderay, was one such place.

East of them was Lake Pend Orelle. They had driven alongside it for quite a while after taking Idaho State Highway 56 south from Troy. It wasn't the quickest route—Idaho State Highway 2 was—but it was becoming clear that these weren't normal times. Roy and Sylvie, as well as the marshal, had agreed with Caleb's desire to minimize encounters with people when they'd chosen a route. Maybe he was being paranoid, but he didn't care. Paranoia had served him well over the years.

As he stretched his back, Caleb couldn't help puzzling over Roy and Sylvie's generosity. A shower, a hot meal, a bed for the night, and then the motorcycle. What did they get out of it? He and the marshal offered nothing in return. Maybe some people were just... good. The idea made him uncomfortable. He'd spent so many years expecting the worst of people that genuine kindness felt like a trap. Maybe this was disaster's silver lining—it reminded people they needed each other.

Maybe, like Roy had said, he was the one who needed reminding.

Here, the land was flat. They couldn't see the residential streets and commercial strips along the highway unless they left the road to investigate. Highway 56 had been in the valley between two mountain ridges. There had been nothing to see, apart from the stunning pine forests. Now, they were coming up on Sandpoint, where Highway 200 became Interstate 95. Caleb wanted to scout ahead, but he didn't want to leave the motorcycle with the marshal.

He didn't think the marshal would leave without him. Trying to drive the bike with the broken bones in his foot would be excruciating. He worried the marshal might get jumped by someone who wanted their working motorcycle. He had a gun now but one injured man—even an armed one—was still an easier mark than two.

The marshal limped out from behind the car he'd been pissing behind and walked in Caleb's direction. His eyes narrowed and his mouth pinched tight as he walked. He'd left the crutch behind, the stubborn fool. When he reached Caleb, Caleb said, "We're coming up on Sandpoint. Maybe five miles."

The marshal's head canted to one side. "You look worried."

Caleb blinked. He'd thought his concern wasn't obvious. "There's a bridge south of Sandpoint that goes over the lake. It's not even a quarter of a mile long, but it's a choke point."

"Oh," the marshal said. "Do you think there will be that sort of trouble?"

Caleb shrugged. "Maybe."

The motorcycle's engine revved to life, the tremor of its horses buzzing against Caleb's legs. So far, the motorcycle's temperamental quirks were absent. Caleb glanced at the gas gauge. A sliver of anxiety snaked its way inside his gut. They were down to a third of a tank—enough to get to Specter Lake, but not enough to continue to Coeur d'Alene.

The first community they encountered after leaving Troy was the little town of Clark Fork. They had seen little from the road, despite slowing for abandoned vehicles. Apart from the occasional shout, it had been quiet, the sort Caleb associated with the wilderness. With more ground to cover before the day was over, they hadn't stopped.

Caleb checked the snap under his chin while he waited for the marshal to climb onto the bike. After the marshal settled, his hands lightly holding Caleb's waist, they resumed their journey. The marshal's spirits seemed better than yesterday. Caleb had wondered how he might feel this morning after the bargain they had struck. Would the Clark Kent part of his personality feel conflicted about their deal? His improved mood made Caleb think the marshal could live with it.

Caleb intended to hold up his side of the bargain. He would get the man home to his family, to the pretty little thing of a daughter who hadn't let him leave her father in the wilderness. Caleb did not share the marshal's hope that the CME's effects might be localized. Call it intuition, a soldier's sixth sense, whatever you liked; Caleb had a bad feeling about all of it. He didn't believe they would arrive to find life chugging along as usual in Specter Lake.

Caleb believed the marshal would hold up his end, too. The irony of the marshal's Clark Kent streak working in his favor was not lost on him. Besides, the marshal needed to rest and let that foot heal properly. He needed to be whole for what was coming, not permanently impaired. Had circumstances been different, he would have said so.

But the facts on the ground were what they were. A shadow of a smile lifted his lips. A lawman and an outlaw walk into a bar... For Christ's sake. The situation was beyond weird. He would get the man home and then set out on his own. If things played out as he feared they might, his status as a fugitive armed bank robber would not be at the top of anyone's priority list. If his imagination had gotten the better of him and the world still ticked along like always, he would melt away into the background, as he had so many times before.

Abruptly, the lush green gave way to low industrial buildings, then a commercial strip of small shopping plazas and parking lots. Cars clogged the road. Caleb concentrated as he wove the motorcycle through the abandoned vehicles. His fight-or-flight instinct amped up. His training would keep those instincts from affecting him. If he had to fight, he would. And if he had to get out, he'd get out, just like he had with his unit and later, his crew.

People in shorts and tee shirts milling in the parking lot near a fast-food restaurant stared as the motorcycle cruised. Cardboard and other junk littered the small shopping plaza's parking lot. Caleb noticed groups of people being directed toward various shopping areas by men and women wearing orange vests. Outside the gas station doors stood a man with a rifle and a woman with a shotgun. Both stepped forward as they drove by. Armed guards already? That wasn't a good sign.

A hundred yards down the road, the windows of a SureWay supermarket glinted in the sun. A police officer stood at the entrance, where an orderly line snaked past the storefronts for admittance. The crash of shattering glass sliced through the motorcycle's engine noise. One of the large windows on the far side had broken. Small groups of people raced away from it, struggling to push three overfilled carts across the parking lot. A flash of movement caught Caleb's eye. A man with a rifle stepped into the bed of a pickup truck parked alongside the SureWay's entrance. He raised the rifle to his shoulder. The crack of a shot pierced the motorcycle's roar. The man fired again and again. After the third shot, Caleb quit counting. People fell to the ground or darted between abandoned cars, running for their lives.

Then Caleb saw the sign above the door: LOOTERS WILL BE SHOT.

"Stop!" the marshal yelled, gripping Caleb's shoulder. "We have to help!"

Caleb didn't stop.

"Dammit, Frost! People are dying!"

Caleb turned the motorcycle down a side street a few blocks away before stopping. The marshal was off the bike so fast it might as well have been on fire. By the time Caleb dismounted, the marshal was halfway down the block despite his broken foot. "You have got to be kidding me," he said, taking off after him.

Although the marshal might be motivated, Caleb was quick and whole. Whole enough, anyway. The bruises all over his torso were lodging a protest. He grabbed the marshal by his shoulders and yanked him to a halt.

"Let me go!"

Caleb turned the marshal around, then snapped up his helmet visor. "There's a sign, warning that looters will be shot. If we intervene, we'll get shot, too."

"I don't care what it said on a sign. People can't take the law into their own hands!"

"They weren't," Caleb snapped. "There was a police officer at the door, letting people lined up inside. He didn't bat an eye. He never moved, let alone tried to stop that shooter."

Color drained from the marshal's face. "What?"

"You didn't see him?" Caleb asked.

"No," the marshal said, sounding stunned. "I didn't."

"It's not our fight," Caleb said, not without sympathy. The marshal's idea of what it meant to be in his line of work wasn't what had happened in that parking lot. Shooting people, even looters, shouldn't happen. It shouldn't be sanctioned by law enforcement, but it had.

The marshal's jaw clenched as he rallied. Righteous Clark Kent's anger flared in his eyes. Caleb tightened his grip on the marshal's shoulder. "Think about your wife and baby. They're who you need to protect. Going back there won't help you do that."

For a second Caleb thought he hadn't gotten through. Then the marshal slumped, the fight and righteous fury draining from his frame. They proceeded with more care, scanning for movement that might mean trouble. He'd always thought smaller communities would fare better in a disaster because of a more closely knit populace. Maybe Sandpoint had passed whatever threshold that applied to, if it applied at all. A few blocks later, Caleb saw the raised roadway of what must be the interstate. He turned the bike left and throttled up when he saw the ramp. From here, Specter Lake was fifty miles away. He still had to figure out gas, but with any luck, he might reach Coeur d'Alene today after reuniting the marshal with his family.

The cars on the ramp were pushed to one side. Caleb's spirits lightened, then fell to his toes with a *plop*. Cars and two sections of freestanding chain-link fence blocked the top of the ramp. He slowed the motorcycle to a halt halfway up the ramp, planting his feet on the ground before turning the engine off. He undid the snap and pulled off his helmet. The breeze cooled his sweaty scalp.

The marshal said, "Why are we stopping?" And then, a moment later, "Shit."

"Yeah," Caleb said. "It's starting."

chapter
nineteen

EMMA

MONDAY, JULY 14
   12:00 NOON

Emma stood at the kitchen sink and turned the faucet. Nothing. No drop, drip, nor trickle. Not even a hiss or sputter of air. She twisted the faucet harder, as if the water was only stuck. "Shit," she muttered, letting her head drop forward. Her loose bun wobbled, wisps of hair sticking to her damp neck.

Two days since the power went out. Two days of ignorance and uncertainty. If something didn't change soon, maybe even chaos.

Emma's throat constricted as it hit her again. No more water. A semi-hysterical laugh slipped from her mouth. "You live by a lake, Emma. There's water. There's just no water..." Tears sprang to her eyes, a longing so sharp it punched through her chest like a fist.

Goddammit, Cody, of all the times to not be here.

A soft snuffling from the portable bassinet in the kitchen

made her turn from the sink to look at Grace. She stirred in her sleep, then settled down. Thank you, Universe, Emma thought as she watched her baby. The heat had made poor little Grace fussy all day, as sticky with sweat as her mother. The house was cooler than outside, but the still air felt as cloying as overly sweet perfume.

"Emma." Martha's voice carried from the front porch. The screen door creaked. "Emma?"

"In the kitchen," Emma called, keeping her voice low.

Martha appeared in the doorway from the hall, her silver ponytail neat despite the heat. The older woman's eyes, dark and shrewd, zeroed in on Emma's face. "Your water's out, too."

Emma nodded. "Yes. Just now."

"I've been checking with neighbors. Most of the street is dry." Martha sighed, her eyes roaming over the water-filled containers stacked on every available surface. "It's a good thing you got a jump on this."

"I hope it's enough," Emma said, knowing it wasn't.

Martha ran a fingertip along the rim of a ceramic mixing bowl filled with water and covered with plastic wrap. "Tom's spreading the word about your meeting. One o'clock, right? That's in an hour."

Emma's shoulders tensed. Her meeting? When had it become her meeting? She'd just offered to host, though what she'd been thinking she couldn't fathom. Her house wasn't even fully unpacked. "Do you think anyone will come?"

"Oh, they'll come," Martha said. "The only question is how many. People are scared. They want answers."

"I don't have answers."

Martha put a hand on Emma's arm. "No, but you're thinking ahead. You're trying."

"I don't want to seem like I'm overreacting."

"Overreacting?" Martha's laugh held no humor. "The power has been out for two days. Cars don't work, phones are dead, and now the water's gone. Given all that, this..." She gestured at the bottles, bowls, and vases filled with water. "Doesn't feel like over-reacting."

Despite the warmth of Martha's presence, ice settled in Emma's stomach. Apparently, she was leading a meeting of neighbors she didn't know, with no concrete information about what was happening, with a fussy ten-week-old baby. And without Cody.

She ran her hand lightly over Grace's downy head. "This is going to be a train wreck."

Every window in the house stood open, but the breeze was negligible, barely stirring the limp curtains. The sweat trickling down Emma's ribs made her skin itch. She sighed, thinking they should have set up on the patio.

"We'll be hot no matter where we are," Martha said. She looked out the front window. "Kate said she was coming, right?" Emma nodded, and Martha's lips pressed together in a stiff line. Almost to herself, she murmured, "She's usually so punctual."

A knock on the door sent nervous butterflies alight in Emma's stomach. She met Tom and Carrie Wilson at the door. Tom's weathered face was creased with concern, his short silver-white hair sticking up, like he'd been running his hand through it. Carrie was on the plump side with eyes that made Emma think she tried to give everyone the benefit of the doubt.

"We've been storing water since Y2K," Carrie said after being introduced. She smiled self-consciously and handed Emma a covered pitcher. "We rotate it through. I thought right now it's better than bringing a snack."

"Thank you," Emma said, touched by the gesture. She set the pitcher on the coffee table by the cups she'd set out. "Please, take a seat."

"Folks are on their way," Tom said, sitting on the love seat where Carrie joined him. "We saw Chuy and Maria coming down the street."

As if on cue, Chuy Rodriguez appeared at the door with his

wife, Maria. Both were lean and bronze-skinned, Chuy's black hair close-cropped. Maria's long braid looked like melted caramel.

"Water's out all over town," Chuy said, dabbing at his brow with a napkin. "I rode my bike into town to make sure the shop was locked up tight. Same story everywhere."

"Did you see Kate?" Martha asked. "She said she was walking over with you."

"We knocked, but she didn't answer," Maria said. "We figured she was already here."

Emma's worry uncoiled like a snake at the base of her skull. She'd only just met Kate, but she hadn't looked well. The door opened again. A slender Asian woman in her sixties, her black hair streaked with silver, introduced herself as Susan. She lifted a small basket covered with a cloth. When she pulled the cloth back, Emma saw jars of golden liquid inside. "Honey from Iris's hives— my wife," she said, setting it on the coffee table. "We meant to stop by to welcome you to the neighborhood. Iri isn't feeling well, so she stayed home."

"Oh," Emma said, surprised. Who thought about bringing a housewarming present in the middle of a crisis? Someone with her act together, Cody's voice whispered in her ear.

Diane from across the street arrived next, her copper braid coming loose. Her freckled face was pink like a rose. "Sorry I'm late. Randy had me inventorying what's left of the perishables." She glanced around the room and said, "This whole thing is crazy. The power being out is bad enough, but no water—"

The screen door banged open. Diane jumped, her hand clutching her chest. "Hey, Pete," she said, as a stocky, balding man with what looked like a permanent frown strode inside. "Good think you knocked, or I'd have had a heart attack."

"This is a waste of time," he said, scowling like his life depended on it. He examined the chaotic, half-unpacked living room with hard gray eyes. "The backup for the water system here is a joke."

He glared at everyone, but his expression transformed when

he saw Maria. "I didn't know you were coming," he said, his voice warming. "Guess nothing's getting done now."

Maria laughed. "Come sit by me, *idiota*."

Pete grinned, then seemed to remember that he thought the meeting was a waste of time. He resumed scowling and sat by Maria. He must be here for the water, Emma thought.

"Good to see you too, Pete," Martha said, her tone dry.

Emma looked down to hide a smile. The final arrivals, Janice Miller and her husband, and Karen White, arrived together—and not. Janice swept into the house. Emma looked at the HOA president in stunned awe as she made a grand and ridiculous entrance into a regular ranch home. Janice had traded her stylish athleisure wear for pristine linen pants that looked crisp from ironing and a sleeveless blouse, her makeup still perfect despite the heat. She looks like a real estate agent, Emma thought. She pegged Janice as in her early fifties and revised her assessment. She looked like a real estate agent as a second career after she'd raised perfect but oppressed children who were old enough to do more for themselves.

"I brought cookies," Janice announced, holding out a plate wrapped in plastic. When she pulled back the plastic wrap, the smell of slightly scorched chocolate made Emma's nose wrinkle. "Baked them before... well, you know," she said, her hand fluttering in the air.

"How thoughtful," Emma said. Janice smiled, as if praise was her due, and set the cookies on the coffee table beside the pitcher of water. She didn't bother to introduce her husband, a tall man with thinning hair, who slipped through the door like an afterthought. Karen trailed in Janice's wake like the plain stepsister, hovering at Janice's shoulder like a nervous bird.

Janice's eyes swept the room, cataloging those present. Her gaze lingered on the water containers on the kitchen table that were visible through the doorway. "I see you've been busy, Mrs. Greer."

Emma breathed through a flash of irritation. Even during a

crisis, it wasn't against the law to fill containers with water. "Please, call me Emma. And yes, I was worried the water would quit working. I filled up as many containers as I could."

"How proactive of you," Janice said, a chill in her voice. Her tight smile didn't reach her eyes. She took a seat beside her husband, arranging herself with practiced poise. Karen perched on the chair next to her, twisting her thin hands in her lap.

Emma looked around the room. Eleven people from a neighborhood of seventy homes. It didn't feel like much, but they had to start somewhere. She'd prepared a mental list of topics, but now her throat tightened. She was a newcomer with a baby and a husband who was only God knew where. When her eyes prickled, warning of tears, she blinked a few times. *I can't think about that now.*

"Thank you all for coming," she began, her voice steadier than she felt. "I know it's hot and uncomfortable, and I'm not sure what I was thinking when I said we could meet here." She gestured around the room. "We're not even unpacked. But I think we all realize we need to look after each other."

"That's putting it mildly," Pete muttered. "This could go on for months."

A ripple of unease passed through the room. "Let's focus on what we know," Emma said. "The power's been out for almost two days and anything with electronics doesn't work—cell phones, cars. And now the water's stopped."

"Older vehicles still run," Pete said. "Tom's truck, Chuy's Charger, my Suburban. Older generators, too, or anything in a—" He stopped, as if catching himself.

When he didn't say more, Chuy said, "I think I have the same idea as Pete about what may have happened."

All eyes turned to Chuy, but Pete interrupted. "It's a coronal mass ejection. Anyone with half a brain knows that." He looked around the room, his scowl suggesting he thought most of them didn't.

Don't wanna share the glory, huh? Emma thought. This guy was a piece of work.

"I agree," Chuy said. "I've been interested in astronomy since I was a kid. I really got into it when I was in the Peace Corps, in Mongolia." His eyes softened, his voice becoming dreamy. "You wouldn't believe the stars there. Anyway, now I watch the NOAA website—the National Oceanic and Atmospheric Administration. They have a Space Weather Prediction Center that I follow pretty closely. Everyone got the text about the solar flare the other day, right?"

Heads around the room nodded. Emma has missed the text. At this point, it didn't matter.

Chuy continued. "Usually, solar flares are no big deal. I think the flare was a lot stronger than they realized, or there was a coronal mass ejection at the same time."

Maria said to her husband, "Chuy, get to the point. Everyone's eyes are glazing over."

"I'd like to know what he's talking about," Karen said.

"I'll make it quick," Chuy said, now a little pink in the face, though he gave Maria a warm smile. "A CME is a massive burst of energy and magnetic field from the sun. If one hits the Earth's magnetic field just right, it can fry electronics, power grids, anything with modern circuitry. That's why only older vehicles still run. And it makes sense that communication is so difficult.

"I almost said something when we were all talking the other day, and again at the town meeting, but I didn't want to scare people. And the meeting... well." He shrugged, adding, "Everything fits."

Pete pounced. "This country's grid has been vulnerable to a CME or EMP for years, but nothing ever got done about it. Every administration just kicks the can down the road." He looked around the room at every person. "Now it's hit the fan."

Emma tried not to roll her eyes. *There's always a head case, every freaking time.*

It was why she'd hated group projects from kindergarten

through law school. It wasn't simply vindication, probably after years of snickers behind his back, burning in Pete's eye. The guy sounded excited.

Emma said, "I thought it might be an EMP. I'm a patent attorney. One of my clients made hardened electronics for the military, so I figure it was—"

"An EMP is caused by a nuclear weapon detonated in the atmosphere," Pete said, interrupting her. "A CME is a natural phenomenon. It might not seem it, but we're lucky it's not an EMP. Then we'd be at war."

Emma narrowed her gaze. "Okay. Like I was saying, if we're right about it being a *C M E*"—she emphasized every letter, a wisp of sarcasm in her voice—"how long until things are fixed?"

Chuy exchanged a glance with Pete. "That's the problem. We don't know the extent of the places affected. If it's localized, the recovery will be a lot faster. But if it's widespread—if it hit a large portion of the country or beyond—repairs could take months, maybe years."

The room fell silent as the implications sank in. Nothing electronic would work, which meant all the things they were used to —electricity, clean water, access to food and health care, even weather reports—would no longer function as they had.

Karen's voice wavered as she said, "That's impossible. The government would have emergency systems. The military—"

"My understanding is that some military equipment is hardened against EMPs, but not all," Emma said.

"Civilian infrastructure isn't the same as military," Pete said. "That's why you have to prepare yourself."

"But the mayor said they're working on solving the water and power problems," Janice said, as if this settled the matter. She dabbed at her forehead with a napkin. "We need to follow proper, official channels."

"The mayor doesn't know anything more than we do," Martha said. "You saw how unprepared they were at the meeting."

"I've known Ken Dawson for thirty years," Tom said. "He's a good man, but he's out of his depth."

"That's why we're here," Emma said. "To figure out what we can do as a neighborhood while we wait for larger solutions."

"We should vote on a neighborhood committee," Janice declared. "With proper representation and leadership."

Emma fought the urge to roll her eyes. "I think making sure everyone is okay and establishing a committee can happen at the same time. And we can coordinate with the police department to avoid duplication of effort where we can."

Pete snorted. "Police can't handle this. Seven officers for the whole town? They're overwhelmed already."

"We can still work with them," Emma countered.

"I disagree," Janice said. "The HOA has emergency protocols—"

"For normal power outages and snowstorms," Martha said. "Not for this."

Janice's mouth tightened. "The principles are the same. We need to maintain order and property standards—"

"We need to ensure people have water and food," Emma interrupted, unable to keep the incredulity from her voice. "Property standards are pretty low on the list right now."

Janice sniffed. "Easy for you to say as a renter. Some of us have investments to protect."

For a moment, Emma just stared at her. What was the woman on? "We bought this house, not that it's relevant."

Janice wrinkled her nose like she smelled something nasty. "The HOA bylaws give us authority to protect community standards—"

"Do you have a copy of those bylaws, Janice?" Emma said, her voice snapping like a whip.

Janice blinked, as if she wasn't used to her authority being challenged. "Well, no. They're on my laptop and the community website. I don't have a printed copy."

"So, they're inaccessible without power or the internet,"

Emma said, her irritation plain. "Too bad you don't have a printed copy. I *am* an attorney. I'd love to review them."

Chuy couldn't suppress a smile and tried to cover it by yawning. Karen's eyes shifted between her friend and Emma, like she was trying to weigh which would be the winning side. Pete didn't bother hiding his smirk.

"Then what do you suggest, *Mrs. Greer*?" Janice asked, emphasizing Emma's name as if to remind everyone she was a newcomer. "That we panic? Start hoarding supplies?"

"Just the opposite," Emma said, looking Janice in the eye. "I'm suggesting we work together. Share information and check on vulnerable neighbors. Make sure everyone has what they need to get through this until help arrives."

"It sounds like you've got it all figured out," Janice snapped. She stood up so fast she looked like a jack-in-the-box leaping up on its spring. She snatched the cookies from the table and gave Emma a tight smile. "I'll leave you to it."

She turned on her heel and marched out the door. Her husband smiled apologetically. "She's a little wound up," he murmured before following her out the door.

Karen rose as well. "I think I'll go. You seem to have things in hand."

"I wish you wouldn't," Emma said. Her brain hadn't quite caught up to Janice's outburst. Janice had taken the cookies and gone home, like a spoiled child.

Karen bit her lip, then added, "Thanks for having me."

Quiet settled over the room. After Karen left, Emma said, "Wow. Did she really just take her cookies and go home?"

"Janice is going to be a problem," Carrie said with a sigh. "She's a member of our church and—well, I hate to be unchristian, but when Tom was on the board..." Her voice faded. That seemed to be as far as she was willing to go, but the implication was clear.

Tom's mouth turned down at the corners, the wrinkles around his blue eyes deepening. "Carrie's right."

Emma said. "So, what do we do?"

"Start without her," Diane answered. "Randy can't get through to the regional office. He and I were talking about distributing what's left at the grocery store, especially the perishables. We've only got another day's worth of fuel for the backup generators."

"Hasn't anyone from the mayor's office approached you about using your refrigerators? Surely they can get fuel for them. It would really help people out and save a lot of food," Emma asked.

Pete snorted. Diane said, "We approached them about it yesterday. They still haven't gotten back to us like they promised."

Emma would swear her brain wasn't working right. "They— What? Are you kidding me?"

"Of course she's not," Pete said, sounding impatient and unsurprised. "The authorities are never up to dealing with anything unexpected."

"Maybe we should try again," Emma said.

"I've spent a lot of time preparing," Pete said, folding his arms. "I'm not giving away my supplies. If other people aren't prepared, that's not my problem."

Emma saw Tom wince, as if he'd been expecting Pete's reaction. Susan Chau spoke up for the first time, her voice soft but firm. "I was a nurse practitioner for forty years. Community health doesn't work that way. If your neighbors suffer, eventually you will too." Pete snorted but didn't argue. She carried on, saying, "In situations like this, basic needs come first. Water, food, medicine, shelter, security. Everything else is luxury."

"Exactly," Martha said. "We need to be systematic."

Susan nodded. "Actions speak louder than committee meetings."

A spark of hope ignited inside Emma as the group started planning. Even Pete, for all his not wanting to share bluster, hadn't left. Grace whimpered, then started to cry. Emma lifted her daughter, discovering a wet diaper. "I've got to change her. I'll be right back. And it might be cooler on the patio if anyone wants to go outside."

Emma carried Grace to the nursery and lay her on the changing table. She glanced out the open window as she bent down to get a diaper. The sun blazed in a clear sky, not a cloud in sight. She couldn't recall any rain in the last forecast she'd heard. The water in the containers in her kitchen, which had seemed so plentiful when she'd filled them, now seemed pitifully inadequate. And Cody was out there somewhere, if he was still alive. The thought came unbidden, a stab of fear almost taking Emma's breath away.

"Stop it," she said aloud. She straightened up and set the diaper on the changing table. "You poor thing," she said to Grace as she unfastened the wet diaper. "No wonder you're so unhappy."

A minute later, Grace's little bottom was dry. When Emma held her close, she gnawed at Emma's breast with her gummy little mouth. "Hungry too, huh?"

Emma sat down in the gliding rocker, the closeness between she and her baby wrapping around her like a hug. Emma brushed her finger over Grace's head before Grace caught Emma's pinky in her tiny hand. The curve of her cheek looked so much like Cody's that tears welled in Emma's eyes. "Daddy will be home soon, sweetheart," she said through the tightness that gripped her throat. "I know he will."

Grace squeezed her finger like she agreed. The voices of her neighbors in the living room were a soft murmur, like a song Emma could hear without making out the words. She barely knew the women and men down the hall, but here they were. Whatever came next, she and Grace weren't alone. They had people to help them until Cody got home. The small, imperfect, determined circle of neighbors in her living room might not be enough, but it was a start.

chapter
twenty

CODY

MONDAY, JULY 14
12:04 PM

Shock jolted through Cody when he saw the chain-link barrier at the top of the ramp. But beneath the shock, in the part of himself that knew but refused to believe how quickly things could collapse, resigned acceptance settled like a stone in his chest. An armed guard stood at the fence—added insurance against anyone trying to breach the barrier. Farther down the bridge crossing Lake Pend Orelle, Cody glimpsed another sharp corner of chain-link fence.

"I'm going to talk to him," he said. He swung his right foot over the bike, lowering his left foot to the pavement at the same time. He didn't want to land on his injured foot with all his weight, even for a moment. Despite heat radiating from the pavement, the weak breeze felt wonderful on his sweaty scalp. Even with the wind from their ride, the sun overhead promised the day's worst heat was yet to come.

Frost removed his helmet but stayed astride the motorcycle. "Think it'll do any good? They might be the same group shooting people in the back at the SureWay."

Cody had the same thought. He wouldn't get home if he ran afoul of people like that, but he also wouldn't be getting home if he gave up at every obstacle. He shrugged. "Won't know unless we try."

Frost pursed his lips like he'd tasted something sour. Then he switched off the motorcycle and dismounted. After a few steps up the ramp, with a better view of the bridge, Frost pointed. He'd seen what Cody had, though now Cody grasped what they faced. A hundred feet from the exit ramp stood several sections of free-standing chain-link fencing positioned beyond two police cruisers and three civilian SUVs. A sizeable crowd pressed against the far side of the fence. Beyond them, near the other end of the bridge, another blockade rose from the asphalt. They were trapped.

"This is bad," Frost muttered.

Cody nodded, half expecting Frost to suggest they leave. Foreboding roiled in the pit of Cody's stomach. Everything about what he saw here stank. The people trapped between the two chain-link barriers roasted in the brutal sun. No shade existed, not even a cloud for momentary relief—just gray concrete radiating heat like a forge.

A baby's wail cut through the drone of discontent, along with pleas for water. At the front by the chain-link fence, a woman gripped two small children's hands to keep them close. All three were red-faced and wilted like flowers tossed roadside. An elderly woman slumped against the chain-link toward the center of the bridge. Nobody helped her. They lacked the strength to spare. How long had these people been trapped here? And what did the local authorities think this would achieve beyond adding misery to everyone's predicament? Sweat trickled between Cody's shoulder blades and several damp patches of sweat had formed on his shirt front by the time they completed their short walk to the top of the ramp. A lot of people stuck on the bridge weren't dressed for protection from the sun, but many were. Most had some kind of rolling suitcase or duffel bag. They had not left their homes without some degree of planning.

When they reached the chain-link barrier, Cody and Frost waited in silence. A man stood with his back turned beyond one of the two vehicles reinforcing the chain link. Anger radiated from Frost like a predator coiling around Cody's body. "Keep your cool," Cody said to him.

Frost's contemptuous sidelong glance—his mouth a hard, downturned line below flashing, narrowed eyes—sent a shiver over Cody's shoulders. He never wanted that glare directed at him. A small start of surprise flared inside him at Frost's reaction to the suffering of these people. It didn't fit with what Cody thought he knew of Frost, the criminal. Maybe he had misjudged Frost the man by giving more weight to his crimes. Cody realized he didn't know why Frost had left the Army, nor the circumstances. The man had excelled as a Ranger. Why leave that behind to become a criminal?

"Don't worry about me," Frost said, his tone the kind used to bait a bully into a fight the bully didn't realize they were going to lose.

Cody didn't feel better despite Frost's reassurance. He shoved his concerns about Frost aside and called to the man beyond the chain-link barrier, "Hey there."

The man turned around. He wore a red baseball cap, the rounded, old-fashioned type. Cody saw he was just a kid, maybe twenty, and in civilian clothes. Upon seeing Cody and Frost, the young man's face hardened. "You can't come on the bridge."

"I can see that," Cody said. He tilted his head toward the people on the bridge. "What's going on there?"

"Refugees from farther south started arriving yesterday," the young man said. "We don't have room."

"Refugees?" Cody said, taken aback.

"From Coeur d'Alene mostly, but other places, too."

Speaking for the first time, Frost said, voice neutral, "It's bad in Coeur d'Alene?"

The young man shifted his attention to Caleb. "Same as here, just more people with fewer supplies. They lost water yesterday from what I understand, just like we did."

Cody's brain had filled with so many questions he didn't know where to start. He had read how urban centers would run out of food within days if there was a significant supply chain disruption. Given the hot weather, the situation might deteriorate more quickly simply because people were hot and uncomfortable. Settling on the simplest question, he said, "Why are they stuck on the bridge?"

"We don't have enough for them, so we put up the roadblock. But they don't want them farther south either, so they put up a roadblock, too."

"How long have they been there?" Cody asked, his stomach tightening. He was pretty sure he wasn't going to like the answer.

"Since yesterday," the young man said.

Cody blinked. They'd been on the bridge since yesterday? He opened his mouth, anger hot, but Frost cut him off. "Are you in charge here?"

The young man shook his head. "Chief Roberts is— damn, I mean Chief Estes is in charge. I'm just helping out."

"You have a new chief?" Frost said.

Something about his tone made Cody wonder what he had picked up on. Was the police chief just new, or had something happened to the previous one?

"Chief Roberts died yesterday."

"Oh," Cody said. Suddenly, the situation on the bridge made more sense. If they'd lost the police chief yesterday, it might be that someone with a lot less experience had gotten a battlefield promotion. Perhaps someone who wasn't ready for the job, let alone an emergency like this.

Frost said, "May we speak to Chief Estes, please? Is he here?"

When the young man didn't answer, Cody added, "I'm law enforcement, United States Marshal Service."

The young man pushed his baseball cap back from his forehead. "He's here but... Lemme see."

He turned away and shouted. A few minutes later, another man, this one an actual adult, joined him. After a hushed conversation, the older man nodded and left. The young man in the baseball cap said, "He's going to check, but no promises."

"Thank you." Cody stepped back from the chain-link barrier beside Frost. Lowering his voice, he said, "This is a real mess."

"If they haven't figured out they need to take some of those people by now, I don't think they will. Especially after what went down at SureWay. If they're willing to shoot looters, they won't think twice about letting people die of heatstroke."

Uneasy silence settled between them. Cody wanted to find a flaw in Frost's logic but couldn't. What were the cities like right now? How was Specter Lake handling this? Cody had thought it was a good place to settle—close enough to commute to Coeur d'Alene but small enough for the advantages of tight-knit communities. This place would have seemed the same.

A man in a police officer's uniform approached. "I'm Chief Estes," he said when he reached the fence. "I understand you're law enforcement."

Estes had the distracted bearing of someone trying to juggle too many balls, never mind keeping them in the air. Cody said, "Yes. I'm Deputy US Marshal Cody Greer. Is it okay if I reach into my back pocket to get my credentials for you?"

The police chief nodded, though his posture became more alert. Cody reached into his back pocket with care, keeping his movements slow and easy. The smooth leather of his badge wallet under his fingertips felt reassuring. This was something he had done countless times, although usually he kept his credentials in his front jacket pocket.

He held them up for Estes' inspection. The man's posture relaxed. "I've got a situation brewing here and not a lot of time.

How can I help you?" Then he added, directing his next comment to the young man in the red baseball cap, "Help me move this so I can talk here."

The younger man hurried over and helped move the barrier enough for him to slip through. Raised voices from the bridge barrier swelled, accompanied by chain link rattling. Shouts and demands to be let through carried on the slight breeze. Estes looked over, then back to Cody. Whatever the situation and bad calls that had been made, he was willing to speak to them. That counted for something.

"We need to cross the bridge," Cody said.

"Not possible," Estes answered.

"Then can we get some gasoline? We're headed to Specter Lake and don't have enough to backtrack. From the looks of things in town, I don't think we're getting gas there."

Estes frowned. "I can't help you with that. The guards are just a precaution to avoid problems. We need what gas we've got." He fished a handkerchief from his pocket and dabbed at his forehead. "Water stopped running yesterday and people are scared. We're a small police force. I've had to recruit other first responders and civilians to keep order. Even if I let you through, they won't let you pass on the other side. It's a waste of time."

"And you don't want those people rushing your fence if you let us through," Frost said. "What happens to them?"

"Hell if I know," Estes said. "We don't have the resources for refugees. Too many of them are coming north from Coeur d'Alene. I'm trying to get our neighbors on the other side to take some of these refugees. We can help some but not all of them."

There it was again—refugees. Cody looked over his shoulder at the shoreline of the lake the bridge spanned. "How do you plan to keep people out? You've got miles of lakeshore."

A flash of irritation in Estes' eyes made Cody regret his comment. "We're organizing a patrol of the lakefront. Look, I can't help you. You're going to have to figure it out."

"Chief Estes, please," Cody said. "As a professional courtesy, will you let us over the bridge?"

"No."

As Estes turned away, Frost said with an edge to his voice, "You might want to check in at the SureWay. If you've got rules of engagement—"

Estes rounded on them. "We won't tolerate looting," he spat, his face red with heat and anger. "Anyone who goes there is warned. I cannot have people hoarding supplies to the detriment of everyone else."

"So you're shooting them?" Cody said. "Are you going to let them die of heat and thirst, too?"

The murmurs of the crowd at the barrier on the bridge grew louder. Cody realized the rattling on the chain-link fence had been almost constant while he and Frost spoke to Chief Estes, that the murmur of the crowd had become cries of anger. Desperation. The men at the barrier tried to shout down the hundred strong crowd. The air crackled, like the fizz of a burning fuse.

"You can't pass, Marshal," Estes said, all pretense of friendliness gone. "Get out of here."

Cody said, "They're not refugees. They're Americans."

Estes didn't stop as he stalked away.

"We need to go," Frost said. "That barricade is about—"

The crowd's shouts erupted as a roar, drowning out Frost's words. The chain-link fence swayed, forward and back, forward and back. Then the swaying paused. As one, the desperate people pulled the fence toward themselves and then scattered away like marbles. The fence teetered, motionless for a split second. Then it fell, the guards unprepared. They had never considered it might be pulled down in that direction.

The crowd surged forward like water breaching a dam. Those too slow to clear the falling fence were pinned beneath, the metal trapping them rattling like dry bones. Cody's chest seized as the guards raised their weapons.

The first shot cracked sharp as a thunderclap.

A young woman in a faded jean shorts and a blue top jolted like she'd touched a subway third rail. Her mouth opened in surprise. She looked down at a crimson stain spreading across her stomach. Two little girls still held her hands, their matching pink shorts now splattered with red. The woman doubled over, clutching her belly. Blood seeped between her fingers under the blazing sun.

"Mommy?"

She collapsed between the little girls, her legs giving out all at once.

More shots. *Pop-pop-pop.*

A man in work coveralls spun as a bullet caught his shoulder. He stumbled forward against the tide of the panicked crowd. A second shot punched his back with a wet thud. His thick fingers clutched at the air before he pitched face-first to the scorching concrete.

Cody stood frozen, horror engulfing him as the guards kept firing. It did them no good. The fence was down.

chapter
twenty-one

CALEB

MONDAY, JULY 14
12:26 PM

Caleb felt the shift a heartbeat before it happened. The collective intake of breath. The air was charged like before a thunderstorm, when ionized energy buzzed against skin. The blink that crystallized a crowd into a mob, resignation transformed into desperation. The tension on the bridge crackled with it like static electricity. Then it broke.

"We need to go," he told Greer, his voice tight. "That barricade is about to—"

His words died as the crowd's pleas and anger became a roar. The chain-link fence swayed like a metal tide—forward and back, forward and back. Then came the pull. The fence wobbled, teetered, then crashed down onto some of the people closest to it.

Sweaty bodies surged forward in a wave. The fallen barrier rattled as people scrambled over. Pinned beneath the chain link, the unlucky souls too slow to get away screamed. Caleb's muscles had tensed, ready to run, when the first shot cracked through the air.

"Jesus Christ," Greer whispered beside him. Blood bloomed on a middle-aged man's chest like a bright-red poppy, jarring against his grimy white tee shirt. A look of confusion—like an accountant puzzling over numbers that didn't add up—filled his face as he fell forward.

More shots followed. The police chief yelled to cease fire, but most of the men posted at the barrier weren't trained for this. The contagion of fear kept them firing into the crowd.

Caleb's gaze locked on the woman he'd seen at the edge of the bridge. Her wide eyes reflected the fear swirling around all of them, sticky as honey. She had cleared the fallen fence and pushed through a gap between the police cruisers. She dragged her children with her, a boy about five and a girl about three. Her white knuckles clutched their hands as she pulled them through the melee.

Ruth.

She wasn't his sister, and yet the sight of her with two kids at her side made his brain stutter and his heart clench. The same desperation and fierce protectiveness that he felt for his sister during their moves between foster homes, never knowing if he could keep them together, hit Caleb like a brick.

A uniformed officer broke from the melee. He grabbed the woman by the hair, yanking her backward. Her mouth flew open, the din swallowing her scream. She was thrown to the concrete, torn from the screaming children's grasp. The officer raised his baton.

Caleb shoved aside the kid in the red baseball cap and bolted onto the bridge. His body used what he wanted to forget—how to find gaps and move through chaos, how to navigate the battlefield the bridge had become.

The officer's baton struck the woman at the crook of her neck and shoulder. Then Caleb barreled into him, driving his shoulder into the officer's rib cage. He'd forgotten about the ballistic vest the man wore. The impact rebounded into his shoulder even though the officer's feet lifted from the ground. The officer landed on the concrete hard, his breath knocked from his lungs with an *oof*.

In combat, he wouldn't stop there. He'd make sure the man stayed down. No time for that now. He turned to the woman. She stared up at him, dazed. Blood trickled from a fresh cut on her cheekbone. "Get up," Caleb shouted, extending his hand. "Now!"

She took his hand. Caleb pulled her up, so hard her toes dragged on the concrete. Eyes darting wildly, she zeroed in on her daughter. The girl stood frozen a few feet away, too overwhelmed to cry. Caleb scooped her up and shoved her into her mother's arms. Caleb snatched at the boy, just an arm's length away. His finger grazed the collar of his shirt, the cotton soft against his fingertips. Then the boy bolted into the surging crowd.

He saw a flash of the boy's blue shirt, then he was swallowed by the heaving mass of bodies. "Stay with me," Caleb said, gripping the woman's hand tighter.

He plunged them into the crowd after her son. The mob pushed against them like a living thing. Caleb used his size and strength to carve a path, ignoring the throb in his shoulder and jaw from his foolish tackle. Another flash of blue darted between two men ahead of him. Caleb lunged. His hand closed around the boy's arm, as skinny as a pencil. The child fought against his grip, his thrashing limbs clutching at the people surrounding them.

"Tyler! It's me, baby. It's Mommy!"

The boy's shriek stabbed through Caleb's chest. He hoisted the boy onto his hip and dragged the small family free of the crush. The boy reached for his mother. Caleb pulled them in his wake to the top of the ramp. The marshal's face, white as chalk, sagged with relief when he saw them. The men trying to hold the line at the downed barrier were losing. Gunfire kept erupting from their weapons.

Flesh tore. Bone cracked. A man dropped, his leg twisted wrong beneath him. A teenaged boy tripped, stumbled, clutching his chest. Blood spilled from between his fingers. An elderly woman collapsed, her white blouse turning ruby red. Screams echoed off the water below. The bridge had become a charnel house.

"Can you drive with your foot?" Caleb barked at Greer as he shoved the woman and children through the gap.

Greer's eyes snapped to his. "Yes."

"Let's go." They ran down the ramp to the motorcycle faster than the marshal could have managed before. To the woman, Caleb said, "Get on the motorcycle with your daughter in front of you. I'll take your son."

She nodded. The marshal, then the woman, mounted the motorcycle. The girl squeezed between them. "Hold on to him," Caleb instructed, pulling her closest hand to Greer's waist. "Don't move, just sit still."

The boy watched, his eyes as wide as dinner plates. "Mama!"

Caleb said, "Do you trust your mom?" The boy nodded, his mouth puckered from crying. "Then trust me, too. Go," he said to the marshal, jutting his chin west. "Ten blocks if you can. I'll catch up."

Greer hesitated. "Are you sure?"

"I'm sure. Just go."

The motorcycle growled to life. Greer let the bike drift backward. When the back tire touched the ramp's side barrier, he turned and accelerated down, disappearing from view.

chapter
twenty-two

CALEB

MONDAY, JULY 14
12:40 PM

Caleb bolted down the ramp, the boy in his arms. Carrying the child piggyback was out of the question; he was too big and the boy too small. The boy's arms wrapped around his neck like a small octopus. Once clear of the ramp, Caleb broke into a flat-out run. He cut through an alley between two commercial buildings, hugging close to a wall. He looked for cover, knowing ahead there'd be open spaces where they'd be more vulnerable.

"Where's my mommy?" the boy asked, his voice shaking.

The distant gunfire had stopped. "Somewhere safe," Caleb said. "We'll see her in a few minutes."

What he had told the boy could be the truth. That didn't stop him from hoping like hell he wasn't misleading him. They emerged from the alley onto a residential street. It was so quiet, so... tranquil.

A rush of vertigo slashed through Caleb's head. "Whoa," he

said softly. He'd never felt this before—like stepping into a new world conjured into being, a world that wasn't real. Even returning from combat hadn't triggered this disorientation of light limbs and foggy brain. He studied the houses they passed, trim ranch homes and Craftsman era bungalows with tidy yards. Children's toys on the porches, a swing hanging from a tree. It felt so normal. The only hint something had changed was the lack of sprinklers and the sleeping bags on porches, presumably to escape the heat of houses lacking air-conditioning. But even those subtle clues didn't feel out of the ordinary.

Caleb shook himself and the dreamy quality dissipated, leaking away like air from a punctured bicycle tire. He kept moving, noticing the streets were all straight. The neighborhood used a grid system. The familiar burn of his muscles made him more aware of his legs and his breath, heavy but not labored. The weight of the child in his arm felt heavy somehow, so heavy he might drop him. The dreamy feeling washed over him again. It was the heat, he realized, and not enough water. Sweat soaked his shirt as the sun beat down like his drill sergeant from basic. He was still sweating, which was good. That meant he didn't have heatstroke yet.

After eight blocks, the neighborhood changed. Larger lots, bigger houses, but the biggest difference was the trees. Massive maples lined both sides of the street. Their branches stretched out to touch those from the other side, providing shade so deep his eyes needed a moment to adjust. The temperature dropped beneath the leafy canopy, sending a shiver up Caleb's spine. It was still hot, surely eighty degrees, but it felt much cooler.

Caleb slowed his pace, scanning for signs of the marshal and the motorcycle. Had he taken this street or was he on another block? His ears pricked up at a rumble drifting on the breeze. Caleb followed the sound. He turned the corner and slowed to a walk. Fifty yards ahead, a single-story ranch house of red brick sat beneath the shade of two enormous beech trees and underneath the canopy was the marshal on the motorcycle. He killed the engine. For a moment, they just sat there. Then the woman dismounted awkwardly. Once on the ground, she scooped up the rag doll limp girl. The marshal dismounted.

"There's your mommy," Caleb said, pointing ahead.

When the boy lifted his head from Caleb's shoulder, a wave of emotion hit him like a freight train. The weight of the boy's sweaty head when it had rested on his shoulder, the small, too warm body close to Caleb's own. He'd held his niece like this when she was small. Cradled his infant nephew in his arm. His stomach hollowed when he thought of how much bigger they were now. He had missed so much, given up his life to wage a pointless rebellion against a system that had wronged him. Like an idea that had percolated inside him for years, he knew. All this time, all he'd accomplished was keeping the pain of his loss alive. He'd pulled it into the present, insisting on its poisonous presence. Even worse, he had done it to himself.

The marshal turned around, as if sensing his approach, his hand halfway behind him, reaching for his gun. He huffed out a breath when he saw it was Caleb. "You okay?"

The boy called out, "Mommy!"

The woman whirled around, relief flooding her face. "Tyler! Oh, baby..."

She rushed forward as Caleb lowered the boy to the ground. Tyler shot away like a comet burning across the night sky. He collided with his mother as she dropped to her knees. Children wrapped in her arms, she started to weep.

"How are you just getting here?" Caleb asked. "I can't run that fast."

"I went too far before I realized it. Had to circle back."

The front door of the house opened. Caleb turned, instantly wary. A man in his mid-thirties stepped out, barefoot, dressed in cargo shorts and a faded tee shirt. His blond hair riffled in the breeze. He was halfway down the walk when a dark-haired woman with light-bronze skin appeared in the door and followed.

"Are you okay?" the man asked, eyes roving from the tearful family to the marshal and finally to Caleb.

The marshal reached toward his back pocket. "I'm US Deputy Marshal Cody Greer," he said, pulling out his badge wallet and flipping it open for the man to see. "We need help."

The man stepped closer, squinting as he inspected the marshal's credentials. Then he stepped back. His wife, or so Caleb assumed, had followed and stopped behind him. Her light-blue eyes were startling, like pale sapphires that popped against her darker skin. Her brow wrinkled, concern pinching the edges of her mouth. "We thought we heard gunshots but weren't sure."

The man's gaze shifted to the woman's bloodied face and torn shirt. Already a bruise purpled her neck and shoulder from the blow she had suffered. His posture tensed, and he shot a wary glance at Caleb and the marshal. Crouching beside her, he said, "Are you okay? You'll be safe with us."

The woman looked at him, blinking like a prisoner pulled into the light after months in a dungeon. "No, I'm okay," she said, sounding confused. When she shrugged, she winced. "Oh. Oh no, they didn't do this."

The man looked at his wife, a question in his eyes. He wanted to know what she thought, if she believed this woman's story. His wife bit her lip, then sized them up. Caleb saw the change in her eyes as she decided. "You should come inside. Maybe pull your motorcycle around the side of the house? I'm Lisa, by the way." She motioned to the mother and children to follow her. "Let's get you cleaned up."

"I'm Dan," the man said as he stood. He extended his hand first to the marshal, then to Caleb, his grip firm. He was friendly enough, but the way he'd checked in with the woman meant he wasn't accepting anything at face value. That alone made Caleb like him. "What happened to you?" he said.

Caleb said. "You probably wouldn't believe it."

"Is there room in your garage to park the motorcycle there?"

the marshal asked, and Caleb understood immediately. Getting it out of sight was better than parking in the driveway.

"Sure," Dan said. "Just give me a sec. I need to pull the manual release."

After the marshal parked the motorcycle and they pulled the door down, Dan led them inside.

Gooseflesh rippled up Caleb's arms as they stepped into a tiled entryway. He didn't like following a stranger into an unfamiliar house, and didn't hear the background hum of air-conditioning, but the house was still cool. Candles and a battery-operated lantern were on a table just inside the front door.

Parallel to the street, along the front wall of the house, a hallway was lost in shadows. Ahead him, at the house's rear, was a combination living and dining room, the back wall almost entirely glass from floor-to-ceiling. Dan led them in that direction to the kitchen, which was on the right before the living area, directly behind the garage. The woman Caleb had rescued sat at the kitchen table, her daughter in her lap and son pressed against her side. Lisa set a package of wet wipes on the table. "I can clean that cut, if that's okay."

The woman nodded. To Caleb and the marshal, she said, "I'm Jenny. Thank you... both of you." Her brown eyes filled with tears that spilled down her pale cheeks. She pushed her light-brown hair behind her ear and said, voice breaking, "I don't know what I would have done..."

The marshal stepped closer to her and squeezed her shoulder. "You're safe now." He smiled, looked at the little girl, and said, "Who are these little monkeys?" Both children burrowed against Jenny, hiding their faces. "Or maybe they're little baby kangaroos."

Jenny smiled. "This is Nora. She's three. And this is Tyler. He's five and a bit of an escape artist."

"Nice to meet you both. I'm Cody."

Nora chanced a peek, revealing a strong resemblance to her mother. Tyler stayed where he was, safe against his mother's side.

Greer glanced at Caleb as he stepped back, his eyes reflecting that he knew how hollow his promise of safety might be. When Dan returned with bottled water, Caleb realized he hadn't noticed him leave. I'm getting sloppy, he thought, or the dehydration is affecting me more than I realized. Now that the rush of helping Jenny and her children and running from the bridge was over, his body felt heavy and his mind sluggish. He cracked open the water and drank it all in one go.

After indulging in the water, the marshal said, "It's cool in here."

"You picked a good street to stop," Dan said, gesturing for them to sit at the table. "The trees keep the house comfortable. This neighborhood has trees like this on every street. Before the power went out, we hardly ever used the A/C."

The marshal sat at the table to Jenny's right, the wall the kitchen shared with the garage behind him. Caleb walked to the side of the table opposite Jenny, where an open door led to a narrow side yard. There was a six-foot privacy fence made of wood; that was good. Hard for anyone to see them outdoors. He relaxed a little as he leaned against the wall next to the door. Out of habit, Caleb scanned the house, noting windows and exits.

Lisa collected the discarded wipes that Jenny had used to wipe her and her kids' faces and threw them away. She turned toward them. "What's going on?"

No one answered. Lisa and Dan looked at them, then each other, as a tense silence fell. Caleb glanced to the marshal, who he was pretty sure shared his thoughts. While they were showing kindness now, this couple lived here. They might know some of the men on the bridge. They might be related to the police chief for all they knew. They needed more information.

"How long has the power been out?" Caleb asked.

Dan's brow furrowed, his surprise at the change of subject plain. "This is the third day."

"The same as in Montana."

Lisa perked up at that. "Is that where you were? Dan's from

outside Helena. We can't get hold of his folks with the phones out. We moved back here a couple of years ago." She crossed her arms and rubbed them like she was cold. "Everything not working... it's unnerving."

Caleb had relaxed the tiniest fraction when he heard Dan was from Montana, but when Lisa said they'd 'moved back,' his wariness flared again. "I guess you've seen the auroras."

Lisa huffed out a breath. "They're pretty hard to miss. People are saying it's an EMP."

"Caleb thinks it's a CME, a coronal mass ejection. It does the same thing as an EMP," Cody said.

Dan slipped his arm around Lisa's shoulders. She leaned into him, for the first time seeming not as self-assured. "I told you," she said, nudging her husband with an elbow. "Without the internet to check for the answer, he didn't believe it was a CME because of who was saying it."

"Not without good reason," Dan countered.

"I know, but still," she said. "It's our neighbor who said it was a natural event, not an EMP. Growing up, Mister Harrison was that crabby, weird neighbor. The one who sees government conspiracies under every rock. He's harmless, but..." She shrugged.

"Strange," Caleb supplied.

She nodded. "But when I thought about it, it made sense. There was a solar flare the same day. Did you know about that?"

Caleb nodded. "Yeah. Are your folks local? Are they okay?"

"They passed last year," Lisa said. "Car accident."

"Oh," Caleb said. "I'm sorry to hear it."

The gears of his mind whirred and clicked. He wasn't sure how to play this. That uncertainty itched at the base of his skull and sent an electric tingle across his skin. Reading people, a room —he'd learned that of necessity when he was a child. It was part of why he had excelled when he was in the service, and after. Even though it hadn't been his or the marshal's doing, Lisa and Dan might fault them for what had happened at the bridge. Lisa had grown up here, even if she hadn't spent her entire life here. Caleb knew he had done the right thing, but why would they take the word of strangers—one of whom had assaulted a police officer— over people they knew?

He caught the marshal's eye, hoping the marshal had a better idea of how much they should reveal, because all he saw was downside. The marshal's troubled gaze suggested he wasn't sure what their play should be, either.

"I live in Specter Lake," the marshal said. "We tried to get over the bridge, but it was closed."

"Ugh," Lisa said. "I heard about that yesterday. I wanted to go see if it was true, see if I could help, but Dan asked me not to. He was afraid there might be trouble."

"It was the right call," the marshal answered. He bit his lip, the calculation in his eyes plain. "Look," he said, lifting his chin. "I don't know who you know and I'm not trying to put my foot in it. We talked to the police chief at the bridge right before things got out of hand. That's what the gunshots were from, but we weren't part of it."

Lisa and Dan stared at him. Dan's posture tensed. He took a step forward, like he was readying to shield his wife. Lisa's gaze slid to Jenny and her kids. Her sharp study of them made Caleb feel like he was seeing them for the first time, too. The small family was sunburned, exhausted, and scared.

Lisa put her hand on Dan's shoulder. "The police chief—Mr. Roberts—died yesterday. He had a heart attack. I think his pacemaker quit working when all this"—she motioned at the ceiling— "started." She shook her head and sighed. "Bobby Estes took his place. I dated Bobby in high school. He's a nice guy but he couldn't keep order at a bingo night. What happened?"

Caleb almost sighed aloud in relief. He didn't feel like they were out of the woods, but Lisa seemed willing to hear them out. The marshal's posture had relaxed, too. He said, "Caleb and I started out in Montana."

As he told their story, the marshal glossed over the fact that he'd gone to Montana to take Caleb into custody. He didn't explain why they'd been traveling together. Rather than being reassured by this, tension coiled in Caleb's shoulders and neck. The marshal's attitude seemed different since they'd arrived here. Nothing Caleb could put his finger on but the way he talked about their journey here was different. Caleb could see questions in the man's eyes as he spoke, like he was working on a puzzle whose pieces had changed halfway through and no longer fit together.

Jenny reminded Caleb of his sister, Ruth. They didn't resemble one another, but Jenny's kids were little, her daughter's age in the same ballpark as Ruth's daughter the last time he'd seen her in person. It had twigged his emotions in a way he hadn't expected. Muscle memory, from combat and years of training, had done the rest.

He had compromised himself back there. Shown the marshal a side of himself he kept hidden. The side willing to put himself in danger to protect those who needed protection. Hiding that side of himself wasn't a habit born of the past few years since he'd started robbing banks, but one he'd had since he was a kid. Since their father had abandoned him and Ruth to the mercy of strangers. He only felt comfortable with that part of himself during deployment. There, it had been an asset, not a liability.

Shit, he thought, closing his eyes for a long moment. If he was going down this rabbit hole, he was more tired and mentally taxed than he'd realized.

Dan had pulled lunch meat, cheeses, and mayonnaise from a cooler by the sink while the marshal spoke. While they listened to the marshal, he and Lisa had made sandwiches that they now passed around. Caleb accepted a sandwich from Lisa with a genuine nod of thanks. He had eaten that morning but it felt like twenty years ago.

Nora had curled up in her mother's lap and fallen asleep. Tyler had wandered to the couch and lay across it, sacked out, his thumb in his mouth, his dark hair a jumble. Caleb felt himself soften as he watched the sleeping boy. He said a silent prayer for Ruth, Jodi, and Peter. That they were safe—together—and if they ran into trouble, someone was willing to step in and help them.

Longing to see his sister, to make up for the time he had wasted, burned hot in Caleb's chest. It tightened his throat, so much that he found it hard to swallow his food. A prickle in the corners of his eyes warned of tears. Caleb couldn't remember the last time he'd cried. He couldn't remember the last time he had let himself feel as much as he had these last few days. He took a deep breath, blinking hard to will the tears and emotion away.

The marshal could plan to take him in to his heart's content. Caleb didn't care. He had plans of his own. First, he was going to Coeur d'Alene to find his sister, niece, and nephew. Then he would get them somewhere safe and take care of them, like he should have been doing all along. He couldn't do so right now, as much as he wanted to. It made sense to keep a low profile in case anyone was looking for them, and they needed more fuel.

For now, he would do the one thing he could: make sure Jenny and her kids were safe. That was what his sister would expect of him. What the man he used to be would have expected, too.

chapter
twenty-three

CODY

MONDAY, JULY 14
1:10 PM

Cody's fingers trembled as he took another bite of his sandwich. Fatigue had woven its way between his muscle fibers and into his bones. He flexed his injured foot beneath the table, wincing. The pain was a persistent throb he could ignore during their flight from the bridge. Ignoring it was no longer an option.

He watched Frost from the table. Frost leaned against the wall, keeping an eye on the windows and doors, but not like when they'd first arrived. Cody had assumed his hypervigilance was a byproduct of his time in the service or his line of 'work.' Now, he wasn't so sure.

Cody had read Frost's file, so he knew Frost's father was in prison for killing a man at a bar. The file hadn't mentioned Frost's father was an alcoholic, but there was no reason it would. His father's substance abuse hadn't been relevant to Frost's crimes, at least on the surface. Frost had a younger sister. The two of them had gone into foster care since their mother had died of cancer before the shooting. Going into the system might have led to any number of poor outcomes. That hadn't happened. His sister went to college and became a nurse while Frost had joined the Army, becoming a Ranger. By all indications, he'd been good at his job.

What had happened? Why had he gone from decorated soldier to armed bank robbery? Not just a soldier, but a special operator. The dedication necessary was extraordinary. Many graduates of Ranger School—a grueling test of mettle, dedication, and resourcefulness—went on to other assignments. Frost had gone on to join the Ranger Regiment to be a special operator. There'd been some kind of dustup with a former commanding officer. The file had been light on details, but Frost had been honorably discharged. It couldn't have been that serious. And then he'd become a criminal. How did that make sense?

Today, Frost jumped in to help Jenny and her kids. Cody didn't know what to think. Frost had come back to the plane and helped him, but there was self-interest in that. If the CME was localized and Frost escaped while Cody died, he would be looking at a manslaughter charge at the very least. He would have been held responsible. Cody got the motivation there. But throwing himself in harm's way for strangers who meant nothing to him? How did that fit?

The image of him barreling into that officer replayed in Cody's mind: the arc of the baton raised to rain down another blow. Frost's speed—he was like the goddamned Flash—and the force he'd used to take the officer down. To Cody's eye, it had been the minimum required. Once he had the officer beating Jenny on the ground, he hadn't bothered to do more. It hadn't been necessary. Maybe if there hadn't been a melee around them, he'd have done more, but Cody didn't think so. His goal had been to help a defenseless woman and her small children. Frost had acted with a moral clarity that contradicted everything Cody thought he knew about the man. Criminals as good as Frost had been—nine robberies in six years, millions of dollars, with no shots fired and no casualties—didn't risk their freedom for random strangers.

Frost had a sister, though. The FBI had never made a connection between them criminally. They'd never been able to establish that they were in contact after his first year as a fugitive. Even then, it had been Ruth Frost who informed the authorities when her brother contacted her. If they were using phones, it would be burners—impossible to trace. It was purchasing the phones where people got sloppy, but that hadn't happened. Frost was too smart for email, the same for mail. Cody had assumed they were estranged, but Frost wanted to find his sister and her kids. He had never said more than that; it was how he said it. Their connection was deep and present, not an artifact.

So what was it? What was going on with the guy?

Lisa said, "Think they're down for the count?"

Cody refocused his attention, the non sequitur question pulling him away from a puzzle he didn't have the pieces to solve. Jenny had returned from settling Nora on the couch next to her brother. The bruise on her neck had darkened to a deep purple black against her pale skin. Lisa got up from her chair and gestured for Jenny to take it, then leaned against the wall by the kitchen door a few steps away. Jenny sat, her eyes red-rimmed with exhaustion. "We'd been walking for a day before getting stuck on the bridge. They're exhausted." She sighed. "Me too."

Cody smiled. "I feel you there." More gently, he asked, "How did you end up there?"

Jenny rubbed at her eyes, then sighed again. "We live in Coeur d'Alene. When everything went dark, I thought it was just a regular power failure. Everyone did. We stayed home the first day and went out to watch the sky that night like everyone else."

She tucked a strand of her dark hair behind her ear. "But the next night things changed. There was no news, like none. Everyone was getting antsy, me included, and it was so hot.

Tempers get short when it's hot, you know? I didn't have much food in the house. I heard gunshots that night.

"My neighbors, Mark and Betsy, came over real late. They watch the kids for me sometimes. Their car still worked—Bill said because it was old. They were leaving for their summer place, north of Sandpoint, early the next morning. When they asked if I wanted to come, I said yes.

"The water went out overnight. We left so early, it was barely light out. There was already looting, people fighting in store parking lots. I was so glad we were leaving."

Jenny's voice trailed off for a moment before she continued. "We were stopped at a roadblock near Cocolalla. They were dressed like police but it was obvious pretty fast they weren't, and they had guns. They took the car. Took everything. We've been walking since."

"What happened to your neighbors?" Caleb asked.

"I don't know," she said. Her voice tightened and tears flooded her eyes. "Tyler wanted to see if there were any fish in the water, so I took him and Nora to the side so they could see the lake. Anything to distract them, you know? We got pushed forward when the fence fell. I don't know what happened to them."

Lisa stepped closer and placed a hand on Jenny's shoulder. "Dan and I will look for them. You don't have to go anywhere. You and your kids can stay with us for as long as you need."

Jenny twisted in her chair and looked up at Lisa. "We can't impose—"

"You can," Dan said. "There's plenty of room. Besides, we're safer together."

Cody caught the approving nod Frost gave Dan. To Jenny, he said, "You've seen what it's like out there. It's gonna get worse before it gets better. You have your kids to think of." Frost's ice-blue eyes held Jenny's gaze and something passed between them. Recognition, maybe?

"Why don't you get some rest?" Lisa said to Jenny. "Dan

made up the foldout in the basement. We'll wake you up for dinner if you want, or you can just sleep. Whatever you want."

Jenny nodded. After she and Lisa left, Cody said to Frost, "We should see if we can find some gas and head out soon. Can you help us figure out a route?" he asked Dan.

Dan's eyebrows knitted together in confusion. "You should at least stay the night. You both look exhausted." To Cody, he added, "And you're hurt. I've seen you limping."

"We're so close to Specter Lake," Cody said. Lisa returned and stood in the doorway. "I just want to get home to my wife. Besides, we don't want to cause you any trouble."

"What if she's not there?" Lisa said. "Jenny left her home. She might have needed to go, too."

Cody's whole body contracted at the suggestion. Emma wouldn't leave unless she had to, and Specter Lake wasn't a big place like Sandpoint. "She'll be there. She'll wait for me."

The confidence in his voice sounded hollow, even to himself. Emma was smart—if it wasn't safe, she'd leave for somewhere that was. If he got home to an empty house, he'd just have to hope she left a note saying where she'd gone.

"Staying overnight might not be a bad idea," Frost said.

Cody stared at him. They were so close. If they didn't leave now, he might explode. "Why?"

"We've got an old motorcycle, which is memorable, and it works, which makes it even more memorable. We can probably get more gas somewhere, but if anyone is looking for us because of what I did, we'll stick out like a sore thumb." Then he added, looking at Lisa and Dan, "But we don't want to cause trouble for you. We can go tonight."

"You saved a woman with two small kids from being beaten, maybe killed," Lisa said, her eyes flashing. "It wasn't Jenny's fault they were where they were. If anyone has a problem with that, let them try to be assholes about it. They'll have to come through me first."

Dan smiled and pulled Lisa to him. "She's my little wallflower."

Even Frost smiled at that but persisted. "They were firing on unarmed civilians. Most of them weren't actual law enforcement, but they were acting in that capacity. This could blow back on you hard."

Before Lisa could respond, Cody said, "We saw people shot in the SureWay parking lot, shot in the back. When we told Estes, he said they wouldn't tolerate looters and hoarding. I know the situation on the bridge was getting tense when we were talking to him, but..." Cody shrugged. "He didn't seem to have a problem being judge, jury, and executioner."

Lisa's face had sobered. In a more measured tone, she said, "We're having a special service Wednesday evening. I'll get out to see more people tomorrow before I work on my sermon. I'll get a better sense of what they need and how they're handling this."

"You're a minister?" Cody asked in surprise.

Lisa nodded. "United Church of Christ."

Cody didn't know what to say, so he kept his mouth shut. Frost grinned. "I bet you're a spitfire in the pulpit."

Lisa laughed. "I like to think so. When I need to be, anyway."

Dan said, "If you leave early in the morning, I don't think you'll have problems. I might have gas in the gas can for the lawn mower."

"I already know your route," Lisa added. To Dan, she said, "Highway 2 and over the bridge."

He nodded. "That's what I was thinking."

When Dan left for the garage, Frost pushed off the wall. "I'll look outside. Make sure no one followed us."

Cody watched Frost leave the kitchen by the side door. The man who'd been his prisoner was making a security sweep, and he was letting him. As if he had control of Frost or their situation. The absurdity of it almost made him laugh.

"Your friend. He's kind of... intense," Lisa said when he'd gone.

Without thinking, Cody said, "He's not my friend." Realizing how that sounded, he winced. "I mean, I don't know him well. But he's a good guy to have around when things go sideways."

"How do you two know each other?"

Cody chose his words with more care this time. "We were on the same plane and stuck together."

"That was a lucky coincidence," she said.

Cody snorted. "Yeah. Something like that."

chapter
twenty-four

EMMA

MONDAY, JULY 14
    2:17 PM

Emma uncapped her permanent marker with her teeth, the acrid chemical smell stinging her nostrils as she wrote the last item on the action list. The word WATER stared back at her in bold capitals, underlined three times.

"That's everything," she said, pulling the cap from between her teeth and pressing it back onto the marker with a click. "Tom and Chuy will get the operational vehicles and generator census and coordinate supply runs. Susan and Maria will inventory medical needs. Martha and I are checking on and compiling a list of vulnerable residents. Pete—"

"I know my job," Pete said. The words seemed to force themselves from between tight lips. "Security assessment. That leaves Diane and Carrie to talk to people about how much food and water they have."

"That's going to suck," Diane said. She cast Pete a baleful

glance. "Some people won't want to share even when we explain we want to pool resources for everyone till we see how things are going, especially with the water treatment plant."

Carrie gave Diane an encouraging smile. "I believe people will be more cooperative than you think."

"If you say so," Diane muttered. The way she bit her lip, expecting she was going to see the selfish side of human nature, belied her words.

Forty-eight hours since the power died. Already, everything Emma counted on—light at the flick of a switch, water at the twist of a faucet, cell phones and laptops that connected you with people halfway around the world—felt antiquated, like a half-remembered dream.

"We'll meet at Tom and Carrie's tomorrow at nine, see where we're at, then ask to meet with the mayor and city council," Emma said. She stood, energized by having a course of action to follow.

Tom's weathered hand squeezed her shoulder. "You're good at this, Emma."

"They don't tell you in school, but half of being an attorney is managing chaos."

"Women seem to be pretty good at that, in my experience," he said, a twinkle in his eye.

"Maria and I will check on Kate on our way home," Chuy said, as people started heading for the door.

"I'll do it, Chuy," Martha said. "I was planning to ask her to come have dinner with me. You're invited, too, Emma, if you want to join us."

"I'll come with you," Emma said. She didn't want to be alone, not after spending more time with other adults than she had in weeks since moving. "Let me change Grace."

Five minutes later, Emma had Grace in the Baby Bjorn carrier, its straps snug on her shoulders. She was only eleven pounds, but Emma hoped the carrier would still be as comfortable as Grace got bigger. Grace fussed before settling in, her tiny head resting against Emma's chest.

"Kate's down past the first bend on your side," Martha said. "The bungalow with yellow siding and blue shutters."

Emma nodded, having noticed that bungalow before. It had the sort of flower beds Emma aspired to every spring, only to again confront the reality that she wasn't a *work in the yard* person. The breeze picked up. Not cool, but its caress against Emma's bare arms and legs was welcome. More people sat on their front porches than usual with no air-conditioning or television to escape to.

Kate's tidy bungalow was soon in their sights. Once up the front walk, Martha rapped sharply on the front door. No answer. She knocked again, more insistently. "Kate? It's Martha."

After another round of knocks with no reply, Emma stepped off the small square of porch and peeked inside a front window. Seeing nothing out of the ordinary, she circled to the side of the house. "Her car's in the carport," she called, then felt foolish. A parked car in a driveway meant nothing.

Martha left the porch to join her. "Let's try the back. She might be in the garden." Martha sounded worried, which made Emma worried, too. They rounded the house to find an empty patio filled with potted plants wilting in the heat. Martha tried the sliding glass door—locked.

"Is there a spare key?" Emma asked.

Martha nodded. "There's a hide-a-key rock under the hydrangea." She crossed the patio toward a huge pink hydrangea. After a quick search, Martha returned, looking triumphant. The key slipping into the lock seemed to echo in the silence. Martha pushed the door panel aside and stepped into the kitchen. "Kate?" Martha called, her voice hollow in the silence. "Kate, are you here?"

Emma followed Martha into the kitchen. Similar to Emma's kitchen, an assortment of bowls, bottles, and other containers filled with water littered the counter. "Kate?" she called out.

Warm stuffy air filled Emma's lungs . She realized all the windows were closed, just like the front windows. "Kate, it's Emma Greer from down the street."

Martha went to the dining area off the kitchen. Emma headed for the hallway toward the front of the house. The light dimmed as the deeper interior shadows of the hallway pooled in front of her, except for a brighter patch near an open door. A crumpled form lay on the floor in a pale puddle of light.

"Kate!"

Lightning seemed to electrify every cell of Emma's body, propelling her forward. Kate lay sprawled on her side, wearing a halter top and shorts. One of her arms stretched overhead, the hand out of sight, having crossed the threshold of the bathroom door. Emma dropped to her knees beside Kate's still form. A cheep, like the hungry cries of a baby bird, accompanied the startled jerk of Grace's body. The fingers of Kate's outstretched hand curled, as if she'd been grasping for something just beyond reach. She looked sleepy, her eyes half-closed.

Emma felt Martha's presence behind her more than heard her hurried footsteps. The older woman's breaths came shallow and fast.

"Kate?" Emma asked. She shook Kate's shoulder. No rebound, no spring, no stir. No... anything. Kate wasn't chilled, but she wasn't as warm as she ought to be. Her skin was dry in the hot, stuffy house when it should have been damp from perspiration, or at least dewy. Still, she pressed her hand to Kate's chest, praying to feel it rise and fall.

"She's dead," Emma whispered, her throat so tight the words felt like boulders being squeezed through a funnel with a pinhole opening. "I think— I don't know how long."

Emma closed Kate's eyelids with her fingertips. The slight stiffness and waxy texture of the dead woman's skin sent Emma's stomach lurching out of place. A sound like a whimpering puppy pulled her attention to Grace, but it wasn't Grace making the pitiful sound; it was Martha. "We need to get help," Emma said, getting to her feet. Martha had sagged against the wall, her mouth opening and closing. Emma took her hand and said, "I'll go. Come sit down."

Martha shook her head, her voice hoarse when she said, "No. I'll stay with her." She roused herself, her focus sharpening. "Cut across the yard of the house across the street, and the house behind it. You'll come out across the street from Tom and Carrie, number 114."

Emma hesitated, about to ask if Martha was sure about staying behind, but Martha had already sunk to her knees. Emma walked back through the kitchen rather than taking the front door, the route imprinted on her brain. She hurried down the driveway, curling her hand behind Grace's head and breaking into a jog when she reached the street. Concrete and asphalt jarred her feet through the thin soles of her canvas sandals before the give of soft earth and grass.

She followed Martha's directions. Her mind raced faster than her feet. As the days without electricity dragged on, Emma knew people with health conditions were at risk. This made it real. Martha had mentioned Kate's pacemaker, but it hadn't seemed serious enough that her heart would stop if the pacemaker quit working. Had she fallen and hit her head? That had been the reason for Kate's pacemaker. How many people in Specter Lake depended on devices that no longer worked?

Emma pounded on the door, not stopping until it opened.

"Kate's dead," she blurted out, her breath coming in short bursts. Carrie stood just inside the threshold, her hand still holding the doorknob. She wore a light cardigan sweater, like Emma's grandmother, who had always been cold. Tom strode down the hall, just a few steps behind his wife. "I don't know what happened. Martha is with her now."

"Where is she?" Carrie asked.

"Her house. We found her on the floor." The words tumbled from Emma's mouth so fast she almost tripped on them. "We need to go door-to-door and check on people."

Grace began to fuss. Carrie nodded. "I'm coming with you." She turned to her husband. "See if Dr. Meyers can come. Susan might be better; she's here in the neighborhood."

"I'll meet you at Kate's." Tom grabbed a flashlight from the hall table.

When Emma and Carrie reached the bottom of the porch steps, Carrie caught her elbow. "What?" Emma said.

Carrie pulled Emma into a side hug. "That must have been a terrible shock."

"I—" Emma stepped out from under Carrie's arm, her anxiety growing. "We have to get back."

"Emma," Carrie said, her voice soft but filled with authority. "Settle down, okay? You have Grace, and she can feel how upset you are. There's nothing we can do for Kate now."

Emma stepped back, pulled up short. Grace was whimpering, not quite ready to cry, but it had that quality to it. Emma took some deep breaths, for the first time noticing how shaky they were.

"Better?" Carrie asked after she'd taken a few more deep breaths.

Emma nodded. "Yeah."

They cut back through the yards Emma had just traversed. She walked at a slower pace than before, matching Carrie's stride, and rubbed Grace's back. Already, the baby was settling down. Her lawyer's organizational mind kicked into gear. "We need a list," Emma said. "We need to find every vulnerable person, especially those with no one checking on them."

When they reached Kate's house, Martha stood outside on the patio. "I found this," she said, holding up a piece of paper. "It's a letter Kate's doctor wrote to her insurance company. Her condition had gotten worse, and they denied the procedure she needed to treat it." Martha's tears contradicted the anger in her voice. "They said she was too young."

"Oh my God," Emma said, feeling sick. She wished she could be surprised that a health insurance company would deny life-saving care, but she wasn't. They made money by paying for as little as possible.

"Her mother had a bad heart," Carrie said.

When Tom and Susan arrived, Emma stayed outside with Carrie, following her advice to stay as calm as she could for Grace. When Grace started crying, Emma's breasts grew heavy with the swift rush of milk coming down. She carried Grace to a chair and nestled her in the crook of her arm, pushing down the scooped neckline of her tank top to expose her breast. She undid the snap on her nursing bra. If anyone was scandalized, they could suck it.

Grace settled as soon as she latched on, opening and closing her tiny hand. Emma looked to the sky, a barely perceptible rose petal pink evident. Now the aurora was visible in the day? A shiver ran down her spine. An irrational desire to snatch Grace up and run, to hide, to protect her from the deadly beauty lurking in the sky above washed over Emma. She had never witnessed such beauty as the aurora, but with the discovery of Kate's body, it felt ominous.

When the others returned, they joined Emma where she sat. The thoughtfulness touched her; not everyone would realize it might be awkward for her to stand while nursing the baby.

Susan said, "Her pacemaker must have stopped working after the CME because of the electronics."

"Wouldn't that have killed her right away?" Tom asked.

Susan shook her head. "It depends on a person's condition. Milder conditions, like Kate's initial diagnosis, didn't get pacemakers in the past. People lived their lives with a heart that was just a little off. Kate's condition had worsened, so she was more vulnerable. That wouldn't have changed, even if she had a different device."

Tom nodded, the set of his mouth grim. As he took Carrie's hand, he said, "This is terrible."

"Her mother had a bad heart," Carrie said again, her voice thready. She wiped at her eyes. "We were best friends since high school and I found out by accident. She was private that way, and Kate was just like her."

Emma switched Grace from one breast to the other. The severity of their situation felt like a bomb exploding inside her head. "There must be others, then."

Susan nodded. "I'm sure of it."

"We can't let this happen to anyone else," Emma said, her voice hardening. "We need to find out who's in trouble now."

"Emma, we won't be able to help them all," Susan said. "We'll get Doctor Meyers' opinion, but if I'm right, there are others who've died that we don't know about. And others who will die if this continues."

Emma shivered again despite the warm temperature. An icy dread made it hard to breathe. She let the conversation wash over her as Grace finished nursing. A leaden exhaustion settled in her limbs.

"You look done in, Emma," Martha said. "Go home for a while, till Susan and I get the others organized."

Emma frowned. "I can't sit around doing nothing."

Martha said, "I'll come get you when we're ready to knock on doors."

Conflicted feelings filled Emma with indecision. She wanted to stay and do something, even though she could do nothing for Kate. She also wanted to flee—follow the primal instinct to get far from the dead woman and the signal fire her death represented. "Okay," she said. "But please come get me. I want to help."

Even though it was midafternoon, as she neared home, Emma's feet plodded like a tired child's. Halfway down the stretch of their wooded lot, she saw a man near Diane's house. He walked around the corner from the backyard and onto the sidewalk. Her heart soared, relief bursting from her chest and rushing through her body. Cody! It was Cody! She opened her mouth to call his name when she realized it wasn't. Her elation bled away, the disappointment replacing it crushing, like being inside a tightening fist. If it were Cody, he'd be crossing the street toward their house—or straight to her if he'd seen her. But this man was headed the same way she was. He was walking away.

When she reached the house, she stood on the front walk, unable to stomach going inside. Cody wasn't there to greet them. He wasn't there to take Grace from her, to wrap his arms around her, where she could find strength and comfort and protection.

Minutes ticked by, taking the world Emma had always known—the one she'd assumed would always be—with them. Now, so much was unwelcome. Scary. The safety rails she'd never noticed stood in stark relief.

Grace wriggled against her chest. Emma could only imagine the stress and anxiety she was exposing Grace to. How much of it would stick? Was she rewiring Grace's brain into one more prone to anxiety or depression? Emma sat on the porch step, a sucking despair pulling her down. She curled her hand over Grace's head like a touchstone that could keep them both safe. Tears filled her eyes as she thought of her family. What had happened to her parents and sisters? She had no way to reach them. They lived in the suburbs of Washington, DC., as she had until a few weeks ago. Was it better there? Worse? Were people pulling together, or was America turning into a disaster movie?

A misery sharper than knives carved up her insides. Tremors crawled over her skin like microscopic earthquakes. Where the hell was Cody? He would reach them, come home, whatever it took—she had told herself this over and over, but what if she was wrong? What if he wasn't coming back? What if their last conversation was his tiptoeing appeasement and her overtired annoyance? What if the last time she'd seen him really was the last?

Emma swiped at the tears dripping from her chin. Her head bowed as the sobs overtook her, like the monsters of childhood leaping out from the dark. If Cody didn't come back, what would she do?

chapter
twenty-five

CODY

MONDAY, JULY 14
    9:00 PM

The sun had almost set. Already the aurora shimmered, a swirl of red, green, and violet that would brighten even more as the canvas of the night sky darkened. Lisa and Dan had gone to check on an elderly neighbor, hoping they might hear any gossip about had happened on the bridge. In a town this small, Cody was sure they'd learn something. For a paranoid moment, he worried they might alert the police to their presence, then checked himself. Nothing about them set off his spidey sense, and Frost didn't seem concerned. Frost was probably better at reading people, much as it rubbed Cody the wrong way to admit it.

Cody sat on the back patio with his injured foot propped up on a chair. Frost had remained outside since his initial sweep, no doubt keeping an eye out for anything unusual. He sat a few chairs away at the oblong patio table. The temperature had cooled but the night air was still warm. Summers here must be beautiful,

Cody thought. If only he were home and none of this had happened.

"Do you think they'd come after Lisa and Dan if they find out they helped us?" he asked Frost, trying to distract himself from thoughts of Emma and Grace that were never far away.

Frost shrugged. "I don't know. People are scared and scared people do stupid things. She is a minister, which makes her a leader in the community. If there's any fallout, that should help them." His jaw tightened. "I don't want anyone getting hurt because of me."

After the rescue on the bridge, Frost's concern for Lisa and Dan didn't surprise Cody. An almost companionable silence fell between them. Cody wasn't sure how close Frost and his sister were, but now, since the bridge, he wondered. He opened his mouth, then stopped. He could ask, but Frost wouldn't answer. Then he thought, what the hell? He had nothing to lose. "Jenny reminded you of your sister, didn't she?"

Frost's gaze snapped toward him like steel shutters slamming shut against a storm. "What do you know about my sister?" His voice sounded like a growl. If he were a dog, his ruff would bristle and the hair along his spine would stand on end.

"Nothing," Cody said, flustered by the ferociousness of his response. "Just that you've got one." Frost looked away. As Cody had thought, he wasn't going to answer. After his reaction, Cody wasn't sure he wanted him to.

After several minutes had passed, Frost said, "Yeah. She did."

Keep your mouth shut, Cody. His curiosity got the better of him. "And that's why you jumped in."

"I didn't think. I saw the kids, saw her trying to protect them, and something clicked." He rubbed a hand across his face. "Ruth —my sister—has two kids. I haven't seen them in a while. Jodi was about their age the last time I saw them. Peter was a baby. I don't know either of them."

Cody tried to be surreptitious as he studied Frost. Apart from his military service, nothing Frost had done since had hinted he would commit the selfless act Cody had witnessed. Risking your life for a member of your unit, knowing they'd do the same, was different from today. "I've never seen anyone move that fast."

A ghost of a smile touched Frost's lips. "It was my training. Old habits."

"Those old habits saved their lives."

Frost shrugged and looked down, seeming uncomfortable with the praise. Cody asked another question. "Why did you become a Ranger?"

Frost thought for a moment, his gaze becoming distant. Then he said, "Because it was hard, and I was good at it. Because it meant something."

Cody felt the rigid categories he used to order his life—to make sense of the world—warp at the edges: good and bad, right and wrong, criminal and lawman. Like everyone else, he'd done the wrong thing: at work, at home, with Emma. The pain of losing his father as a boy, never far from the surface, erupted from those hidden depths and swallowed him whole, like Jonah and the whale. If he'd only made a different choice, gone on the damn camping trip, his whole life would be different. His family would be different. His mother, his grandparents, his pastor, even his sisters—only kids themselves—had told him it wasn't his fault. Cody knew better.

He knew the pain of making the wrong choice and how it can shape your life—how it leads from one thing to the next with no intent on your part. Frost had done bad things. He had broken the law. Maybe that's how it had started for him, too. One bad choice led to another, until bad choices were all there was.

But maybe now things were different. Maybe the collapse of their world—the chaos and fear it had unleashed—had given Caleb Frost the chance to make the right choice. Coming back to the plane instead of running. Helping the man trying to lock him up. Saving a woman and her children with nowhere to turn.

Whatever had turned Frost into a criminal, Cody was sure it had started when he left the Army—something tied to that dustup with the officer. He didn't know how he knew this; he just did.

Frost hadn't softened. He still watched everyone like they might turn on him. But his actions—coming back, not running, protecting others—hinted at a man trying to decide if he wanted to be different.

"I may have misjudged you."

Frost's eyes met his, the surprise in them as bright as the aurora. A streak of light blazed across the night sky, its bright trail there and gone in the blink of an eye.

Then another streak of light. And another. And another.

"What the hell?" Cody said, getting to his feet, his attention fixed on the sky. "Are those shooting stars?"

Frost didn't answer for a long time. When he did, his voice was grim. "I think they're satellites."

They watched in silence as more flares of white raced across the sky, silent harbingers of a world changed forever.

"Ruth, I should be with you," Frost said, his voice soft, like falling snow.

Cody's heart thudded in his chest. "Emma. Grace."

The heavy weight of Frost's hand gripped Cody's shoulder. "We'll find them, Marshal. We have to."

chapter
twenty-six

MONDAY, JULY 14
    9:19 PM

Emma's gaze followed the wavering flame of the beeswax candle. Iris, Susan's wife, had brought it to their informal command center at Tom and Carrie's dining room table. Iris was a tall, raw-boned woman, soft-spoken, and reminded Emma of a Valkyrie. Its light cast elongated shadows up the wall, turning familiar shapes into things distorted and alien.

Emma took another sip of coffee. She'd given it up when she got pregnant and stayed away since she was nursing Grace, until tonight. When she'd smelled the coffee, it was like encountering the Borg from *Star Trek*: resistance had been futile.

"Four," Martha said, her voice hollow as she tallied the marks in the notebook for the tenth time. "Four dead in our neighborhood alone. Five, including Kate."

Emma looked into the living room, to the deep love seat where Grace slept with a fort of pillows surrounding her. Her arms were flung up along her head, like she was playing a game of stick-up. She'd been fussy all evening, too warm like everyone else. After finding three elderly neighbors dead in their homes, Emma couldn't decide if her daughter felt too warm from the weather or something more sinister.

"That's only who we know about," Pete added. His gruff demeanor from when they'd met at Emma's house had softened somewhat. It made Emma think his bark was worse than his bite. Pete's jaw remained clenched, like he was holding something back. "There are a dozen houses we couldn't get into."

Susan's slim fingers traced the list of names. "Mrs. Abernathy's insulin wouldn't stay cold without refrigeration. Mr. Cheney's oxygen ran out without the home healthcare delivery."

"And the Fletcher twins," Iris said, shaking her head. Emma had never met the elderly identical twins, two women in their nineties. They had never married and instead traveled the world. They must have been something special, for the morale of their small group had plummeted with that discovery. Beyond those who had died, they had found people with other needs. One had been severely dehydrated; others had run out of medication or needed medical attention.

The flickering candlelight, which she'd normally have enjoyed, heightened the feeling of instability. Emma's stomach churned as she thought of Kate's body—how still it had been and the wrongness of it. She had been in her thirties. How many people had died without the medical care they needed? How many more would they find? Not just here but in all of Specter Lake, maybe in all the country?

A thin, reedy cry that grated against Emma's ear announced Grace had woken. "I need to head home," Emma said, rising from her chair. The wooden legs scraped against the floor with a jarring screech that made Emma wince. "Grace will sleep better in her own bed."

"You look ready to drop yourself," Martha said, her shrewd gaze passing over Emma like she was conducting an examination.

Emma nodded. Whatever Martha had seen just now, Emma knew she was right. "If Tom and Chuy come back with any news, will someone let me know?"

The sound of an engine rumbling up the driveway made them all freeze. Tom and Chuy had returned from their trip into town. Footsteps thudded on the porch and the front door swung open. Tom reached the dining room first, eyes glittering in the candle-light, with Chuy a few steps behind. Both men looked grim.

"What did they say?" Martha asked, pushing away from the table.

Tom twisted the cap in his hands and raked his fingers through his hair. "There have been other fatalities. The morgue has no room. It's running on generators as it is."

"They're planning to turn them off in the morning to conserve the fuel," Chuy added, his jaw tight. "They told us to bring the bodies to the cemetery."

"The cemetery?" Emma said, her voice cracking. "What about notifying their families? They can't just..." Her voice trailed. She couldn't say it out loud.

"Bury them," Tom finished for her. His words hung in the air like the ringing of an off-key bell. "That's exactly what they're telling us to do. There's a backhoe that still works. They're digging a common grave."

The room fell silent, the only sound the drone of cicadas through the open windows and Grace's agitated whimpers. Emma felt the world tilting beneath her, reality becoming more fractured. "This can't be happening," she whispered. She walked into the next room and picked up Grace, who quieted in her mother's familiar arms. "We're burying them without... anything?"

"It's happening," Pete said, the finality in his voice echoing in Emma's head like a judge's gavel. "And it's going to keep happening. We need to face reality. Things will only get worse."

Emma's throat tightened. She thought of finding Kate on her floor like discarded clothing. Her mind's eye filled with others they didn't know about. Cody was out there somewhere, if he was still alive. "I have to go," she said abruptly, her voice thick with emotion. "Grace needs to be home."

Martha stood. "I'll walk with you."

Emma didn't protest. Walking alone with just her baby under the crimson night sky felt menacing. She adjusted her hold on her squirmy daughter, said good night to the others, and followed Martha out the door. They walked in silence, the weight of what they'd learned pressing down on them. Emma focused on placing one foot in front of the other, on breathing, on trying to soothe Grace with the smooth movements of her body. Rounding the bend to the cluster of hers, Martha's, and Diane's homes, raised voices carried in the stillness. Emma stopped, listening, then zeroed in on Diane's house. A dim light, probably from a battery-powered lantern, glowed through the front windows. "Is that Diane?"

"No," Martha said, her voice hardening. "That's Heath." She took off at a trot, then turned back. "Go get Chuy or Pete or Tom. Now."

Emma hesitated, torn between following Martha's instruction and not wanting to leave her alone. "I don't think—"

"Go!" Martha hissed before turning away and jogging across the street. Martha reached Diane's front door. She banged on it with a force that belied her age. Grace, startled by the noise, burst into full-throated wails.

The door flew open, the dim light spilling onto the porch. Diane tumbled through it and Martha followed her. In the aurora's glow, Emma could see Diane's long braid was beginning to unravel. A heavyset man stepped into the doorway, his shoulders hunched like a boxer, ready to charge. Emma didn't remember moving, just that she now stood at the end of the walk to Diane's house.

"What's going on here?" Martha demanded.

Diane said, her voice trembling, "You need to leave, Heath. Right now!"

Emma took a step back. Was Heath the man she had seen before?

He strolled toward Martha, who had planted herself between Diane and her ex-husband. "Martha, this is between me and my wife."

Emma blinked, unprepared for the reasonableness of his tone. He sounded like a teacher explaining how something worked for a student, not a man pursuing a woman who was clearly afraid of him.

"I am not your wife!" Diane said, her voice cracking. "I haven't been your wife for two years!"

Martha drew herself up, imposing despite her small stature. "You know you're not supposed to be here, Heath. There's a restraining order against you. You'll be arrested."

"With all that's going on, the police have bigger fish to fry than a family disagreement," he said.

"That's not what this looks like to me," Emma said, clutching Grace tight. Grace's wails only added to the tension charging the air. "If she has a restraining order, this is intimidation and criminal harassment. It's criminal contempt of a court order. That makes it aggravated stalking which is a felony—once an emergency is declared. That's going to happen by tomorrow if it hasn't already."

"Who the hell are you?" Heath demanded. His posture stiffened. He seemed to swell in size. The boxer's hunch of his shoulders returned. That single gesture, that hunch, and Emma understood why Diane was afraid.

This was where she should turn, run into her house, and lock the doors. This was where Cody's coaching about what to do during a confrontation should kick in. This was where she should realize she held her daughter and that she had to protect Grace from the threat this man posed.

This was where her temper—and dislike of bullies—got the better of her.

Emma ignored his question. "Add criminal trespass during a

declared disaster and intimidation of a protected person? That's another five years, easy."

In the bright light of the aurora, she saw his eyes widen. For the first time since he'd appeared, his confidence seemed to falter. Emma could smell it in the air: the moment when a person caves. She'd realized pretty quickly after joining the district attorney's office that she didn't want the stress of criminal trial work, despite being good at it. But if anything might have kept her in the courtroom, it would have been this smell.

"Emergency powers legislation allows for expedited prosecution of crimes that exploit disaster situations," Emma said, closing in for the kill. "That makes it federal, because FEMA's going to get involved. Then you're really screwed. I don't know the history here, but you're playing with fire every second you stay."

Grace let out an earsplitting squall, her eyes screwed tight and body rigid. Heath took an involuntary step backward. "You're bluffing," he said, but his voice was now tinged with uncertainty.

"I used to be a district attorney, and my husband is a US Marshal. But if you want to make it worse, stay, by all means."

Her eyes locked on his. The frustration and fear of the last few days, the fury of her baby's wails, thundered in Emma's ears. If the aurora hadn't been making everything glow red, her anger would have.

Heath's gaze darted between the three women. Then his hard posture softened. The easygoing demeanor he had begun the encounter with returned. "There's no reason to get upset," he said, holding his hands up in surrender. He smiled, and goddamn if it wasn't charming despite how menacing he'd been a moment ago. "I just wanted to talk, but I can see I'm not welcome."

"You're not," Emma said, her anger making her voice hard as flint. "Don't come back. And don't come near me ever."

He smiled at Diane, then skirted around her and Martha. As he cut the corner of the yard to stay clear of Emma, a mix of anger and contempt flashed across his face. He walked into the street and sauntered away like he'd been out for a stroll. They watched until he disappeared around the bend in the road. Finally, Grace's crying ceased. She sagged against Emma's body, having cried herself out.

"Are you okay?" Martha asked Diane.

Diane nodded, but Emma could see that she was shaking. "He showed up half an hour ago to 'check on me,'" she said, her tone making clear what she thought of his excuse. "He wouldn't leave and was getting angry."

"Your threats worked," Martha said to Emma, admiration in her voice. "Where did all that come from?"

Emma managed a weak smile. "I was an assistant district attorney for a year. Sometimes I lose my temper, usually when it would be smarter not to."

"You were amazing," Diane whispered. Her eyes glistened in the crimson light. "Thank you."

"You're staying with me tonight," Martha said to Diane.

"I don't want to be a bother—"

"It's not a bother," Martha said, cutting her off. "It's what neighbors do."

Emma shifted Grace in her arms. Her tiny body bucked from soft hiccups. "Will you two be okay?"

"You aren't coming with us?" Martha asked, surprise in her voice.

Emma shook her head. "I'll be fine. I need to get Grace to bed."

"I'd feel better if you stayed with us. You really pissed Heath off," Martha said.

"I can take care of myself," Emma said. "Cody's in law enforcement. We have guns."

Martha pursed her lips, her eyes boring into Emma. Then she nodded reluctantly. "Come over if you change your mind. I'll check on you in the morning."

The walk to her house felt longer than ever before. Grace had settled to whimpering, her face hot against Emma's neck. By the time she reached the front door, Emma couldn't stop trembling.

That had been so stupid, so incredibly stupid. She had Grace to think of, to protect. What had she been thinking?

Emma opened the door, sagging against it as she slid the deadbolt into place. She fumbled for the headlamp she'd left on the kitchen table. She locked the back door and the door to the garage. It had a deadbolt, too, which Cody had liked. At the time, she'd found it amusing. Now, she was grateful.

She carried Grace to the nursery to change her diaper and remove her light tee shirt. Then she carried her to the bedroom she and Cody shared and lay her gently in the bassinet. In the harsh light of the headlamp, Grace's cheeks looked flushed, her hair damp with sweat. Emma's heart clenched with fear. She'd take Grace's temperature, but the baby thermometer was digital. If the confrontation with Diane's ex-husband hadn't occurred, she'd find Susan and ask her to examine Grace, since Susan was a nurse practitioner. Emma didn't know her specialty, but she could still assess Grace. But the confrontation had happened, and now Emma was afraid to walk alone.

We need the fucking power to come back on.

Without pediatricians, without medicine, what could she do if Grace got ill? "You're going to be fine, Gracie," she whispered, as much to convince herself as anything. "It's just the heat."

She found a clean washcloth in the master bath and dampened it with precious water. Gently, she wiped Grace's forehead and neck, then her torso and limbs. Grace settled after a minute of the cool cloth on her skin, her eyes fluttering shut almost immediately.

Grace now settled, Emma moved with purpose. She pushed the sliding door of the bedroom closet aside, then Cody's clothes. The tall metal gun safe stood against the wall at one end of the closet. Her fingers trembled slightly as she turned the combination lock—Cody's badge number, then the month and day they'd met.

Thank God this isn't electronic, she thought. If the gun safe were newer, the locking mechanism would probably be electronic.

Right now, that meant the safe would stay locked. Electronic gun safes weren't fail-safe; they didn't unlock when the power failed. They were fail-secure, so they stayed locked. Only a mechanical override key would open one if the power failed. Cody hadn't liked the idea of being dependent on a separate object to open the safe. Between the move, the half-unpacked house, and new parent sleep deprivation, never mind the stress of the last couple days, if they'd had an electronic safe, Emma wouldn't have counted on remembering where the key was if her life depended on it.

She pushed the handle down and pulled the safe open. The case of Cody's personal firearm, a Glock 23 9mm, the same as his department-issued firearm, lay on the shelf above his hunting rifles. Beside it was the case for her Walther PDP-F. Emma lifted both cases out, their weights familiar and not, for she hadn't picked up either in some time. When it was clear things between them were getting serious, Emma asked Cody to teach her how to shoot. "If we're going to live together, I need to know," she had said.

Then her stomach had plunged to her feet. She could see the words floating in the air and wanted to snatch them back and stuff them in her mouth. They hadn't broached the subject yet, and she hadn't meant to. Not now, not like this. And then Cody had smiled.

Emma closed her eyes. The memory of that smile, slow to start but setting his face aglow, hit her like a train. She could feel his warmth behind her during the lessons that followed as he adjusted her stance, his voice calm and steady in her ear. And later, the feel of his skin against hers, his breath hot on her neck while their bodies twined together, the passion burning between them so intense it was blinding.

Emma gasped, the wave of longing rushing through her so strong she felt like maple sugar candy dissolving in a downpour. Then she opened her eyes and took a shaky breath. She checked the preloaded magazines—124-grain HSTs for the Walther, Gold Dot +Ps for the Glock—then seated the magazine for each firearm with a firm push of her hand and racked the slides, just as Cody had taught her. She set each firearm in its open case and loaded the spare magazines. She performed the actions with both intention and by rote and felt her body relax, the tightly coiled muscles unwinding. Firearms were tools. Dangerous weapons. Equalizers.

Emma made sure to put the correct spare magazine with each weapon. They could use the same ammunition, but the magazines weren't interchangeable. She considered which one she preferred, settling on her Walther. It was designed with the smaller hands of women in mind. She considered placing it on the bedside table, within easy reach, the image of Heath's angry face flashing through her mind. But Grace was in the room, in the bassinet beside the bed. The danger a loaded weapon posed wasn't worth it, especially if someone broke in while she slept.

If Heath broke in.

A wave of shame crashed over Emma, rough like ocean surf after a storm. She should have protected her daughter first, but she hadn't. She had ignored that first instinct: to run inside and get Grace out of harm's way. Instead, she'd acted on the more immediate threat. She didn't regret helping Diane, but she should have done it without putting Grace in danger. Without painting a target on her own back.

Emma put the Glock back in the gun case and closed it. She returned the Walther to its case but left it open on the top shelf of the closet, the spare magazine and another box of ammunition beside it. Close enough if she needed it during the night, but not out in the open where anyone could see it.

Emma sank to the edge of the bed, the darkness pressing in around her. Five people gone. People who had been alive only yesterday, who would now be buried without ceremony. A common grave dug, their bodies lowered into it. How many would follow? She didn't know. The world she knew was slipping away so fast she couldn't keep up.

Emma curled onto her side, pulling Cody's pillow against her chest. It still smelled faintly of him, the mix of soap and aftershave and an earthy scent that was just him. She pressed her face into it, allowing the tears to come, her body shaking with silent sobs.

"Please come home," she whispered into the darkness. "We need you. I need you. Please come home."

Through the window, the aurora continued its ghostly dance across the sky, bathing the world in its bloodred light, indifferent to the suffering below.

day four

chapter
twenty-seven

CALEB

TUESDAY, JULY 15
  6:30 AM

Frustration bubbled underneath Caleb's skin, sticky as hot tar. Even with the ratty old blanket Lisa had folded up for him to use as a mat, the concrete garage floor chilled his knees. He looked up at Greer, murder in his eyes. "Try it again."

The 1952 Indian Chief motorcycle that Roy had given Caleb and the marshal had run flawlessly yesterday. This morning, however, it refused to start. Caleb had a smattering of knowledge about motorcycle maintenance, but only a smattering. He'd never ridden an Indian before this, nor any other motorcycle this old. Its age should—all things being equal—make fixing it easier since the engine was simpler. Without YouTube—his go-to source for fixing almost anything he didn't already know how to do—Caleb was out of his depth.

Greer turned the key in the motorcycle's ignition. The engine gave a half-hearted cough. "Goddammit," Greer said. Then to Lisa, he added, "Sorry. I know you're a pastor."

Lisa rolled her eyes. "I swear, too."

Caleb rocked back on his heels, almost ready to call it, because they were burning daylight. It was still early—6:30 in the morning—but they'd been at this for an hour. If they didn't leave soon, they'd lose any advantage leaving early might give them in terms of fewer people seeing them.

"Roy said something about the spark plugs," Greer said. He dismounted and leaned closer to the motorcycle, pointing at the stylized letter I on the side. "They're here, right?"

Caleb frowned as he tried to remember everything Roy had told them about the motorcycle. "I think so." He craned his neck and peered under the concave piece. "I think that's it. Might as well try."

After finding the right crescent wrench, he applied pressure, steady but firm. *Come on, come on...*

The wrench slipped off the plug. Caleb's knuckles raked over the sharp edges of the engine fins, lighting them up like a flaring match.

"Goddammit," he shouted as he shook out his hand. It didn't ease the pain at all. He kicked the wrench across the floor. "You fucker!" He glared at the wrench, like his skinned knuckles were its fault. Then he turned to Greer and Lisa. Through clenched teeth, he said, "We need a new plan."

"We can walk," Greer said, his voice tight with frustration.

"With your foot?" Caleb raised an eyebrow. "That'll never work."

"We'll give you some bikes," Lisa said. "But let's eat first. Dan's making oatmeal. And your knuckles need to be bandaged."

Caleb inspected his throbbing knuckles. The first three were skinned and bleeding. Dammit, he thought. It felt like the bad karma he'd racked up the last few years was coming due, starting with the plane plummeting from the sky.

Dan had bowls of oatmeal with chopped nuts and honey

ready. A camping stove was visible through the kitchen window from where it sat on the patio table. Caleb thumped into a seat at the kitchen table and started shoveling food into his mouth.

"This is what you're going to do," Lisa said, nudging Dan out of the way. She spread a map on the table. Greer leaned closer. "There's a route we take all the time—west on Highway 2 to Priests River. You can cross the river at the Dover Bridge. There's a great coffee shop there. We ride out and have lunch all the time." Then she paused, her cheeks pinkened with embarrassment. "Not that you're going to be stopping for coffee.

"You'll go east after the bridge and take Dufort Road," she said, her finger moving left on the map along a body of water. "Specter Lake Cutoff Road is just a couple of miles at a T inter-section. It goes all the way to Specter Lake. The entire trip is about"—she looked at Dan—"twenty-five miles, give or take?"

Dan nodded. "About that."

Greer studied the map. "On a good day I could manage, but with my foot the way it is, I don't know."

"It'll be slow going," Caleb said. "And it'll suck, but it's doable."

Greer snorted. "If you say so."

"Cycling's our thing and I know you can do it," Lisa insisted. "The bikes aren't the most important thing. Decide you can do it and you will. Where the mind goes, the body follows."

"Okay," Greer said. "If you think so."

Lisa shook her head. "You need to think so."

Greer looked a little daunted. Caleb tried to hide his smile. He knew Lisa was right. The biggest fight was always the mental part.

He considered their options, all of which were subpar. Walking would take days and be brutal for Greer with broken bones. The motorcycle would not fix itself. Even if they managed a repair, they'd be screwed if it happened on the road. Or they could take the offered bikes and push on. He looked at Lisa, frowning. "Aren't you going to need your bikes?"

Dan laughed out loud. Lisa grinned at him. "You did not pay attention to our garage, did you?"

Forty minutes later, they were ready to go, and Caleb had realized he had not paid the least bit of attention to the contents of Lisa and Dan's garage. There were ten bikes at least, some for road cycling and others for mountain biking. The couple adjusted the seats and checked the tires and brakes on two mountain bikes—a black Santa Cruz for Caleb and a blue Specialized for Greer. They also stuffed their backpacks with water bottles, oranges, a squeeze tube of peanut butter, and some first aid supplies.

"The route's pretty straightforward," Dan said, handing Caleb the map they'd insisted the men take. "Just go west on Highway 2 until Priests River. It's the only bridge. You can't miss it."

Caleb nodded, feeling nonplussed. He gripped the handlebars of his bike, grateful he had something to do to cover his disquiet. Lisa and Dan had brought them into their home and were letting Jenny and her kids stay with them, even if it might blow back on them. Apart from rescuing Jenny yesterday, Caleb couldn't remember the last time he'd helped someone without calculating what he'd get back. Maybe it was Lisa being a minister, but his selfishness felt raw and exposed now.

Jenny stood inside the garage door, her children clinging to her legs. "Thank you," she said when he and Greer stopped to say goodbye. "I don't know what would have happened if you hadn't been there."

Caleb looked at the floor, embarrassed by her gratitude. No one would call his behavior since leaving the Army altruistic, but you didn't stand by when a woman was being beaten. Even he hadn't sunk that low.

Keeping a hand on one handlebar, he squatted down to eye level with Tyler and Nora. Their small faces were solemn but no longer frightened. Both children sported gravity defying bedheads. "You mind your mom and take care of each other, okay?"

Nora nodded. When Jenny's hand touched Tyler's head, he leaned against her and buried his face in his mother's leg. Lisa hugged Cody and Caleb in turn. "I'll be praying for you both. I have a feeling you'll need it. If you need to come back, you're welcome anytime."

As they pushed their bikes down the driveway, Caleb glanced back. Dan stood with his arm around Lisa's waist, Jenny beside them with her children. They were a family of sorts, rising from the chaos like a phoenix from fire. A painful twist in Caleb's chest —of longing or loss, maybe both—made his breath catch.

"Let's go," Greer said, pulling Caleb back to himself. "We're not getting any younger."

chapter
twenty-eight

EMMA

TUESDAY, JULY 15
   7:03 AM

A blade of sunlight sliced through the curtains, cutting across Emma's face like a heated knife. She groaned, rolling away from the glare. She lay still, unmoving, the torpor of her limbs too much to fight. She'd done far too much since the power went out on too little sleep. Her body was rebelling—if she could be an asshole, it could be one too. She summoned the energy to rub at her eyes and then check the windup wristwatch Carrie had given her—5:27 in the morning, assuming it wasn't running slow.

She'd managed maybe four hours of broken sleep in the stuffy house, waking at every creak, heart thundering in her chest. Had Heath returned to make good on the threat his eyes had promised? The first time this happened, she'd gone to the closet for the Walther and placed it on the floor beneath her bed. At two months old, Grace would not find the gun and shoot herself. Every time she or Grace woke after that, she reached beneath the bed, her fingers brushing the metal and polymer grip. Other times she listened for the sounds of Grace breathing, telling herself that she was so keyed up from the earlier confrontation that she'd crossed the line from normal concern into paranoid hyper-vigilance.

Emma pushed herself upright, her spine popping. Outside, the birds sang in melodies and counterpoints high and sweet. They sang as if their birdsong alone could tug the sun from its sleep and push it up in the sky. Grace lay in the bassinet beside the bed, her tiny chest rising and falling in a steady rhythm. Emma crawled from the bed to lay the back of her hand against Grace's cheek. Warm, but not overly so. At least she didn't think so. She'd been told the evenings here were cooler. Even with this heat wave, overnight temperatures were still fifteen to twenty degrees cooler than the day's high. Under normal circumstances, she'd have flung the windows wide to let the cooler air inside. After her confrontation last night, no power on earth could have persuaded Emma to crack a window, much less leave one open.

The house felt like a tomb—too silent and oppressive No hum of the refrigerator, no faint whisper of the air-conditioning, just the heat and quiet pressing down like a boulder. The bottle of water on her nightstand was warm, but Emma drank it greedily.

She crept to the window, peeling back the curtain. The eastern sky blushed pink and orange, heralding what she expected to be another scorching day. Through the trees, she saw silhou-ettes of men and women in the predawn light, heading toward the lake with buckets in hand. They'd agreed last night to meet at first light.

Emma ate a granola bar and an apple, then dressed in a tank top, shorts, and her Teva hiking sandals. She couldn't remember the last time she'd gone hiking. Cody had tried to use it as a selling point when it was clear he was being sent to the professional equivalent of Siberia after working out of Washington, DC. She missed him. And hiking. And coffee. And every other thing that had bothered her last week. If she'd known what lay ahead—

"Stop it," she muttered to herself. "Self-pity's not a good look."

She hated to wake Grace, but she had to get her ready. Carrie was expecting them. Her stomach lurched as she lifted Grace from the bassinet. Leaving her—even for an hour—felt like cutting off a limb, but they needed water. She had to do her part.

"It's not much of a choice, is it, sweetheart?" she whispered as she sat in the rocker to nurse.

Thirty minutes later, Emma stood on Carrie and Tom's front porch, Grace asleep against her shoulder. She hadn't woken even when Emma picked her up from the stroller. Emma wished she could be as oblivious to the transfer about to take place. Carrie smiled when she opened the door and invited Emma in. They stood in the front hall, Emma feeling like she faced a gallows. She'd always thought women who carried on about leaving their babies with a sitter or at daycare melodramatic. Sure, it must be hard, especially at first, but it wasn't like they were leaving a sickly child exposed on the rocks. They weren't pretending the fairies were taking the baby away to live in the Summerlands while leaving a dead changeling in its place.

How little she'd known. That was exactly how it felt.

Her words tumbled out in a nervous rush. "She hasn't really woken up yet, so I wasn't able to nurse her properly. She's been really fussy... I think it's the heat. She feels warm sometimes, but it's been so hot, so I'm not sure. Cody's mom gave me a manual breast pump, just in case," Emma said. "So there's breast milk in the diaper bag. Will you be able to keep it cold enough? Oh, forget that. Of course you will, with the freezer."

Carrie nodded, an understanding smile curling her lips upward. "We're running the generator just enough to keep what's in the basement freezer frozen. I'll put your breast milk there. You don't have to worry about anything. She'll be fine."

Emma nodded, swallowing the lump in her throat. Carrie held out her arms. Emma kept hold of Grace, as if she didn't understand what the gesture meant, tears welling in her eyes. "I know. I just... I haven't left her before, not like this. I've been next door at Martha's when she was asleep, just since this all started, but never for long."

"The first time's always the hardest."

Emma forced herself to put Grace in Carrie's arms. Losing a limb wouldn't hurt as much. Carrie smiled at Grace, the wrinkles around her eyes only making her seem more gentle. "You won't even notice, will you?" she said to Grace. "But momma's gonna cry all morning."

Emma swiped at a tear. "You'd think I was leaving her at an orphanage."

"She'll be right here when you get back, so scoot," Carrie said, a mock severity creeping into her voice. "The sooner you leave, the sooner you'll be back."

Emma turned and walked away through sheer force of will, each step coaxed like a confession. She knew this was the right choice, even though it felt like her heart lay in a puddle of blood on the porch. She had to make their home as safe as possible for Grace, their neighbors, and herself. For Cody, when he came home.

You better get your ass here or I'll murder you, Cody. I did not sign up for single motherhood.

The path to the lake wound through the stands of ponderosa pines that ringed it, the dappled morning light filtering through the branches. Emma's footsteps crunched on the carpet of dried needles. Three days without rain, two days without water, and temperatures over eighty-five degrees. Every plant drooped, their leaves curling at the edges. It felt like even the trees were holding their breath.

The lake opened before her like a brilliant mirror reflecting the dawn sky. A dozen figures moved along the shoreline beyond the paved path that circled the lake, staggering like zombies under the weight of the buckets they lugged along the shore. Maria waved, her long ponytail swinging as she straightened.

"Emma! Over here!"

Emma picked her way down the gravelly embankment to where Maria and Chuy worked, filling gallon milk containers with the opaque lake water. "You look like you barely slept," Maria said, her nose wrinkling.

"I got five hours. Maybe," Emma said, trying—and failing—to stifle a yawn. Emma looked at the small mountain of gallon milk containers. "Where did you get all these?"

"We were digging through everyone's recycling last night like trash pandas," Maria said. "My hands were so gross by the time we finished. It was foul." She dipped her free hand in the water like she still felt the sticky residue. "Pete says we'll use them for the filtered water once we have filtered water to wash them out."

"How's the little one?" Chuy asked, handing her an empty bucket.

Emma crouched beside them and dipped the jug in the lake to hide the tears in her eyes. It had been, what? Fifteen minutes, and Chuy asking about Grace was reducing her to tears? "She's with Carrie," she said, working hard to keep her voice even.

Chuy looked at her sidelong, a sympathetic twist to his mouth. "First time you've left her?"

Emma laughed a little shakily. "Yeah. How'd you know?"

"You look like you wanted to cry, that's how," Maria said. She pulled her filled jug from the water and screwed on the cap. "Chuy was like that about his nieces and nephews when we moved here."

"I was not," he said.

Maria rolled her eyes as she stood up. "Oh yes, you were. But it's cute, *mijo*."

The cool water sloshed over Emma's toes, making her glad she'd worn her Tevas. Damp, squelching tennies would have sucked, but with the sandals, the water on her toes was refreshing. They worked in silence for a few minutes, the rhythm of dip and fill meditative. The lake water had to be purified to make sure it was safe enough to drink. That part wasn't Emma's area of expertise, but she was about to learn. If they got desperate enough, even untreated lake water would be better than nothing. It was already better than the nothing coming from their taps.

"Chuy," Emma said. "Do you know if there's going to be a service for the people buried yesterday?"

Chuy's hand tightened on the jug he was filling. His broad shoulders slumped a little. "I haven't heard anything, but I'm sure there will be." Under his breath, he added, "Eventually."

The heaviness in his voice made Emma's chest ache. She shied away from the thought of Kate lying in the common grave with no ceremony to mark her passing. Right now, it was all brutal efficiency to avoid disease. "It doesn't seem right," she said.

"No," he agreed. "It doesn't."

Emma's optimism of yesterday afternoon fizzled and settled in her stomach like a stone. If this was how they treated their dead after only four days without power, what would the coming weeks bring? She thought of Grace sleeping at Carrie's house, of Cody out there somewhere. The uncertainty felt like it would swallow her whole.

Fuck feeling like this. I'm not a helpless woman from a nineteen fifties movie. Aloud, Emma said, "We'll do something, then, once we've got the water situation under control. Even if it's just a prayer or saying the rosary, or whatever people want to do."

Chuy grinned at her. "You're right. It's not like we're waiting around for someone else to do what we're doing now. We can get people together and say some words."

"Hey!" Pete's gruff voice carried down the shoreline. "Stop with the buckets and get over here!"

Emma looked up, squinting against the morning sun now cresting the trees. Pete stood by an older pickup truck parked at the edge of the clearing. In its bed sat a jumble of buckets, pipes, and hoses.

"That's how we're going to purify the water?" Emma said, unable to keep the dubiousness out of her voice.

Chuy shrugged, but he grinned, too. The brightness in his brown eyes, the dimple in one cheek, chased away the heaviness of their burial conversation. He reminded Emma of a teenager delighted to be getting away with something. "That's what he says. He's not called Prepper Pete for nothing. At least I hope not."

"How did you convince him to help?" Emma asked, watching as Pete barked orders at two younger men helping him assemble his contraption.

"I didn't," Chuy said. "That was all Maria."

"It was nothing," Maria said, dismissing Chuy's praise with a wave of her hand. "I just appealed to his better nature."

"Does Pete even have a better nature?" Emma asked, speaking without thinking. She clapped her hand over her mouth. "Did I say that out loud?"

Maria's laugh was high and bright, Chuy's a deep rumble. "Okay," Maria relented, her brown skin setting off her smile. "I told him this was his chance to show everyone he was right all along."

"Oh," Emma said, her face still hot with embarrassment. "He gets to be the expert." Pete was gruff and seemingly reluctant. Despite his protestations that he was prepared and anyone who wasn't was not his problem, he'd been helpful. He'd come to her meeting, which was more than most.

"He's always been one of my favorite clients," Maria said, standing and brushing dirt from her knees. At Emma's raised eyebrow, she added, "I cut his hair. Have for years. He's my favorite gringo and I'm his favorite Mexican, even though I'm from Arizona."

Emma shook her head, bemused. "I'd have pegged him as a barber kind of guy."

"He was, but the barber retired. Everyone needs haircuts," Maria said with a shrug. "Even doomsday preppers."

As Emma followed them, she scanned the tree line, searching for a familiar silhouette. For Cody. She'd been angry with him before he left—angry and fed up and just trying to get through this transition. To reach the other side of the unhappiness between them that she'd hoped wasn't as far away as it seemed. It felt like a distant memory now compared to never seeing him again.

"You coming?" Maria said. Emma realized she had slowed as she searched the far shore. Maria and Chuy were several paces ahead.

Emma nodded and hurried to catch up. Cody would be here as soon as he could. She knew it like she knew the sun rose and set and the moon waxed and waned. It might take a while, but he would be here. He had to be, because the alternative was unthinkable.

chapter
twenty-nine

CALEB

The ride to Priests River was easier than Caleb had expected. Highway 2 was mostly clear. Idaho was sparsely populated in relation to its size. That meant fewer abandoned cars to navigate around than one might expect, especially on secondary highways. The mercury climbed steadily as the morning wore on, but the wind of their ride kept them comfortable.

Greer showed signs of fatigue from pain more than anything, Caleb thought. He had to hand it to the marshal. He might be struggling because of his injury, but he mostly kept the pace and didn't bitch. Caleb had to allow a grudging respect for the man's determination. He could have given up a dozen times over the past few days. His broken foot even gave him a reason, yet he never faltered. He was determined to get back to his family.

With Greer's impairment, it took almost four hours to reach the sign welcoming them to Priests River. The town seemed calm compared to Sandpoint. The people watching them pass looked hungry for information rather than wary. Caleb wasn't deceived by the calm. He felt the undercurrent of anxiety, of not knowing what was happening or if help was coming. He coasted to a halt and waited for Greer to catch up. "If we turn on Main, the coffee shop's that way, toward the bridge."

"I could use a break." Greer's sweaty forehead shined in the sunlight. Caleb saw the pain in the set of his mouth and squinting eyes.

"Let's see if anyone's at that coffee shop. I doubt we'll get lattes, but maybe we can get some information."

They turned and coasted down a pretty shopping street toward the river. Slowing at the corner several blocks from the highway, Caleb saw a small group clustered on the sidewalk of a cross street, just as Lisa and Dan had described. The group fell silent as Caleb and Greer approached. Caleb could feel the weight of their collective curiosity. His pulse sped up even though no one's body language was threatening. Tense, yes, but the vibe wasn't that of people ready to throw down.

Greer dismounted from his bike with a wince. "Any chance of getting something to drink?"

A woman in her forties with a gray-streaked ponytail and light-blue eyes stepped forward. The white apron around her waist accentuated her slim build. "We're brewing coffee on a camp stove since the regulars won't stop coming." She looked them over. "You boys aren't from around here."

"We aren't," Caleb said, keeping his tone friendly but neutral. "We're going to Specter Lake."

A buzz, like a swarm of bees, came to life among those gathered. A younger man in his twenties perked up and stood. He resembled the elderly man sitting in the chair beside him, with the same square jaw and heavy brow. "Specter Lake?"

Greer nodded. "Yes."

The young man stepped forward and partly in front of the

young woman next to him. "We just came from that direction yesterday. Not Specter Lake but Coleman."

The woman's straight black hair was pulled back from her face. Her fair skin was pink from sunburn. There was a subtle difference to the shape of her brown eyes. Asian ancestry, maybe, but maybe not. Caleb couldn't say with any certainty, and he sure as hell didn't care. What caught his attention most, apart from the way the young man was shielding her with his body, was her rigid posture. She studied Caleb and Greer like a deer, trying to decide if it should stand its ground or run.

"Did you drive or bike?" Greer asked when the young man didn't answer. If he'd noticed the couple's body language and the tense undercurrent, he wasn't letting on.

"We biked. My grandparents live here and I wanted to check on them when the power stayed out." The young man paused. "You know there was an EMP, right?"

"Yes, we do." Greer extended his hand but didn't move closer. "I'm Deputy US Marshal Cody Greer. This is my colleague, Caleb. He thinks it was a coronal mass ejection, not an EMP." Greer ducked his chin with a smile. "He understands this stuff. I just take his word for it."

Maybe Greer had noticed the couple's body language, since he was employing self-deprecating humor. And apparently, the two of them were colleagues. Wonders never did cease. The young man hesitated, then said, "What's a US Marshal doing here?"

"Trying to get home. I live in Specter Lake."

The young man and the rest of the group relaxed. The young man extended his hand. "I'm Ben. This is my fiancée, Mei. And that's my grandfather. He's Ben, too."

While Greer introduced himself and showed his credentials, Caleb scanned the area. The coffee shop crowd seemed harmless enough, but something had happened to make the couple so jumpy. When there was a break in the conversation, he said, "How's the route to Specter Lake?"

Ben and Mei exchanged glances. "Okay," Mei said, though her

tone didn't match her words. "Mostly." She paused, looked at Ben, and then continued. "But there are these roadblocks set up by locals. Three of them."

Here it is, Caleb thought.

Greer's brow furrowed. "Roadblocks?"

"More like citizen checkpoints, I guess you'd call them," Ben explained. "Two of them were fine. Just neighbors making sure people knew where they were, probably trying to keep trouble-makers out. They offered us water and directions, just like you'd expect in an emergency."

"But one was different," Caleb said.

Mei bit her lip and looked at her feet. Ben took her hand. "It was the middle one, about halfway on the cutoff road," he said. "Those guys were... intense."

"They were scary," Mei said. "I'd have turned around when we saw the next one, but going back..." She shook her head. "I wasn't going back there. I'd hike around with my bike first."

Greer leaned forward. "Scary how?"

Caleb felt a familiar tension coiling in his shoulders. Whatever was coming wasn't good. "They had a lot of guns," Ben said slowly. "And wanted to know where we lived."

"They were really aggressive about it," Mei said.

Ben nodded. "They kept talking about securing the area from undesirables and criminals coming to our country. And I was like, 'Guys, I just wanna check on my grandma and grandpa.'"

"Were they dressed a particular way?" Greer asked. "Wearing anything distinctive, like an informal uniform? Tattoos? Anything like that?"

Both Ben and Mei shook their heads. Then Mei said, "They were really checking me out. Not because they thought I was pretty or anything," she said, her face reddening. "They freaked me out. I don't know what they were looking for but—" She stopped, looked at her feet, and bit her lip. Her shoulders slumped, and she huffed out a short breath, the kind that often precedes tears.

"That's not true," she said, her voice now tight and squeaky. "My grandmother was from China. Her husband was Caucasian, and so was my mom. Sometimes people sense a difference about my features, usually my eyes, but can't put their finger on it. I think that's what was bothering the guy hassling us the most."

Ben pulled Mei closer, his arm slipping around her shoulders. "When they started with the foreigner stuff, that's when I said it was cool and we'd go back, but they let us through. We were almost afraid to go on, you know? But it might have made them more suspicious if we didn't."

"I won't go that way again," Mei said, her features pinched. "I don't care if it's longer to go around or if I have to carry Ben."

Caleb and Greer exchanged glances. In addition to sucking on its own merits, this complicated things. Caleb heard Greer curse under his breath, then ask, "Is there a way around?"

The coffee shop owner returned then, a tray with several cups of coffee on it. "It's on the house." As she pressed a steaming cup into Caleb's hands, she said, "I'm Barbara, by the way, and you're gonna need the coffee. You won't like the alternatives."

After telling everyone else the rest of the coffee was first come, first served, Barbara leaned against one of the sidewalk tables to join the conversation. A middle-aged man, doughy around the middle with a kindly face, said, "After you cross the bridge, you either take Dufort Road all the way to I-95 and go south or take the HooDoo Valley Trail."

Caleb saw Greer's shoulders slump. He felt his own body fizz like a deflating balloon. They'd already seen some of what I-95 had to offer at Sandpoint. He could only imagine how much worse it might be near more populated areas. And the Hoo what? In Caleb's experience, 'trail' usually meant 'long and out of the way.'

Having seen their reaction, the man who had made the suggestion frowned. "I hate to say it, but if I were you, I'd take HooDoo Valley Trail."

"Jerry's right," Mei said, nodding at the doughy man. "That's the way I'd go if we had to do it again." Then, with a note of apology, she added, "It's a lot longer, but it's remote and peaceful, and it's paved. I can't imagine you'll run into problems out there."

"Just how long are we talking about?" Caleb asked.

An uncomfortable silence that no one seemed willing to break was filled with reluctant glances between the locals. Then the man who had suggested it said, "The trail is twenty-seven miles, plus getting to and from it."

"How bad is your foot?" Barbara asked Greer. "You're limping."

"It's sprained," the marshal said quickly.

"He's got two metatarsal fractures," Caleb said, feeling suddenly testy. What the hell did Greer think saying it was sprained would achieve?

The murmur of conversation picked up around Caleb. Barbara disappeared inside and returned with a small pill bottle. "Take this," she said, handing the bottle to Greer. "It's oxycodone left over from my rotator cuff surgery. My physical therapist suggested I take one before our sessions." Greer started to protest, but she waved him off. "I don't need them anymore. You do."

While Greer and Barbara talked, Ben and Mei told Caleb about the trail that everyone thought they should take. "I know that look," Jerry said. Caleb hadn't noticed him join them. Jesus, he thought, appalled by the lapse. If he kept this up, he'd be like every other person who lost all situational awareness the second they entered Costco.

"What look is that?" Caleb said.

Jerry smiled wryly. "You're figuring out how much longer this is going to take."

Caleb nodded. "A lot longer than I want it to."

"I've got a '74 Ford pickup that's still running. I'll drive you boys as far as the trailhead. It's not much, but it'll save you a few miles."

It took Caleb a moment to react. "Why would you do that? You should conserve your gas or at least get a trade."

Jerry shrugged, confusion wrinkling his brow. "Because I can. And I feel bad about suggesting the trail."

"But—"

"I've got my family to look after so I can't take you any farther. You're right, that gas is too precious to waste. But the trailhead? That I can do."

"Jerry's good people," Barbara called over to them. "If he's offering, take it."

Greer hobbled over to join them. "What's the offer?"

"A ride to the trailhead," Caleb explained, still puzzled by the man's generosity. "We can't pay you anything."

"I didn't ask you to," Jerry said simply, as if the matter were closed.

While they worked out the details with Jerry, the other locals got them a trail map, more water, some trail mix, and dried fruit. When they protested, for they had supplies, no one would hear of taking anything back. Caleb watched it all unfold with a growing sense of confusion. These people didn't know them. They owed him and Greer nothing.

Greer pulled him aside, fidgeting like he was nervous. "I know you have no reason to and I know it's asking too much, but— Would you be willing to go ahead to Specter Lake? I'm slowing us down, but you could make better time if you're willing to do it."

It felt like it took a year for Caleb to catch up. "Will I— You trust me to go check on your family and not just take off?"

Greer leveled his blue-eyed gaze straight at Caleb. "Yeah. I guess I do."

For a split second, Caleb considered it. He could be free of Greer and make better time to Coeur d'Alene to find his sister. He didn't have to go to Specter Lake; he could just go. But Greer stood before him, banged up from head to toe, fear for his family and hope that Caleb might grant him this favor tangled in his eyes, and he knew he couldn't. He couldn't be the reason Greer's daughter grew up without a father. He'd lived that life and it was bad enough in the world they knew. It was bound to be worse in this one. He didn't want to be lumped in with those men Ben and Mei had met on the road who seemed to be doing whatever they wanted.

His fear for Ruth's safety, for her children, still coiled in his chest and muddled his thinking. His sister was smart—smarter than he ever was. His fear of never making things right, that was what whispered she needed him. The truth was, he'd been absent for years. Ruth and her kids got along just fine without him. Caleb was the one who couldn't say the same. He shook his head. "No. We stick together."

Surprise, and something like respect, flickered in Greer's eyes. "She'll be okay, your sister."

"You don't know that," Caleb said, sharper than he intended.

"You're right, I don't," Greer admitted, a conciliatory note in his voice now. "But if she's anything like you, she's tough. A survivor."

Caleb didn't respond. The tightness in his throat wouldn't allow it. He nodded and turned away. Greer was right that Ruth was a survivor, but wrong about her being tough like him. When it came to inner strength, it had always been the other way around.

An hour later, they were loading their bikes into the back of Jerry's pickup truck. The locals from the coffee shop had gathered to see them off, offering final bits of advice and encouragement. "Stick to the HooDoo," Ben said. "It'll take longer, but you'll avoid those checkpoints."

"Watch for bears," Barbara said, her voice teasing.

Jerry slammed the tailgate shut. "Let's go, boys."

As he waited for Greer to get in the truck, Caleb struggled to process the kindness they'd been shown. After years of keeping to himself, of assuming the worst about people's motives, of building walls to protect himself from disappointment, this outpouring of generosity left him... He didn't know what it left him feeling. He couldn't even hazard a guess. He had believed his life couldn't get better, that he would always be alone, but these people gave freely. They created community instead of division and, for the brief time he was here, made him feel part of it.

As Jerry's truck pulled away, Caleb looked back at the people waving goodbye. Maybe his choices hadn't just been about rebelling against a system that wronged him, but reinforcing his belief that people couldn't be trusted. Now, he wondered if he'd been wrong.

chapter
thirty

TUESDAY, JULY 15
    9:12 AM

Pete stood at the back of his weathered pickup truck, his face gleaming with sweat as he arranged a complex assembly of plastic barrels, PVC pipes, and garden hoses. He worked with the confidence of someone familiar with how all the pieces of his device worked. When he noticed their approach, he straightened up with a grunt.

"About time," he said, sounding gruff, but there was no real bite to his words. "Get those containers lined up over there."

Emma, Maria, and Chuy joined the small crowd gathering around Pete's contraption. "What are we looking at here, Pete?" Chuy asked.

Pete's gaze swept over the group. He took his time. His scowl, hard eyes, and knitted brow made it seem as if he found every single one of them an imbecile. Then the scowl softened. "This," he said, tapping the largest barrel, "is a gravity-fed water filtration system. It's simple, but effective." He pointed to the different layers visible through the semitransparent plastic. "We've got sand, activated charcoal, and cloth. Water goes in dirty at the top and comes out clean at the bottom."

"Does that work?" a woman Emma hadn't met asked in a voice brimmed with skepticism.

"You bet your ass it does," Pete said, sounding as if she'd just called his new puppy homely. "This process alone removes most pathogens and sediment."

Emma peered inside. Assembled from rain barrels and five-gallon buckets, the system looked too simplistic for the task at hand. The same woman followed up with, "Most pathogens doesn't sound drinkable."

"If you'll let me continue," Pete said, his tone so frosty Emma almost shivered. "After filtering, the water still needs chemical treatment to remove whatever the gravity-fed system can't." He hoisted high a gallon jug bottle of bleach sitting on the truck tailgate. "Eight drops of regular unscented bleach per gallon for clear water, sixteen if it's cloudy. Let it stand for thirty minutes to let the bleach do its work, and you've got potable water."

From the surrounding murmurs, the others seemed as impressed as Emma. "How many gallons can this process?" Chuy asked.

"About five gallons every fifteen minutes," Pete said. "We need an assembly line. Two or three people filling, two filtering, two treating and labeling."

"How often do we need to change out the sand and charcoal?" Maria asked.

Pete nodded at Maria as if he approved of her question. From the little Emma had seen of his prepping mentality, he probably did.

"Good question," he said. "Sand and charcoal don't last forever. Replace the sand every two to three months, sooner if water comes through slow or cloudy. The charcoal's trickier. It loses effectiveness after about a month, depending on how much we're running through it. The cloth you can rinse and reuse until it's shot."

He knocked on a barrel. "It's not just the layers, though. These barrels need scrubbing every couple months. Mold loves damp plastic."

"Sounds like a full-time job," Maria said.

Pete almost smiled at her. "That's where recordkeeping comes in. We need to mark the dates when we rotate materials and log the output. If we keep the system healthy, it does the same for us."

Maria whistled. "Look at you, Mister Organized. How much charcoal do you have in your garage? I bet it looks like you've got a Costco in there."

Pete shot her a mock glare. "Like I'd ever let the likes of you in my garage."

Maria shrugged, smiling. "I'll get to see that stash someday, Pete. Unless you want to find someone else who can stand cutting your hair."

"Yeah, yeah," he said, waving her off. "You're a pain in the ass, Maria, but you're all right for a Mexican."

Maria laughed. "You know I'm from Arizona, *listillo*."

Emma didn't need to speak Spanish to see the sassy affection in Pete and Maria's banter. When she'd first met him, Emma had never considered Pete might be affectionate with anyone. As Pete divided them into teams, a tentative flicker of hope ignited in Emma's heart. This was tangible progress, a solution to one of their most pressing problems. Paired with Maria for treating and labeling, Emma had nothing to do yet. "I need to talk to Pete," she told Maria. "Be right back."

Pete stood at the filling station, explaining how to pour without backsplash. Emma waited, then said, "Pete, can I talk to you for a second?"

Pete gave her a look that was more like a glare, but he nodded. "You got this?" he said to Chuy.

When Chuy nodded, Pete said, "C'mon," and walked twenty feet away. Emma's brow furrowed. Pete didn't know what she wanted to talk about, so why walk away? Then again, he was paranoid. Maybe that's just how he did things. Pete stopped and crossed his arms like he was prepared to hold his ground. "What's on your mind?"

Emma's stomach fluttered, her palms clammy. Pete might be an affectionate pain in the ass with Maria, but with his downturned mouth, beetled brow, and squinting gray eyes, he looked ready for a fight. She didn't want to make him angry, but this was important. "Do you know Dave Harper? I'm told he runs the city water treatment plant."

Pete's eyes narrowed even more. "Yeah, I know Dave. Why?"

"Um... well... I haven't met him myself. I just remember him being talked about at the Town Hall meeting." At her mention of the Town Hall, Pete rolled his eyes. "I was thinking—if your system works this well for a small group, maybe Dave could use your expertise to help get some kind of municipal solution going. Or at least something..."

Her voice trailed away. Pete's scowl had, if anything, changed to one of disgust. "They don't want my help. They've got their own ways of doing things, just like I've got mine."

"But those ways aren't working right now," Emma pressed. "People are getting desperate. We need to avoid that."

Pete's jaw worked. He looked like he had a foul taste in his mouth. "I don't play well with bureaucrats."

"I don't think anyone does," she said, trying to build rapport. Unfortunately, she had recent experience with men unreceptive to her suggestions. It was why she was here. "Will you at least think about talking to him?" Then, inspired, she added, "I might have to sic Maria on you otherwise."

Pete's laugh was short but genuine, lighting his face like a firefly. His posture relaxed. He looked like a different person. "Christ, anything but that." His gaze drifted to where Maria was organizing empty jugs. "That woman could talk a fish into climbing a tree."

Emma smiled. "So you'll think about it?"

He didn't answer right away. It seemed to Emma that he was trying to pull his frowny face back together. "I'll think about it." Under his breath, he muttered, "I had to try a Mexican for a haircut and look where it's got me."

"Didn't she say she's from Arizona?"

"Yeah, yeah," Pete said, but there was a millisecond flash of amusement in his eye. "Believe what you want. It's still a free country."

Emma smiled, counting this as a victory.

"I hear you had a run-in with Diane's ex last night."

Emma's eyes widened in surprise. "How did you hear about that?" The altercation last night hadn't been loud enough for people beyond the bend to hear, had it?

Pete stepped closer. His eyes had that hard, flinty look again. "Small neighborhood. Even smaller now. Let's just say Heath Landry's reputation precedes him. The county prosecutor had to ask for a change of venue to get Diane that restraining order."

"How do you know that?" Emma asked.

Emma had been practicing law for six years now. Many factors justified a prosecutor or defense attorney's request for a venue change. In a small town, the most common reasons for a change were probably the judge had some connection with the defendant or plaintiff and needed to recuse him or herself, or the prosecution or defense—sometimes both—felt the jury pool was tainted. Either circumstance could make a fair trial impossible. Both scenarios made sense in a small community like Specter Lake. Still, the news felt ominous. Emma's trepidation about the incident, already high, ramped up a notch.

"Public record," he said, almost a little too quickly. "I retired up here from Los Angeles. I was a police officer for twenty-five years. When you're on the job that long, you become a good judge of character. I knew Heath Landry was trouble the first time I met him."

The revelation sent a chill down Emma's spine.

Then Pete said, "I was told a guy who's no longer on the force went to high school with Landry. The guy who told me never came out and said it, but I think incidents got downplayed for quite some time."

A wave of light-headedness made the world at the edges of her vision move too fast. "Is he dangerous?"

"Any man who beats his wife is dangerous."

It made more sense now that Heath had so blatantly violated the order. Even if his friend was no longer around to run interference, Heath was right about one thing. With everything else going on, someone violating a restraining order wouldn't be at the top of any police department's priority list.

Now that she thought about it, Heath's confidence hadn't faltered until she'd mentioned declared emergencies and federal involvement. Well, that's fucking great, she thought. Maybe keeping the gun at her bed last night hadn't been paranoid. Mouth dry, Emma said, "Thanks for telling me, Pete."

"If he comes around again, don't hesitate. Get help. Your husband's law enforcement, right?" Emma nodded, and Pete said, "Then I expect you have firearms." When she nodded again, Pete's face darkened like a thunderhead. "The self-defense statute in Idaho is Stand Your Ground. There's no duty to retreat if you believe your life is in danger."

Emma swallowed hard and nodded. Her stomach roiled like those machines used to train astronauts that whirled around so fast they simulated different intensities of G-forces. Did he really think it was that bad?

"Hey now," Pete said, his voice returning to its usual level of gruffness. "I didn't mean to scare you. Just thought you should know. How about we get this water filtered before we all die of thirst?"

chapter
thirty-one

EMMA

TUESDAY, JULY 15
11:12 AM

A few hours later, the water filtration operation was running smoothly. Everyone had rotated through conducting and monitoring all stages of the process. Five-gallon containers stood filled and treated. Distribution would begin with households that had the greatest need. Emma's back ached from bending and lifting, but the rhythm of work kept her mind from spinning on any one thing too much—like if Grace was okay and where Cody might be. Or if Diane's ex-husband was going to be a much bigger problem.

The rumble of an approaching engine caught Emma's ear. Tom's old pickup emerged from the tree line. He parked at the edge of the clearing and climbed out, his silver hair catching the sunlight.

"Tom!" Chuy called, waving him over. "You're just in time to haul water."

"I've got some news," he said as he approached. Tom's shoulders were a little slumped. He was tired, just like everyone else, but his face was lit with excitement. "The National Guard has arrived from Boise."

Emma's heart leaped in her chest. The zing of energy leaping from person to person felt like a high-tension wire electrifying the small group. This meant news about what was happening and help. The gargantuan weight of fear and responsibility sloughed from Emma's shoulders like a two-ton icefall. "Any word about what's happening?"

"It's not good. I thought you'd like to meet the officer in charge, so I came straight over."

"Maria and I can handle things here," Pete said. "You go."

Emma hesitated, torn between their need for water and for information.

"Go," Maria said. "Find out what's happening."

———

Specter Lake's town square hummed with activity. A military Humvee and two olive-drab trucks were parked in front of Town Hall. National Guardsmen in camouflage uniforms directed a line of people toward tables where supplies were being distributed. Emma squinted, noting they handed out bottles of water, MRE rations, and basic medical supplies.

The soldiers looked about to drop, their faces streaked with dirt and eyes puffy with fatigue. Emma counted only eight of them, not enough for a relief operation. A young lieutenant stood near the tailgate of the closest truck, pointing at something while she spoke with another soldier.

"That's her," Tom said. "Come on."

When Tom approached, she looked up. Her expression changed from politely attentive to one of recognition. "Lieutenant Vargas," Tom said, holding out his hand, which the young woman shook. "These are the folks I mentioned. Emma Greer and Jesús Rodriguez."

"Lieutenant Angela Vargas, 116th Cavalry Brigade Combat Team, ma'am, sire" she said, shaking Emma's and Chuy's hands in turn. Her brown hair was pulled into a tight bun at the nape of her neck, low enough not to catch on her cap. Her light-brown eyes were alert, even though dark circles below them signified a lack of sleep. She smiled, and most of the fatigue slipped from her face, lightening her features.

To Emma, she said, "Mister..." She hesitated, then looked at Tom and said, "Wilson?" At his nod, she smiled again. "He says you're organizing your neighborhood."

"We're trying," Emma said. "What is going on? You're the only relief effort we've seen."

Lieutenant Vargas glanced around, then gestured for them to follow her to a quieter spot beside one of the trucks. "It was the solar flare. Do you know about that?" When they nodded, she said, "It knocked out most electronics across the Western United States. It might be nationwide. We don't know for sure. Communications are spotty at best."

Emma gasped and took a step back. She felt the blow in her whole body, like a concrete building collapsing on top of her.

"Wh— What?" Chuy said, his speech stumbling. "All the western states?"

"I'm afraid so, sir. The power grid is confirmed down in at least seven states—California, Oregon, Washington, Idaho, Nevada, Arizona, and Colorado, but it's probably more. Every major city that command has made contact with is experiencing the same issues: no electricity, no running water, severely limited transportation, and medical need that is off the charts."

Emma's chest felt so tight she could barely breathe. Nationwide? "What about federal assistance?" she said, her voice squeaking. "FEMA or Homeland Security?"

A flicker of something—frustration? resignation?—passed across the lieutenant's face. "This is bigger than that. FEMA's resources are stretched beyond capacity; Homeland Security, too. I've heard they're organizing a response but I haven't seen anything myself." She added, her voice apologetic, "Major population centers are the priority."

Tom sounded resigned when he said, "And we're not a major population center."

Lieutenant Vargas' eyes seemed to beg an apology. "We're only stopping because you're on our route. We have three more towns to reach today. I'm afraid we can only leave limited supplies."

"So we're on our own," Chuy said, his voice barely more than a whisper.

"For the foreseeable future, yes." Vargas' voice softened. "I won't sugarcoat it. Boise and Idaho Falls are a mess. If it's not refugees clogging the roads, it's vehicles that can't start, civil unrest, and casualties are high. Hospitals are overwhelmed. It's the same thing everywhere we've had reports: Salt Lake City, Portland, Seattle, Oakland, San Jose, Denver. Coeur d'Alene wasn't so bad at first, but..." She shrugged. "You'll have displaced people here soon if you don't already."

Emma asked, her voice barely above a whisper, "How long until things start getting back to normal?"

Lieutenant Vargas met her gaze directly. "Ma'am, there is no 'back to normal.' The infrastructure damage is catastrophic. Even with every functional resource deployed, we're looking at months, maybe years."

Lieutenant Vargas kept talking, but Emma didn't hear it over the static roaring inside her skull. Months, maybe years. *Years.* The implications crashed through her brain like a sledgehammer, so hard she couldn't keep up. No power. No running water. No medical services. No supply chains. Just whatever they could cobble together.

And Grace. Tiny, vulnerable Grace. How was she supposed to keep her safe? Keep her alive?

"...winter," the lieutenant said.

The word snagged on Emma's ear. "What about winter?"

"You need to think about food stores, alternative heat sources, security."

"Idaho winters are no joke," Tom said, sounding as serious as a heart attack. "Is there anything else you can tell us?"

A voice called out, "Lieutenant."

Vargas looked over her shoulder. A woman of about thirty approached from the rear of the truck. Her light-brown hair was pulled back in a ponytail and a stethoscope hung around her neck. Dark smudges under her eyes attested to long hours of taking care of people, but she had the purposeful stride of someone accustomed to dealing with high-stress situations. Vargas said to them, "Give me a sec," and turned away. "What's up, Ruth?"

"Word's gotten out that we're here. There are a lot more residents arriving. How much time do we have to triage and identify those we can help before we go?"

"I'm meeting with the town council and local law enforcement soon." Vargas checked her watch. "Crap, right now, actually. We'll be here a couple hours, anyway. I'll follow up with you afterward. You and the docs just use your best judgment."

Ruth nodded, offering Emma and the others a brief, tired smile. As she walked away, Emma saw a girl and a boy chasing one another at the back of the truck. Ruth called after them, but Emma didn't hear what she said. She didn't recognize the children, but she didn't recognize most people yet.

Vargas returned her attention to them. "We've been ordered to report to Fairchild Air Force Base, east of Spokane. They have operational facilities." She shrugged. "More than most, anyway. Command is concentrating military assets there to better respond to the crisis."

"Oh," Emma whispered.

"Is anyone coming?" Tom asked.

"I honestly don't know, sir," Vargas said. "I wish I had better news."

"Thank you for your honesty," Emma said, sounding like an

automaton programmed to maintain an appropriate level of professional courtesy.

The lieutenant turned and walked away, heading for the town hall. They stood in stunned silence. Emma was having trouble processing what she'd been told. It was too big. Tom sounded stunned as he said, "All the western states? It's one thing to suspect..."

When his voice trailed, Chuy finished the thought. "And another to have it confirmed."

Emma stared at the line of people waiting for their meager rations. Tired, pinched faces, some cast with a premonition of gauntness that spoke of missed meals. This was just the beginning. It was only going to get worse.

"We should get supplies while we can," Tom said. "Then head back and spread the word. People need to know."

Chuy sighed. "The mayor and town council are going to screw this up. *Querido Dios.*"

Emma nodded, mutely following as Tom led them toward the distribution line, but her mind raced. They needed to expand the water filtration on a vastly larger scale. Organize food distribution. Establish security. Find out what, if anything, the town council and local emergency services were doing. And as much as it seemed irrelevant in the broiling July heat, prepare for cold weather. They faced a mountain of need with a molehill of resources. It would only get harder as supplies dwindled and desperation grew.

An hour later, with three bags of supplies in the truck bed, they climbed into the truck. "Emma," Tom said gently. "Should we drop you at my house to check on Grace? Maybe get some rest? You look dead on your feet."

The mention of her daughter sent a spike of longing through Emma. Her breasts, full with milk, throbbed. She wanted to hold Grace, breathe in the sweet scent of her hair, feel the weight of her in her arms. She wanted to pretend that the world wasn't crumbling around them, that any minute now, Cody would stroll through the door. But pretending wouldn't filter water. It wouldn't gather supplies. It wouldn't do a damn thing they needed. "I can put in another hour or two at the lake," she said, straightening her spine. "I'll rest later."

Tom's eyes were so full of concern for her that her eyes flooded with tears. "Are you sure?" he said.

Emma nodded. "Yeah. We have work to do."

Tom steered the truck onto the road to return to the lake and their makeshift solution for one problem among more than Emma could count. It was an imperfect solution, perhaps, but real. One small answer in a world now full of questions she didn't have answers for. It would have to be enough—they would have to be enough—because now they knew. No one was coming to save them.

day five

chapter
thirty-two

EMMA

WEDNESDAY, JULY 16
 3:00 PM

Emma dabbed her cheek with a cloth moistened from her dwindling water supply, then bent over the bassinet where Grace slept. Again. The baby's chest rose and fell in a rhythm that should have reassured her, but a cold tendril of worry circled nonstop in Emma's brain. Grace had slept far more than usual today, even for her age. The times she'd been awake, her fussing had an edge to it that Emma hadn't heard before.

She brushed her fingertips against Grace's forehead. Still warm. The same warmth that had troubled her when she'd nursed Grace thirty minutes ago. She hadn't nursed well. The same warmth that had kept her checking and rechecking the rise and fall of her tiny chest.

Emma rubbed at her eyes before her gaze drifted to the purple edges of paper on the kitchen table—the so-called "Emergency Guidelines" that someone from the mayor's office had tacked on her front door while she'd been at the lake or in town. Emma scanned the list again.

Conserve water by flushing toilets only once per day. Because they had water to flush toilets.

Report to designated congregation points for daily updates. For what, the memo didn't say, nor were the 'congregation points' specified.

Register household medical needs at Town Hall between 10 AM and 2 PM daily.

Maybe they were doing something useful with that last one, but how realistic was it for people who lived far from town? What about people who were infirm or had limited mobility? Not everyone could walk into town like she could. She stood and looked down at Grace. "What do you think, Gracie?" she whispered, running the back of her forefinger over the swell of Grace's cheek. "Yeah... I think we're screwed, too."

A knock on the front door sent her pulse spiking. She flinched. Heath's threatening posture flashed through her mind. She forced herself to peek through the window first instead of going to the bedroom for the Walther. Martha stood on the porch, her silver hair pulled back from her face. Emma released her suspended breath and opened the door.

"Did you see this?" Martha asked, waving her own guidelines sheet.

"Yep," Emma said, opening the screen door.

Martha entered, following Emma to the kitchen. "You know what I want to know? Where did they find the one functioning manual mimeograph machine in the county to print these? I didn't know they still made the ink."

"Is that how they did it?" Emma asked, looking again at the purply blue ink. "I wondered about that."

Martha tossed her sheet of paper on the table. It drifted lazily on a pocket of air before settling on the polished wood. "We called these dittoes. When Sister Mary Catherine handed out new ones, all of us kids had them up to our faces like we were huffing glue.

They smelled like grape Kool-Aid spiked with nail polish remover." She laughed. "It sounds terrible, but I loved that smell, especially when they were right off the machine and the paper was still cold."

Martha sat down at the table. A corner of her mouth quirked up. "If they're going to insult us with this crap, they could have at least given them to us fresh. You look exhausted. Trouble sleeping?"

Emma glanced away. "Yeah. Grace was restless last night." It wasn't entirely a lie, but worrying about Heath accounted for ninety-five percent of her lack of sleep.

"You weren't jumpy after the run-in with Heath the other day? I am, and Diane's staying with me."

Emma sighed. "Every noise had me reaching for my gun." The admission felt like a release valve on the pressure building in her chest. "I'm not kidding. I learned to shoot when Cody and I got serious. I figured if there was going to be a firearm in the house, I should know how to handle it safely. Having it under the bed like that... I failed the gun safety test." Emma shook her head, still surprised at herself. "I can't believe I confronted him when I had Grace with me. I keep thinking about what might have happened if he hadn't left."

"You did a good job of intimidating him." Martha's face lit up and her voice had a distinct note of gleeful gloating. "Were you really a district attorney?"

Emma nodded. "I worked in the Anne Arundel County district attorney's office outside of DC, but not for long. Going to court was too stressful, even as third chair, and I had tons of student loans. Private practice paid better."

Martha covered her mouth with her hand but didn't quite stifle her yawn. "Are you still planning to come to Janice's meeting?"

Emma glanced at Grace, then shook her head. "Grace still feels warm, and I don't think it's just the heat. I'm going to Susan's to ask her to look at Grace."

Martha frowned, stretching her neck to look at the sleeping baby. "Susan left early this morning with Doctor Meyers. They're doing house calls for people who can't get to the clinic."

"Right, of course," Emma said. Of course, Susan was helping. Not that Emma knew her well, but the combination of Susan's nursing and Iris's beekeeping made her think the couple were the kind of people you could depend on when things got tough.

"She'll be at the meeting unless something's changed," Martha added. "She told Tom so when he saw her this morning."

"Then I guess I'm going to the meeting. When is it?"

Martha checked the watch on her wrist. She must have found an older one. "In about fifteen minutes."

"Just give me a minute to get the diaper bag together." Emma stood, a wave of dizziness making her blink. She probably needed to drink some water. She went to the nursery and packed up the diaper bag. As she stepped into the hall, she hesitated, then went to the bedroom and retrieved the gun from under the bed. With no safety to check—not the kind with a button, anyway—she slipped the weapon into the diaper bag beneath the extra diapers.

Martha had already gotten the umbrella stroller out. Emma checked Grace's diaper, then lifted her from the bassinet. Grace's whimper made her wince. She buckled her into the stroller and snapped the sunshade into place, then tucked a cloth diaper under Grace's chin. Grace had been drooling all day, and she was far too young for it to be teething related. Another symptom that wrung Emma's stomach like a rag.

"Do you want me to carry that?" Martha asked when Emma picked up the diaper bag.

Emma shook her head as she slipped the diaper bag over her shoulder. "It's fine. I've got it."

There was no way she was letting anyone touch the diaper bag. Martha would notice its weight and Emma wasn't getting into explanations. She found the weight of the gun reassuring. And kind of terrifying that she'd been reduced to feeling so unsafe in her own home—and neighborhood—that she felt like she needed it.

"I brought this," Martha said. She pulled a tiny battery-powered handheld fan from her front shorts pocket. "I thought it might help with Grace."

A rush of gratitude brought tears to Emma's eyes. "Thank you," she said, her voice getting tight. The small kindness felt enormous. I am really overtired, she thought.

As they walked toward the clubhouse, Emma scanned every yard, every shadowy space. "Do you think he's still around?"

Martha didn't pretend not to understand. "Heath? I doubt it. He's a coward when it comes down to it. Men like him always are. Besides, there are too many witnesses in the daytime."

Her words were meant to reassure but instead fueled Emma's worst disaster scenarios. There was no way to know what might happen next in the dark.

The community clubhouse was located just inside the entrance to the neighborhood, a low-slung building with a brightly colored sign that read Welcome to Lakeside Pines Estates, Where Dreams Come to Live. When she'd first seen the sign, Emma had laughed out loud. "They get points for enthusiasm, I guess," she'd said to Cody.

"Emma! Martha!" Pete's gruff voice called from the side of the building. He stood in the shade and held up his copy of the mayor's office guidelines. "Have you seen this horseshit?"

Martha nodded as they met him. "Sure did."

Pete snorted, jabbing a finger at the paper. "'Limit cooking to one meal per day to conserve fuel.' What fuel? Half the neighborhood is on electric."

"Maybe they think we'll have campfires?" Martha said.

"Here's my favorite," Pete continued. "'Maintain normal hygiene routines to avoid illness.' Without water? And this one—'Prepare to evacuate if directed.' To where? In what?"

Grace stirred in her stroller. Emma peeked around the sunshade. Her tiny face scrunched, making her look like a grumpy old man. Straightening up, she said, "I think whoever wrote this doesn't grasp what's happening."

"Ya think?" Pete said, his voice dripping with derision. He glanced at the doors to the community clubhouse, then back to Emma and Martha, rising on his toes and raising his eyebrows. "This meeting's gonna be a waste of time, but I'm not missing the show. Shoulda brought popcorn." He nodded, then headed for the doors.

"He's a ray of sunshine," Martha said.

Despite her anxiety, one corner of Emma's mouth lifted. Not a smile, but not a frown. Pete was a curmudgeon, but she was starting to see why Maria liked him so much. "He knew about what happened with Diane the other night. Did you tell him?"

Martha shook her head. "No, but Diane may have. It doesn't hurt to have Pete on your side, whatever the problem is. He's a crusty old fart, but he comes through when the chips are down." Her expression brightened. "Ready for nothing?"

Emma huffed out a breath. "As I'll ever be," she said and followed Martha inside.

chapter
thirty-three

EMMA

WEDNESDAY, JULY 16
  3:30 PM

The inside of the clubhouse had the stale smell of a building not often used. The press of bodies and a few days without showers weren't improving the aroma. Every window stood open, but the air remained thick and unmoving. Rows of metal folding chairs, most with an occupant, faced a small raised platform at the front.

Emma spotted Tom and Carrie near the front row, their silver heads catching the light. Diane sat in the row in front of them, her copper braid immediately recognizable. Emma searched the room. Still no sign of Diane's ex-husband. As if sensing her thoughts, Diane turned and caught Emma's eye. She offered a small smile Emma returned.

Martha squeezed Emma's arm. "I see Susan and Iris with Maria and Chuy," she said, pointing toward the middle of the room. "There are two seats."

Emma shook her head. "I'll stand in the back. If Grace cries, I don't want to disturb everyone. I do want to talk to Susan, though. Do you mind staying here? Then I don't have to push the stroller through. I'll tell them to save you a seat."

Martha agreed, so Emma crossed to where Susan sat. "Susan, Iris, hi," she said, offering a smile. The two women looked up. They looked tired, but no more than anyone else. "Could you check Grace after the meeting? She's been warm and fussy and sleeping more than usual. I'm worried it's not just the heat."

Susan's face softened with a look of concern. "Of course. Are you sure waiting until after the meeting is okay?"

Relief loosened the band that had been tightening around Emma's chest all day. "Yes, thank you. And can you save a seat for Martha? She'll be over as soon as I get back to Grace."

Emma walked back to relieve Martha, then found a spot near an open window. A wisp of a breeze caressed her shoulder. Grace stirred again in the stroller and made an unhappy gurgle. Emma attached the fan Martha had given her to the sunshade of the stroller and turned it on. Its low, mechanical whirr—not to mention the tiny breeze it generated—seemed to soothe Grace.

While Emma waited for the meeting to start, she thought about what they'd learned from the National Guard. That they were on their own. She'd never realized just how fragile the infrastructure they depended on was; or rather, she'd never run up against it herself. She knew America's infrastructure had been neglected for decades, had read countless news stories about crumbling bridges and roads, and the fragility of the electrical grid, but it wasn't the kind of thing that stayed top of mind. And even if the grid wasn't antiquated, there didn't seem to be any way to protect all of it from what had just happened. Even the military didn't have all of its systems hardened for something like this.

We are so screwed.

She looked around the room at her neighbors, whom she was only now getting to know. It was obvious that everyone was scared and nervous. Emma was, too. But others—Chuy, Maria,

Martha, Pete, Carrie, and Tom—seemed resolved, which made her feel less alone.

As she looked around the room, Emma realized that she had stood where she could see every entrance and exit. On their third or fourth date, Emma had teased Cody, telling him she hoped he wasn't one of those guys who always had to sit with his back to a wall. Even now, she could hear his laugh. "Doors and corners," he'd said, grinning. "They're always what screws you, but no. I am not that guy."

I'd sell my soul to know where you are right now, she thought. She chewed on her lower lip, feeling the doom spiral, trying to take hold. Cody is fine, she said to herself. He's fine and will be home soon.

Janice appeared at the front of the room, as meticulous about her appearance as ever. "Ladies and gentlemen, if we can begin," she said, raising her voice. After the buzz of conversation quieted down, she began, "I'd like to take a moment of silence for the neighbors we've lost."

Emma closed her eyes, thinking of Kate's still form and the four other neighbors they'd found. Of all the people out there who had no one to check on them. And of Cody, who might be among the lost for all she—

Cody is fine, she told herself again. *He's zippity fucking sunshine and tweeting birds and bunnies fine.*

After a respectful pause, Janice continued. "Thank you. As president of the Lakeside Pines Estates Homeowners Association, I've called this emergency meeting to address the crisis we're facing."

Emma shifted her weight from one foot to the other, already regretting her decision to attend. The oppressive heat made it hard to concentrate. The diaper bag pulled on her shoulder and lay heavy against her hip, like an accusation. What kind of mother brought a gun to a community meeting? With the world falling apart, and after putting herself in the crosshairs of a violent man, what kind didn't?

"The HOA board has implemented several measures to ease problems during this unfortunate situation," Janice announced. "First, we've established a neighborhood watch rotation. Four-hour shifts, two people per shift, to patrol the perimeter of our community." Murmurs rippled through the crowd. Emma saw Pete, standing along the adjacent wall, roll his eyes. "Second," Janice continued, "we've authorized the use of HOA emergency funds to purchase additional supplies once services are restored."

"When that will be?" someone called out.

Janice's smile tightened. "The mayor has assured me that progress is being made." More murmurs, but with an undercurrent of dissatisfaction. "And our third measure," she said. "We've designated the clubhouse as our community hub. The board will post all official information here and maintain office hours to address concerns."

Emma noticed several people exchange incredulous glances. Someone near the front raised a hand.

"Yes, Rob?" Janice acknowledged.

"What about the neighborhood census? The folks who were checking door-to-door the other day are the only reason I have water. What's planned next? I want to pitch in."

"That was an unsanctioned effort," Janice said, her tone cooling. "While well intentioned, they didn't follow proper protocols."

"Proper protocols?" A middle-aged man stepped out from the wall on Emma's left. "It took me three days to get here from Coeur d'Alene. Those 'unsanctioned efforts' saved my mother's life. She's elderly and had passed out from dehydration when they went to her house."

"They got Mr. Davis his heart medication," someone else said.

Diane stood, her copper braid falling from her shoulder to trail down her back. "We're also helping people who need to get to town for medical attention find rides from those who have working vehicles. If that's something you need, please come talk to me, or Susan and Iris."

Janice's smile looked frozen as Diane sat down. "Again, while these efforts are well meaning, they're not being coordinated through proper channels. The HOA board needs to—"

"The board needs to get off its high horse," Pete called out. "People are dying while you're worrying about 'proper channels' and not being able to water your lawn."

That's a cheap shot, Emma thought, but she didn't disagree.

"I will not tolerate this kind of disrespect," Janice snapped. "We have procedures—"

"Your procedures are useless," a young woman said, standing up from her chair. "You say you're working with the mayor's office? What the heck is this?" She flapped the copy of the emergency guidelines clutched in her hand. "I went to town hall. All they did was give me the runaround. The police weren't much better. Can you tell us anything? Did you talk to the National Guard when they were here? I hear this might drag on for months."

The room erupted into overlapping voices and questions. Janice banged a gavel, its sharp crack cutting through the noise. She has a gavel? Emma thought. For an HOA meeting?

Janice shouted, "Order! I will have order!"

Grace chose that moment to wake up—no surprise, given the noise. Her pink face contorted as she let out a wail that pierced the cacophony of questions. For a moment, the room fell silent. Then the frustrated questions started up again.

Emma's cheeks burned as she headed for the door. She'd been so impatient with people and their crying children before having Grace. Now she was getting her comeuppance. Once outside, she cradled Grace's rigid body in her arms. Her diaper was dry, yet she continued to wail. Even in only a diaper, she felt too warm. Emma set down the diaper bag and paced in the shade on the grass beside the clubhouse sign saying Stay off the Grass.

"Shh, it's okay," she whispered, though nothing felt okay. Grace felt warmer than before, her small face flushed. What if this was something serious?

The clubhouse door banged open. Emma flinched, her heart racing. The diaper bag and gun were ten feet away. Then she realized it was only Susan. "I saw you leave," Susan said, approaching Emma. "Let's see what's going on with Grace."

They spread out a baby blanket Emma had stuffed below the seat of the stroller and lay Grace down. She promptly began to cry. "That's right, tell me all about it," Susan murmured as she felt Grace's forehead, then felt the glands in her neck. To Emma, she said, "You're right. She's running a fever. How long has she been like this?"

The question felt like a blow. What if this was measles or polio or something worse? Grace was only ten weeks old. She hadn't had all her vaccinations yet. "She was a little warm yesterday. No, the day before. I thought it was just the heat."

"Emma," Susan said. "Take a deep breath. Grace will be fine."

Emma blinked back tears, the stress of the past days hitting her all at once. "I'm sorry, I just— Cody's gone, and now Grace—"

"The last couple days have been a lot," Susan said, rubbing Emma's arm. "Believe me, I know. Is there anything else you've noticed?"

Emma took a deep, hitching breath. "Um, today she's sleeping more. She's fussy when she's awake. And she's drooling more than usual."

Susan nodded. "And you noticed her first symptoms two days ago?"

Emma nodded and bit her lip. Susan looked at the soles of Grace's feet, then turned her palms up. Tiny red spots dotted Grace's hands, clustered near the wrist.

"Has she been nursing okay?" Susan asked.

Emma shook her head. "Less than usual. She seems uncomfortable when she tries."

Susan nodded. "I think she has hand, foot, and mouth disease. It's common in babies and children. Uncomfortable, but it's usually not dangerous."

"Hand, foot, and mouth?" Emma repeated. "Isn't that what cows get?"

"No, that's a different disease. This is a viral infection that causes fever, fussiness, and a rash on hands and feet. Sometimes in the mouth, too, which makes eating painful." Susan stroked Grace's head. "The good news is that it will only last a week or so. The bad news is there's no specific treatment. We just keep her comfortable."

Emma was glad she was already kneeling because her legs felt weak. "So what do I do?"

"Keep her hydrated—that's the most important thing. You can't catch this, so nurse as much as she'll tolerate. Use cool compresses for the fever. We have children's acetaminophen from the last time the grandkids were visiting. It will bring her fever down."

"Thank you," Emma whispered, tears pricking her eyes. "I don't know what I would have done if—"

The clubhouse door banged open again. People streamed out, voices raised in dissatisfaction. Susan's mouth twisted in a wry grimace. "Looks like Janice's attempt to assert control didn't go well."

Emma barely noticed the people streaming by. Her world had narrowed to the feverish, unhappy baby on the blanket. Without Cody, without easy access to health care, without the safety net she'd always taken for granted, she felt stripped bare. Then she gave herself a mental shake. She was an adult, smart and capable, a member of the Virginia bar, for crying out loud. Susan had said this wasn't serious. She could handle it. She had to. "I should get her home."

"I'll walk you home, then get you the medicine."

"Don't you want to wait for Iris?"

Susan shook her head. "She'll probably confab with Pete a while. They love to make fun of Janice."

As they made their way down the street, passing neighbors having disgruntled conversations about Janice and her meeting, the mayor's office and its pointless guidelines, no power and no water, Emma felt disconnected from it all. The petty politics, the power struggles—none of it mattered compared to her daughter.

"Do you think—" Emma started, then swallowed hard. "Will we get back to normal?"

Susan took a moment before she replied. "I don't know, but people adapt. We find new normals."

Grace whimpered. She held her tiny arms out from under the stroller's sunshade. Her fingers clutched at the air, grasping for her mother or comfort or just because it was what babies did. Emma understood more than ever that she would do anything—absolutely anything—to protect her daughter. It didn't matter if the world was the one she'd always known or something else entirely. Protecting Grace would always come first.

As they approached Susan's house, Emma found herself scanning the street again. The weight of the gun in the diaper bag felt reassuring instead of troubling. Did that make this even more screwed up? It probably did. She was still glad she had it. "I wish Cody were here," she said, the words catching in her throat.

Susan nodded. "I know you do."

Above them, the afternoon sky had taken on that unnatural reddish tinge again as the aurora prepared for its nightly display. The beautiful lights that had filled Emma with wonder the first time she'd seen them now felt like a mocking reminder of all they had lost, and all they still might lose.

chapter
thirty-four

CODY

WEDNESDAY, JULY 16
   7:56 PM

My foot...

Cody's forehead wrinkled as his right foot pushed on the bicycle pedal.

Feels fine. My foot...

A hot lance of pain ripped through the top of his foot. "Goddammit!"

Cody quit pedaling and shifted his weight to touch his left foot to the ground. He must have cursed louder than he realized, for Frost stopped and looked back. Frost shook his head, then coasted back and stopped a few feet from Cody. "You let the pain get ahead of you again, didn't you?"

Cody sucked in a breath. He knew this mountain ridge wasn't high enough for thin air, but that didn't stop it feeling that way. When he met Frost's eyes, he expected a snarky comment.

Instead, Frost said with an exasperated edge, "Let's walk the rest of the way. You can take a painkiller when we get there."

Letting the bike bear some of his weight as he hobbled behind Frost didn't feel good, but his foot didn't feel like it was being sliced in half anymore. An hour ago, they'd seen the silhouette of the fire lookout tower above the pine forest canopy. Dark rain clouds had grown foreboding as they traveled north, carried on the warm wind that wicked away the sweat from Cody's face.

They stepped off the winding HooDoo Trail as fat raindrops dropped from the clouds. The hard dirt and springing pine needles cushioned Cody's feet. He stopped and tipped his head back. The cool raindrops pattered—light at first, then with more commitment. Within a few seconds, the rain wetted his face and ran down his neck.

The lookout tower had flights of stairs on three sides. He caught up with Frost, whose mountain bike leaned against the structure. Frost climbed, his lead increasing. When Cody reached the second landing, thunder cracked overhead with a percussive *boom*. The skies opened, unleashing the full force of the storm. Two jagged spears of lightning stabbed at the earth. Then a bright flash illuminated the landscape for miles, like a paparazzo's camera.

Frost waited for him at the last landing. Together, they opened the gate and stepped onto the balcony ringing the square structure. Cody took care to close the gate behind them. He wasn't getting this close to home, only to fall down the stairs in the dark and kill himself. Frost tried the door, which was locked. Not missing a beat, he pulled a multi-tool from a pocket and set to work picking the lock. That tracks, Cody thought, smothering a chuckle. "Breaking and entering," he said as they entered the small cabin. "Remind me to add it to the list."

Frost chuffed a laugh.

As Cody took in their surroundings, he felt his muscles relax. The fresh air coming through the open door helped dispel the stuffiness of the closed-up tower. The square room was small and what they needed: dry, elevated, and empty. Windows on all sides offered a panoramic view of the surrounding wilderness. Storm clouds obscured the aurora, muting its otherworldly glow to disjointed patches in the sky. Rain lashed against the glass in a staccato beat, the runnels of water turning the landscape into a blur of gray and green.

The simple furnishings included a single bed in one corner with faded mattress ticking, a long, low desk along one wall with cabinets below it, and a round wood table and chairs. Cody eased himself into a chair and stretched his leg out, sighing. "Take one of those painkillers," Frost said. "It'll take longer to get the pain under control because you skipped the last one."

The authority in his voice gave Cody a shiver. Frost could give Nurse Ratched a run for her money. Cody took a pill and peered into the bottle. In the fading light, eight pills remained. Taken every four to five hours, he had at least thirty-two hours of medicine left. Frost was right that he shouldn't have waited, but he'd never admit it. Frost searched the surfaces and cabinets with the efficient curiosity Cody recognized. If what he sought was here, Frost would find it. He looked under the desk, examined the window locks, and inspected the bed. Cody watched, part of him still struggling to reconcile the bank robber in the case file with the man he'd spent the past few days with. The man who saved Jenny and her children on the bridge, who worried for the couple who'd taken them in, who came back for him at the crash site when he could have made a clean escape.

"Jackpot," Frost said. He turned, brandishing a lantern in front of him in a flood of light. He kicked the door closed with his foot, then joined Cody, setting the lantern in the center of the table. Beside it he plunked down a three-quarters-full bottle of bourbon and a short glass on the table beside it. "This is the real find," he said, swishing the contents of the bottle. "But not for you, Marshal. You're taking opiates."

"That's convenient," Cody said. "How is the lantern working?"

"The base is a battery. If the battery is good and wasn't in use when the CME hit, it'll still work."

"I did not know that," Cody said.

"I'm not surprised," Frost said, almost grinning.

Cody bent over to loosen the laces of his boot and ease it from his foot. He peeled off his sock and unwound the athletic bandage. Without asking and before Cody could object, Frost knelt in front of him and took Cody's foot by the heel. He knew the painkiller was kicking in because if Frost had manhandled his foot like that before, he'd be howling like a wolf.

Frost gently pressed his fingers, now bandaged after their run-in with the Indian's spark plugs, along the top of his foot. Cody sucked in a breath. Frost said, "Still pretty swollen but not any worse. You might be able to wear your shoes in a day or two."

Cody looked at him, surprised. "You think?"

"Yeah. I've seen lots worse."

Before taking his seat, Frost pushed the third chair at Cody so he could rest his leg on it. Cody picked up his small backpack and fished out an apple and the squeeze tube of peanut butter. The apple's skin yielded with a juicy snap, moisture spraying on Cody's lips. His gaze drifted to a narrow table tucked against the wall near the door. He hadn't noticed it before; the open door had blocked it from view. In the warm glow of the lantern light, Cody spotted... something. An electric tingle rushed through his body. "By the door..." he said, pointing with his half-eaten apple. "Is that what I think it is?"

Frost followed his gaze. "Holy shit." In three steps, he stood in front of the HAM radio, lantern in hand. He set it beside the radio and looked it over. "It's an old one. Let's see if it works."

Cody followed Frost and stood a few paces behind him, the wood plank floor rough against his still bare foot. He held his breath. Frost looked at the wires attached to the radio and flipped the switches.

Nothing happened.

The buzz of energy that had filled the room, zipping and

weaving like the bright light of a fairy, fizzled. Cody sighed, releasing a held breath. After flipping more switches and fiddling with wires, Frost shoved the radio back in place with a sigh. "Even if the components aren't fried, the power source it's hooked up to probably is. We just don't have that kind of luck, do we, Marshal?"

The tone of his voice had a devil may care quality, but Cody could see he was crestfallen. When he rejoined Frost at the table, he saw he'd poured himself a very generous three fingers of bourbon. Frost swallowed it all in one go, then poured himself another. Frost was a big guy, and the kind who knew his limits. Cody wasn't about to start critiquing his drinking habits.

Cody stared into the lantern's glow. The painkiller had dulled the throbbing in his foot. He yawned, the physical exertion of the day catching up with him. If anyone had told him last week that he would hike out of the wilderness and then bicycle close to twenty miles with broken bones in his foot, he'd never have believed it.

The fire lookout tower creaked as the wind and rain lashed the roof and windows. Was it raining in Specter Lake? *What are you doing, Emma? Are you and Grace okay?* Cody closed his eyes and took a deep breath. The desire to hold them both close, to feel their warm bodies tight in his arms, filled him with a yearning he almost couldn't bear.

"We're almost there, Marshal," Frost said, sipping of his drink. "You'll be with them tomorrow."

Cody's eyes snapped open. Frost regarded him with a steady gaze even as he flipped an Army Ranger bottle opener over and over in his fingers. His gaze shifted from Cody to the inoperable HAM radio, then back again. It must be worse for Frost, he thought. Cody knew nothing about how to operate a HAM radio. Forget about fixing it. Frost seemed to know enough that with the right tools, he could get it working. It had to be maddening. "I hope so."

"If you've found a woman who can stand being married to you, she's tougher than you're giving her credit for."

Cody smiled, an absent one. He looked out the dark windows. "I used to love this stuff. The woods. Camping. If the world stays like this, we'll be getting back to basics."

Frost snorted. "The basics aren't all they're cracked up to be. Indoor plumbing and modern medicine are where it's at. There's a reason life expectancy was so low in the 'good old days.'" When Cody didn't reply, Frost said, "You don't like the outdoors anymore?"

Cody rubbed his jaw, feeling the prickle of stubble that wasn't as sharp as the day before. Since the moment he left his house on Saturday, everything had gone topsy-turvy. From the broken foot he couldn't depend on to a prisoner he couldn't control and the family he wasn't there to protect. Frost should have legged it at the first opportunity, but he hadn't. Instead, he'd helped Cody and others, too. The lines between lawman and criminal were so blurred that the conversation felt like one between friends. Maybe he had Stockholm syndrome.

Instead of ignoring Frost's question, Cody sighed. "I still like the woods. I just— My dad and I were supposed to go camping. There was a party, and a girl I liked was going so..."

"So you bailed," Frost said. He tipped the bottle, pouring more bourbon into his glass, an indulgent smile curving his lips.

"Yeah," Cody said, feeling as if he was wading through two feet of wet concrete. "He was killed in a liquor store robbery the same night as the party. Just stumbled into it. He wasn't on duty because he wasn't supposed to be home." He shrugged, words too small for the emotions exploding inside them. "If I hadn't been such a selfish brat, he wouldn't have been there. My mom wouldn't have been a widow at forty-two. My sister wouldn't have needed to settle for me walking her down the aisle. Nothing was the same without him, especially the woods."

Frost was quiet for a long time. Then he said, "How old were you?"

Cody looked away, blinking hard against tears that made him feel like a child. "Fifteen."

"Fifteen-year-olds are supposed to be selfish brats," Frost said. "It's... an appropriate developmental stage."

"I guess." Cody shrugged, his words and the gesture inadequate to the guilt he still felt. The guilt he would always feel. "I'll always wish I'd gone camping."

Frost nodded. He knocked back his bourbon, then grimaced. "This is terrible stuff," he said, pouring more. "That's the thing. Life's a capricious motherfucker. Kids are just too dumb to know it. I felt like I couldn't get out from under the cloud of what my dad had done, so I did all the wrong things. When I joined the Army, and especially when I became a Ranger, it was the first time since he went to prison that I felt like I belonged anywhere."

"Until you didn't," Cody said.

Frost's face hardened. "Yeah, well... Reporting a C.O. who's stealing weapons and selling them on the black market was not a smart career move."

Cody stared at him. A dustup with an officer. An honorable discharge. Then a life of crime. "Wait a minute... The guy who wrote the book." Cody snapped his fingers, as if it might jog his memory. "The one the president pardoned. That was your commanding officer? You were the person who blew the whistle?"

Frost snorted, his laugh jagged as splintered glass. "I'm not anything."

Frost's denial was about as convincing as a virgin in a whorehouse. "Did he do it?" Frost didn't answer. "Come on," Cody persisted. "I want to know."

"Of course he fucking did it," Frost said with a resigned snap in his voice. "Why the hell else would I turn on another Ranger, even an asshole like Avery Scott?"

Cody blinked. Frost had surprised him more than once since their plane fell from the sky, but this... He didn't see it coming. "It was the right thing to do."

"It was the right thing?" Frost said, incredulous. "I got

drummed out of the Army for 'the right thing.' The second the president got involved, they couldn't kick me to the curb fast enough." He sucked down his drink, then sloshed more into the glass. "They gave me an honorable discharge all wrapped in a bow, but I was out on my ass and they knew he'd done it. The court marital convicted him, for Christ's sake." Frost glared at him, as if daring Cody to say it was otherwise.

"So why rob banks? You're a smart guy. You could have done anything."

Frost scowled. "Hell if I know now. I guess I thought what did it matter? I might as well get mine. If I could stick it to Uncle Sam in the process? That was gravy."

"A one-man crusade, huh?"

"More like one-man stupidity." He fixed Cody with a glassy stare that seemed to lay his soul bare. "You became a lawman because your dad died enforcing the law. I ended up robbing banks after my dad broke it. How's that for a sob story?"

The bottle of terrible bourbon was empty. Cody realized Frost was drunk.

Frost raised his glass. "To good fathers and bad." He finished his drink in one swallow, banging the scuffed glass too hard as he set it down. His ice-blue eyes studied Cody's face, like he was searching for the answer to a question he didn't know how to ask. "You'll be one of the good ones, Marshal."

Cody swallowed, surprised by the prickle of tears at the corners of his eyes. Surprised by how much Frost's opinion mattered. Their eyes held a moment longer, an unspoken recognition passing between them. They stood on different sides of the law, both still trying to escape the shadows cast by their fathers.

day six

chapter
thirty-five

CALEB

THURSDAY, JULY 17
   7:30 AM

Caleb's gritty eyes peeled open like they'd been filled with sand. He smacked his lips, the inside of his mouth tacky as glue. A headache thumped behind his eyes, annoying but not terrible. What had he been thinking, drinking all that crappy bourbon? He sat up, stiff from sleeping on the floor. The marshal had put up a feeble protest that Caleb snuffed out with a long stare.

As a rule, Caleb didn't drink. He didn't like the sloppy feeling of disconnection that felt like interacting with the world on a ten-second delay. When he decided to train to apply to Ranger school, he couldn't afford to lose time to hangovers. Before setting his sights on Ranger school, he'd had a rule that he couldn't drink if he didn't work out. He had followed that rule like a religious zealot intent on going to Heaven. The trainings were half-assed compared to the ones when he'd gone to bed sober. After a while, it was simpler to skip the drinking altogether.

After he was pushed out of the Army, he'd had a bad patch. He woke up hungover one morning—not unusual at the time— and grabbed a beer to take the edge off. To this day he could hear the pop and hiss of the can cracking open, its whispered promise of relief in his ear, because he glimpsed his reflection in the kitchen window. He'd seen his father looking back at him. He couldn't claim to have made the best choices after that, but he'd quit using alcohol as a crutch.

Instead, I started robbing banks.

He'd traded one crutch, alcohol, for his go-to: adrenaline. He could see that now. Over the last year, the realization had become clearer. The dissatisfaction, the feeling of drift, the low-grade depression were easy to dismiss at first. But unhappiness was a stubborn S.O.B. It didn't like being ignored.

Caleb sighed, scrubbed at his face, and sat up. His muscles felt like overwound guitar strings—not so tight they were in danger of snapping but needing attention. He lay back down on the floor to stretch. The gym and daily runs were one thing; the exertion of the past couple of days after a plane crash was another. The achiness felt good, like his loosening muscles. Not like being in the field, but a comfortable echo.

Greer slept on his back, one hand flung over his head. Even asleep, he looked righteous somehow. Clear in his purpose. Despite the anxiety and worry for his family, Greer seemed secure in his belief that his vocation—for it wasn't just a job with him— mattered. That it held chaos at bay and that he had ground to make up. Blaming yourself for your father's death would do that to a man.

Caleb climbed to his feet to stretch his upper body. He leaned into the sensations: tightness, resistance, loosening, then the cycle repeating as he deepened the stretch. Banishing thought—his life, his sister, Greer and his family, the people he had met since the plane had crashed—was easier when he focused on easing the tension in his frame. As his muscles and sinews loosened, replaced by a supple ease, he found his mind wandering again.

What was happening? There'd been a CME, obviously. What he wondered about was how it changed people. The mismanagement and chaos of the bridge, he understood. He expected the bad. He expected the wolves who took advantage of the lack of shepherds, the incompetence of people who couldn't admit they were in over their heads. That was what had happened at the bridge. Where the wrong people ended up in charge, the cycle would repeat itself. Ben and Mei had encountered this on their way to Priests River.

But the others—like Amy and Dan, Roy and Sylvie Jenkins, the people at the coffee shop—puzzled him. Greer didn't seem to think it unusual that strangers would help them. He didn't wonder what was in it for them, like Caleb did. Is it me? Caleb thought. Had he spent so long holding people at bay that expecting the worst made it inevitable?

Before he joined the Army— No, that wasn't right. Before he'd been in Mister Jacobs' history class, he'd trusted no one but his sister. Being in the system had taught him trust was dangerous. He looked out for himself and Ruth, no one else. He learned to figure out what others wanted so he could use it to get what he wanted. He'd been charming, quick to please, the kind of kid good foster parents felt they might make a difference for. He thought of those people now with shame. They had cared, wanted to help him and Ruth, maybe even loved him. He hadn't been able to see it.

Mister Jacobs had changed all that. Caleb still didn't know what he'd seen in the shutdown, angry, manipulative boy he had been. The JROTC sponsor had somehow gotten Caleb to join. He must have thought he could get something from his teacher. Instead, he'd gotten everything. Friends—real ones—and the structure he had sorely needed. A glimpse of a future where his past didn't have to matter. Mister Jacobs had seen a leader under all the crap and helped Caleb feel safe enough to feel again. He'd already decided to enlist when Mister Jacobs broached the idea. His teacher wanted Caleb to apply to West Point and begin his service as an officer. Caleb hadn't had the confidence for that. He'd enlisted and never regretted it.

And then he'd blown it. By then, he should have known. You took your lumps and moved on, learned the lesson and let the rest go, but he'd still been that scared kid underneath. Losing that place to belong and the family he'd found there had been a blow he couldn't absorb, not then.

Caleb was halfway through chewing off his fingernails, a habit he'd broken years ago, when he caught himself. A hot rush of annoyance heated his face. He didn't have time for pointless questions he couldn't answer. They needed to get moving. He needed to get his head in the game, focus on the task at hand and what it took to execute it.

He turned away from the windows to wake Greer. From the corner of his eye, he saw the radio and paused. They might have information about what was happening if the damn thing worked. Was it worth another look? Probably not, but what were five more minutes of doing something pointless?

Caleb knelt beside the radio he'd attempted to fix the previous night. Dawn's pale light filtered through the fire tower's grimy windows. Rather than jump in, he took a moment to examine the radio. He noticed a wire running up the wall from the unit. It disappeared through a small hole drilled into the plank wall. He hadn't seen it last night.

I must have been more tired than I realized.

Time to find the fried component that made the radio useless. He eased the door open and stepped out onto the balcony. The morning air warmed his arms, promising yet another hot day. A small utility cabinet was mounted to the wall where the wire had gone through it. A wire snaked to the roof from the cabinet. Caleb took a step back and squinted at the roof.

Solar panels.

His heart sped up, like a small rabbit hopping over a field. Don't get excited, he told himself. He pulled the cabinet open.

The cabinet had two shelves, the upper held batteries. A small black component sat on the lower shelf. The brand, maybe the model, SunSaver, was printed in white letters on the top left corner. Across the front near the top were stylized symbols: a yellow sun labeled SOLAR, a battery labeled BATTERY, and something that looked like a plug labeled LOAD. Below that were a row of shiny screws across the unit's face under the solar, battery, and load icons, for connecting wires. Caleb sucked in a sharp breath. Nothing was hooked up. Not the wire from the roof to connect the solar panels to the batteries, nor the batteries to the component.

Caleb's heart began to race. It might not be that the radio didn't work, just that it wasn't connected properly. Old analog equipment like this, likely maintained by some underfunded forestry department, should still work where cutting-edge technology across the nation had failed. Caleb stepped back, trying to get a better look at the solar panels. If they were newer, they'd be useless, but if they were old, they might still work. On the left of the slim black component were three battery icons, the status lights beside them dark. He dug in his jeans pocket for the multitool he carried with him and connected all the wires. The indicator lights lit up.

Caleb blinked at the glowing lights, his mouth going dry, and raced inside. A growing buzz of excitement, like the distant pulse of war drums, filled Caleb's stomach. He crouched in front of the radio. With sweaty fingers, he flicked the switch. The radio hummed to life.

"Holy shit," he breathed, his heart now pounding hard. His hand shook as he turned the tuning dial. The hiss and pop of empty airwaves scratched through the speaker, a discordant counterpoint to the birdsong outside. A voice broke through the white noise.

"...broadcasting on emergency frequency 7.255 MHz," a voice said, breaking through the white noise.

Caleb's hand froze.

"This is Shoshone Medical Center Emergency Coordination

in Kellogg, Idaho. Repeat, this is Shoshone Medical Center Emergency Coordination broadcasting on emergency frequency 7.255 MHz. Any stations receiving, please respond…"

Caleb's eyes widened. "Greer!" he barked, looking over his shoulder. "Get up!"

Greer pushed halfway up in the cot, blinking at him. "What?"

"The radio works!"

"…we have limited medical supplies, food, and water. Repeating message."

Greer stumbled out of his cot. The broadcast began again.

"This is Shoshone Medical Center Emergency Coordination," the voice said again. "Repeat, this is Shoshone Medical Center Emergency Coordination broadcasting on emergency frequency 7.255 MHz. Any stations receiving, please respond."

Caleb looked at Greer, stunned. Any stations. Any stations was them. He reached for the microphone, then hesitated. What identity should he claim? He'd make one up. He picked up the microphone and pressed the talk button. "Shoshone Medical, this is Ranger Station 16. We read you. We're on the HooDoo—"

"Any medical professionals able to reach Kellogg, your help is requested. We are coordinating care for the community but are overwhelmed." The voice continued, as if Caleb hadn't responded.

"They can't hear us," Greer said.

"We have many patients with chronic conditions and medical equipment that's failed. Heart conditions, dialysis patients, and…"

"Oh my God," Caleb said, sucking in a breath. The edges of his vision sparkled, like a meteor shower rained down around his head. He put out a hand to steady himself, for his knees had loosened like melting chocolate. "Ruth."

Greer looked at him sharply. "Your sister?"

Caleb nodded. The motion of his head felt like a film he was watching. Greer turned up the volume as Ruth's voice continued.

"There are roadblocks and checkpoints along Interstate 90 and the surrounding area. There's a confirmed National Guard checkpoint set up at the Fourth of July Summit. They're limiting eastbound travel. There's an unofficial checkpoint reported just west of Cataldo Mission, by the river bend near the old rest stop. Several travelers reported being fired on or robbed near Rose Lake, where the road dips by the old rail tracks. If you're trying to bypass I-90, Old Highway 10 is open between Coeur d'Alene and Kingston. Forest Route 9 and 612 south of Pinehurst is an alternate route, but it's not advised unless you're in a 4x4 and know how to navigate switchbacks. We're told Fernan Saddle Lost Mines Road via Linford is okay."

Caleb leaned on the shelf, disbelief clogging his brain as his sister's voice filled the small cabin. Ruth sounded tired but composed. He'd heard that tone before when they talked after she'd finished a difficult shift.

"We need anyone with medical training. We are waiting for National Guard support to evacuate critical patients. For now, we're stabilizing those we can."

"Kellogg," Caleb said, more to himself than to Greer. "That's about a hundred miles east of here."

Ruth's voice continued through the static. "Supplies of blood, insulin, and other refrigeration dependent medications will begin to spoil once the generators fail. If anyone has access to these supplies, we can negotiate with you. We will assist with casualties, no strings attached."

"Sounds like she's in charge," Greer said.

Caleb nodded and said absently, "She would be."

"This broadcast will repeat hourly with updates as we get them," Ruth said. "Stay safe, everyone. This is Shoshone Medical Center Emergency Coordination broadcasting on emergency frequency 7.255 MHz signing off."

Static hissed from the radio's speakers again. Caleb's feet felt rooted to the floor. He stared at the radio, as if the hour had passed and the message would begin again. Ruth was in Kellogg, not in Coeur d'Alene. He knew she hadn't moved. She would have told him. Had she gone there for work or to visit a friend, or had it gotten bad in Coeur d'Alene and she and the kids left?

Her voice echoed in his ears, a steady beacon cutting through the chaotic thoughts swirling in his head. Ruth was alive, apparently well, a hundred miles away and nowhere near Specter Lake.

A daughter, Grace. She's such a pretty little thing.

Caleb looked at Greer, overwhelmed and frozen. His stomach roiled so much he thought he'd be sick. The lawman's blue eyes were as full of urgent longing to reach his family as ever, but there was something else in them now. "You have to go find her," he said.

Caleb stared at him, uncomprehending.

"Go find your sister," Greer said. "Specter Lake isn't that far. I can make it there today." He gestured at his foot, adding, "Even with this."

Caleb blinked. His stomach churned, acid bile burning at the back of his throat. Ruth was okay. She wasn't even that far away, but... How could he leave the marshal to get home on his own? Greer could make it, but what if something happened? What was the point of all they'd gone through if his little girl still ended up an orphan? "You'll just let me go?"

Greer huffed a low laugh. "I'm acknowledging reality. You're not my prisoner. You haven't been since the plane crashed."

Greer's statement hung in the air between them, growing larger until it seemed to fill the small room. Caleb could have escaped ten times over if he'd wanted. After the crash or when they reached Troy. During the night at Dan and Amy's place or at any point along this trail. He hadn't because of Greer's daughter. No matter how much the man had pissed him off at the start, every time he thought of leaving, he remembered what Greer had said to the pilot. When had things changed between them? Caleb didn't know, but at some point they had. "And you trust me to just walk away after everything I've done?"

The question wasn't rhetorical. He wanted to know. Why

would Cody Greer, upholder of law and order, let him go? He was a bank robber, a fugitive.

Greer shook his head and shrugged, the gesture almost helpless. "You lost your way, Caleb, but I've seen enough to trust that you'll do the right thing, even when it's hard. Even if it costs you."

Hearing Greer repeat his own words back to him hit Caleb like a blow. He couldn't remember the last time anyone besides Ruth had expressed so much faith in him. Not to execute a plan or pull off a job, but to do the right thing. "You're sure about this?"

"I'm not sure about anything anymore, but it feels right."

They looked at one another. Caleb could feel the pull of his sister's voice. Every molecule in his body leaned into it. The ache to find her, embrace her, be there for her, cut so deep it felt like he was being ripped apart.

A daughter, Grace. She's such a pretty little thing.

Caleb knew he'd lost his way. He hadn't simply believed he'd never find his way back; he'd never bothered to try. But now, things were different. It might be possible, but only if the rest of what Greer had said was also true. Leaving to find Ruth would be easy. It would feel right, even be right, because she was his sister. Taking care of her was his job. It was what he'd always done until he'd let his pain and bitterness get in the way.

There was so much he needed to make up for. He wouldn't fool himself that it would be easy, but it wouldn't be hard, not like this would be. Leaving now would feel right, but he'd lose his way again. It would be about what he wanted. If this really was his second chance, his wants couldn't come at the expense of others.

Caleb opened his mouth. Nothing came out. He took a shallow breath and tried again. "If she's able to do her job, then she's okay. She's with other good people. I said I'd get you home to your daughter."

Greer stared at him, dumbfounded. "You don't have to—"

"I do."

Greer looked at him a moment longer, then limped over to

the table. Caleb followed. They sat in silence, the morning sun breaking through the clouds. Ruth's voice lingered in the quiet of the small lookout tower, but it didn't hurt like it had moments before. It didn't feel like an accusation, but encouragement. He would find Ruth after he did right by Greer. He knew she would understand.

Caleb said, "We should get moving."

Greer didn't move, his gaze distant. Then he said, "I've got rifles at home. When we get to Specter Lake, you should take one of them."

Caleb looked at the marshal, then burst out laughing.

"What's so funny?" the marshal asked.

Caleb couldn't stop chuckling as he got his backpack and dug inside it. When he found the small bundle, he pulled it out and set it on the table. "What's this?" Greer asked.

"Take a look."

Greer gave him a quizzical look. He looked at the bundle like it might contain a hive of angry bees. He unwrapped it, revealing the revolver. He blinked up at Caleb, a look of profound shock on his face. "You had this the whole time?"

Caleb shook his head, the laughter, if not his amusement, under control. "Roy gave it to me."

"You have got to be kidding me," Greer said. "This is why you gave back my gun."

"It's not," Caleb said. "He gave it to me the next morning before we left. He thought you had one. Well, he believed you did, since you didn't rat me out."

Greer considered the revolver, then looked up at Caleb, as if seeing him for the first time. "You're not who I thought you were."

Caleb shrugged. "Neither are you."

chapter
thirty-six

CODY

THURSDAY, JULY 17
7:30 AM

Cody's foot screamed like a victim in a horror movie. The winding Hoodoo Trail had become his personal nightmare. Since all of this started, he'd been walking or riding on a broken foot for more miles than he cared to count. Sometimes Frost rode ahead, probably out of sheer boredom. Cody's pace wasn't a crawl, but he couldn't go fast. The painkiller was wearing off. He needed another before the pain got ahead of him.

Sweat plastered his clothes to his body like an itchy second skin. The afternoon sun beat down without mercy, and exhaustion dragged at him with the relentlessness of an annoying younger sibling. Still, Emma and Grace waited. He kept going.

Frost staying with him still surprised Cody. If their roles were reversed, Cody wasn't sure he'd be as selfless. Ironic, considering his attitude toward Frost when he'd gone to retrieve him. Then, Caleb Frost had been a name on a page, a one-dimensional criminal. He'd turned out to be far more complex and honorable than Cody imagined. He'd half expected Frost's mood to sour now that he knew where his sister was, only to be heading in the opposite direction. Instead, Frost seemed lighter than before, like uncertainty had lifted from him. He knew for a fact that his sister was alive. Perhaps knowing, rather than hoping, made his decision easier.

Sunlight dappled the trail ahead where it filtered through the trees. It would have been beautiful were desperation not clawing at his insides. He needed to get home. He was so close he could feel Emma's arms around him, smell the baby powder scent of Grace's skin.

The gray-brown blur of a rabbit darted across the trail. Cody jerked the handlebars. His injured foot slipped off the pedal, toes catching the ground. White-hot agony blasted through his leg. He jerked the handlebars, again overcorrecting. The bike careened off the path. The front wheel hit a hole and *thunked* down. Cody flew over the handlebars and slammed into the ground. His face raked over twigs and stones. Dust filled his nose. His injured foot caught in the bike frame and twisted.

"Ugghh!"

Birds exploded from the treetops. Through the flapping of wings, Cody heard Frost's shout and pounding footsteps. He lay sprawled face down on the hard-packed earth. It had happened so fast he hadn't even gotten his hands up. "Fuck," he groaned. "Fucking perfect."

"Don't move," Caleb said, crouching beside him. His large hands untangled Cody's foot from the bike frame. "You have a goddamned talent, Marshal. Let me check—"

"I'm fine," Cody said through gritted teeth, but his vision swam when he tried to sit up.

"Like hell you are." Caleb's face was grim as he gently pressed on Cody's foot through the boot. Cody couldn't suppress his strangled grunt of pain. "Can you move your toes?"

The simple task felt like trying to lift a mountain. Cody

nodded. He could do it—barely—though the effort sent fresh waves of nausea through him.

"The front wheel's shot," Frost said after inspecting the bike. "And you're in no shape to walk far." He looked up at the sun, already past its zenith.

"I'm not stopping," Cody said.

If the crash hadn't already, Frost's agitated glare would have pinned Cody in place. "Quit being so damn stubborn, just this once. Take this."

Caleb handed him a painkiller and the last of their water. Cody slumped against the nearest tree trunk, sweat trickling down his neck. The pill crawled down his throat like a reluctant child. Frost ran his hand through his hair, his frustration palpable. "We've got maybe fifteen miles left. I'll walk and you'll ride." Cody opened his mouth. Frost sounded like a lion when he growled, "This isn't a debate."

By the time they set out again, the painkiller had taken the edge off. The broken bones of Cody's foot felt like grinding glass when he pushed the bike pedals. They moved slower now, Frost's long stride eating up the ground beside him. Midday bled into afternoon. When they reached the main road, neither man spoke. Their destination felt farther away rather than closer, to Cody at least. It felt so unfair, but when had fairness ever mattered?

Cody glanced at Frost, his jaw set while he scanned ahead like he was on patrol. Something stole across his face that Cody hadn't seen before.

"You okay?" Cody asked.

Caleb's gaze flicked to him, then back to the road. "I just want to get you home."

But Cody saw more than that. The tightness around Frost's eyes, the way his fingers flexed into fists, then relaxed in a steady rhythm. It wasn't fatigue. It seemed like coiled energy about to erupt. Like Frost was holding himself back. Was he angling for something beyond just dropping Cody off and moving on?

Maybe, but Cody couldn't think what, and he sure as hell wouldn't pry.

As they neared the outskirts of Specter Lake, Caleb's pace increased. Cody winced as the bike swooped over subtle dips in the road, but he didn't complain. Each painful rotation of the pedals brought him closer to home. They entered the neighborhood from a smaller backstreet to the west, bypassing the welcome sign that never failed to earn a snarky comment from Emma. When they reached the last house before the bend in the road, just as Cody thought he'd collapse, he saw his house nestled among the tall pines. A soft light glowed in the living room window.

His vision blurred with sudden tears. If there was a light, then Emma and Grace must be here. Safe. "That one," he managed, his voice rough.

Caleb's stride hitched for just a moment. The big man's shoulders tensed, then relaxed, as if he'd just set down a heavy load he'd been carrying too long. His eyes fixed on the house like it contained a precious treasure.

They crossed the last stretch in silence. Cody's legs quivered as he stopped the bike at the end of the driveway. Then the front door was flung open and Emma appeared. The head rush of relief and love and joy made him dizzy. For a heartbeat, no one moved, as if time held its breath.

"Cody?"

Emma's voice cracked on his name. He didn't register dropping the bike and didn't feel any pain as he stumbled forward. His world narrowed to Emma's face—eyes wide, lips parted, cheeks wet with tears. Then she ran to him, colliding so hard Cody's leg almost gave out.

Emma's arms wrapped around him, holding tight like a swan curling into its mate. Everything else fell away. He buried his face in her hair, breathing in the familiar scent of her shampoo. A sob of relief and need and his desperate love for her made his body shudder.

"You're here," Emma whispered against his neck, her breath hitching in fits and starts. She looked up, running her hands alongside his face.

"I'm sorry it took so long," he said, voice thick with tears. "Oh God, Em."

He pulled her close again, memorizing the feel of her—the weight of her head, the curve of her waist. Emma pulled away, but only enough to look at him. Her eyes scanned his face, taking in the scrapes, the exhaustion, the relief. Her hand hovered over his bruised cheek. "What happened to you?"

Cody pressed his forehead to hers. "It's a long story. Is Grace okay?"

Emma nodded. "She's sleeping."

A low rattle made him turn his head. Frost was righting the bike. He stood beside it, looking like an awkward boy, his massive frame somehow diminished. Cody blinked hard. Frost's presence, always commanding, wasn't now. The guy keeping hold of the bicycle looked like someone else. Cody broke the embrace but kept hold of Emma's waist. "Emma, this is Caleb."

Emma blinked. She gave Cody a sidelong stare. "The bank robber?"

Cody saw a glint of amusement flicker in Frost's eyes. "He's the guy who got me here."

Emma looked at Cody a second longer, a lifetime's worth of 'What the fuck?' in her eyes. When Frost stepped forward, she held out her hand. "I'm Emma," she said. Then, her voice cracking, "Thank you for getting him home."

The house smelled of candle wax and something floral—tea, maybe. Lanterns cast pools of golden light in the living room. Even in the chaos of the last few days, Emma had made it feel like home. The bassinet sat between the couch and the chair. It pulled Cody across the room like a fish on a hook.

Grace lay on her back, sleeping, arms out at her sides. Tears flooded Cody's eyes. He thought he'd known how much he missed her, how deep his worry for her was, but he'd been mistaken. He dropped to his knees. His chest grew tight, squeezed by invisible pincers. "Hey, baby girl."

He stroked her plump cheek with the back of his index finger, careful not to wake her. Her skin felt warm and downy soft. She stirred, so he pulled his hand away. He slipped his pinky finger into her hand and smiled when she gripped it. "Oh, Grace, I was so worried about you."

Emma's hand lighted on his shoulder when she stepped close beside him. Cody sagged against her legs, so tired he could have lay down on the floor. "I was so worried about you, Cody."

Her fingers stroked along his temple, sending ripples of comfort through Cody's body. "Not as much as I was about you." Cody looked up at her. Emma's eyes shined with tears. "Thank you, Em, for keeping her safe."

She smiled. "I'm going to get you something to eat. You must be starving." Cody didn't want her to leave, but the mention of food made his stomach rumble.

Cody watched her walk across the room. His girls were here and okay. He couldn't believe his luck. When he felt Frost's gaze, he looked up. Frost had moved closer to peer in the bassinet. Cody moved to the side, his pinky still in Grace's tiny fist. "This is Grace."

"She's beautiful," Frost said, his voice a low rumble. "She looks like her mother."

Cody nodded. "She does."

Something between longing and loss stole over Frost's face, raw with emotion, so tender that Cody felt like he was intruding. "This is worth it, all of it," Frost murmured. Then he seemed to remember he wasn't alone. He stiffened, like he was battening down the hatches.

Cody stood and pointed at the chair near the bassinet. "Sit down before you fall down."

"You're projecting, Marshal," Frost said, his tone dryly mocking, but he sat down anyway.

Cody sank onto the couch with a groan, feeling the toll of his journey. Frost's eyes were on Grace again. She whimpered, stirring in her sleep. Cody didn't know what he expected, but it wasn't for Frost to lean forward and make a soft shushing sound. "It's okay, sweetheart," he murmured. "It's okay."

The tension in Frost's shoulders melted away. An unguarded smile transformed his rugged features, the hard edges softening. He looked to Cody like the man he might have been if life had been kinder, his choices wiser. Emma returned with a makeshift cookie sheet tray with sandwiches and beers. "It's peanut butter and jelly, and the beer's warm," she said, setting the food on the coffee table.

She handed Cody a plate, and Frost stood to get his. Emma sat beside Cody, her thigh pressed against his, a hand on his shoulder, as if she couldn't bear to lose contact.

"It's perfect," Cody said, taking her hand and squeezing it. His gaze swept over the room, taking in the water containers stacked against the wall, the papers with lists. "You've been busy."

"We all have," she said with a tired smile. "The neighborhood's pulling together. We're lucky, so lucky, Cody. There are so many good people here."

As they ate, Cody filled Emma in on the plane crash, their trek through the wilderness, and finding the HAM radio at the fire lookout tower. Emma perked up at the last, grilling him about where the lookout tower was, then Frost, when Cody couldn't provide answers to her satisfaction. "We need to go get it," she said. "We need to know what's happening out there." She said to Frost, "So you're the bank robber."

He had just taken a sip of his beer and choked. Coughing, he managed, "I was."

Emma looked at Cody. He could see the gears of her mind whizzing around, the questions she had. "Caleb is—" He stopped, not sure what he'd been going to say. That Frost had been transformed by the last few days was clear. So had he, but into what?

When he didn't finish the sentence, Emma said, "You both

look about to fall over. The guest room's not set up yet, Caleb, but we have the couch."

"That's more than enough," Frost said. "Thank you for... for letting me stay."

"Thank you for getting Cody home," she said in that direct way she had. "You're not going to kill us in our sleep, are you? 'Cause I've got a gun."

Frost stifled a laugh. A real one. "No, ma'am. I am not."

Emma nodded. "All right then."

Later, after they'd gotten Frost set up on the couch and Cody had washed up as best he could with limited water, he found Emma in the nursery, watching Grace sleep. A candle on the windowsill cast a fragile net of light. Outside, the aurora lit the night sky. Cody wrapped his arms around Emma from behind, breathing in the scent of her skin.

"I was so afraid," she whispered. She turned in his arms, her face tilted up to his. Tears glittered in her eyes. "I didn't know if you were alive or dead, if I'd ever see you again."

"I'm here now," he murmured against her hair. "I'm not going anywhere."

She tipped her head toward the nursery door. "Do you trust him? Enough to have him in our home, with Grace?"

Cody thought about everything that had happened since their plane fell from the sky. Frost had so many opportunities to look out for himself... When the plane first crashed. In Troy, Montana, after they met Roy and Sylvie. On the bridge in Sandpoint or when they'd reached Priests River. Frost had never wavered, always honoring his side of what Cody had thought was a Faustian bargain to get home to Emma and Grace. At every point along the way, Frost could have chosen himself. Instead, he'd helped others. "I do. He could have left me behind a dozen times, but he didn't, and he got me home to you." Cody paused. "Caleb's not a bad person, Emma. He just... lost his way."

Emma nodded as a tear trailed down her cheek. She brushed it away. She took a deep breath and puffed it out all at once. "That's good enough for me. It's a little creepy, you seeing right and wrong in shades of gray."

He pulled her tighter. "Maybe you just need to get used to it."

Outside, the aurora painted the sky in rippling ribbons of light. The world had changed, perhaps forever. In this moment, he and Emma and Grace were together. They were still a family, intact and whole. That was all that mattered.

day seven

chapter
thirty-seven

CALEB

FRIDAY, JULY 18
11:45 AM

Caleb woke to the soft murmur of a woman's voice and the scent of hot oil. His stomach growled. The couch cushions felt like a cocoon. For a disorienting second, he couldn't place where he was. He had a groggy sense of being somewhere he could let down his guard. Then it all rushed back—Greer's reunion with his wife Emma and daughter Grace, that pretty little thing of a baby. He half smiled, half winced, recalling Emma's query about whether he planned to murder them while they slept.

He rolled onto his side and pushed himself up, his body stiff and sore, and glanced at his watch. 11:45? He held it to his ear, but it ticked. He couldn't remember the last time he had slept this late, for almost fifteen hours. It accounted for the fuzziness making it hard to wake up. The woman's voice would be Greer's wife. Was Greer still sleeping? Caleb hoped so. He'd seen soldiers with better training give up when faced with less daunting odds. Greer had pushed himself past the breaking point to get home.

Caleb stood, stretching his arms overhead until his spine popped. He walked to the kitchen, pausing on the threshold. Emma stood a few steps back from the stove, her profile defined by the windows along the kitchen's back wall. She was a looker, all right—tall and slender-limbed, with long blond hair pulled back from her face that showed off the graceful curve of her neck. Greer's determination to get home to her made even more sense now. She sang to Grace, who was strapped to her chest in one of those baby harnesses. Grace's tiny feet kicked against her mother's stomach. Caleb cleared his throat from the doorway. "Good morning."

Emma turned and gave him a warm smile. "He lives." She gestured at the table with a spatula. "Coffee's in the press. I'm making pancakes."

"You don't have to cook for me."

Emma raised an eyebrow. "You trekked through half of Idaho to bring my husband home. I think I can make you pancakes. Besides, my gas stove is one of the few things that still works."

Caleb nodded, then hooked his thumb toward the hallway. "Bathroom's that way?"

Emma nodded. "There might be a spare toothbrush under the sink, I'm not sure. We just moved in. Half of our stuff's still in boxes."

In the bathroom, Caleb found the toothbrush. A small thing but appreciated. Knocking your host over with morning breath was no way to start an acquaintance. His face in the mirror looked different. Still his, of course, but also kind of... He wasn't sure. Less closed, maybe. He turned the faucet. Nothing. Then he saw the baby wipes tucked behind the faucet, which he used to clean his hands. He wrinkled his nose at the grime and dirt on them when he finished.

Back in the kitchen, Caleb poured himself coffee from the French press, then retreated to the doorway. He felt too big for the room, even though the kitchen was a decent size. "Sit down," Emma said.

"No water I take it?" Caleb asked, taking the nearest chair.

Emma shook her head. "None. But we've got a stop gap for now. A guy in the neighborhood set it up. He's a prepper type." She raised her eyebrow. Sarcasm laced her voice when she added, "He's enjoying being right about the fall of civilization, but his heart is in the right place once you get past the prickles."

Grace made a small sound. Emma bounced a little on her toes, the movement so natural it looked like breathing. A minute later, she set a plate of pancakes in front of Caleb and sat down. "So, Caleb. Are all bank robbers helpful in emergencies, or just you?"

Caleb choked on his coffee. "I wouldn't know. We don't have conventions."

Emma laughed. "That's fair. Cody told me a little more of what happened before he conked out." She paused, then added, her voice thoughtful, "It's almost like he's been swapped out for a pod person."

"Um... okay," Caleb said. Spending time with her husband had not prepared him for Emma Greer. How had Greer landed her?

"He's always been so sure of where things fit—black and white, you know? You follow the rules or you don't, and people who break the law are criminals. End of story."

"And now?"

Emma smiled a little. "Now he's brought home a bank robber."

Caleb didn't know how to respond. He'd always been the charmer, knowing just what to say, and when, to get what he wanted from caseworkers, foster parents, officers, and his unit. Now, he had no clue. "We just helped each other out."

"Do you want more?" Emma asked, tipping her chin at his empty plate.

Caleb did, but he wouldn't have more until everyone else had eaten. "No, that was great. Thank you."

Grace wriggled in the harness. It seemed to Caleb the baby was working herself up to something. "Can you take her?" Emma asked. "I shouldn't hold her while I'm cooking, but she's been sick, so she's fussy."

"Sure," he said.

Last night, Emma asked if he was going to murder them all in their sleep. This morning she was handing him her child. The marshal must have reassured her. The marshal was so uptight that Caleb had expected his wife to be the same. So far, she wasn't. He pushed his mug well back from the table's edge. Grace was too young to pull one of those sudden lunges that caught adults unawares, but he'd rather be cautious. Emma pulled Grace from the harness and held her out to him. Caleb took the baby, engulfing her in his large hands. She weighed almost nothing.

"Support her head," Emma said, guiding his hand. "There you go."

Grace's eyes, unfocused but bright, stared up at him. Her skin was translucent, veins visible at her temples. A tuft of downy hair stood up on her crown. She had a rash of red spots on her hands and wrists. Caleb looked at her feet; she had them there, too. He settled the baby into the crook of his arm. Déjà vu so vivid it stole his breath made the scene feel like a repeat of holding Peter for the first time. He'd been a little smaller than Grace, but no less miraculous.

Grace's face contorted, a whine of protest escaping her. "Just —" Emma said, then stopped when he rocked Grace, a gentle sway from side to side.

"Hey there, Grace. I've got you, and your mama's right there." Grace's whine petered out. Caleb kept up the gentle motion. "She has hand, foot, and mouth?"

"Yeah," Emma said, surprise in her voice as she looked over from the stove.

"My niece had it once. She had the same rash on her hands and feet." A singsong quality crept into his voice. "She was a grumposaurus, just like you."

"How the hell did you end up robbing banks?"

Caleb blinked up at Emma, taken aback. She stared at him like she'd never seen a man before and had no idea what one was. When she kept looking at him, her eyebrows drawn together, he realized she wanted an answer. "I didn't exactly plan it," he said. "After the first one, the next one was easier."

She bit her lip, her eyes narrowed, then turned back to the stove. The sizzle of batter hitting the hot pan followed a moment later. When she didn't say more, he didn't either. Her questions were so direct it felt like being mugged. Caleb took a breath, then smiled at Grace. She really was a pretty little thing. He took another careful sip of coffee, leaning away from Grace as he did. He didn't know what to talk about with the wife of the man who was supposed to put him in prison, and was kind of afraid of what she might ask next.

A few minutes later, Emma took the seat across from him, slathering peanut butter on her pancakes. "Cody says you could have left a dozen times, but you didn't." Her voice softened. "Thank you. I don't know—" Her eyes flooded with tears. She sniffed and blinked hard. "Just... thank you."

Caleb gave her a slight nod and looked away. It seemed the marshal hadn't told her that Caleb had left him and then returned. He said, "What's happening here in Specter Lake?"

Emma allowed the subject change, though her eyes told him she knew he was trying to shift attention from himself. "The mayor's office doesn't have a clue. Some of us in the neighborhood are winging it." She described their water filtration system, the neighborhood census, the deaths so far, and helping people with medical needs. "I didn't know anyone a few days ago. Now I'm running meetings in my living room."

"Leadership finds the right person in a crisis," Caleb said.

Emma snorted. "Or the idiot stupid enough to volunteer."

Caleb laughed—a real one. Grace startled at the sound, then settled again.

"You're good with her," Emma said. "Are you—"

The marshal's limping footsteps drawing near saved him. Greer appeared in the doorway, looking like he'd just woken up from a three-day bender. Emma rose and wrapped her arms around him. Greer held her tight. A twinge of envy flared inside Caleb. Not for Greer's wife, but for the idea of having a woman be that happy to see him. I'm getting soft, he thought, looking down at Grace. It had to be holding the baby. If a baby as cute as this one couldn't soften a man, he was made of stone.

"I made pancakes to celebrate," Emma said to Greer when she loosened her embrace enough to look him in the face. "And coffee."

"You're amazing," he said, then collapsed into a chair. He looked over to Caleb, his gaze lighting on Grace.

"You weren't kidding, Greer," Caleb said. "She's a pretty little thing."

Greer's smile widened. Emma set a plate in front of him. He dug into his meal with the focus of a man running on empty for months. A sense of satisfaction, like he'd completed a mission and achieved all the objectives, settled over Caleb. Greer was home, reunited with his family. Despite all the things he'd screwed up, he had helped make this happen. It didn't balance the scales, but it was a start.

Grace began to fuss again. Caleb passed her back to Emma, who settled Grace against her shoulder. Greer finished chewing his last bite of pancakes, then said to Caleb, "When are you leaving?"

"Soon as I can."

Emma looked from Caleb to Greer, then back to Caleb, almost as if this wasn't what she'd expected. "You're going to find your sister? When did you last see her?"

Caleb's jaw tightened. He'd wasted so much time. "Six years ago."

"Before all—" Emma said, then stopped, a blush coloring her cheeks. "Well, before."

Caleb nodded. "Ruth lives in Coeur d'Alene but we heard a

broadcast she did from the medical center in Kellogg, so that's where I'm going."

"Her name is Ruth?" Emma said, sounding surprised. "I just met, well, I didn't meet but came across someone named Ruth the other day. It's not a common name anymore."

A prickle of awareness—of premonition—crawled up Caleb's spine. "She's a trauma nurse."

Emma's fingers stilled between Grace's shoulder blades. Her eyes flicked to Greer, then back to Caleb. "About thirty, with light-brown hair?"

An electric jolt shot through Caleb's chest. He sat forward in his seat, his skin buzzing. "You know her?"

"I— No," Emma said. "But a National Guard unit came through town. There was a nurse named Ruth with them."

The room shrank around Caleb. The air got so thick he couldn't catch his breath.

"We were talking to the unit's commander, me and Tom and Chuy, trying to get information about what's happening" Emma continued. "A nurse—she had a stethoscope, anyway—came to talk to the lieutenant about triage for people needing medical help. It sounded like she was the one doing it. The lieutenant called her Ruth."

Caleb's heart hammered against his ribs. "Did she have children with her? A girl and a boy?"

Emma's brow furrowed in concentration. "Some kids were running around near the trucks, but I didn't pay much attention. I don't know if they were with her... I was focused on the lieutenant. She'd just told us we were on our own." Emma paused. "But now that I've met you, I see a resemblance. Your eyes are like hers, and the shape of your mouth and chin."

Caleb felt hot and cold at once. His mind raced. He and Ruth both had their mother's eyes and their dad's mouth and chin. "How old were they, the kids? What did they look like?"

Emma shook her head. "I don't know... maybe nine for the girl, and the boy was four or five? The little boy had that white-blond hair, but I just caught a glimpse. They might have been kids from Specter Lake, I just don't know." She paused, then said, almost hesitantly, "The National Guard unit was heading to Fairchild Air Force Base. They said it was east, no, west of Spokane. The lieutenant said the military is consolidating units from Idaho and Eastern Washington there."

Caleb felt the blood drain from his face. He felt light-headed, like if he turned his head too fast, he'd spin away. Ruth had been here, with little kids nearby, one a boy with bright-blond hair. Emma had seen his sister. He knew it. Idaho was that small, and the details, the description, matched. He'd been less than twenty miles away when she passed through Specter Lake.

"Frost, are you all right?" Greer said.

Caleb pushed back from the table and stood, unable to stay still. He paced to the window, his hands clenching and unclenching at his sides. Ruth and her kids had been here. If they'd pushed harder, if he'd left Greer to go to Kellogg on his own, he might have—

He shut the thought down. He'd made his choice, and it had been the right one. The timing couldn't be more perverse if the world was trying to fuck with him.

"Caleb, are you okay?" Emma asked.

He nodded, the movement stilted. He didn't trust his voice enough to speak. Six years of self-imposed exile and he'd missed finding his sister when she was so nearby. "Did you talk to her at all?"

Emma shook her head, her mouth downturned. "I just overheard her name while she spoke with the lieutenant, but she was going with them."

Caleb ran a hand through his hair, his mind going in ten directions. Security at a military base would be heavier than normal with all that had happened. Gaining entry would be a challenge, but first he had to get there.

Greer stood and limped over. He gripped Caleb's shoulder. "We'll get you there."

Caleb nodded, swallowing around the sudden lump in his throat. The surety in Greer's voice felt reassuring but also unwelcome. Greer had no reason to care about Caleb's family reunion. By rights, he had every reason to want him locked away.

"Maybe I should go with you. My badge might help get you through checkpoints."

Emma's head snapped up. "Absolutely not." Her flat voice brooked no argument, though tears flooded her blue eyes. "You just got home and can barely walk. You are not leaving again."

Greer opened his mouth, then closed it. "I wasn't thinking, Em." He hobbled to her, proving her point. "I promise, I'm not going anywhere."

"You're damn right you promise," she said, a flash of temper slipping past the tears she swiped from her face.

"She's right, and from what I've seen, a damn sight smarter than you, Marshal," Caleb said. "Your place is here, with your wife and daughter."

Emma's shoulders relaxed the littlest bit. Greer pulled her and Grace close, and she melted against him. He's too Clark Kent for his own good, Caleb thought.

"Caleb, I'm not sure it was your sister I saw," Emma said after she was a little more composed. Caleb could see the worry in her eyes that she was sending him astray.

He said to her, "I am."

chapter
thirty-eight

CODY

FRIDAY, JULY 18
12:40 PM

"A bike won't cut it," Cody said after Frost had helped Emma clear the breakfast dishes.

Cody had tried to help, only for Emma to order him to sit his ass down. She had softened the reprimand with a throw cushion from the couch for his foot, which was propped on the extra kitchen chair. The last painkiller had dulled the sharp edge, but his bones still ground together with each step. The bruises covering his foot were still spreading like an oil slick days later.

Frost said, "I'll be fine."

"What about checkpoints?" Cody persisted.

"Real ones or impromptu?" Frost said, leaning against the counter, his arms crossed over his body. His tone made plain that he thought Cody's objection was nonsensical. "I've been in combat, Marshal. I'll be fine using the bike."

The morning sun streamed through the kitchen windows,

backlighting Frost in a sunlit glow. Emma peeked through to the living room, where she'd put the portable bassinet after Grace finished nursing. She said to Frost, "How far is Fairchild?"

Frost shrugged. "It's about sixty miles to Spokane and Fairchild isn't too much farther. Let's say eighty miles total."

"Is that using the interstate?" Cody said. "That might be dicey."

Emma took the chair next to Cody, scooching hers closer so she could take his hand. When her fingers threaded between his, Cody felt his body relax. Only now that he was home with them did he understand just how scared he'd been for hers and Grace's safety.

"Cody's right," Emma said, her voice carrying the quiet authority he knew so well. "The interstate won't be as usable. You should take a car if we can find one. It'll give you more flexibility."

Cody noticed how Emma's watchful gaze fixed on Frost. He knew that look—she was trying to figure him out. She'd been looking at him the same way. Cody would never have helped a fugitive before this happened. He had a lot to explain once he got it straight in his own head.

It's not helping, he reminded himself. *It's aiding and abetting.*

While he'd been getting dressed, Emma had told Cody about hers and Frost's breakfast conversation before he joined them. "You should have seen him with Grace. It was like she was his own. I asked him why he robbed banks. He looked so taken aback you'd think I asked him if he only dates hookers."

"I don't think he knows, Em. Not really," Cody said.

Emma moved closer, her voice low. "Why are you helping him, Cody? Your job is to bring him back to answer for what he's done."

"It's not that simple anymore."

"I gathered." Emma traced small circles on the back of his hand that sent electric sparks up Cody's arm. "What I don't get is why you're helping him. This isn't your style, Cody. Criminals have to pay for their crimes; that's your style. You aren't even pretending he's in your custody."

"He's not what I thought he'd be, and he saved my life, Emma. He got me back to you and Grace. I honestly believe he's left all that behind. I think he's been looking for a way back for a long time. Now he has one."

"People shouldn't need the world to end for that."

"I know that, Cody said. "You seemed to get along with him well enough. What do you think?"

Emma's gaze went distant. She bit her lip, thinking. "I think you're right, but I don't want this blowing back on you."

"It won't," he told her.

"You don't know that."

"Are you doing that lawyer playing devil's advocate thing just for the hell of it?"

Emma had shaken her head. "No," she'd said. "I'm trying to understand what happened to you."

Cody roused himself from the earlier conversation he'd let his mind wander to. Frost's frame seemed to fill the room as he said, "A car is harder to hide, needs gas, and might break down."

"Like the motorcycle," Cody conceded.

"Besides," Frost added. "Anyone with a running car won't lend it to a stranger."

"Chuy," Emma said.

Cody frowned at her. "Bless you?"

"No," Emma said, almost laughing. Her voice felt like cool water. "Jesús Rodriguez, he lives in the neighborhood. Everyone calls him Chuy. He's a mechanic who specializes in classic cars. I met him and his wife when all this started." She glanced at her watch. "Keep an eye on Grace, Cody. I'll go find him. If anyone can help us out, it's him."

"I don't want a car," Frost said.

"What about once you've found your sister?" Emma asked. "There will be four of you."

Cody nodded. "If you come back here, or wherever you go, do you want to do it on bikes with little kids?"

Frost's eyes narrowed. "You better be careful, Marshal. That almost sounded like an invitation."

Cody blinked, surprised. "I guess it was."

Frost smirked. "You want to know where I am so you can lock me up when things go back to normal?"

Cody considered the question. Before all this, that would have been true—apart from the small detail that he would never let a fugitive go free. Frost wasn't just a fugitive anymore. He wasn't a friend, either. Cody hadn't done enough to qualify as a brother-in-arms, but something was there between them that might become that.

Cody said, "Emma says the National Guard told her the western states they'd been in contact with are all affected. They haven't been able to establish contact beyond that, which makes me think the whole country is crippled. If that's true, nothing is going back to how it was. You're a useful man to have around."

Frost's face did something complicated, a mixture of uncertainty and suspicion and longing flashing over his features, and Cody knew. *He needs a place to land.*

If Frost had found something to be part of after such a traumatic childhood, and it was taken away unjustly, he might not have been able to respond constructively. That wasn't an excuse. Lots of people got a raw deal and didn't turn to bank robbery, but the realization that he had nowhere to belong—and Frost's reaction—made sense to Cody.

"We'll see what Emma's friend can do." Frost's voice was rough, as if a swell of emotion had caught him unawares. "But I'm not sticking around beyond today."

chapter
thirty-nine

CALEB

"Gotta hand it to you, Chuy," Caleb said, wiping grease from his hands with an old rag. The smell of motor oil and gasoline clung to him like a second skin, familiar and comforting. "I didn't think we'd get this running."

The stuffy air in Chuy's garage had Caleb's shirt sticking to his back, even with both doors open and despite the cooling evening air. The heat wave seemed to be loosening its grip. Across from him, Cody shifted his weight, leaning more heavily on a borrowed crutch Chuy had found while they looked for parts. The marshal's face was pale with exhaustion, but he'd refused to go home until they finished.

"She just needed the right touch once we found a fuel pump," Chuy said, pushing down on the hood to make sure it latched. "I was close to giving up. I'm glad we didn't."

"How long were we looking for that part? Three hours?" Cody asked.

Chuy nodded. "Just about."

After all their work, the truck's engine purred. It was a distinct improvement from the sputtering death rattle the first time they'd tried to start it. The pickup wasn't fancy, with faded paint and a few spots of rust, but it ran.

Caleb liked Chuy. The stocky mechanic had an easy smile, calloused hands, and zero bullshit. When Emma had introduced him and Cody, and told Chuy what they hoped to do, he hadn't batted an eye apart from an enthusiastic, 'It's the missing husband! I'm so glad to meet you, man.' There had been no questions about Caleb. Trust—never Caleb's strong suit—felt like more of a luxury than ever. Chuy's straightforward willingness to help felt almost surreal. Even now, maybe especially now, Caleb still couldn't bring himself to trust anyone, but this felt close, like it did with Greer.

"Just needed the right touch," Chuy repeated, handing Caleb the keys. "She'll get you to Fairchild and back."

Caleb hesitated, his hand stopping short of taking the keys. The weight of what they represented settled heavy in his chest. Freedom. A chance to find Ruth. A way out. The feeling should be light, shouldn't it? This was everything he wanted. A chance to do the right thing, to take care of his family, to stay out of prison. Why did it rub like a blister forming on his heel?

Cody cast a sidelong glance at Chuy that was almost a wince. Yeah... that was why. Chuy assumed he would be back. Caleb wasn't sure that was true. "I can't guarantee I'll be back, Chuy."

Chuy shrugged. "Take the keys, man. It's no problem. Just take care of her. I had plans for this lady, but now my hands are kinda full with survival shit."

Caleb took the keys and slipped them into his front pocket. The marshal straightened up, his face contorting with a grimace. He'd been pushing himself too hard, hanging in to help when he could—which had been more than Caleb would have thought—and it showed.

Chuy noticed too. "You look dead on your feet, Cody. You guys should head home."

"I'm fine," Cody said, though it was obvious he wasn't.

"I don't need your wife mad at me," Chuy said. "And I don't need my wife mad at me because Emma's annoyed."

Caleb smiled, and Cody did, too. Then Chuy snapped his fingers. "Let me find you a jack. You should have one, just in case."

Several minutes of searching and lots of swearing, Caleb assumed, in Spanish later revealed the jack Chuy was looking for wasn't there. "It must be at home," he said. "I'll walk it over."

Caleb said, "I'll come with you and then walk to— Cody's." It felt weird calling him Cody, but it might seem weird to others if he called him the marshal. "You've already done enough." He looked at the marshal. "Can you manage driving?"

The marshal nodded. "I can drive that far."

"You've got your gun if anyone tries to mess with you," Chuy said, amusement filling his voice and flashing in his eyes. "I guess it's just habit with you, Cody. Some people in the neighborhood who are walking around with them all of a sudden? It's like they think their next-door neighbor's gonna settle the score about not mowing the lawn enough."

Cody grimaced. While he took Chuy's ribbing in good humor, Caleb could tell the news of this change in behavior wasn't welcome news. Welcome to Idaho, marshal, Caleb thought wryly.

"I'll see you at the house, Caleb."

Caleb. It sounded strange, coming from the marshal. Something about his tone seemed off. Caleb narrowed his eyes, making a quick study of the man. After everything they'd been through—the plane crash, the bear, the bridge riot, the countless miles hiking and cycling through the wilderness of Montana and Idaho—did Greer think he'd just leave? That would be hard to do, what with Greer being the one driving away with Chuy's truck. Greer was the kind of guy who'd want to say goodbye. Caleb realized he did, too.

He'd robbed banks for six years because he thought he'd lost his place in the world when the Army kicked him out. These past few days had shown Caleb his world could be more. He'd been reminded of the man he'd been before, who had helped and protected others. The man he could be again, if he chose to be.

Ruth had been right. It was time to figure out what the hell he was doing with his life.

chapter
forty

EMMA

FRIDAY, JULY 18
  7:30 PM

Outside, the light was pink, a harbinger of the aurora's imminent arrival. Yesterday, the aurora's crimson hues stirred a primal fear in Emma's chest. The color seeping through the curtains, casting bloodstained shadows across the kitchen floor, had seemed like a curse. Then Cody came home, battered and exhausted but alive. Her heart fluttered at the thought. Their survival felt balanced on a knife's edge but with Cody at her side, she wouldn't face it alone.

Not that the jerk was here this minute. If he didn't come home soon, she was going to be 'that wife' and go get him. "If he were a sheep, he wouldn't have the sense to come in out of the rain," she muttered.

Emma looked out the kitchen window at the yellow and amber sunset as it morphed into the familiar crimson glow. It didn't feel as ominous as it had last night. She picked up the apple she'd come to the kitchen for and cut it into quarters, then began cutting out the cores from each wedge. The knife caught on the core of the first wedge. When she applied more pressure, it sliced through the apple so fast it kept going, right into the meaty section of her hand below the thumb.

"Ow!" she cried out. Blood ran over her palm and dripped onto the counter. She didn't remember them being this sharp. Cody must have sharpened them before he left for Montana.

She set the knife on the counter, then cleaned and disinfected the cut. A dab of antibiotic ointment and a bandage finished the job. She sighed, looking at the apple, which no longer seemed appetizing. She filled a cup with precious water from a pitcher. The liquid wetted her mouth and throat, warm with an under-taste of plastic and bleach, but still a luxury. Emma rubbed at her itchy eyes. Now that Cody was home, she'd relaxed, and the stress of the past week hit her like a linebacker.

A knock at the back door made her startle. Water sloshed over the rim of her cup. "It's me," Diane called through the door.

Emma's shoulders relaxed. She set down the cup and crossed the room to open the door. Diane stood on the back step, her copper braid hanging over her shoulder. Dark circles shadowed her eyes, making her look gaunt in the dying light. "I came to check on Grace," she said, stepping inside. "Martha told me she's sick and that Cody's back."

"He is," Emma said, smiling. "Though he's with Chuy and his friend Caleb right now. They're working on a truck for Caleb to take to Spokane."

"Spokane's kind of far," Diane said.

"His sister's there, he thinks."

Diane nodded. "And Grace?"

"She's much better. Her fever broke right before Cody got home. I just got her down a little while ago." When Diane didn't leave, Emma remembered that Martha had said she was going over to see Tom and Carrie. With everything that had happened, Diane might not want to be alone. "Do you want to come in?"

"Yeah, that'd be great."

In the living room, Diane's eyes drifted to the window. The red glow had intensified, spilling over Diane's face like a wound. "I swear it gets brighter every night."

The undulating ripples of scarlet in the darkening sky looked like banners snapping in an invisible wind. "I thought it was so pretty that first night, then it felt like a bad omen. It doesn't seem so scary now that Cody's home. I don't think I realized how worried I was."

"Of course you were worried," Diane said.

"Do you want something to drink?" Emma asked. "I've got some soda."

Diane nodded. "A soda would be great."

"It's warm," Emma said, an apology in her voice.

"That's fine."

Emma got the drinks and rejoined Diane in the living room. Diane almost flopped on the couch under the large front window while Emma took the love seat. Diane sipped her soda and sighed. "Mmm... that's nice." She paused, then said, "I can't believe the last few days. Part of me wants to head south for the winter like a bird, where it won't be so cold."

Emma nodded. She knew how Diane felt. "How did people do it in pioneer days?"

Diane shrugged. "I guess we'll find out."

"I'm just glad Grace doesn't have something serious. If that happened, I'd snap. It'd be one thing too many." Emma set her soda can on the coffee table and picked up a book of matches that lay on it. The polished paper of the cover felt smooth against her fingers. She didn't want to upset Diane, but she had to know. "Any sign of Heath?"

Diane stiffened. "No, thank God."

"That's good," Emma said. "And Cody's home now. You've got a gen-yoo-ine marshal next door."

Diane tucked a stray strand of hair behind her ear. "I shouldn't have gotten you involved. I'm so sorry."

"You have nothing to apologize for," Emma said. "You weren't the one violating a court order."

Diane bit her lip, looking unconvinced. A soft coo from the bassinet caught Emma's ear. "Grace," she groaned. "Why are you waking up?" She stood and leaned over the bassinet beside the couch. Grace stirred, her tiny nose wrinkling. Then her eyes opened, and Emma couldn't help but smile. The rash seemed redder in the light filtering through the windows. Emma scooped Grace up and cradled her against her chest. "Shh, it's okay," she murmured. "You're fine."

She pressed her lips to the top of her daughter's downy head, breathing in her scent. Diane joined them, her expression softening at the sight of Grace. "She's so tiny."

"But she'll be fierce, I think."

"That's good," Diane said. "If you ne—"

A sharp *crack* against the front door jerked Emma's head up. A rush of adrenaline electrified her body and rushed into her limbs. Grace startled against her chest, letting out a tiny whimper of protest.

"What was that?" Diane whispered, her body tensing like a taut wire.

"Back door," Emma said, already moving toward the kitchen. "Now."

She reached the kitchen before she realized Diane hadn't followed. She hurried back to the living room and grabbed Diane's arm. "Diane, come on!"

The front door splintered inward with a sound like a gunshot. Grace screamed, her sudden bawling like knives to Emma's ears. Diane yelped. It reminded Emma of her childhood dog, Buster, when someone tripped on his tail.

Heath filled the doorway, his broad shoulders in the same hunched boxer's stance. The aurora's crimson glow caught the angular planes of his face, distorting it like a funny house mirror. Emma saw the matte black shape of a pistol in his hand and froze.

Diane swayed in place while Heath's eyes swept the room. His lips curled, somewhere between a smile and a sneer. "Isn't this cozy?"

"Get out of my house," Emma said, taking a step back. She was near the back door. If Diane weren't so frozen in Heath's presence, she'd make a run for it and get help.

Heath snorted. "I need to talk to my wife."

His voice, so sure and angry, sent shivers down Emma's spine. Her throat closed like a Venus flytrap, making it hard to breathe. Her armpits were wet, her heart like an out-of-time drumbeat. Grace squirmed against her chest, still wailing.

"Heath," Diane's voice cracked. "Please. Just leave."

Heath's mask slipped, revealing the rage beneath his flat, cold eyes. "Just go, okay?" Emma said, her voice shaking. She wanted to soothe Grace, whose cries now included hiccupping sobs, but was afraid to provoke him. "Whatever you think this will—"

Heath's voice cracked through the room like a whip. "You know nothing about this." He looked at Diane and something shifted. His face filled with a terrible tenderness that chilled Emma more than his rage. "You're my wife, Diane. You always will be. No piece of paper changes that."

"Heath," Diane whispered. Beside her, Emma could see that Diane's face was as pale as chalk. "Please, Heath. Don't do this."

His face hardened. "You think I don't know what you've been saying about me? Telling everyone I'm some kind of monster? You think I didn't see you in Chuy's car the other day? Are you fucking him?" He crossed the room with frightening speed, grabbing Diane's arm and yanking her toward him. "After everything I've done for you, you're fucking a mechanic?"

Emma took a careful step back. While he was distracted, she would run and get help. Then her cheek exploded in a starburst of pain. She stumbled backward, almost losing hold of Grace, and banged into the wall. She slid down the wall like a spray of window cleaner, fast and all at once. Grace's tiny body was as rigid as a board, her squalls like an air raid siren.

"Stay there," Heath snarled at Emma. Diane cried out in pain when he twisted her arm. "This is between me and my wife."

"I'm not your wife," Diane said.

The blow came fast. A blur, a low *thwack*, the copper swish of Diane's braid whipping like a flag in the wind. Diane's head snapped to the side. She fell like a stone. Blood coursed down the side of her face where the pistol butt had cut her above the temple. It slicked her ear, cheek, and jaw, the steady drip spattering on the hardwood floor.

"Stop!" Emma cried out, clutching Grace tighter.

Heath loomed over Diane's crumpled form. "Get up."

Diane struggled to get to her hands and knees. Her eyes were unfocused, dazed from the blow. She couldn't get her body to cooperate. Her bloody face looked like a reflection of the scarlet aurora growing brighter against the dusky sky.

"I said, GET UP!" Heath grabbed Diane's braid. He yanked her to her knees. Her hands scrabbled to gain purchase while he dragged her into the front room and threw her on the sofa.

"You'll kill her!" Emma cried, scrambling to her feet. She held Grace tight as a starfish clinging to a rock.

Heath turned on her, his face contorted like a gargoyle. "Shut that kid up or I'll do it for you."

Icy terror flooded Emma's body, her nerve endings popping and sparking like a downed electrical line. "Please," she begged, her voice breaking. "She's just a baby. She doesn't understand."

"Put her in the crib and sit on the couch."

On unsteady legs, Emma obeyed, her mind racing while she searched for a way out of this nightmare. Her attempt to murmur something soothing to the baby came out as garbled whimpers. Diane's eyes locked on Emma's, a silent apology pouring from them. Even in the middle of this attack, she was still apologizing for Heath's actions. Despite her terror, a spark of anger kindled behind Emma's breastbone. She sat on the couch, clutching the side of the bassinet with one hand so she could rock it back and forth. Grace continued to cry.

Heath paced before them, the gun in his hand. The aurora's glow was in full bloom, bathing the room in a bloodred light that lent a nightmarish quality. "I tried to be reasonable, Diane," he said. "I just wanted to talk but you had to make it difficult. Why do you do that?"

"What do you want, Heath?" Diane asked. She'd managed to sit up but still looked dazed.

He barked out an astonished laugh, brittle as breaking glass. "I want the life you destroyed when you left. You're coming with me. We're going to start over somewhere else."

"Everything's falling apart," Diane said. "We can't just—"

The gun swung up, pointing at her face. "Don't tell me what I can't do."

Grace's cries escalated again, her face mottled red with distress. Emma's breasts ached in response to her daughter's wails.

"Can't you shut her up?" Heath snapped, his agitation growing. "Jesus Christ, how hard is it?"

"She's a baby, she's sick," Emma said, her voice shaking. "Please don't hurt her. Please."

"I'll go with you, wherever you want," Diane said, looking up at Heath. She held her hands out in supplication. "I'll do whatever you want. Just let them go. The baby's sick. She needs a doctor."

Heath jutted his chin at the window behind them. "There are no doctors anymore. There's nothing."

"Then she needs her mother even more," Diane said, sensing an advantage she could press. How she could think after the blow she'd suffered, Emma couldn't fathom. "I'm the one you want. Let them go."

Emma's heart lurched. "Diane—"

"You think I'm stupid?" Heath said, his lip curled into a sneer. "If I leave her, she'll run next door."

"Martha's not home! You can tie her up," Diane suggested, her voice steadier now. "Then we'll go. No one is here to follow us. Heath, please."

He stared at Diane like she was a booby trap. Then he pushed aside one of the front window curtains, wrapped his hands around the top of the cord, and yanked down. Emma heard the rod groan and loosen in the wall, then the cord snapped. Her stomach heaved. It wasn't difficult to pull a rod from the wall, but snapping the cord like it was a piece of thread?

Emma's face throbbed harder as she thought of his strength. Her cheek and jaw had swollen. Heath had backhanded her and it felt like he'd used a baseball bat. Emma looked up at him in mute horror, imagining his strength and fury focused on Diane time after time after time.

Heath said, "Get up and turn around, hands behind your back."

Emma complied, trembling as she felt Heath approach. He bound her wrists, the cord cutting into her skin when he cinched it too tight.

"Sit," he ordered, shoving her toward the couch. "Don't make a fucking sound."

Emma nodded, her throat too tight for words, and dug her hands into the cushions behind her. Her wrists ached against the unyielding cord. There was no way she could wriggle her hands free.

Heath crouched to tie her feet. Diane held out her hand to him. "Heath, honey, let's go. I want to go right now."

Heath looked at her, surprised, the piece of cord clutched tight in his hand. He looked back at Emma's still untied feet.

"Heath," Diane said. She smiled at him when he looked at her, the quirk of her lips tremulous and warm and terrified. "Let's go right now. It's been so long since we were together on our own. You're right, I see that now, and I'm so, so sorry. I'm so sorry for what I've done. Let's not waste any more time."

Heath hesitated, then dropped the cord. He grabbed Diane by the arm. Diane allowed herself to be led. At the door's threshold she tried to speak, but Heath pushed her out ahead of him. Then he looked at Emma, his shadowed eyes like dark tarry pits. "You move an inch, say a word? I'll kill you."

As soon as he was out the door, Emma vaulted from the couch and ran to the kitchen, tripping over her own feet in her haste. She backed up to the sink and reached around, finding the knife she had used before when she cut her hand. Precious seconds slipped by as she fumbled with it, her hands shaking and slick with sweat. In the living room, Grace howled.

Emma turned the knife in her awkward fingers and sawed at the cord. Then she lost her grip. The knife clattered to the floor.

"Shit!" Frustration bubbled up, mixing with her fear in a toxic cocktail. Emma dropped to the floor. The kitchen was darker than the living room, the tile floor a deep terra cotta orange. She couldn't see the knife. She sat on her ass and scooted around, feeling the cool tiles with fingers that were going numb.

Outside, she heard Heath ranting over Diane's low, placating murmurs. Her finger scraped something that spun away. The knife! Frantic, Emma's fingers reached, searching. There. She caught the knife's handle between her pinky and fourth finger and inched it toward her palm. She slid the knife closer until she could grip the handle, her hands gritty from dirt on the floor.

It took a few attempts to twist the knife into position. Grace's shrieks thundered in her ears. She sawed at the cord, jabbing the insides of her wrists. She had to get this damn thing—

The cord snapped.

Emma scrambled to her feet and flat-out ran to the bedroom. Her fingers felt disconnected from her body as she fumbled with the gun safe lock, almost overshooting the middle number. Emma snapped the handle down and pulled the door open.

For the second time, she heard a sharp *crack*.

This time, it came from a gun.

chapter
forty-one

CODY

FRIDAY, JULY 18
7:47 PM

Cody eased the truck to a halt in the driveway. Inside, he could hear Grace crying like her little life depended on it. He knew Emma was happy and relieved he was alive, but if this was how her evening with Grace had gone, she must be exhausted.

She hadn't wanted him to go out in the first place, and there was the small matter of her being right about that. He couldn't do anything about that right now, but he could get his ass inside and take Grace off Emma's hands. He climbed out of the truck, feeling as stiff as an iron rod. He pushed the door shut and limped around the cab.

A man—solid as a brick—burst through the front door, shoving someone ahead of him. A woman, her copper hair disheveled and face bruised. Cody froze. Recognition dawned like ice water down his spine. It was Diane, his neighbor from across the street. Another piercing wail from Grace cut through the quiet evening air. Cody cried out, "Grace!"

The man's head snapped up. Diane struggled against his grip and he yanked her closer, an arm around her throat. In his other hand, Cody saw the glint of metal from a gun.

His training kicked in. He reached across his body for the sidearm in his shoulder holster. "US Marshal! Drop your weapon," he said, projecting his voice with cool authority. On the inside, fear howled like an injured animal. Where was Emma? Why was Grace screaming?

The man didn't comply. He turned, pulling Diane with him. He kept her in front, using her as a shield. His face contorted with rage. "Stay back!"

"Let her go," Cody said. He slowed his approach, but his gun stayed trained on the pair. "You don't want to do this."

"You don't know what I want!" the man snarled. Diane cried out when he tightened his grip. One side of her face was covered in blood.

Inside the house, Grace's cries continued unabated. "Is my wife inside? Is our baby unharmed?"

The man's eyes, wild and unfocused, darted between Cody and the house. "They're inside," Diane said.

"Shut up!" the man shouted, jerking her roughly.

Cody said again, "You need to lower your weapon." Rage roared inside his skull like a forest fire. He shut it down. He didn't have backup, didn't have a clear shot. He couldn't let fear for Emma and Grace distract him. Still, his mind raced. He needed to distract the man and get him away from the house. "Listen to me," Cody said. "This doesn't have to get any worse. Put the gun down and—"

The bullet hit Cody like a punch, knocking him backward against the truck. He hit the concrete hard. Rubber and the sharp copper scent of blood overwhelmed Cody's senses. Wet warmth spread across his torso. The world tilted, then righted itself. Cody couldn't feel his hand or gun.

The gunman advanced, dragging a struggling Diane with him. "Look at the hero now," he sneered.

Cody tried to push himself up, but his arms wouldn't cooperate. The edges of his vision blurred. Not like this, he thought, desperate. *Not like this, not now.*

"Cody!"

Emma's voice. He had wanted to know if she was all right. Now, he wanted her far away. "Run!" he said, the words sticky in his throat. "Get away!"

Diane twisted in her captor's grip. She sank her teeth into his hand. The man howled, his rage unearthly.

The bite loosened his grip.

Diane broke free.

Another shot rang out.

The gunman staggered, confusion spreading over his face. A dark stain bloomed on his chest, spreading like spilled ink. He turned toward the house, raising his gun.

Emma stood outside the front door, legs shoulder-width apart, holding the gun in front of her in a two-handed grip. She fired again. And again. And again. The gunman jerked like a marionette, staggering back with each impact. Then he fell, the gun tumbling from his hand.

"Cody!"

Emma was on her knees beside him. Her hands pressed against him, trying to staunch the blood flowing from his body. "Cody," she sobbed. "Stay with me. Don't you go. You stay with me!"

The world swam in and out of focus. Emma's face, lit pink from the aurora stretching across the sky, hovered above him. Fear and love mingled in her bright-blue eyes.

"Grace..."

"She's okay," Emma said, her face wet with tears. She looked up and shouted, "Help! I need help!"

Inside the house, Grace continued to cry. Cody wanted to cry, too. She was alive. She was safe. They were both okay. "I'm sorry," he whispered, the words stumbling through lips that didn't want to work right. "I should... have been here."

Shouting. Voices drawing near. The aurora ignited, pirouetting across the sky like a celestial ballet.

"Don't die on me, Cody," Emma said, her voice like steel. "Don't you dare!"

Cody's vision flickered. Emma's face swam in and out of focus. He wanted to tell her he loved her. That he'd do better, be better. That she was all he'd ever wanted.

Footsteps pounded on the pavement. Emma's face contorted as she screamed for help. The sky had gotten so dark. Even the aurora seemed dimmer. Darkness swallowed the edges of Cody's vision. Someone pushed Emma aside, their silhouette blocking the aurora's glow. He spoke words Cody couldn't hear as a heavy weight pushed against his torso.

"Emma," Cody sighed.

Emma.

now what?

IF YOU ENJOYED DARKEST LIGHT, **please leave a review!**
Reviews don't need to be long to make a difference in the willingness of others to try out a book. Leave a review here: https://amzn.to/3FXS00p

Want to know what happens to Samantha Young, the witness Cody was trying to call when the CME happened? Find out by reading *Fear the Dark* by T.W. Piperbrook! Get your copy here: https://amzn.to/465naxR

Sign up for my Stories from the Edge newsletter. It will keep you up-to-date about what I'm doing and where you can see me at live events. Plus you'll get advance notice of new releases, pre-sales, and other special goodies I only give to newsletter subscribers. Sign up here: http://bit.ly/newsamgeev

the ravaged skies
world

The project that ended up being the Ravaged Skies World is the brainchild of author Baileigh Higgins. It goes something like this: a bunch of zombie authors walk into a bar talking about writing a different kind of apocalypse and voilà! Ravaged Skies was born.

As soon as Baileigh floated the idea, I was in. I knew many of the authors from our mutual internet haunts and had already read, or soon did read, their books. We settled on a devastating solar storm that plunges the world into darkness where people face the unthinkable: a world without power.

The final line up is an incredible group of storytellers who have created their stories within the larger shared world. Every first book by every author has a crossover moment with another Ravaged Skies series. If you read them all, and I strongly suggest you do because the roster of authors is remarkable, you'll find all those little Easter eggs.

Group projects are the definition of hell. As hells go, this one has been a lot of fun. If you happen to see Baileigh, buy her a drink. After wrangling all of us, she probably needs one.

You can find out more about the project, including where to get all the books, at

- Ravaged Skies World website - https://ravagedskies.wordpeddlersociety.com/
- Ravaged Skies World Facebook Group - https://www.facebook.com/RavagedSkies

From the untamed American West to the lush jungles of Africa, from the ancient British Isles to New England's salt-sprayed shores, humanity faces its darkest hour beneath the Ravaged Skies.

acknowledgments

Thanks to my readers, who are the reason I do this in the first place. I hope you like this new apocalyptic world, even if it doesn't have zombies.

Never fear, EMP/CME (and adjacent) disaster readers! I know that ending was rough but there's lots more story in the works for the Fire in the Sky gang.

The Most Humungous Thanks to Sarah Lyons Fleming for making this book the best it can be, even if your critique meant I had to rewrite the ending. Jerk.

Very Special Thanks to Baileigh Higgins. I don't think Baileigh understood that wrangling a bunch of writers to work on this shared world project was a terrible idea, because herding cats would have been easier by a factor of a gazillion. I wouldn't have taken the leap from zombies to plain old disasters (ha ha) without the nudge, at least not now. I'm grateful that you provided this opportunity for me and everyone else associated with Ravaged Skies. I'm not so grateful about working to a deadline, but you win some, you lose some.

Creatives: Molly Phipps of We Got You Covered Book Design for the, as usual, amazing covers. As I've come to expect, your ideas surpassed my expectations.

Editing: Kimberly at Kimberly Dawn Editing

I want to thank and acknowledge all of the authors writing in the Ravaged Skies World: Scott M. Baker, Kate L. Mary, Marie Lanza, Kellee L. Greene, Courtney Konstantin, Chris Philbrook, DJ Cooper, Boyd Craven, JS Patrick, T.W. Piperbrook, Baileigh Higgins, and Ryan Colley. I'm so grateful to have been a part of the project and look forward to doing more cool things together.

As always, thank you to my wonderful family, whether by birth, marriage, or honorary association.

And endless thanks to my husband Drew, whose unfailing support makes up for all the dirty dishes he leaves in the sink. Sort of… but not really. This isn't exactly an apples to apples thing going on here, but I thank and love him all the same.

— June 28, 2025

also by a.m. geever

THE UNDEAD AGE

Love in an Undead Age, Book 1

Damage in an Undead Age, Book 2

Reckoning in an Undead Age, Book 3

Undead Age: The Complete Series, Books 1 - 3

STEEL CITY APOCALYPSE

Undead Menagerie, Book 1

Undead Sanctuary, Book 2

Undead Impact (pre-order), Book 3

Available at retailers everywhere, including direct from the author. Signed paperback copies are available at live events and direct from the author.

about the author

A.M. Geever is the award-winning author of *The Undead Age* and *Steel City Apocalypse* zombie apocalypse adventures. She also writes gritty post-collapse fiction in her *Fire in the Sky* series, where a solar flare brings modern civilization to its knees. A sci-fi enthusiast who dreamed of Starfleet command, she loves to write about impossible choices, no-win scenarios, and bad behavior. She shares her home with her husband, two cats with impeccable manners, and a pair of Blue Heeler/Catahoula hellhounds who have two speeds: fast and snuggle.